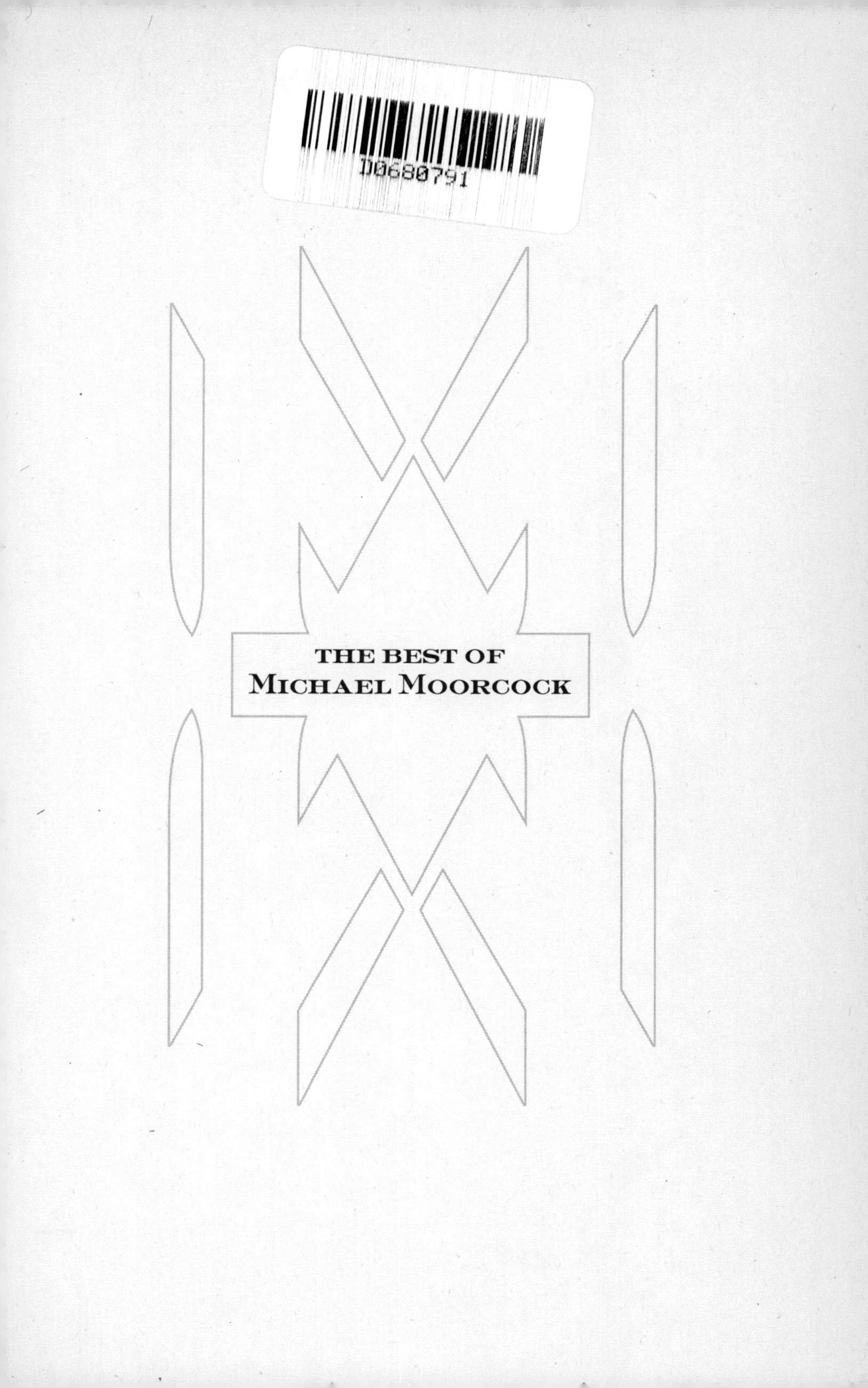
D0680791
THE BEST OF
MICHAEL MOORCOCK

TACHYON PUBLICATIONS

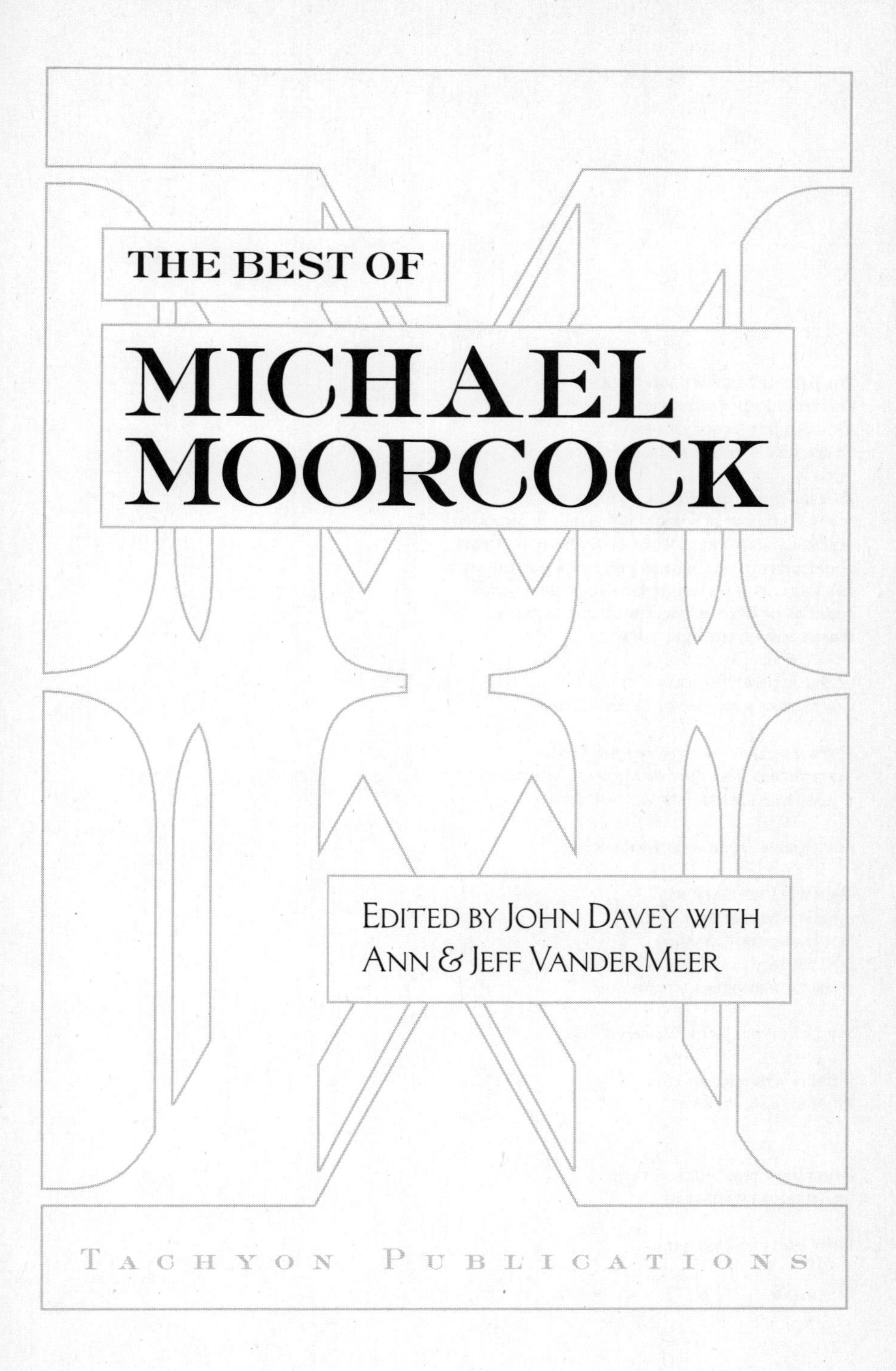

THE BEST OF MICHAEL MOORCOCK

EDITED BY JOHN DAVEY WITH
ANN & JEFF VANDERMEER

TACHYON PUBLICATIONS

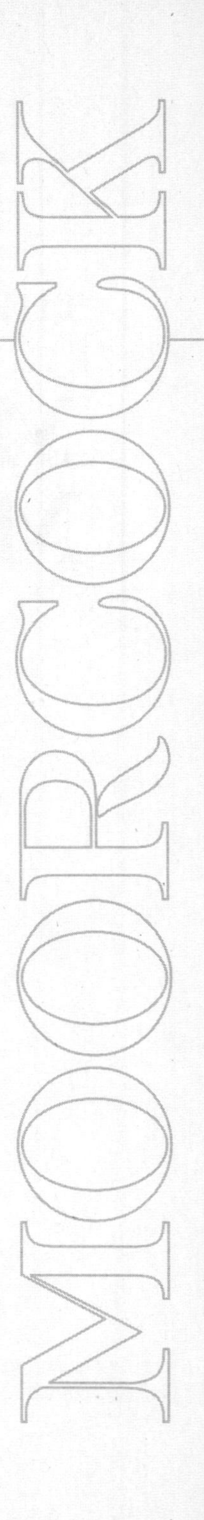

The Best of Michael Moorcock
Edited by John Davey with
Ann and Jeff VanderMeer

Interior design by John Coulthart
Cover design and image by Ann Monn

Tachyon Publications
1459 18th Street #139
San Francisco CA 94107
(415) 285-5615
www.tachyonpublications.com

Series Editor: Jacob Weisman

ISBN 13: 978-1-892391-86-5
ISBN 10: 1-892391-86-4

Printed in the United States
of America by Worzalla

First Edition: May 2009

0 9 8 7 6 5 4 3 2 1

CONTENTS

INTRODUCTION

Some time ago, I compiled a selection of the best of Michael Moorcock's short fiction, and "published" it in the ultimate limited edition—three copies—one file copy, one for Moorcock's sixty-fifth birthday, and first and foremost one for my youngest daughter's sixteenth (the same year).

When Michael Moorcock later asked me to assist Jeff and Ann VanderMeer in editing a *Best of...* for public consumption, using my earlier, somewhat uncommercially large selection as its basis, I had little hesitation in agreeing to do so.

What you see here is the result: a mixture of stories chosen by me and/or the VanderMeers—with a marked emphasis on what can be seen as a golden decade for Moorcock's short fiction (the 1990s)—some of which have until now remained unpublished or uncollected in the U.S.A.

How to arrange the stories posed one of the major problems. They actually span a period of more than forty years, from 1964 to 2006, and any attempt to arrange things chronologically was deemed unwise, as the book would end up front-loaded with stories which, whilst often no less powerful than their latter-day counterparts, might seem representative of a less mature talent.

Instead, we opted for an almost random selection, trying merely to give, across the book as a whole, a reasonable mix of the old and the new, the long and the short, the fantastical and the comparatively down-to-earth. If this means that there is occasionally a stylistic jarring of the senses to be found—instances of which do indeed occur here and there—then so be it.

I think that is all to be said by way of general introduction to this collection, although there is a mini-preface to each story in which its source and, where needed, its context are duly set out.

The original, limited-edition collection, which this book resembles in more than a few ways, was dedicated to my youngest daughter, Rebecca. This version I dedicate, with every bit as much love, to my eldest, Emma.

John Davey,
London,
August 2008

In memory of
Barry Bayley and Tom Disch

THE BEST OF
MICHAEL
MOORCOCK

A Portrait in Ivory (2005)

We begin this collection with a tale of Elric of Melniboné. Proud prince of ruins. Kinslayer. Call him what you will. He remains, together with maybe Jerry Cornelius, Moorcock's most enduring, if not always most endearing, character.

Elric started life in response to a request from John Carnell, editor of *Science Fantasy* magazine, for a series akin to Robert E. Howard's Conan the Barbarian stories. What Carnell received, while steeped in sword-and-sorcery images, was something quite different. The first tale to feature the albino emperor of Melniboné was "The Dreaming City" in 1961. In all, nine Elric stories appeared in the magazine between then and 1964. They formed the basis of two books, *The Stealer of Souls* and *Stormbringer*, although Moorcock has gone on to write many prequels and sequels to events therein.

"A Portrait in Ivory" was written in 2005, for an anthology of stories crafted around winning words from the Scripps National Spelling Bee. The editor asked contributors to choose a word; Moorcock picked "insouciant." This particular tale is set after the sacking of Imrryr, capital city of the Dragon Isle of Melniboné. It finds Elric—a shunned, outcast mercenary, wandering the Young Kingdoms over which his nation once ruled—in a contemplative, rather than a combative, mood. It was originally published in 2007, in *Logorrhea: Good Words Make Good Stories* (Bantam), edited by John Klima.

A Portrait in Ivory

1 An Encounter with a Lady

Elric, who had slept well and revived himself with fresh-brewed herbs, was in improved humour as he mixed honey and water into his glass of green breakfast wine. Typically, his night had been filled with distressing dreams, but any observer would see only a tall, insouciant "silverskin" with high cheekbones, slightly sloping eyes and tapering ears, revealing nothing of his inner thoughts.

He had found a quiet hostelry away from the noisy centre of Séred-Öma, this city of tall palms. Here, merchants from all over the Young Kingdoms gathered to trade their goods in return for the region's most valuable produce. This was not the dates or livestock, on which Séred-Öma's original wealth had been founded, but the extraordinary creations of artists famed everywhere in the lands bordering the Sighing Desert. Their carvings, especially of animals and human portraits, were coveted by kings and princes. It was the reputation of these works of art which brought the crimson-eyed albino out of his way to see them for himself. Even in Melniboné, where barbarian art for the most part was regarded with distaste, the sculptors of Séred-Öma had been admired.

Though Elric had left the scabbarded runesword and black armour of his new calling in his chamber and wore the simple chequered clothing of a regional traveller, his fellow guests tended to keep a certain distance from him. Those who had heard little of Melniboné's fall had celebrated the Bright Empire's destruction with great glee until the implications of that sudden defeat were understood. Certainly, Melniboné no longer controlled the world's trade and could no longer demand ransom from the Young Kingdoms, but the world was these days in confusion as upstart nations vied to seize the power for themselves. And meanwhile, Melnibonéan mercenaries found employment in the armies of rival countries. Without being certain of his identity, they could tell at once that Elric was one of those misplaced unhuman warriors, infamous for their cold good manners and edgy pride.

Rather than find themselves in a quarrel with him, the customers of the Rolling Pig kept their distance. The haughty albino too seemed indisposed to open a conversation. Instead, he sat at his corner table staring into his morning wine, brooding on what could not be forgotten. His history was written on handsome features which would have been youthful were it not for his thoughts. He reflected on an unsettled past and an uneasy future. Even had someone dared approach him, however sympathetically, to ask what concerned him, he would have answered lightly and coldly, for, save in his nightmares, he refused to confront most of those concerns. Thus, he did not look up when a woman, wearing the conical russet hat and dark veil of her caste, approached him through the crowd of busy dealers.

"Sir?" Her voice was a dying melody. "Master Melnibonéan, could you tolerate my presence at your table?" Falling rose petals, sweet and brittle from the sun.

"Lady," said Elric, in the courteous tone his people reserved for their own high-born kin, "I am at my breakfast. But I will gladly order more wine..."

"Thank you, sir. I did not come here to share your hospitality. I came to ask a favour." Behind the veil her eyes were grey-green. Her skin had the golden bloom of the Na'äne, who had once ruled here and were said to be a race as ancient as Elric's own. "A favour you have every reason to refuse."

The albino was almost amused, perhaps because, as he looked into her eyes, he detected beauty behind the veil, an unexpected intelligence he had not encountered since he had left Imrryr's burning ruins behind him. How he had longed to hear the swift wit of his own people, the eloquent argument, the careless insults. All that and more had been denied him for too long. To himself he had become sluggish, almost as dull as the conniving princelings and self-important merchants to whom he sold his sword. Now, there was something in the music of her speech, something in the lilt of irony colouring each phrase she uttered, that spoke to his own sleeping intellect. "You know me too well, lady. Clearly, my fate is in your hands, for you're able to anticipate my every attitude and response. I have good reason not to grant you a favour, yet you still come to ask one, so either you are prescient or I am already your servant."

"I would serve you, sir," she said gently. Her half-hidden lips curved in a narrow smile. She shrugged. "And, in so doing, serve myself."

"I thought my curiosity atrophied," he answered. "My imagination a petrified knot. Here you pick at threads to bring it back to life. This loosening is unlikely to be pleasant. Should I fear you?" He lifted a dented pewter cup to his lips and tasted the remains of his wine. "You are a witch, perhaps? Do you seek to revive the dead? I am not sure..."

"I am not sure, either," she told him. "Will you trust me enough to come with me to my house?"

"I regret, madam, I am only lately bereaved—"

"I'm no sensation-seeker, sir, but an honest woman with an honest ambition. I do not tempt you with the pleasures of the flesh, but of the soul. Something which might engage you for a while, even ease your mind a little. I can more readily convince you of this if you come to my house. I live there alone, save for servants. You may bring your sword, if you wish. Indeed, if you have fellows, bring them also. Thus I offer you every advantage."

The albino rose slowly from his bench and placed the empty goblet carefully on the well-worn wood. His own smile reflected hers. He bowed. "Lead on, madam." And he followed her through a crowd which parted like corn before the reaper, leaving a momentary silence behind him.

2 The Material

She had brought him to the depth of the city's oldest quarter, where artists of every skill, she told him, were licensed to work unhindered by landlord or, save in the gravest cases, the law. This ancient sanctuary was created by time-honoured tradition and the granting of certain guarantees by the clerics whose great university had once been the centre of the settlement. These guarantees had been strengthened during the reign of the great King Alo'ofd, an accomplished player of the nine-stringed *murmerlan*, who loved all the arts and struggled with a desire to throw off the burdens of his office and become a musician. King Alo'ofd's decrees had been law for the past millennium and his successors had never dared challenge them.

"Thus, this quarter harbours not only artists of great talent," she told him, "but many who have only the minimum of talent. Enough to allow them to live according to our ancient freedoms. Sadly, sir, there is as much forgery practised here, of every kind, as there is originality."

"Yours is not the only such quarter." He spoke absently, his eyes inspecting the colourful paintings, sculptures and manuscripts displayed on every side. They were of varied quality, but only a few showed genuine inspiration and beauty. Yet the accomplishment was generally higher than Elric had usually observed in the Young Kingdoms. "Even in Melniboné we had these districts. Two of my cousins, for instance, were calligraphers. Another composed for the flute."

"I have heard of Melnibonéan arts," she said. "But we are too distant from your island home to have seen many examples. There are stories, of course." She smiled. "Some of them are decidedly sinister..."

"Oh, they are doubtless true. We had no trouble if audiences, for instance, died for an artist's work. Many great composers would experiment, for instance, with the human voice." His eyes again clouded, remembering not a crime but his lost passion.

It seemed she misinterpreted him. "I feel for you, sir. I am not one of those who celebrated the fall of the Dreaming City."

"You could not know its influence, so far away," he murmured, picking up a remarkable little pot and studying its design. "But those who were our neighbours were glad to see us humiliated. I do not blame them. Our time was over." His expression was again one of cultivated insouciance. She turned her own gaze towards a house which leaned like an amiable drunkard on the buttressed walls of two neighbours, giving the impression that if it fell, then all would fall together. The house was of wood and sandy brick, of many floors, each at an angle to the rest, covered by a waved roof.

"This is the residence," she told him, "where my forefathers and myself have lived and worked. It is the House of the Th'ee and I am Rai-u Th'ee, last of my line. It is my ambition to leave a single great work of art behind, carved in a material which has been in our possession for centuries, yet until now always considered too valuable to use. It is a rare material, at least to us, and possessed of a number of qualities, some of which our ancestors only hinted at."

"My curiosity grows," said Elric, though now he found himself wishing that he had accepted her offer and brought his sword. "What is this material?"

"It is a kind of ivory," she said, leading him into the ramshackle house which, for all its age and decrepitude, had clearly once been rich. Even the wall-hangings, now in rags, revealed traces of their former quality. There were paintings from floor to ceiling which, Elric knew, would have commanded magnificent prices at any market. The furniture was carved by genuine artists and showed the passing of a hundred fashions, from the plain, somewhat austere style of the city's secular period, to the ornate enrichments of her pagan age. Some were inset with jewels, as were the many mirrors, framed with exquisite and elaborate ornament. Elric was surprised, given what she had told him of the quarter, that the House of Th'ee had never been robbed.

Apparently reading his thoughts, she said: "This place has been afforded certain protections down the years." She led him into a tall studio, lit by a single, unpapered window through which a great deal of light entered, illuminating the scrolls and boxed books lining the walls. Crowded on tables and shelves stood sculptures in every conceivable material. They were in bone and granite and hardwood and limestone. They were in clay and bronze, in iron and sea-green basalt. Bright, glinting whites, deep, swirling blacks. Colours of every possible shade from darkest blue to the lightest pinks and yellows. There was gold, silver and delicate porphyry. There were heads and torsos and reclining figures, beasts of every kind, some believed extinct. There were representations of the Lords and Ladies of Chaos and of Law, every supernatural aristocrat who had ever ruled in heaven, hell or limbo. Elementals. Animal-bodied men, birds in flight, leaping deer, men and women at rest, historical subjects, group subjects and half-finished subjects which hinted at something still to be discovered in the stone. They were the work of genius, decided the albino, and his respect for this bold woman grew.

"Yes." Again she anticipated a question, speaking with firm pride. "They are all mine. I love to work. Many of these are taken from life..."

He thought it impolitic to ask which.

"But you will note," she added, "that I have never had the pleasure of sculpting the head of a Melnibonéan. This could be my only opportunity."

"Ah," he began regretfully, but with great grace she silenced him, drawing him to a table on which sat a tall, shrouded object. She took away the cloth. "This is the material we have owned down the generations but for which we had never yet found an appropriate subject."

He recognised the material. He reached to run his hand over its warm smoothness. He had seen more than one of these in the old caves of the Phoorn, to whom his folk were related. He had seen them in living creatures who even now slept in Melniboné, wearied by their work of destruction, their old master made an exile, with no one to care for them save a few mad old men who knew how to do nothing else.

"Yes," she whispered, "it is what you know it is. It cost my forefathers a great fortune for, as you can imagine, your folk were not readily forthcoming with such things. It was smuggled from Melniboné and traded through many nations before it reached us, some two-and-a-half centuries ago."

Elric found himself almost singing to the thing as he caressed it. He felt a mixture of nostalgia and deep sadness.

"It is dragon ivory, of course." Her hand joined his on the hard, brilliant surface of the great curved tusk. Few Phoorn had owned such fangs. Only the greatest of the patriarchs, legendary creatures of astonishing ferocity and wisdom, who had come from their old world to this, following their kin, the humanlike folk of Melniboné. The Phoorn, too, had not been native to this world, but had fled another. They, too, had always been alien and cruel, impossibly beautiful, impossibly strange. Elric felt kinship even now for this piece of bone. It was perhaps all that remained of the first generation to settle on this plane.

"It is a holy thing." His voice was growing cold again. Inexplicable pain forced him to withdraw from her. "It is my own kin. Blood for blood, the Phoorn and the folk of Melniboné are one. It was our power. It was our strength. It was our continuity. This is ancestral bone. Stolen bone. It would be sacrilege…"

"No, Prince Elric, in my hands it would be a unification. A resolution. A completion. You know why I have brought you here."

"Yes." His hand fell to his side. He swayed, as if faint. He felt a need for the herbs he carried with him. "But it is still sacrilege…"

"Not if I am the one to give it life." Her veil was drawn back now and he saw how impossibly young she was, what beauty she had: a beauty mirrored in all the things she had carved and moulded. Her desire was, he was sure, an honest one. Two very different emotions warred within him. Part of him felt she was right, that she could unite the two kinsfolk in a single image and bring honour to all his ancestors, a kind of resolution to their mutual history. Part of him feared what she might create. In honouring his past, would she be destroying the future? Then some fundamental part of him made him gather himself up and turn to her. She gasped at what she saw burning in those terrible, ruby eyes.

"Life?"

"Yes," she said. "A new life honouring the old. Will you sit for me?" She too was caught up in his mood, for she too was endangering everything she valued, possibly her own soul, to make what might be her very last great work. "Will you allow me to create your memorial? Will you help me redeem that destruction whose burden is so heavy upon you? A symbol for everything that was Melniboné?"

He let go of his caution but felt no responsive glee. The fire dulled in his eyes. His mask returned. "I will need you to help me brew certain herbs, madam. They will sustain me while I sit for you."

Her step was light as she led him into a room where she had lit a stove and on which water already boiled, but his own face still resembled the stone of her carvings. His gaze was turned inward, his eyes alternately flared and faded like a dying candle. His chest moved with deep, almost dying breaths as he gave himself up to her art.

3 The Sitting

How many hours did he sit, still and silent in the chair? At one time she remarked on the fact that he scarcely moved. He said that he had developed the habit over several hundred years and, when she voiced surprise, permitted himself a smile. "You have not heard of Melniboné's dream couches? They are doubtless destroyed with the rest. It is how we learn so much when young. The couches let us dream for a year, even centuries, while the time passing for those awake was but minutes. I appear to you as a relatively young man, lady. But actually I have lived for centuries. It took me that time to pursue my dream-quests, which in turn taught me my craft and prepared me for…" And then he stopped speaking, his pale lids falling over his troubled, unlikely eyes.

She drew breath, as if to ask a further question, then thought better of it. She brewed him cup after cup of invigorating herbs and she continued to work, her delicate chisels fashioning an extraordinary likeness. She had genius in her hands. Every line of the albino's head was rapidly reproduced. And Elric, almost dreaming again, stared into the middle-distance. His thoughts were far away and in the past, where he had left the corpse of his beloved Cymoril to burn on the pyre he had made of his own ancient home, the great and beautiful Imrryr, the Dreaming City, the dreamer's city, which many had considered indestructible, had believed to be more conjuring than reality, created by the Melnibonéan Sorcerer Kings into a delicate reality, whose towers, so tall they disappeared amongst clouds, were actually the result of supernatural will rather than the creation of architects and masons.

Yet Elric had proven such theories false when Melniboné burned. Now all knew him for a traitor and none trusted him, even those whose ambition he had served. They said he was twice a traitor, once to his own folk, second to those he had led on the raid which had razed Imrryr and upon whom he had turned. But in his own mind he was thrice a traitor, for he had slain his beloved Cymoril, beautiful sister of cousin Yyrkoon, who had tricked Elric into killing her with that terrible black blade whose energy both sustained and drained him.

It was for Cymoril, more than Imrryr, that Elric mourned. But he showed none of this to the world and never spoke of it. Only in his dreams, those terrible, troubled dreams, did he see her again, which is why he almost always slept alone and presented a carefully cultivated air of insouciance to the world at large.

Had he agreed to the sculptress's request because she reminded him of his cousin?

Hour upon tireless hour she worked with her exquisitely made instruments until at last she had finished. She sighed and it seemed her breath was a gentle witch-wind, filling the head with vitality. She turned the portrait for his inspection.

It was as if he stared into a mirror. For a moment he thought he saw movement in the bust, as if his own essence had been absorbed by it. Save for the blank eyes, the carving might have been himself. Even the hair had been carved to add to the portrait's lifelike qualities.

She looked to him for his approval and received the faintest of smiles. "You have made the likeness of a monster," he murmured. "I congratulate you. Now history will know the face of the man they call Elric Kinslayer."

"Ah," she said, "you curse yourself too much, my lord. Do you look into the face of one who bears a guilt-weighted conscience?"

And of course, he did. She had captured exactly that quality of melancholy and self-hatred behind the mask of insouciance which characterised the albino in repose.

"Whoever looks on this will not say you were careless of your crimes." Her voice was so soft it was almost a whisper now.

At this he rose suddenly, putting down his cup. "I need no sentimental forgiveness," he said coldly. "There is no forgiveness, no understanding, of that crime. History will be right to curse me for a coward, a traitor, a killer of women and of his own blood. You have done well, madam, to brew me those herbs, for I now feel strong enough to put all this and your city behind me!"

She watched him leave, walking a little unsteadily like a man carrying a heavy burden, through the busy night, back to the inn where he had left his sword and armour. She knew that by morning he would be gone, riding out of Séred-Öma, never to return. Her hands caressed the likeness she had made, the blind, staring eyes, the mouth which was set in a grimace of self-mocking carelessness.

And she knew he would always wonder, even as he put a thousand leagues between them, if he had not left at least a little of his yearning, desperate soul behind him.

The Visible Men (2006)

Now we move on to Moorcock's other most famous and influential character, Jerry Cornelius, the ambiguous, androgynous "English Assassin."

Jerry started life in *New Worlds*—the seminal speculative fiction magazine which Moorcock edited for many years and with which he remains closely associated—in 1965, with "Preliminary Data," an extract from what was to become the first of several Cornelius novels, *The Final Programme*, published in 1968. A later novel, *The Condition of Muzak* (1977), won the prestigious Guardian Fiction Prize.

"The Visible Men" is a much more recent outing for Jerry and his bizarre circle of family, friends and foes. It is by far the shortest story in this collection, and possibly one of the strangest. It first appeared in *Nature* magazine (No. 7,091) in May 2006.

THE VISIBLE MEN

Or, Down the Multiversal Rabbit Hole

"That a cat's cradle?" Miss Brunner peered down at a naked Jerry Cornelius tangling his hands in a mess of guitar strings. A red Rickenbacker twelve lay beside him.

"It's twine theory," he said. Frank was absorbed in his own calculations covering the large slate propped on his mum's kitchen table. "He got a bit confused. Too many Es. Too much reverb." He followed her gaze. "G? Somewhere in the seventh dimension."

"He's a simple soul at heart. Easily led…" Major Nye stroked his pale moustache. He'd come in with Miss Brunner hoping to take Mrs. Cornelius out. "Is she here at all?"

"Pictures with Colonel Pyat." Frank spoke spitefully. "IT at the Electric. I'll tell her you called." His horrible feet in a bowl of soapy water, he frowned over his equations. What had been in that third syringe?

"Pip," said Jerry. "Pip. Pip." The strings coiled into a neat pile and vanished. He beamed.

Frank wondered why Jerry could charm and he couldn't?

Jerry strolled into the basement room sniffing. At the window, Jerry stopped to test the bars. In the kitchen Jerry cursed as he felt about in the toaster. From the front door upstairs Jerry called through the letter box. They were all naked, save for black car-coats. Jerry stood up pulling on his underpants. "Sorry I'm not decent."

Miss Brunner turned away with a strangled word. "What…?"

"Interdimensional travel." Jerry knotted his wide tie, copping Frank's calculations. "Though not very sophisticated." He reached to rub out a figure.

Pettishly, Frank slapped him. "Just the air cooling. Entropy factor. Anyway, your sizes are all slightly different."

"All?" Jerry frowned at the versions of himself. "If I had a black hole they'd follow me into it. As it is…"

Frank scowled. "You and your bloody multiverse. Energy's bound to thin out if you're that profligate."

"Crap." Jerry holstered his vibragun. "Effectively energy's limitless. It's Mandelbrot, Frank. Each set's invisibly smaller. Or invisibly bigger. Depending where you start. You don't go through the multiverse—you go up and down scales of almost infinite but tiny variability. Only the mass varies enormously, making them invisible. That's why we're all essentially the same." With scarcely any echo, identical voices came from each identical mouth: "Only after travelling through billions of sets do you start spotting major differences. The quasi-infinite, Frank. Think how many billions of multiversal planes of the Universe there are! Vast as it is, with my box you can step from one end to the other in about ten minutes. Go all the way round. Your mass compresses or expands accordingly. Once I realised space is a dimension of time, the rest was easy!"

"Pervert! You and your proliferating clones."

"Clones?" Miss Brunner licked her lips. "Are they edible?" She adjusted her powder-blue two-piece.

"They're not clones, they're versions. When you dash about the multiverse, this sort of thing happens. I prefer to shrink. But denser, you rip holes; drag things in. Nobody sees the universe next door because it's too big or too small. Fractional, of course, in multiversal terms. Problem is, bits of one universe get sucked into another. They're all so close. Déjà vu…?"

"Carry on like this, young man," Major Nye straightened his cap, "and you'll cause the end of matter. You'll have your chaos, all right!" Feelings hurt, he made for the basement door.

"That's ridiculous." Miss Brunner repaired her face. "Why aren't your clones—"

"Duplicates."

"Why aren't they too big or too small to see?"

"That's the whole trick." Jerry preened. Now in sync, his rippling duplicates followed his every move. "Getting us all to the same scale. Expansion and compression. Your atoms only change mass, maintaining identity. See, we're either too huge to perceive the next universe or we're so massively tiny we merely pass through it without noticing it. Either way you can't see 'em. Until I use this little gadget."

With a disapproving pout, she clicked across the parquet.

"You change your mass relative to theirs, or vice versa, and they become visible. At first you feel a bit queasy, but you get used to it." Picking up the small black box from the table, he showed her the display, the triggers. "Have a go. It's easy. Everything's digitalised."

"Certainly not. I have enough trouble controlling my own world."

"But this gives you millions of alternatives. Immortality of sorts. Admittedly, the nearest billion or so are boringly alike. But most people, like you, love repetition..."

"Rot! Utter dissipation! Double Deutsch, I call it!" Grumpily, Major Nye closed the door. Through the bars they saw him climb area steps, pushing aside three more Jerrys staring at one another in some confusion.

Upstairs the front door opened.

"Oh, blimey!" Dismayed, Jerry peered around for a hiding place. "Mum's back early."

"You'll have some explaining to do." Frank smirked.

But Jerry was already fiddling with his box and wires. As Mrs. Cornelius waddled into the room, exuding a delicious smell of greasy fish, Jerry shrank into a corner, his duplicates following. Everyone stared after him.

"Fairyland again!" Miss Brunner was contemptuous.

"The major said Jerry 'ad a message. Where's 'e gorn?" Mrs. Cornelius lifted huge blue suspicious eyes. A plump hand carried chips from her newspaper to her mouth.

"Climbing the bloody beanstalk, as usual." Defeated, Frank faded.

Mrs. C. roared.

A Dead Singer (1974)

One of Jerry Cornelius's most stalwart companions, throughout his many adventures, is Shakey Mo Collier.

In 1974, Mo got his own story, originally published in an anthology, *Factions* (Michael Joseph), edited by Giles Gordon and Alex Hamilton. In "A Dead Singer" he is (amongst other things) an ex-roadie for rock bands including the Deep Fix, the name of Moorcock's own band.

A Dead Singer

In memory, among others, of Smiling Mike and John the Bog

I

"IT'S NOT THE speed, Jimi," said Shakey Mo, "it's the H you got to look out for."

Jimi was amused. "Well, it never did me much good."

"It didn't do you no harm in the long run." Mo laughed. He could hardly hold on to the steering wheel.

The big Mercedes camper took another badly lit bend. It was raining hard against the windscreen. He switched on the lamps. With his left hand he fumbled a cartridge from the case on the floor beside him and slotted it into the stereo. The heavy, driving drumming and moody synthesisers of Hawkwind's latest album made Mo feel much better. "That's the stuff for energy," said Mo.

Jimi leaned back. Relaxed, he nodded. The music filled the camper.

Mo kept getting speed hallucinations on the road ahead. Armies marched across his path; Nazis set up road blocks; scampering children chased balls; big fires suddenly started and ghouls appeared and disappeared. He had a bad time controlling himself enough to keep on driving through it all. The images were familiar and he wasn't freaked out by them. He was content to be driving for Jimi. Since his comeback (or resurrection as Mo privately called it) Jimi hadn't touched a guitar or sung a note, preferring to listen to other people's music. He was taking a long while to recover from what had happened to him in Ladbroke Grove. Only recently his colour had started to return and he was still wearing the white silk shirt and jeans in which he'd been dressed when Mo first saw him, standing casually on the cowling of the Imperial Airways flying boat as it taxied towards the landing stage on Derwent Water. What a summer that had been, thought Mo. Beautiful.

The tape began to go round for the second time. Mo touched the stud to switch tracks, then thought better of it. He turned the stereo off altogether.

"Nice one." Jimi was looking thoughtful again. He was almost asleep as he lay stretched out over the bench seat, his hooded eyes fixed on the black road.

"It's got to build up again soon," said Mo. "It can't last, can it? I mean, everything's so dead. Where's the energy going to come from, Jimi?"

"It's where it keeps going to that bothers me, man. You know?"

"I guess you're right." Mo didn't understand.

But Jimi had to be right.

Jimi had known what he was doing, even when he died. Eric Burden had gone on TV to say so. "Jimi knew it was time to go," he'd said. It was like that with the records and performances. Some of them hadn't seemed to be as tight as others; some of them were even a bit rambling. Hard to turn on to. But Jimi had known what he was doing. You had to have faith in him.

Mo felt the weight of his responsibilities. He was a good roadie, but there were better roadies than him. More together people who could be trusted with a big secret. Jimi hadn't spelled it out but it was obvious he felt that the world wasn't yet ready for his return. But why hadn't Jimi chosen one of the really ace roadies? Everything had to be prepared for the big gig. Maybe at Shea Stadium or the Albert Hall or the Paris Olympia? Anyway, some classic venue. Or at a festival? A special festival celebrating the resurrection. Woodstock or Glastonbury. Probably something new altogether, some new holy place. India, maybe? Jimi would say when the time came. After Jimi had contacted him and told him where to be picked up, Mo had soon stopped asking questions. With all his old gentleness, Jimi had turned the questions aside. He had been kind, but it was clear he hadn't wanted to answer.

Mo respected that.

The only really painful request Jimi had made was that Mo stop playing his old records, including "Hey, Joe" the first single. Previously there hadn't been a day when Mo hadn't put something of Jimi's on. In his room in Lancaster Road, in the truck when he was roading for Light and later the Deep Fix, even when he'd gone to the House during his short-lived conversion to Scientology he'd been able to plug his earbead into his cassette recorder for an hour or so. While Jimi's physical presence made up for a lot and stopped the worst of the withdrawal symptoms, it was still difficult. No amount of mandrax, speed or booze could counter his need for the music and, consequently, the shakes were getting just a little bit worse each day. Mo sometimes felt that he was paying some kind of price for Jimi's trust in him. That was good karma so he didn't mind. He was used to the shakes anyway. You could get used to anything. He looked at his sinewy, tattooed arms stretched before him, the hands gripping the steering wheel. The world snake was wriggling again. Black, red and green, it coiled slowly down his skin, round his wrist and began to inch towards his elbow. He fixed his eyes back on the road.

2

Jimi had fallen into a deep sleep. He lay along the seat behind Mo, his head resting on the empty guitar case. He was breathing heavily, almost as if something were pressing down on his chest.

The sky ahead was wide and pink. In the distance was a line of blue hills. Mo was tired. He could feel the old paranoia creeping in. He took a fresh joint from the ledge and lit it, but he knew that dope wouldn't do a lot of good. He needed a couple of hours of sleep himself.

Without waking Jimi, Mo pulled the truck into the side of the road, near a wide, shallow river full of flat, white limestone rocks. He opened his door and climbed slowly to the grass. He wasn't sure where they were; maybe somewhere in Yorkshire. There were hills all around. It was a mild autumn morning but Mo felt cold. He clambered down to the bank and knelt there, cupping his hands in the clear water, sucking up the river. He stretched out and put his tattered straw hat over his face. It was a very heavy scene at the moment. Maybe that was why it was taking Jimi so long to get it together.

Mo felt much better when he woke up. It must have been noon. The sun was hot on his skin. He took a deep breath of the rich air and cautiously removed his hat from his face. The black Mercedes camper with its chrome trimming was still on the grass near the road. Mo's mouth felt dry. He had another drink of water and rose, shaking the silver drops from his brown fingers. He trudged slowly to the truck, pulled back the door and looked over the edge of the driver's seat. Jimi wasn't there, but sounds came from behind the partition. Mo climbed across the two seats and slid open the connecting door. Jimi sat on one of the beds. He had erected the table and was drawing in a big red notebook. His smile was remote as Mo entered.

"Sleep good?" he asked.

Mo nodded. "I needed it."

"Sure," said Jimi. "Maybe I ought to do a little driving."

"It's okay. Unless you want to make better time."

"No."

"I'll get some breakfast," said Mo. "Are you hungry?"

Jimi shook his head. All through the summer, since he had left the flying boat and got into the truck beside Mo, Jimi appeared to have eaten nothing. Mo cooked himself some sausages and beans on the little Calor stove, opening the back door so that the smell wouldn't fill the camper. "I might go for a swim," he said as he brought his plate to the table and sat as far away from Jimi as possible, so as not to disturb him.

"Okay," said Jimi, absorbed in his drawing.

"What you doing? Looks like a comic strip. I'm really into comics."

Jimi shrugged. "Just doodling, man. You know."

Mo finished his food. "I'll get some comics next time we stop on the motorway. Some of the new ones are really far out, you know."

"Yeah?" Jimi's smile was sardonic.

"Really far out. Cosmic wars, time warps. All the usual stuff but different, you know. Better. Bigger. More spectacular. Sensational, man. Oh, you want to see them. I'll get some."

"Too much," said Jimi distantly but it was obvious he hadn't been listening. He closed the notebook and sat back against the vinyl cushions, folding his arms across his white silk chest. As if it occurred to him that he might have hurt Mo's feelings, he added: "Yeah, I used to be into comics a lot. You seen the Jap kind? Big fat books. Oh, man—they are *really* far out. Kids burning. Rape.

All that stuff." He laughed, shaking his head. "Oh, man!"

"Yeah?" Mo laughed hesitantly.

"Right!" Jimi went to the door, placing a hand either side of the frame and looking into the day. "Where are we, Mo? It's a little like Pennsylvania. The Delaware Valley. Ever been there?"

"Never been to the States."

"Is that right?"

"Somewhere in Yorkshire, I think. Probably north of Leeds. That could be the Lake District over there."

"Is that where I came through?"

"Derwent Water."

"Well, well." Jimi chuckled.

Jimi was livelier today. Maybe it was taking him time to store up all the energy he'd need when he finally decided to reveal himself to the world. Their driving had been completely at random. Jimi had let Mo decide where to go. They had been all over Wales, the Peaks, the West Country, most parts of the Home Counties, everywhere except London. Jimi had been reluctant to go to London. It was obvious why. Bad memories. Mo had been into town a few times, leaving the Mercedes and Jimi in a suburban lay-by and walking and hitching into London to get his mandies and his speed. When he could he scored some coke. He liked to get behind a snort or two once in a while. In Finch's on the corner of Portobello Road he'd wanted to tell his old mates about Jimi, but Jimi had said to keep quiet about it, so when people had asked him what he was doing, where he was living these days, he'd had to give vague answers. There was no problem about money. Jimi didn't have any but Mo had got a lot selling the white Dodge convertible. The Deep Fix had given it to him after they'd stopped going on the road. And there was a big bag of dope in the truck, too. Enough to last two people for months, though Jimi didn't seem to have any taste for that, either.

Jimi came back into the gloom of the truck. "What d'you say we get on the road again?"

Mo took his plate, knife and fork down to the river, washed them and stashed them back in the locker. He got into the driver's seat and turned the key. The Wankel engine started at once. The Mercedes pulled smoothly away, still heading north, bumping off the grass and back onto the asphalt. They were on a narrow road suitable only for one-way traffic, but there was nobody behind them and nobody ahead of them until they left this road and turned onto the A65, making for Kendal.

"You don't mind the Lake District?" Mo asked.

"Suits me," said Jimi. "I'm the mad Gull Warrior, man." He smiled. "Maybe we should make for the ocean?"

"It's not far from here." Mo pointed west. "Morecambe Bay?"

3

The cliff tops were covered in turf as smooth as a fairway. Below them the sea sighed. Jimi and Mo were in good spirits, looning around like kids.

In the distance, round the curve of the bay, were the towers and funfairs and penny arcades of Morecambe, but here it was deserted and still, apart from the occasional cry of a gull.

Mo laughed, then cried out nervously as Jimi danced so near to the cliff edge it seemed he'd fall over.

"Take it easy, Jimi."

"Shit, man. They can't kill me."

He had a broad, euphoric smile on his face and he looked really healthy. "They can't kill Jimi, man!"

Mo remembered him on stage. In total command. Moving through the strobes, his big guitar stuck out in front of him, pointing at each individual member of the audience, making each kid feel that he was in personal touch with Jimi.

"Right!" Mo began to giggle.

Jimi hovered on the edge, still flapping his outstretched arms. "I'm the boy they boogie to. Oh, man! There ain't nothing they can do to me!"

"Right!"

Jimi came zooming round and flung himself down on the turf next to Mo. He was panting. He was grinning. "It's coming back, Mo. All fresh and new."

Mo nodded, still giggling.

"I just know it's there, man."

Mo looked up. The gulls were everywhere. They were screaming. They took on the aspect of an audience. He hated them. They were so thick in the sky now.

"Don't let them fucking feathers stick in your throat," said Mo, suddenly sullen. He got up and returned to the truck.

"Mo. What's the matter with you, man?"

Jimi was concerned as ever, but that only brought Mo down more. It was Jimi's kindness which had killed him the first time. He'd been polite to everyone. He couldn't help it. Really hung-up people had got off on him. And they'd drained Jimi dry.

"They'll get you again, man," said Mo. "I know they will. Every time. There isn't a thing you can do about it. No matter how much energy you build up, you know, they'll still suck it out of you and moan for more. They want your blood, man. They want your sperm and your bones and your flesh, man. They'll take you, man. They'll eat you up again."

"No. I'll—no, not this time."

"Sure." Mo sneered.

"Man, are you trying to bring me down?"

Mo began to twitch. "No. But..."

"Don't worry, man, okay?" Jimi's voice was soft and assured.

"I can't put it into words, Jimi. It's this, sort of, premonition, you know."

"What good did words ever do for anybody?" Jimi laughed his old, deep laugh. "You *are* crazy, Mo. Come on, let's get back in the truck. Where do you want to head for?"

But Mo couldn't reply. He sat at the steering wheel and stared through the windscreen at the sea and the gulls.

Jimi was conciliatory. "Look, Mo, I'll be cool about it, right? I'll take it easy, or maybe you think I don't need you?"

Mo didn't know why he was so down all of a sudden.

"Mo, you stay with me, wherever I go," said Jimi.

4

Outside Carlisle they saw a hitch-hiker, a young guy who looked really wasted. He was leaning on a signpost. He had enough energy to raise his hand. Mo thought they should stop for him. Jimi said: "If you want to," and went into the back of the truck, closing the door as Mo pulled in for the hitch-hiker.

Mo said: "Where you going?"

The hitch-hiker said: "What about Fort William, man?"

Mo said: "Get in."

The hitch-hiker said his name was Chris. "You with a band, man?" He glanced round the cabin at the old stickers and the stereo, at Mo's tattoos, his faded face-paint, his Cawthorn T-shirt, his beaded jacket, his worn jeans with washed-out patches on them, the leather cowboy boots which Mo had bought at the Emperor of Wyoming in Notting Hill Gate last year.

"Used to road for the Deep Fix," said Mo.

The hitch-hiker's eyes were sunken and the sockets were red. His thick black hair was long and hung down to his pale face. He wore a torn Wrangler denim shirt, a dirty white Levi jacket and both legs of his jeans had holes in the knees. He had moccasins on his feet. He was nervous and eager.

"Yeah?"

"Right," said Mo.

"What's in the back?" Chris turned to look at the door. "Gear?"

"You could say that."

"I've been hitching for three days, night and day," said Chris. He had an oil- and weather-stained khaki pack on his lap.

"D'you mind if I get some kip sometime?"

"No," said Mo. There was a service station ahead. He decided to pull in and fill the Merc up. By the time he got to the pumps Chris was asleep.

As he waited to get back into the traffic, Mo crammed his mouth full of pills. Some of them fell from his hand onto the floor. He didn't bother to pick them up. He was feeling bleak.

Chris woke when they were going through Glasgow.

"Is this Glasgow?"

Mo nodded. He couldn't keep the paranoia down. He glared at the cars ahead as they moved slowly through the streets. Every window of every shop had a big steel mesh grille on it. The pubs were like bunkers. He was really pissed off without knowing why.

"Where you going yourself?" Chris asked.

"Fort William?"

"Lucky for me. Know where I can score any grass in Fort William?"

Mo reached forward and pushed a tobacco tin along the edge towards the hitch-hiker. "You can have that."

Chris took the tin and opened it. "Far out! You mean it? And the skins?"

"Sure," said Mo. He hated Chris, he hated everybody. He knew the mood would pass.

"Oh, wow! Thanks, man." Chris put the tin in his pack.

"I'll roll one when we're out of the city, okay?"

"Okay."

"Who are you working for now?" said Chris. "A band?"

"No."

"You on holiday?"

The kid was too speedy. Probably it was just his lack of sleep. "Sort of," he said.

"Me, too. Well, it started like that. I'm at university. Exeter. Or was. I decided to drop out. I'm not going back to that shit heap. One term was enough for me. I thought of heading for the Hebrides. Someone I know's living in a commune out there, on one of the islands. They got their own sheep, goats, a cow. Nobody getting off on them. You know. Really free. It seems okay to me."

Mo nodded.

Chris pushed back his black, greasy hair. "I mean compare something like that with a place like this. How do people stand it, man? Fucking hell."

Mo didn't answer. He moved forward, changing gear as the lights changed.

"Amazing," said Chris. He saw the case of cartridges at his feet. "Can I play some music?"

"Go ahead," said Mo.

Chris picked out an old album, *Who's Next.* He tried to slide it into the slot the wrong way round. Mo took it from his hand and put it in the right way. He felt better when the music started. He noticed, out of the corner of his eye, that Chris tried to talk for a while before he realised he couldn't be heard.

Mo let the tape play over and over again as they drove away from Glasgow. Chris rolled joints and Mo smoked a little, beginning to get on top of his paranoia. By about four in the afternoon, he was feeling better and he switched off the stereo. They were driving beside Loch Lomond. The bracken was turning brown and shone like brass where the sun touched it. Chris had fallen asleep again, but he woke up as the music stopped. "Far out." He dug the scenery. "Fucking far out." He wound his window down. "This is the first time I've been to Scotland."

"Yeah?" said Mo.

"How long before we reach Fort William, man?"

"A few hours. Why are you heading for Fort William?"

"I met this chick. She comes from there. Her old man's a chemist or something."

Mo said softly, on impulse: "Guess who I've got in the back."

"A chick?"

"No."

"Who?"

"Jimi Hendrix."

Chris's jaw dropped. He looked at Mo and snorted, willing to join in the joke. "No? Really? Hendrix, eh? What is it, a refrigerated truck?" He was excited by the fantasy. "You think if we thaw him out he'll play something for us?" He shook his head, grinning.

"He is sitting in the back there. Alive. I'm roading for him."

"Really?"

"Yeah."

"Fantastic." Chris was half-convinced. Mo laughed. Chris looked at the door. After that, he was silent for a while.

Something like a half an hour later, he said: "Hendrix was the best, you know. He was the king, man. Not just the music, but the style, too. Everything. I couldn't believe it when I heard he died. I still can't believe it, you know."

"Sure," said Mo. "Well, he's back."

"Yeah?" Again Chris laughed uncertainly. "In there? Can I see him?"

"He's not ready, yet."

"Sure," said Chris.

It was dark when they reached Fort William. Chris staggered down from the truck. "Thanks, man. That's really nice, you know. Where are you staying?"

"I'm moving on," said Mo. "See you."

"Yeah. See you." Chris still had that baffled look on his face.

Mo smiled to himself as he started the camper, heading for Oban. Once they were moving the door opened and Jimi clambered over the seats to sit beside him.

"You told that kid about me?"

"He didn't believe me," said Mo.

Jimi shrugged.

It began to rain again.

5

They lay together in the damp heather looking out over the hills. There was nobody for miles; no roads, towns or houses. The air was still and empty save for a hawk drifting so high above them it was almost out of sight.

"This'll do, eh?" said Mo. "It's fantastic."

Jimi smiled gently. "It's nice," he said.

Mo took a Mars Bar from his pocket and offered it to Jimi who shook his head. Mo began to eat the Mars Bar.

"What d'you think I am, man?" said Jimi.

"How d'you mean?"

"Devil or angel? You know."

"You're Jimi," said Mo. "That's good enough for me, man."

"Or just a ghost," said Jimi. "Maybe I'm just a ghost."

Mo began to shake. "No," he said.

"Or a killer?" Jimi got up and struck a pose. "The Sonic Assassin. Or the messiah, maybe." He laughed. "You wanna hear my words of wisdom?"

"That's not what it's about," said Mo, frowning. "Words. You just have to be there, Jimi. On the stage. With your guitar. You're above all that stuff—all the hype. Whatever you do—it's right, you know."

"If you say so, Mo." Jimi was on some kind of downer. He lowered himself to the heather and sat there cross-legged, smoothing his white jeans, picking mud off his black patent leather boots. "What is all this *Easy Rider* crap anyway? What are we doing here?"

"You didn't like *Easy Rider*?" Mo was astonished.

"The best thing since *Lassie Come Home*." Jimi shrugged. "All it ever proved was that Hollywood could still turn 'em out, you know. They got a couple of fake freaks and made themselves a lot of money. A rip-off, man. And the kids fell for it. What does that make me?"

"You never ripped anybody off, Jimi."

"Yeah? How d'you know?"

"Well, you never did."

"All that low energy shit creeping in everywhere. Things are bad." Jimi had changed the subject, making a jump Mo couldn't follow. "People all over the Grove playing nothing but fake '50s crap, Simon and Garfunkel. Jesus Christ! Was it ever worth doing?"

"Things go in waves. You can't be up the whole time."

"Sure," Jimi sneered. "This one's for all the soldiers fighting in Chicago. And Milwaukee. And New York... And Vietnam. Down with War and Pollution. What was all that about?"

"Well..." Mo swallowed the remains of the Mars Bar. "Well—it's important, man. I mean, all those kids getting killed."

"While we made fortunes. And came out with a lot of sentimental shit. That's where we were wrong. You're either in the social conscience business or show business. You're just foolish if you think you can combine them like that."

"No, man. I mean, you can say things which people will hear."

"You say what your audience wants. A Frank Sinatra audience gets their shit rapped back to them by Frank Sinatra. Jimi Hendrix gives a Jimi Hendrix audience what they want to hear. Is that what I want to get back into?"

But Mo had lost him. Mo was watching the tattoos crawl up his arms. He said vaguely: "You need different music for different moods. There's nothing wrong with the New Riders, say, if you're trying to get off some paranoia trip. And you get up on Hendrix. That's what it's like. Like uppers and downers, you know."

"Okay," said Jimi. "You're right. But it's the other stuff that's stupid. Why do they always want you to keep saying things? If you're just a musician that's all you should have to be. When you're playing a gig, anyway, or making a record. Anything else should come out of that. If you wanna do benefits, free concerts, okay. But your opinions should be private. They want to turn us into politicians."

"I tol' you," said Mo, staring intensely at his arms. "Nobody asks that. You do what you want to do."

"Nobody asks it, but you always feel you got to give it to 'em." Jimi rolled over and lay on his back, scratching his head. "Then you blame them for it."

"Not everyone thinks they owe anything to anyone," said Mo mildly as his skin undulated over his flesh.

"Maybe that's it," said Jimi. "Maybe that's what kills you. Jesus Christ. Psychologically, man, you know, that means you must be in one hell of a mess. Jesus Christ. That's suicide, man. Creepy."

"They killed you," said Mo.

"No, man. It was suicide."

Mo watched the world snake crawl. Could this Hendrix be an imposter?

6

"So what you going to do, then?" said Mo. They were on the road to Skye and running low on fuel.

"I was a cunt to come back," said Jimi. "I thought I had some kind of duty."

Mo shrugged. "Maybe you have, you know."

"And maybe I haven't."

"Sure." Mo saw a filling station ahead. The gauge read Empty and a red light was flashing on the panel. It always happened like that. He'd hardly ever been stranded. He glanced in the mirror and saw his own mad eyes staring back at him. Momentarily he wondered if he should turn the mirror a little to see if Jimi's reflection was there too. He pushed the thought away. More paranoia. He had to stay on top of it.

While the attendant was filling the truck, Mo went to the toilet. Among the more common bits of graffiti on the wall was the slogan "Hawkwind is Ace." Maybe Jimi was right. Maybe his day was over and he should have stayed dead. Mo felt miserable. Hendrix had been his only hero. He did up his flies and the effort drained off the last of his energy. He staggered against the door and began to slide down towards the messy floor. His mouth was dry; his heart was thumping very fast. He tried to remember how many pills he'd swallowed recently. Maybe he was about to OD.

He put his hands up to the door-handle and hauled himself to his feet. He bent over the lavatory bowl and shoved his finger down his throat. Everything was moving. The bowl was alive. A greedy mouth trying to swallow him. The walls heaved and moved in on him. He heard a whistling noise. Nothing came up. He stopped trying to vomit, turned, steadied himself as best as he could, brushed aside the little white stick-men who tried to grab at him, dragged the door open and plunged through. Outside, the attendant was putting the cap back on the tank. He wiped his big hands on a piece of rag and put the rag back into his overalls, saying something.

Mo found some money in his back pocket and gave it to him. He heard a voice:

"You okay, laddie?"

The man had offered him a genuine look of concern.

Mo mumbled something and clambered into the cab.

The man ran up as Mo started the engine, waving money and green stamps.

"What?" said Mo. He managed to wind the window down. The man's face changed to a malevolent devil's mask. Mo knew enough not to worry about it. "What?"

He thought he heard the attendant say: "Your friend's already paid."

"That's right, man," said Jimi from beside him.

"Keep it," said Mo. He had to get on the road quickly. Once he was driving he would be more in control of himself. He fumbled a cartridge at random from the case. He jammed it into the slot. The tape started halfway through a Stones album. Jagger singing "Let It Bleed" had a calming effect on Mo. The snakes stopped winding up and down his arms and the road ahead became steady and clearer. He'd never liked the Stones much. A load of wankers, really, though you had to admit Jagger had a style of his own which no one could copy. But basically wankers like the rest of the current evil-trippers, like Morrison and Alice Cooper. It occurred to him he was wasting his time thinking about nothing but bands, but what else was there to think about? Anyway how else could you see your life? The mystical thing didn't mean much to him. Scientology was a load of crap. At any rate, he couldn't see anything in it. The guys running all that stuff seemed to be more hung-up than the people they were supposed to be helping. That was true of a lot of things. Most people who told you they wanted to help you were getting off on you in some way. He'd met pretty much every kind of freak by now. Sufis, Hare Krishnas, Jesus freaks, Meditators, Processors, Divine Lighters. They could all talk better than him, but they all seemed to need more from him than they could give. You got into people when you were tripping. Acid had done a lot for him that way. He could suss out the hype-merchants so easily these days. And by that test Jimi couldn't be a fake. Jimi was straight. Fucked up now, possibly, but okay.

The road was long and white and then it became a big boulder. Mo couldn't tell if the boulder was real or not. He drove at it, then changed his mind, braking sharply. A red car behind him swerved and hooted as it went past him through the boulder which disappeared. Mo shook all over. He took out the Stones tape and changed it for the Grateful Dead's *American Beauty*, turned down low.

"You okay, man?" said Hendrix.

"Sure. Just a bit shakey." Mo started the Merc up.

"You want to stop and get some sleep."

"I'll see how I feel later."

It was sunset when Jimi said: "We seem to be heading south."

"Yeah," said Mo. "I need to get back to London."

"You got to score?"

"Yeah."

"Maybe I'll come in with you this time."

"Yeah?"

"Maybe I won't."

7

By the time Mo had hitched to the nearest tube station and reached Ladbroke Grove he was totally wasted. The images were all inside his head now: pictures of Jimi from the first time he'd seen him on TV playing "Hey, Joe" (Mo had still been at school then), pictures of Jimi playing at Woodstock, at festivals and gigs all over the country. Jimi in big, feathered hats, bizarre multicoloured shirts, several rings on each finger, playing that white Strat, flinging the guitar over his head, plucking the strings with his teeth, shoving it under his straddled legs, making it wail and moan and throb, doing more with a guitar than anyone had done before. Only Jimi could make a guitar come alive in that way, turning the machine into an organic creature, simultaneously a prick, a woman, a white horse, a sliding snake. Mo glanced at his arms, but they were still. The sun was beginning to set as he turned into Lancaster Road, driven more by a mixture of habit and momentum than any energy or sense of purpose. He had another image in his head now, of Jimi as a soul thief, taking the energy away from the audience. Instead of a martyr, Jimi became the vampire. Mo knew that the paranoia was really setting in and the sooner he got hold of some uppers the better. He couldn't blame Jimi for how he felt. He hadn't slept for two days. That was all it was. Jimi had given everything to the people in the audience, including his life. How many people in the audience had died for Jimi?

He crawled up the steps of the house in Lancaster Road and rang the third bell down. There was no answer. He was shaking badly. He held on to the concrete steps and tried to calm himself, but it got worse and he thought he was going to pass out.

The door behind him opened.

"Mo?"

It was Dave's chick, Jenny, wearing a purple brocade dress. Her hair was caked with wet henna.

"Mo? You all right?"

Mo swallowed, and said: "Hullo, Jenny. Where's Dave?"

"He went down the Mountain Grill to get something to eat. About half an hour ago. Are you all right, Mo?"

"Tired. Dave got any uppers?"

"He had a lot of mandies in."

Mo accepted the news. "Can you let me have a couple of quid's worth?"

"You'd better ask him yourself, Mo. I don't know who he's promised them to."

Mo nodded and got up carefully.

"You want to come in and wait, Mo?" said Jenny.

Mo shook his head. "I'll go down the Mountain. See you later, Jenny."

"See you later, Mo. Take care, man."

Mo shuffled slowly up Lancaster Road and turned the corner into Portobello Road. He thought he saw the black-and-chrome Merc cross the top of the street. The buildings were all crowding in on him. He saw them grinning at him, leering. He heard them talking about him. There were fuzz everywhere. A woman threw something at him. He kept going until he reached the Mountain Grill and had stumbled through the door. The café was crowded with freaks but there was nobody there he knew. They all had evil, secretive expressions and they were whispering.

"You fuckers," he mumbled, but they pretended they weren't listening. He saw Dave.

"Dave? Dave, man!"

Dave looked up, grinning privately. "Hi, Mo. When did you get back to town?" He was dressed in new, clean denims with fresh patches on them. One of the patches said "Star Rider."

"Just got in." Mo leaned across the tables, careless of the intervening people, and whispered in Dave's ear. "I hear you got some mandies."

Dave's face became serious. "Sure. Now?"

Mo nodded.

Dave rose slowly and paid his bill to the dark, fat lady at the till. "Thanks, Maria."

Dave took Mo by the shoulder and led him out of the café. Mo wondered if Dave was about to finger him. He remembered that Dave had been suspected more than once.

Dave said softly as they went along; "How many d'you need, Mo?"

"How much are they?"

Dave said: "You can have them for ten a piece."

"I'll have five quid's worth. A hundred, yeah?"

"Fifty."

They got back to Lancaster Road and Dave let himself in with two keys, a Yale and a mortise. They went up a dark, dangerous stairway. Dave's room was gloomy, thick with incense, with painted blinds covering the window. Jenny sat on a mattress in the corner listening to Ace on the stereo. She was knitting.

"Hi, Mo," she said. "So you found him."

Mo sat down on the mattress in the opposite corner. "How's it going, Jenny?" he said. He didn't like Dave, but he liked Jenny. He made a big effort to be polite. Dave was standing by a chest of drawers, dragging a box from under a pile of tasselled curtains. Mo looked past him and saw Jimi standing there. He was dressed in a hand-painted silk shirt with roses all over it. There was a jade talisman on a silver chain round his throat. He had the white Strat in his hands. His eyes were closed as he played it. Almost immediately Mo guessed he was looking at a poster.

Dave counted fifty mandies into an aspirin bottle. Mo reached into his jeans and found some money. He gave Dave a five pound note and Dave gave him the bottle. Mo opened the bottle and took out a lot of the pills, swallowing them fast. They didn't act right away, but he felt better for taking them. He got up.

"See you later, Dave."

"See you later, man," said Dave. "Maybe in Finch's tonight."
"Yeah."

8

Mo couldn't remember how the fight started. He'd been sitting quietly in a corner of the pub drinking his pint of bitter when that big fat fart who was always in there causing trouble decided to pick on him. He remembered getting up and punching the fat fart. There had been a lot of confusion then and he had somehow knocked the fat fart over the bar. Then a few people he knew pulled him away and took him back to a basement in Oxford Gardens where he listened to some music.

It was *Band of Gypsys* that woke him up. Listening to "Machine Gun" he realised suddenly that he didn't like it. He went to the pile of records and found other Hendrix albums. He played *Are You Experienced*, the first album, and *Electric Ladyland*, and he liked them much better. Then he played *Band of Gypsys* again.

He looked round the dark room. Everyone seemed to be totally spaced out.

"He died at the right time," he said. "It was over for him, you know. He shouldn't have come back."

He felt in his pocket for his bottle of mandies. There didn't seem to be that many left. Maybe someone had ripped them off in the pub. He took a few more and reached for the bottle of wine on the table, washing them down. He put *Are You Experienced* on the deck again and lay back. "That was really great," he said. He fell asleep. He shook a little bit. His breathing got deeper and deeper. When he started to vomit in his sleep nobody noticed. By that time everyone was right out of it. He choked quietly and then stopped.

9

About an hour later a black man came into the room. He was tall and elegant. He radiated energy. He wore a white silk shirt and white jeans. There were shiny patent leather boots on his feet. A chick started to get up as he came into the room. She looked bemused.

"Hi," said the newcomer. "I'm looking for Shakey Mo. We ought to be going."

He peered at the sleeping bodies and then looked closer at one which lay a little apart from the others. There was vomit all over his face and over his shirt. His skin was a ghastly, dirty green. The black man stepped across the others and knelt beside Mo, feeling his heart, taking his pulse.

The chick stared stupidly at him. "Is he all right?"

"He's OD'd," the newcomer said quietly. "He's gone. D'you want to get a doctor or something, honey?"

"Oh, Jesus," she said.

The black man got up and walked to the door.

"Hey," she said. "You look just like Jimi Hendrix, you know that?"

"Sure."

"You can't be—you're not, are you? I mean, Jimi's dead."

Jimi shook his head and smiled his old smile. "Shit, lady. They can't kill Jimi." He laughed as he left.

The chick glanced down at the small, ruined body covered in its own vomit. She swayed a little, rubbing at her thighs. She frowned. Then she went as quickly as she could from the room, hampered by her long cotton dress, and into the street. It was nearly dawn and it was cold. The tall figure in the white shirt and jeans didn't seem to notice the cold. It strode up to the big Mercedes camper parked near the end of the street.

The chick began to run after the black truck as it started up and rolled a little way before it had to stop on the red light at the Ladbroke Grove intersection.

"Wait," she shouted. "Jimi!"

But the camper was moving before she could reach it.

She saw it heading north towards Kilburn.

She wiped the clammy sweat from her face. She must be freaking. She hoped when she got back to the basement that there wouldn't really be a dead guy there.

She didn't need it.

Lunching with the Antichrist (1993)

In the early '90s, Moorcock began an ambitious project of reordering, revising and republishing much of his back-catalogue in a large set of definitive omnibuses.

The revision process gave him the opportunity to change several character names in order to bring them in line with the developing "Von Bek" series, which had begun in 1981 with *The War Hound and the World's Pain*—although the name's derivation goes back as far as Katinka van Bak in 1973's *The Champion of Garathorm*—and which culminated in the "Second Ether" trilogy of *Blood*, *Fabulous Harbours* and *The War Amongst the Angels* (1995/'96).

So, into many stories, old and new, along came the von Beks and their curious relationships with both Lucifer and the Holy Grail, plus assorted Beggs, Becks, Bekovs, Beckers, Van Beeks and the like.

(For the purposes of this collection, any revised names have been reverted to their original forms.)

Here is one such tale—a new story, rather than a revision—introducing us to Edwin Begg, the Clapham Antichrist. It was originally published in 1993, in an anthology, *Smoke Signals* (Serpent's Tail), edited by the London Arts Board.

"Lunching with the Antichrist" also features another mention of Jerry Cornelius's scurrilous brother Frank.

In memoriam, Horst Grimm

Begg Mansions,
Sporting Club Square

The Editor,
Fulham & Hammersmith Telegraph,
Bishops Palace Avenue,
London W14

13th October 1992

Sir,

SPIRIT OF THE BLITZ

It is heartening to note, as our economy collapses perhaps for the last time, a return to the language and sentiments of mutual self-interest. London was never the kindest of English cities but of late her cold, self-referential greed has been a watchword around the world. Everything we value is threatened in the name of profit.

I say nothing original when I mourn the fact that it took the Blitz to make Londoners achieve a humanity and heroism they never thought to claim for themselves and which no one expected or demanded of them! Could we not again aspire to achieve that spirit, without the threat of Hitler but with the same optimistic courage? Can we not, in what is surely an hour of need, marshal what is best in us and find new means of achieving that justice, equity and security for which we all long? The existing methods appear to create as many victims as they save.

Yours faithfully, Edwin Begg,
former vicar of St. Odhran's, Balham.

HEAR! HEAR! says the Telegraph. This week's Book Token to our Letter of the Week! Remember, your opinions are important to us and we want to see them! A £5.00 Book Token for the best!

1 My First Encounter with the Clapham Antichrist; His Visions & His Public Career; His Expulsion from the Church & Subsequent Notoriety; His Return to Society & Celebrity as a Sage; His Mysterious & Abrupt Departure into Hermitage; His Skills in the Kitchen.

"Spirit of the Blitz" (a sub-editor's caption) was the last public statement of the Clapham Antichrist.

Until I read the letter at a friend's I believed Edwin Begg dead some twenty years ago. The beloved TV eccentric had retired in the 1950s to live as a recluse in Sporting Club Square, West Kensington. I had known him intimately in the '60s and '70s and was shocked to learn he was still alive. I felt a conflicting mixture of emotions, including guilt. Why had I so readily accepted the hearsay of his death? I wrote to him at once. Unless he replied to the contrary I would visit him on the following Wednesday afternoon.

I had met Begg first in 1966 when as a young journalist I interviewed him for a series in the *Star* about London's picturesque obscurities. Then too I had contacted him after reading one of his letters to the *Telegraph*. The paper, still a substantial local voice, was his only source of news, delivered to him weekly. He refused to have a telephone and communicated mostly through the post.

I had hoped to do a few paragraphs on the Antichrist's career, check a couple of facts with him and obtain a short, preferably amusing, comment on our Fab Sixties. I was delighted when, with cheerful courtesy, Edwin Begg had agreed by return to my request. In a barely legible old-fashioned hand he invited me to lunch.

My story was mostly drafted before I set off to see him. Research had been easy. We had half a filing drawer on Edwin Begg's years of notoriety, first before the War then afterwards as a radio and early TV personality. He had lived in at least a dozen foreign cities. His arguments were discussed in every medium and he became a disputed symbol. Many articles about him were merely sensational, gloating over alleged black magic rites, sexual deviation, miracle-working, blasphemy and sorcery. There were the usual photographs and also drawings, some pretending to realism and others cruel cartoons: the Clapham Antichrist as a monster with blazing eyes and glittering fangs, architect of the doom to come. One showed Hitler, Stalin and Mussolini as his progeny.

The facts were pretty prosaic; in 1931 at the age of twenty-four Begg was vicar of St. Odhran's, Balham, a shabby North London living where few parishioners considered themselves respectable enough to visit a church and were darkly suspicious of those who did. The depression years had almost as many homeless and hungry people on the streets as today. Mosley was gathering a more militant flock than Jesus, and those who opposed the Fascists looked to Oxford or the secular left for their moral leadership. Nonetheless the Reverend Begg conscientiously performed his duty, offering the uncertain comforts of his calling to his flock.

Then quite suddenly in 1933 the ordinary hard-working cleric became an urgent proselytiser, an orator. From his late-Victorian pulpit he began preaching a shocking message urging Christians to act according to their principles and sacrifice their own material ambitions to the common good, to take a risk on God being right, as he put it. This Tolstoyan exhortation eventually received enough public attention to make his sermons one of London's most popular free attractions from Southwark to Putney, which of course brought him the attention of the famous Bermondsey barrackers, the disapproval of his establishment and the closer interest of the Press.

The investigators the Church sent down heard a sermon touching mainly on the current state of the Spanish Republic, how anarchists often acted more like ideal Christians than the priests, how people seemed more willing to give their lives to the anarchists than to the cause of Christ. This was reported in *Reynolds News*, tipped off that the investigators would be there, as Begg's urging his congregation to support the coming Antichrist. The report was more or less approving. The disapproving church investigators, happy for a lead to follow, confirmed the reports. Overnight, the Reverend Edwin Begg, preaching his honest Christian message of brotherly love and equity under the law, became the Clapham Antichrist, Arch-Enemy of British Decency, Proud Mocker of All Religion and Hitler's Right Hand, a creature to be driven from our midst.

In the course of a notoriously hasty hearing Edwin Begg was unfrocked, effectively by public demand. In his famous defence Begg confirmed the general opinion of his guilt by challenging the commission to strip itself naked and follow Christ, if they were indeed Christians! He made a disastrous joke: and if they were an example of modern Christians, he said, then after all he probably was the Antichrist!

Begg never returned to his vicarage. He went immediately to Sporting Club Square. Relatives took him in, eventually giving him his own three-roomed flat where it was rumoured he kept a harem of devil-worshipping harlots. The subsequent Siege of Sporting Club Square in which the *News of the World* provoked a riot causing one near-fatality and thousands of pounds' worth of damage was overshadowed by the news of Hitler's massacre of his stormtroopers, the SA.

Goebbels's propaganda became more interesting and rather more in the line of an authentic harbinger of evil, and at last Edwin Begg was left in peace.

Usually attached to a circus or a fair and always billed as "Reverend" Begg, The Famous Clapham Antichrist! he began to travel the country with his message of universal love. After his first tours he was never a great draw since he disappointed audiences with urgent pleas for sanity and the common good and never rose to the jokes or demands for miracles, but at least he had discovered a way of making a living from his vocation. He spent short periods in prison and there were rumours of a woman in his life, someone he had mentioned early on, though not even the worst of the Sundays found evidence to suggest he was anything but confirmed in his chastity.

When the war came Edwin Begg distinguished himself in the ambulance service, was wounded and decorated. Then he again disappeared from public life. This was his first long period of seclusion in Begg Mansions until suddenly on 1st May, 1949, encouraged by his cousin Robert in BBC Talks, he gave at 9:45 p.m. on the Home Service the first of his Fireside Observer chats.

No longer the Old Testament boom of the pulpit or the sideshow, the Fireside Observer's voice was level, reassuring, humorous, a little sardonic sometimes when referring to authority. He reflected on our continuing hardships and what we might gain through them if we kept trying—what we might expect to see for our children. He offered my parents a vision of a wholesome future worth working for, worth making a few sacrifices for, and they loved him.

He seemed the moral spirit of the Festival of Britain, the best we hoped to become, everything that was decent about being British. An entire book was published proving him the object of a plot in 1934 by a Tory bishop, a Fascist sympathiser, and there were dozens of articles, newsreels and talks describing him as the victim of a vicious hoax or showing how Mosley had needed a scapegoat.

Begg snubbed the Church's willingness to review his case in the light of his new public approval and continued to broadcast the reassuring ironies which lightened our 1950s darkness and helped us create the golden years of the 1960s and '70s. He did not believe his dream to be illusory.

By 1950 he was on television, part of the *Thinkers' Club* with Gilbert Harding and Professor Joad, which every week discussed an important contemporary issue. The programme received the accolade of being lampooned in *Radio Fun* as *The Stinker's Club* with Headwind Legg which happened to be one of my own childhood favourites. He appeared, an amiable sage, on panel games, quiz shows, programmes called *A Crisis of Faith* or *Turning Point* and at religious conferences eagerly displaying their tolerance by soliciting the opinion of a redeemed antichrist.

Suddenly, in 1955, Begg refused to renew all broadcasting contracts and retired from public life, first to travel and finally to settle back in Begg Mansions with his books and his journals. He never explained his decision and then the public lost interest. New men with brisker messages were bustling in to build utopia for us in our lifetime.

Contenting himself with a few letters mostly on parochial matters to the Hammersmith *Telegraph*, Edwin Begg lived undisturbed for a decade. His works of popular philosophy sold steadily until British fashion changed.

Writing nothing after 1955, he encouraged his books to go out of print. He kept his disciples, of course, who sought his material in increasingly obscure places and wrote to him concerning his uncanny understanding of their deepest feelings, the ways in which he had dramatically changed their lives, and to whom, it was reported, he never replied.

The first Wednesday I took the 28 from Notting Hill Gate down North Star Road to Greyhound Gardens. I had brought my *A–Z*. I had never been to Sporting Club Square before and was baffled by the surrounding network of tiny twisting streets, none of which seemed to go in the same direction for more than a few blocks, the result of frenzied rival building work during the speculative 1880s when developers had failed to follow the plans agreed between themselves, the freeholder, the architect and the authorities. The consequent recession ensured that nothing was ever done to remedy the mess. Half-finished crescents and abrupt culs-de-sac, odd patches of wasteland, complicated rights of way involving narrow alleys, walls, gates and ancient pathways were interrupted, where bomb damage allowed, by the new council estates, totems of clean enlightenment geometry whose erection would automatically cause all surrounding social evils to wither away. I had not expected to find anything quite so depressing and began to feel sorry for Begg ending his days in such circumstances, but turning out of Margrave Passage I came suddenly upon a cluster of big unkempt oaks and cedars gathered about beautiful wrought-iron gates in the baroque oriental regency style of Old Cogges, that riot of unnatural ruin, the rural scat of the Beggs which William the Goth remodelled in 1798 to rival Strawberry Hill. They were miraculous in the early afternoon sun: the gates to paradise.

The square now has a preservation order and appears in international books of architecture as the finest example of its kind. Sir Hubert Begg, its architect, is mentioned in the same breath as Gaudí and Norman Shaw, which will give you some notion of his peculiar talent. Inspired by the fluid aesthetics of the *fin-de-siècle* he was loyal to his native brick and fired almost every fancy from Buckingham clay to give his vast array of disparate styles an inexplicable coherence. The tennis courts bear the motifs of some Mucha-influenced smith, their floral metalwork garlanded with living roses and honeysuckle from spring until autumn: even the benches are on record as one of the loveliest expressions of public art nouveau.

Until 1960 there had been a black chain across the Square's entrance and a porter on duty day and night. Residents' cars were never seen in the road but garaged in the little William Morris cottages originally designed as studios and running behind the eccentrically magnificent palaces, which had been Begg's Folly until they survived the Blitz to become part of our heritage. When I walked up to the gates in 1966 a few cars had appeared in the gravel road running around gardens enclosed by other leafy ironwork after Charles Rennie Mackintosh, and the Square had a bit of a shamefaced seedy appearance.

There were only a few uniformed porters on part-time duty by then and they too had a slightly hangdog air. The Square was weathering one of its periodic declines, having again failed to connect with South Kensington during a decade of prosperity. Only the bohemian middle classes were actually proud to live there, so the place had filled with actors, music-hall performers, musicians, singers, writers, cheque-kiters and artists of every kind, together with journalists, designers and retired dance instructresses, hair-dressers and disappointed legatees muttering bitterly about any blood not their own, for the Square had taken refugees and immigrants. Others came to be near the tennis courts maintained by the SCS Club affiliated to nearby Queen's.

Several professionals had taken apartments in Wratislaw Villas, so the courts never went down and neither did the gardens which were preserved by an endowment from Gordon Begg, Lord Mauleverer, the botanist and explorer, whose elegant vivarium still pushed its flaking white girders and steamy glass above exotic shrubbery near the Mandrake Road entrance. Other examples of his botanical treasures, the rival of Holland's, flourished here and there about the Square and now feathery exotics mingled with the oaks and hawthorn of the original Saxon meadow.

Arriving in this unexpected tranquillity on a warm September afternoon when the dramatic red sun gave vivid contrast to the terracotta, the deep greens of trees, lawns and shrubbery, I paused in astonished delight. Dreamily I continued around the Square in the direction shown me by the gatehouse porter. I was of a generation which enthused over pre-Raphaelite paint and made Beardsley its own again, who had bought the five-shilling Mackintosh chairs and sixpenny Muchas and ten-bob Lalique glass in Portobello Road to decorate Liberty-oriental pads whose fragrant patchouli never disguised the pungent dope. They were the best examples we could find in this world to remind us of what we had seen on our acid voyages.

To my father's generation the Square would be unspeakably old-fashioned, redolent of the worst suburban pretension, but I had come upon a gorgeous secret. I understood why so few people mentioned it, how almost everyone was either enchanted or repelled. My contemporaries, who thought "Georgian" the absolute height of excellence and imposed their stern developments upon Kensington's levelled memory, found Sporting Club Square hideously "Victorian"—a gigantic, grubby whatnot. Others dreamed of the day when they would have the power to be free of Sporting Club Square, the power to raze her and raise their fake Le Corbusier mile-high concrete in triumph above the West London brick.

I did not know, as I made my way past great mansions of Caligari Tudor and Kremlin De Mille, that I was privileged to find the Square in the final years of her glory. In those days I enjoyed a wonderful innocence and could no more visualise this lovely old place changing for the worse than I could imagine the destruction of Dubrovnik.

Obscured, sometimes, by her trees, the mansion apartments of Sporting Club Square revealed a thousand surprises. I was in danger of being late as I stared at Rossettian gargoyles and Blakean caryatids, copings, gables, corbels of every possible stamp yet all bearing the distinctive style of their time. I was filled with an obscure sense of epiphany.

In 1886, asymmetrical Begg Mansions was the boldest expression of modernism, built by the architect for his own family use, for his offices and studios, his living quarters, a suite to entertain clients, and to display his designs, accommodation for his draughts- and crafts-people whose studios in attics and basements produced the prototype glass, metal, furniture and fabrics which nowadays form the basis of the V&A's extraordinary collection. By the 1920s after Hubert Begg's death the Square became unfashionable. Lady Begg moved to Holland Park and Begg Mansions filled up with the poorer Beggs who paid only the communal fee for general upkeep and agreed to maintain their own flats in good condition. Their acknowledged patron was old Squire Begg, who had the penthouse. By 1966 the building was a labyrinth of oddly twisting corridors and stairways, unexpected landings reached by two old oak-and-copper cage elevators served by their own generator, which worked on an eccentric system devised by the architect and was always going wrong. Later I learned that it was more prudent to walk the six flights to Edwin Begg's rooms but on that first visit I got into the lift, pressed the stud for the sixth floor and was taken up without incident in a shower of sparks and rattling brass to the ill-lit landing where the Antichrist himself awaited me.

I recognised him of course but was surprised that he seemed healthier than I had expected. He was a little plumper and his bone-white hair was cropped in a self-administered pudding-basin cut. He was clean shaven, pink and bright as a mouse, with startling blue eyes, a firm rather feminine mouth and the long sharp nose of his mother's Lowland Presbyterian forefathers. His high voice had an old-fashioned Edwardian elegance and was habitually rather measured. He reminded me of a Wildean *grande dame*, tiny but imposing. I was dressed like most of my Ladbroke Grove peers and he seemed pleased by my appearance, offering me his delicate hand, introducing himself and muttering about my good luck with the lift. He had agreed to this interview, he said, because he'd been feeling unusually optimistic after playing the new Beatles album. We shared our enthusiasm.

He guided me back through those almost organic passages until we approached his flat and a smell so heady, so delicious that I did not at first identify it as food. His front door let directly onto his study which led to a sitting room and bedroom. Only the dining room seemed unchanged since 1900 and still had the original Voysey wallpaper and furniture, a Henry dresser and Benson copperware. Like many reclusive people he enjoyed talking. As he continued to cook he sat me on a sturdy Wilson stool with a glass of wine and asked me about my career, showing keen interest in my answers.

"I hope you don't mind home cooking," he said. "It's a habit I cultivated when I lived on the road. Is there anything you find disagreeable to eat?"

I would have eaten strychnine if it had tasted as that first meal tasted. We had mysterious sauces whose nuances I can still recall, wines of exquisite delicacy, a dessert which contained an entire orchestra of flavours, all prepared in his tiny perfect 1920s "modern" kitchenette to one side of the dining room.

After we had eaten he suggested we take our coffee into the bedroom to sit in big wicker chairs and enjoy another wonderful revelation. He drew the curtains back from his great bay window to reveal over two miles of almost unbroken landscape all the way to the river with the spires and roofs of Old Putney beyond. In the far distance was a familiar London skyline but immediately before us were the Square's half-wild communal gardens and cottage garages, then the ivy-covered walls of St. Mary's Convent, the Convent School sports field and that great forest of shrubs, trees and memorial sculptures, the West London Necropolis, whose Victorian angels raised hopeful swords against the ever-changing sky. Beyond the cemetery was the steeple of St. Swithold's and her churchyard, then a nurtured patchwork of allotments, some old alms cottages and finally the sturdy topiary of the Bishop's Gardens surrounding a distant palace whose Tudor dignity did much to inspire Hubert Begg. The formal hedges marched all the way to the bird sanctuary on a broad, marshy curve where the Thames approached Hammersmith Bridge, a mediaeval fantasy.

It was the pastoral and monumental in perfect harmony which some cities spontaneously create. Edwin Begg said the landscape was an unfailing inspiration. He could dream of Roman galleys beating up the river cautiously alert for Celtic war-parties or Vikings striking at the Bishop's Palace leaving flames and murder behind. He liked to think of other more contemplative eyes looking on a landscape scarcely changed in centuries. "Hogarth, Turner and Whistler amongst them. Wheldrake, writing *Harry Wharton*, looked out from this site when staying at the Sporting Club Tavern and earlier Augusta Begg conceived the whole of *The Bravo of Bohemia* and most of *Yamboo; or, The North American Slave* while seated more or less where I am now! Before he went off to become an orientalist and London's leading painter of discreet seraglios James Lewis Porter painted several large landscapes which show market gardens where the allotments are, a few more cottages, but not much else has changed. I can walk downstairs, out of the back door, through that gate, cross the convent field into the graveyard, take the path through the church down to the allotments all the way to the Bishop's Gardens and be at the bird sanctuary within half an hour, even cross the bridge into Putney and the Heath if I feel like it and hardly see a house, a car or another human being!" He would always stop for a bun, he said, at the old Palace Tea Rooms and usually strolled back via Margrave Avenue's interesting junkyards. Mrs. White, who kept the best used bookshop there, told me he came in at least twice a week.

He loved to wake up before dawn with his curtains drawn open and watch the sun gradually reveal familiar sights. "No small miracle, these days, dear! I'm always afraid that one morning it won't be there." At the time I thought this no more than a mildly philosophical remark.

For me he still had the aura of a mythic figure from my childhood, someone my parents had revered. I was prepared to dislike him but was immediately charmed by his gentle eccentricity, his rather loud plaid shirts and corduroys, his amiable vagueness. The quality of the lunch alone would have convinced me of his virtue!

I was of the 1960s, typically idealistic and opinionated and probably pretty obnoxious to him but he saw something he liked about me and I fell in love with him. He was my ideal father.

I returned home to rewrite my piece. A figure of enormous wisdom, he offered practical common sense, I said, in a world ruled by the abstract sophistries and empty reassurances heralding the new spirit of competition into British society. It was the only piece of mine the *Star* never used, but on that first afternoon Edwin Begg invited me back for lunch and on almost every Wednesday for the next eight years, even after I married, I would take the 28 from the Odeon, Westbourne Grove to Greyhound Gardens and walk through alleys of stained concrete, past shabby red terraces and doorways stinking of rot until I turned that corner and stood again before the magnificent gates of Sporting Club Square.

My friend kept his curiosity about me and I remained flattered by his interest. He was always fascinating company, whether expanding on some moral theme or telling a funny story. One of his closest chums had been Harry Lupino Begg, the music-hall star, and he had also known Al Bowlly. He was a superb and infectious mimic and could reproduce Lupino's patter by heart, making it as topical and fresh as the moment. His imitation of Bowlly singing "Buddy, Can You Spare a Dime?" was uncanny. When carried away by some amusing story or conceit his voice would rise and fall in rapid and entertaining profusion, sometimes taking on a birdlike quality difficult to follow. In the main however he spoke with the deliberate air of one who respected the effect of words upon the world.

By his own admission the Clapham Antichrist was not a great original thinker but he spoke from original experience. He helped me look again at the roots of my beliefs. Through him I came to understand the innocent intellectual excitement of the years before political experiments turned one by one into tyrannical orthodoxies. He loaned me my first Kropotkin, the touching *Memoirs of a Revolutionist*, and helped me understand the difference between moral outrage and social effect. He loved works of popular intellectualism. He was as great an enthusiast for Huxley's *The Perennial Philosophy* as he was for

Winwood Reade's boisterously secular *Martyrdom of Man*. He introduced me to the interesting late work of H. G. Wells and to Elizabeth Bowen. He led me to an enjoyment of Jane Austen I had never known. He infected me with his enthusiasm for the more obscure Victorians who remained part of his own living library and he was generous with his books. But, no matter how magical our afternoons, he insisted I must always be gone before the BBC broadcast *Choral Evensong*. Only in the dead of winter did I ever leave Sporting Club Square in darkness.

Naturally I was curious to know why he had retired so abruptly from public life. Had he told the church of his visions? Why had he felt such an urgent need to preach? To risk so much public disapproval? Eventually I asked him how badly it had hurt him to be branded as the premier agent of the Great Antagonist, the yapping dog as it were at the heels of the Son of the Morning. He said he had retreated from the insults before they had grown unbearable. "But it wasn't difficult to snub people who asked you questions like 'Tell me, Mr. Begg, what does human blood taste like?' Besides, I had my Rose to sustain me, my vision..."

I hoped he would expand on this but he only chuckled over some association he had made with an obscure temptation of St. Anthony and then asked me if I had been to see his cousin Orlando Begg's *Flaming Venus*, now on permanent display at the Tate.

Though I was soon addicted to his company, I always saw him on the same day and time every week. As he grew more comfortable with me he recounted the history of his family and Sporting Club Square. He spoke of his experiences as a young curate, as a circus entertainer, as a television personality, and he always cooked. This was, he said, the one time he indulged his gourmet instincts. In the summer we would stroll in the gardens or look at the tennis matches. Sitting on benches we would watch the birds or the children playing. When I asked him questions about his own life his answers became fuller, though never completely unguarded.

It was easy to see how in his determined naïveté he was once in such frequent conflict with authority.

"I remember saying, my dear, to the magistrate—Who does not admire the free-running, intelligent fox? And few, no matter how inconvenienced, begrudge him his prey which is won by daring raiding and quick wits, risking all. A bandit, your honour, one can admire and prepare against. There is even a stirring or two of romance for the brigand chief. But once the brigand becomes a baron that's where the balance goes wrong, eh, your honour? It gets unfair, I said to him. Our sympathies recognise these differences so why can't our laws? Our courts make us performers in pieces of simplistic fiction! Why do we continue to waste so much time? The magistrate said he found my last remark amusing and gave me the maximum sentence."

Part of Edwin Begg's authority came from his vivacity. As he sat across from me at the table, putting little pieces of chicken into his mouth, pausing to enjoy them, then launching off onto a quite different subject, he seemed determined to relish every experience, every moment. His manner offered a clue to his past. Could he be so entertaining because he might otherwise have to confront an unpleasant truth? Anyone raised in a post-Freudian world could make that guess. But it was not necessarily correct.

Sometimes his bright eyes would dart away to a picture or glance through a window and I learned to interpret this fleeting expression as one of pain or sadness. He admitted readily that he had retreated into his inner life, feeling he had failed in both his public and private missions. I frequently reassured him of his value, the esteem in which he was still held, but he was unconvinced.

"Life isn't a matter of linear consequences," he said. "We only try to make it look like that. Our job is not to force grids upon the world but to achieve harmony with nature."

At that time in my life such phrases made me reach for my hat, if not my revolver, but because I loved him so much I tried to understand what he meant. He believed that in our terror we imposed perverse linearity upon a naturally turbulent universe, that our perceptions of time were at fault since we saw the swirling cosmos as still or slow-moving just as a gnat doubtless sees us. He thought that those who overcame their brute terror of the truth soon attained the state of the angels.

The Clapham Antichrist was disappointed that I was not more sympathetic to the mystical aspects of the alternative society but because of my familiarity with its ideas was glad to have me for a devil's advocate. I was looking for a fast road to utopia and he had almost given up finding any road at all. Our solutions were wrong because our analysis was wrong, he said. We needed to rethink our fundamental principles and find better means of applying them. I argued that this would take too long. Social problems required urgent action.

His attitude was an excuse for inaction. In the right hands there was nothing wrong with the existing tools.

"And what are the right hands, dear?" he asked. "Who makes the rules? Who keeps them, my dear?" He ran his thin fingers through hair which became a milky halo around his earnest face. "And how is it possible to make them and keep them when our logic insists on such oppressive linearity? We took opium into China and bled them of their silver. Now they send heroin to us to lay hands upon our currency! Am I the only one enjoying the irony? The Indians are reclaiming the south-western United States in a massive migration back into the old French and Spanish lands. The world is never still, is it, my dear?"

His alert features were full of tiny signals, humorous and anxious, enquiring and defiant, as he expanded on his philosophy one autumn afternoon. We strolled around the outer path enjoying the late roses and early chrysanthemums forming an archway roofed with fading honeysuckle. He wore his green raglan, his yellow scarf, his hideous turf-accountant's trilby, and gestured with the blackthorn he always carried but hardly used. "The world is never still and yet we continue to live as if turbulence were not the natural order of things. We have no more attained our ultimate state than has our own star! We have scarcely glimpsed any more of the multiverse than a toad under a stone! We are part of the turbulence and it is in turbulence we thrive. Once that's understood, my dear, the rest is surely easy? Brute warfare is our crudest expression of natural turbulence, our least productive. What's the finest? Surely there's no evil in aspiring to be our best? What do we gain by tolerating or even justifying the worst?"

I sat down on the bench looking the length of a bower whose pale golds and browns were given a tawny burnish by the sun. Beyond the hedges was the sound of a tennis game. "And those were the ideas which so offended the Church?" I asked.

He chuckled, his face sharp with self-mockery. "Not really. They had certain grounds I suppose. I don't know. I merely suggested to my congregation, after the newspapers had begun the debate, that perhaps only through Chaos and Anarchy could the Millennium be achieved. There were after all certain clues to that effect in the Bible. I scarcely think I'm to blame if this was interpreted as calling for bloody revolution, or heralding Armageddon and the Age of the Antichrist!"

I was diplomatic. "Perhaps you made the mistake of overestimating your audiences?

Smiling he turned where he sat to offer me a reproving eye. "I did not overestimate them, my dear. They underestimated themselves. They didn't appreciate that I was trying to help them become one with the angels. I have experienced such miracles, my dear! Such wonderful visions!"

And then quite suddenly he had risen and taken me by my arm to the Duke's Elm, the ancient tree which marked the border of the larger square in what was really a cruciform. Beyond the elm were lawns and well-stocked beds of the cross's western bar laid out exactly as Begg had planned. Various residents had brought their deckchairs here to enjoy the last of the summer. There was a leisurely good-humoured holiday air to the day. It was then, quite casually and careless of passers-by, that the Clapham Antichrist described to me the vision which converted him from a mild-mannered Anglican cleric into a national myth.

"It was on a similar evening to this in 1933. Hitler had just taken power. I was staying with my Aunt Constance Cunningham, the actress, who had a flat in D'Yss Mansions and refused to associate with the other Beggs. I had come out here for a stroll to smoke my pipe and think over a few ideas for the next Sunday's sermon which I would deliver, my dear, to a congregation consisting mostly of the miserably senile and the irredeemably small-minded who came to church primarily as a signal to neighbours they believed beneath them…

"It was a bloody miserable prospect. I have since played better audiences on a wet Thursday night in a ploughed field outside Leeds. No matter what happened to me I never regretted leaving those dour ungiving faces behind. I did my best. My sermons were intended to discover the smallest flame of charity and aspiration burning in their tight little chests. I say all this in sad retrospect. At the time I was wrestling with my refusal to recognise certain truths and find a faith not threatened by them.

"I really was doing my best, my dear." He sighed and looked upward through the lattice of branches at the jackdaw nests just visible amongst the fading leaves. "I was quite agitated about my failure to discover a theme appropriate to their lives. I wouldn't give in to temptation and concentrate on the few decent parishioners at the expense of the rest." He turned to look across the lawns at the romantic rococo splendour of Moreau Mansions. "It was a misty evening in the Square with the sun setting through those big trees over there, a hint of pale gold in the haze and bold comforting shadows on the grass. I stood here, my dear, by the Duke's Elm. There was nobody else around. My vision stepped forward, out of the mist, and smiled at me.

"At first I thought that in my tiredness I was hallucinating. I'd been trained to doubt any ecstatic experience. The scent of roses was intense, like a drug! Could this be Carterton's ghost said to haunt the spot where he fell to his death, fighting a duel in the branches after a drunken night at Begg's? But this was no young duke. The woman was about my own height, with graceful beauty and the air of peace I associated with the Virgin. My unconventional madonna stood in a mannish confident way, a hand on her hip, clearly amused by me. She appeared to have emerged from the earth or from the tree. Shadows of bark and leaves still clung to her. There was something plantlike about the set of her limbs, the subtle colours of her flesh, as if a rose had become human and yet remained thoroughly a rose. I was rather frightened at first, my dear.

"I'd grown up with an Anglicanism permitting hardly a hint of the Pit, so I didn't perceive her as a temptress. I was thoroughly aware of her sexuality and in no way threatened by it or by her vitality. After a moment the fear dissipated, then after a few minutes she vanished and I was left with what I could only describe as her inspiration which led me to write my first real sermon that evening and present it on the following Sunday."

"She gave you a message?" I thought of Jeanne D'Arc.

"Oh, no. Our exchange was wordless on that occasion."

"And you spoke of her in church?"

"Never. That would have been a sort of betrayal. No, I based my message simply on the emotion she had aroused in me. A vision of Christ might have done the same. I don't know."

"So it was a Christian message? Not anti-Christian?"

"Not anti-religious, at any rate. Perhaps, as the bishop suggested, a little pagan."

"What brought you so much attention?"

"In the church that Sunday were two young chaps escorting their recently widowed aunt, Mrs. Nye. They told their friends about me. To my delight when I gave my second sermon I found myself with a very receptive congregation. I thanked God for the miracle. It seemed nothing else, my dear. You can't imagine the joy of it! For any chap in my position. I'd received a gift of divine communication, perhaps a small one, but it seemed pretty authentic. And the people began to pack St. Odhran's. We had money for repairs. They seemed so willing suddenly to give themselves to their faith!"

I was mildly disappointed. This Rose did not seem much of a vision. Under the influence of drugs or when overtired I had experienced hallucinations quite as elaborate and inspiring. I asked him if he had seen her again.

"Oh, yes. Of course. Many times. In the end we fell in love. She taught me so much. Later there was a child."

He stood up, adjusted his overcoat and scarf and gave his stick a little flourish. He pointed out how the light fell through the parade of black gnarled maples leading to the tennis courts. "An army of old giants ready to march," he said. "But their roots won't let them."

The next Wednesday when I came to lunch he said no more about his vision.

2 A Brief History of the Begg Family & of Sporting Club Square

In the course of my first four hundred lunches with the Clapham Antichrist I never did discover why he abandoned his career but I learned a great deal about the Begg family, its origins, its connections and its property, especially the Square. I became something of an expert and planned a monograph until the recent publication of two excellent Hubert Begg books made my work only useful as an appendix to real scholarship.

Today the Square, on several tourist itineraries, has lost most traces of its old unselfconscious integrity. Only Begg Mansions remains gated and fenced from casual view, a defiantly private museum of human curiosities. The rest of the Square has been encouraged to maximise its profitability. Bakunin Villas is now the Hotel Romanoff. Ralph Lauren for some time sponsored D'Yss Mansions as a fashion gallery. Beardsley Villas is let as company flats to United Foods, while the council (which invested heavily in BBIC) took another building, the Moorish fantasy of Flecker Mansions, as offices. There is still some talk of an international company "theme-parking" Sporting Club Square, running commercial tennis matches and linking it to a television soap. Following the financial scandals involving Begg Belgravia International and its associate companies, the Residents' Association has had some recent success in reversing this progress.

When I visited Edwin Begg in 1992, he welcomed me as if our routine had never been broken. He mourned his home's decline into a mere fashion, an exploitable commodity instead of a respected eccentricity, and felt it had gone the way of the Château Pantin or Derry & Toms famous Roof Garden, with every feature displayed as an emphatic curiosity, a sensation, a mode, and all her old charm a wistful memory. He had early on warned them about these likely consequences of his nephew's eager speculations. "Barbican wasn't the first to discover what you could do in a boom economy with a lick of paint, but I thought his soiling of his own nest a remote chance, not one of his first moves! The plans of such people are generally far advanced before they achieve power. When they strike, you are almost always taken unawares, aren't you, dear? What cold, patient dreams they must have."

He derived no satisfaction from Barbican Begg's somewhat ignoble ruin but felt deep sympathy for his fellow residents hopelessly trying to recover their stolen past.

"It's too late for us now and soon it won't matter much, but it's hard to imagine the kind of appetite which feeds upon souls like locusts on corn. We might yet drive the locust from our field, my dear, but he has already eaten his fill. He has taken what we cannot replace."

Sometimes he was a little difficult to follow and his similes grew increasingly bucolic.

"The world's changing physically, dear. Can't you feel it?" His eyes were as bright a blue and clear as always, his pink cheeks a little more drawn, his white halo thinner, but he still pecked at the middle-distance when he got excited, as if he could tear the truth from the air with his nose. He was clearly delighted that we had resumed our meetings. He apologised that the snacks were things he could make and microwave. They were still delicious. On our first meeting I was close to tears, wondering why on Earth I had simply assumed him dead and deprived myself of his company for so long. He suggested a stroll if I could stand it.

I admitted that the Square was not improving. I had been appalled at the gaudy golds and purples of the Hotel Romanoff. It was, he said, currently in receivership, and he shrugged. "What is it, my dear, which allows us to become the victims of such villains, time after time! Time after time they take what is best in us and turn it to our disadvantage. It's like being a conspirator in one's own rape."

We had come up to the Duke's Elm again in the winter twilight and he spoke fondly of familiar ancestors.

Cornelius Van Beek, a Dutch cousin of the Saxon von Beks, had settled in London in 1689, shortly after William and Mary. For many Europeans in those days England was a haven of relative enlightenment. A daring merchant banker, Van Beek financed exploratory trading expeditions, accompanying several of them himself, and amassed the honourable fortune enabling him to retire at sixty to Cogges Hall, Sussex. Amongst his properties when he died were the North Star Farm and tavern, west of Kensington, bought on the mistaken assumption that the area was growing more respectable and where he had at one time planned to build a house. This notorious stretch of heath was left to Van Beek's nephew, George Arthur Begg who had anglicised his name upon marriage to Harriet Vernon, his second cousin, in 1738. Their only surviving grandson was Robert Vernon Begg, famous as Dandy Bob Begg and ennobled under the Prince Regent.

As financially impecunious as his patron, Dandy Bob raised money from co-members of the Hellfire, took over the old tavern at North Star Farm, increased its size and magnificence, entertained the picaro captains so they would go elsewhere for their prizes, ran bare-knuckle fights, bear-baitings and other brutal spectacles, and founded the most notorious sporting establishment of its day. Fortunes were commonly lost and won at Begg's; suicides, scandals and duels no rarity. A dozen of our oldest families spilled their blood in the meadow beneath the black elm, and perhaps a score of men and women drowned in the brook now covered and serving as a modern sewer.

Begg's Sporting Club grew so infamous, the activities of its members and their concubines such a public outrage, that when the next William ascended, Begg rapidly declined. By Victoria's crowning the great dandy whom all had courted had become a souse married into the Wadhams for their money, got his wife Charlotte pregnant with male twins and died, whereupon she somewhat boldly married his nephew Captain Russell Begg and had three more children before he died a hero and a colonel in the Crimea. The twins were Ernest Sumara and Louis Palmate Begg, her two girls were Adriana Circe and Juliana Aphrodite and her youngest boy, her favourite child, was Hubert Alhambra born on 18th January, 1855, after his father's fatal fall at Balaclava.

A youthful disciple of Eastlake, by the late 1870s Hubert Begg was a practising architect whose largest single commission was Castle Bothwell on the shores of Loch Ness (his sister had married James Bothwell) which became a victim of the Glasgow blitz. "But it was little more than a bit of quasi-Eastlake and no rival for instance to the V&A," Edwin Begg had told me. He did not share my admiration for his great-uncle's achievement. "Quite frankly, his best work was always his furniture." He was proud of his complete bedroom suite in Begg's rather spare late style but he did not delight in living in "an art nouveau wedding cake." He claimed the Square's buildings cost up to ten times as much to clean as Oakwood Mansions, for instance, at the western end of Kensington High Street. "Because of the crannies and fancy mouldings, those flowing fauns and smirking sylphs the late Victorians found so deliciously sexy. Dust traps all. It's certainly unique, my dear, but so was Quasimodo."

Hubert Begg never struggled for a living. He had married the beautiful Carinthia Hughes, an American heiress, during his two years in Baltimore and it was she who suggested he use family land for his own creation, tearing down that ramshackle old firetrap, the Sporting Club Tavern, which together with a smallholding was rented to a family called Foulsham whom Begg generously resettled on prime land, complete with their children, their cow, their pig and various other domestic animals, near Old Cogges.

The North Star land was cleared. North Star Square was named but lasted briefly as that. It was designed as a true square with four other smaller squares around it to form a sturdy box cross, thus allowing a more flexible way of arranging the buildings, ensuring residents plenty of light, good views and more tennis. Originally there were plans for seven tennis courts. By the 1880s tennis was a social madness rather than a vogue and everybody was playing. Nearby Queen's Club was founded in Begg's shadow. Begg's plans were altogether more magnificent and soon the projected settlement blossomed into Sporting Club Square. The name had a slightly raffish, romantic reference and attracted the more daring young people, the financiers who still saw themselves as athletic privateers and who were already patrons to an artist or two as a matter of form.

Clients were encouraged to commission favourite styles for Begg to adapt. He had already turned his back on earlier influences, so Gothic did not predominate, but was well represented in Lohengrin Villas which was almost an homage to Eastlake, commissioned by the Church to house retired clergy who felt comfortable with its soaring arches and mighty buttresses. Encouraged by the enthusiasm for his scheme, the architect was able to indulge every fantasy, rather in the manner of a precocious Elgar offering adaptations of what Greaves called, in *The British Architect*, "Mediterranean, Oriental, Historical and Modern styles representing the quintessence of contemporary taste." But there were some who even then found it fussy and decadent. When the queen praised it as an example to the world Begg was knighted. Lady Carinthia, who survived him by many years, always credited herself as the Square's real procreator and it must be said it was she who nudged her husband away from the past to embrace a more plastic future.

Work on Sporting Club Square began in 1885 but was not entirely completed until 1901. The slump of the 1890s destroyed the aspirations of the rising bourgeoisie, who were to have been the likely renters; Gibbs and Flew had bankrupted themselves building the Olympia Bridge, and nobody who still had money felt secure enough to cross into the new suburbs. Their dreams of elevation now frustrated, the failed and dispossessed took their new bitter poverty with them into the depths of a North Star development doomed never to rise and to become almost at once a watchword for social decrepitude, populated by loafers, psychopaths, unstable landladies, exploited seamstresses, drunkards, forgers, beaten wives, braggarts, embezzlers, rat-faced children, petty officials and prostitutes who had grown accustomed to the easy prosperity of the previous decade and were now deeply resentful of anyone more fortunate. They swiftly turned the district into everything it remained until the next tide of prosperity lifted it for a while, only to let it fall back almost in relief as another generation lost its hold upon life's ambitions. The terraces were occupied by casual labourers and petty thieves while the impoverished petite bourgeoisie sought the mews and parades. North Star became a synonym for wretchedness and miserable criminality and was usually avoided even by the police.

By 1935 the area was a warren to rival Notting Dale, but Sporting Club Square, the adjoining St. Mary's Convent and the churchyard, retained a rather dreamy, innocent air, untouched by the prevailing mood. Indeed locals almost revered and protected the Square's tranquillity as if it were the only thing they had ever held holy and were proud of it. During the last war the Square was untouched by incendiaries roaring all around, but some of the flats were already abandoned and then taken over by the government to house mostly Jewish political exiles and these added to the cosmopolitan atmosphere. For years a Polish delicatessen stood on the corner of North Star Road; it was possible to buy all kinds of kosher food at Mrs. Green's grocery, Mandrake Terrace, and the Foulsham Road French patisserie remained popular until 1980 when Madame Stejns retired. According to Edwin Begg, the war and the years of austerity were their best, with a marvellous spirit of co-operation everywhere. During the war and until 1954 open-air concerts were regularly performed by local musicians and an excellent theatrical group was eventually absorbed into the Lyric until that was rationalised. A song, "The Rose of Sporting Club Square," was popular in the 1930s and the musical play it was written for was the basis of a Hollywood musical in 1940. The David Glazier Ensemble, perhaps the most innovative modern dance troupe of its day, occupied all the lower flats in Le Gallienne Chambers.

Edwin Begg was not the only resident to become famous with the general public. Wheldrake's association with the old tavern, where he spent two years of exile, is well known. Audrey Vernon lived most of her short life in Dowson Mansions. Her lover, Warwick Harden, took a flat in Ibsen Studios next door and had a door built directly through to her bedroom. John Angus Gilchrist the mass murderer lived here but dispatched his nearest victim three miles away in Shepherds Bush. Others associated with the Square, sometimes briefly, included Pett Ridge, George Robey, Gustav Klimt, Rebecca West, Constance Cummings, Jessie Matthews, Sonny Hale, Jack Parker, Gerald Kersh, Laura Riding, Joseph Kiss, John Lodwick, Edith Sitwell, Lord George Creech, Angela Thirkell, G. K. Chesterton, Max Miller, Sir Compton Mackenzie, Margery Allingham, Ralph Richardson, Eudora Welty, Donald Peers, Max Wall, Dame Fay Westbrook, Graham Greene, Eduardo Paolozzi, Gore Vidal, Bill Butler, Jimi Hendrix, Jack Trevor Story, Laura Ashley, Mario Amayo, Angela Carter, Simon Russell Beale, Ian Dury, Jonathan Carroll and a variety of sports and media personalities. As its preserves were stripped, repackaged and sold off during the feeding frenzy of the 1980s only the most stubborn residents refused to be driven from the little holdings they had once believed their birthright, but it was not until Edwin Begg led me back to his bedroom and raised the newly installed blind that I understood the full effect of his nephew's speculations. "We do not rest, do we," he said, "from mortal toil? But I'm not sure this is my idea of the new Jerusalem. What do you think, dear?"

They had taken his view, all that harmony. I was consumed with a sense of unspeakable outrage! They had turned that beautiful landscape into a muddy wasteland in which it seemed some monstrous, petulant child had scattered at random its filthy Tonka trucks and Corgi cranes, Portakabins, bulldozers in crazed abandon, then in tantrum stepped on everything. That perfect balance was destroyed and the tranquillity of Sporting Club Square was now forever under siege. The convent was gone, as well as the church.

"I read in the *Telegraph* that it required the passage of two private members' bills, the defiance of several preservation orders, the bribery of officials in thirteen different government departments and the blackmailing of a cabinet minister just to annex a third of the cemetery and knock down the chapel and almshouses," Begg said.

Meanwhile the small fry had looted the cemetery of its saleable masonry. Every monument had been chiselled. The severed heads of the angels were already being sold in the antique boutiques of Mayfair and St. Germain-des-Prés. Disappointed in their share of this loot, others had daubed swastikas and obscenities on the remaining stones.

"It's private building land now," said Begg. "They have dogs and fences. They bulldozered St. Swithold's. You can't get to the Necropolis, let alone the river. Still, this is probably better than what they were going to build."

The activities of Barbican Begg and his associates, whose enterprises claimed more victims than Maxwell, have been discussed everywhere, but one of the consequences of BBIC's speculations was that bleak no-man's-land standing in place of Edwin Begg's familiar view. The legal problems of leases sold to and by at least nine separate companies mean that while no further development has added to the Square's decline, attempts to redress the damage and activate the council's preservation orders which they ignored have failed through lack of funds. The project, begun in the name of freedom and civic high-mindedness, always a mark of the scoundrel, remains a symbol and a monument to the asset-stripped '80s. As yet only Frank Cornelius, Begg's close associate, has paid any satisfactory price for ruining so many lives.

"Barbican was born for that age." Edwin Begg drew down the blind against his ruined prospect and sat on his bed, his frail body scarcely denting the great Belgian pillows at his back. "Like a fly born to a dungheap. He could not help himself, my dear. It was his instinct to do what he did. Why are we always surprised by his kind?"

He had grown weak but eagerly asked if I would return the following Wednesday when he would tell me more about his visions and their effect upon his life. I promised to bring the ingredients of a meal. I would cook lunch. He was touched and amused by this. He thought the idea great fun.

I told him to stay where he was. It was easy to let myself out.

"You know," he called as I was leaving, "there's a legend in our family. How we protect the Grail which will one day bring a reconciliation between God and Lucifer. I have no Grail to pass on to you but I think I have its secret."

3 Astonishing Revelations of the Clapham Antichrist; Claims Involvement in the Creation of a New Messiah; His Visions of Paradise & Surrendering His Soul for Knowledge; Further Description of the Sporting Club Square Madonna; Final Days of the Antichrist; His Appearance in Death.

"Perhaps the crowning irony," said the Clapham Antichrist of his unfrocking, "was how devoted a Christian I was then! I argued that we shouldn't wait for God or heroes but seek our solutions at the domestic level. Naturally, it would mean empowering everyone, because only a thoroughly enfranchised democracy ever makes the best of its people. Oh, well, you know the sort of thing. The universal ideal that we all agree on and never seem to achieve. I merely suggested we take a hard look at the systems we used! They were quite evidently faulty! Not an especially revolutionary notion! But it met with considerable antagonism as you know. Politics seems to be a war of labels, one slapped on top of another until any glimmer of truth is thoroughly obscured. It's no wonder how quickly they lose all grip on reality!"

"And that's what you told them?"

He stood in his dressing gown staring down at a square and gardens even BBIC had failed to conquer. The trees were full of the nests crows had built since the first farmers hedged the meadow. His study, with its books and big old-fashioned stereo, had hardly changed but had a deserted air now.

I had brought the ingredients of our lunch and stood in my street clothes with my bag expecting him to lead me to the kitchen, but he remained in his window and wanted me to stay. He pointed mysteriously towards the Duke's Elm and Gilbert's War Memorial, a fanciful drinking fountain that had never worked.

"That's what I told them, my dear. In the pulpit first. Then in the travelling shows. Then on the street. I was arrested for obstruction in 1937, refused to recognise the court and refused to pay the fine. This was my first brief prison sentence. Eventually I got myself in solitary.

"When I left prison I saw a London even more wretched than before. Beggars were everywhere. Vagrants were not in those days tolerated in the West End, but were still permitted in the doorways of Soho and Somers Town. The squalor was as bad as anything Mayhew reported. I thought my anger had been brought under control in prison but I was wrong. The obscene exploitation of the weak by the strong was everywhere displayed. I did whatever I could. I stood on a box at Speakers' Corner. I wrote and printed pamphlets. I sent letters and circulars to everyone, to the newspapers, to the BBC. Nobody took me very seriously. In the main I was ignored. When I was not ignored I was insulted. Eventually, holding a sign in Oxford Street, I was again arrested but this time there was a scuffle with the arresting policeman. I went into Wormwood Scrubs until the outbreak of the Blitz when I was released to volunteer for the ambulance service. Well, I wasn't prepared to return to prison after the war and in fact my ideas had gained a certain currency. Do you remember what Londoners were like then, my dear? After we learned how to look after ourselves rather better than our leaders could? Our morale was never higher. London's last war was a war the people won in spite of the authorities. But somewhere along the line we gave our achievements over to the politicians, the power addicts. The result is that we now live in rookeries and slum courts almost as miserable as our nineteenth-century ancestors', or exist in blanketed luxury as divorced from common experience as a Russian Tsar. I'm not entirely sure about the quality of that progress, are you? These days the lowest common denominators are sought for as if they were principles."

"You're still an example to us," I said, thinking to console him.

He was grateful but shook his head, still looking down at the old elm as if he hoped to see someone there. "I'll never be sure if I did any good. For a while, you know, I was quite a celebrity until they realised I wasn't offering an anti-Christian message and then they mostly lost interest. I couldn't get on with those Jesuits they all cultivated. But I spoke to the Fabians twice and met

Wells, Shaw, Priestley and the rest. I was very cheerful. It appeared that I was spreading my message. I didn't understand that I was merely a vogue. I was quite a favourite with Bloomsbury and there was talk of putting me on Radio Luxembourg. But gradually doors were closed to me and I was rather humiliated on a couple of occasions. I hadn't started all this for fame or approval, so as soon as I realised what was happening I retired to the travelling shows and seaside fairgrounds which proliferated in England in the days before television.

"Eventually I began to doubt the value of my own pronouncements, since my audiences were dwindling and an evil force was progressing unchecked across Europe. We faced a future dominated by a few cruel dictatorships. Some kind of awful war was inevitable. During my final spell in clink I made up my mind to keep my thoughts to myself and consider better ways of getting them across. I saw nothing wrong with the message, but assumed myself to be a bad medium. In my free time I went out into the Square as much as I could. It was still easy to think there, even during the war."

He took a step towards the window, almost as if he had seen someone he recognised and then he shrugged, turning his head away sharply and pretending to take an interest in one of his Sickerts. "I found her there first, as you know, in 1933. And that one sight of her inspired a whole series of sermons. I came back week after week, but it always seemed as if I had just missed her. You could say I was in love with her. I wanted desperately for her to be real. Well, I had seen her again the evening I was 'unfrocked.' Of course I was in a pretty terrible state. I was praying. Since a boy I've always found it easy to pray in the Square. I identified God with the Duke's Elm—or at least I visualised God as a powerful old tree. I never understood why we placed such peculiar prohibitions on how we represented God. That's what they mean by 'pagan.' It has nothing to do with one's intellectual sophistication. I was praying when she appeared for the second time. First there was that strong scent of roses. When I looked up I saw her framed against the great trunk and it seemed a rose drew all her branches, leaves and blooms together and took human form!"

His face had a slight flush as he spoke. "It seemed to me I'd been given a companion to help me make the best use of my life. She had that vibrancy, that uncommon beauty; she was a sentient flower.

"Various church examiners to whom I explained the vision understood my Rose either as an expression of my own unstable mind or as a manifestation of the Devil. It was impossible for me to see her as either.

"She stepped forward and held out her hand to me. I had difficulty distinguishing her exact colours. They were many and subtle—an unbroken haze of pink and green and pale gold—all the shades of the rose. Her figure was slim but it wasn't easy to tell where her clothes met her body or even which was which. Her eyes changed in the light from deep emerald to violet. In spite of her extraordinary aura of power, her manner was almost hesitant. I think I was weeping as I went to her. I probably asked her what I should do. I know I decided to continue with my work. It was years before I saw her again, after I'd come out of prison for the last time."

"But you did see her again?"

"Many times. Especially during the Blitz. But I'd learned my lesson. I kept all that to myself."

"You were afraid of prison?"

"If you like. But I think it was probably more positive. God granted me a dream of the universe and her ever-expanding realities and I helped in the procreation of the new messiah!"

I waited for him to continue but he turned from the window with a broad smile. He was exhausted, tottering a little as he came with me to the kitchen and sat down in my place while I began to cook. He chatted amiably about the price of garlic and I prepared the dishes as he had taught me years before. This time, however, I was determined to encourage him to talk about himself.

He took a second glass of wine, his cheeks a little pinker than usual, his hair already beginning to rise about his head in a pure white fog.

"I suppose I needed her most during the war. There wasn't much time for talk, but I still came out to the Duke's Elm to pray. We began to meet frequently, always in the evenings before dark, and would walk together, comparing experience. She was from a quite different world—although her world sort of included ours. Eventually we became lovers."

"Did she have a name?"

"I think so. I called her the Rose. I travelled with her. She took me to paradise, my dear, nowhere less! She showed me the whole of Creation! And so after a while my enthusiasm returned. Again, I wanted to share my vision but I had become far more cautious. I had a suspicion that I made a mistake the first time and almost lost my Rose as a result. When my nephew, who was in BBC Talks, offered me a new pulpit I was pretty much ready for it. This time I was determined to keep the reality to myself and just apply what I had experienced to ordinary, daily life. The public could not accept the intensity and implications of my pure vision. I cultivated an avuncularity which probably shocked those who knew me well. I became quite the jolly Englishman! I was offered speaking engagements in America. I was such a show-off. I spent less and less time in the Square and eventually months passed before I realised that I had lost contact with my Rose and our child! I felt such an utter fool, my dear. As soon as I understood what was happening I gave everything up. But it was too late."

"You haven't seen her since?"

"Only in dreams."

"What do you believe she was? The spirit of the tree?" I did my best to seem matter-of-fact, but he knew what I was up to and laughed, pouring himself more wine.

"She is her own spirit, my dear, make no mistake."

And then the first course was ready, a *pâté de foie gras* made by my friend Loris Murrail in Paris. Begg agreed that it was as good as his own. For our main course we had Quantock veal in saffron. He ate it with appreciative relish. He had not been able to cook much lately, he said, and his appetite was reduced, but he enjoyed every bite. I was touched by his enthusiasm and made a private decision to come regularly again. Cooking him lunch would be my way of giving him something back. My spirits rose at the prospect and it was only then that I realised how much I had missed his company.

"Perhaps," he said, "she was sent to me to sustain me only when I most needed her. I had thought it a mistake to try to share her with the world. I never spoke of her again after I had told the bishop about her and was accused of militant paganism, primitive nature-worship. I saw his point of view but I always worshipped God in all his manifestations. The bishop seemed to argue that paganism was indistinguishable from common experience and therefore could not be considered a religion at all!"

"You worshipped her?"

"In a sense, my dear. As a man worships his wife."

I had made him a *tiesen sinamon* and he took his time with the meringue, lifting it up to his lips on the delicate silver fork which Begg's Cotswold benches had produced for Liberty in 1903. "I don't know if it's better or worse, dear, but the world is changing profoundly, you know. Our methods of making it safe just aren't really working any more. The danger of the simple answer is always with us and is inclined to lead to some sort of Final Solution. We are affected by turbulence as a leaf in the wind, but still we insist that the best way of dealing with the fact is to deny it or ignore it. And so we go on, hopelessly attempting to contain the thunder and the lightning and creating only further confusion! We're always caught by surprise! Yet it would require so little, surely, in the way of courage and imagination to find a way out, especially with today's wonderful computers?"

I had been depressed by the level and the outcome of the recent British election and was not optimistic. He agreed. "How we love to cling to the wrecks which took us onto the rocks in the first place. In our panic we don't even see the empty lifeboats within easy swimming distance."

He did not have the demeanour of a disappointed prophet. He remained lively and humorous. There was no sense of defeat about him, rather of quiet victory, of conquered pain. He did not at first seem disposed to tell me any more but when we were having coffee a casual remark set him off on a train of thought which led naturally back to that most significant event of his life. "We aren't flawed," he said, "just as God isn't flawed. What we perceive as flaws are a reflection of our own failure to see the whole." He spoke of a richly populated multiverse which was both within us and outside us. "We're all reflections and echoes, one of another, and our originals, dear, are lost, probably for ever. That was what I understood from my vision. I wrote it in my journal. Perhaps, very rarely, we're granted a glimpse of God's entire plan? Perhaps only when our need is desperate. I have no doubt that God sent me my Rose."

I am still of a secular disposition. "Or perhaps," I suggested, "as God you sent yourself a vision?"

He did not find this blasphemous but neither did he think it worth pursuing. "It's much of muchness, that," he said.

He was content in his beliefs. He had questioned them once but now he was convinced. "God sent me a vision and I followed her. She was made flesh. A miracle. I went with her to where she lived, in the fields of colour, in the far ether. We were married. We gave birth to a new human creature, neither male nor female but self-reproducing, a new messiah, and it set us free at last to dwell on that vast multiplicity of the heavens, to contemplate a quasi-infinity of versions of ourselves, our histories, our experience. That was what God granted me, my dear, when he sent me my Rose. Perhaps I was the Antichrist, after all, or at least its parent."

"In your vision did you see what became of the child?"

He spoke with light-hearted familiarity, not recalling some distant dream but describing an immediate reality. "Oh, yes. It grew to lead the world upon a new stage in our evolution. I'm not sure you'd believe the details, my dear, or find them very palatable."

I smiled at this, but for the first time in my life felt a hint of profound terror and I suppressed a sudden urge to shout at him, to tell him how ridiculous I considered his visions, a bizarre blend of popular prophecy and alchemical mumbo-jumbo which even a New Age traveller would take with a pinch of E. My anger overwhelmed me. Though I regained control of it he recognised it. He continued to speak but with growing reluctance and perhaps melancholy. "I saw a peculiar inevitability to the process. What, after all, do most of us live for? Ourselves? And what use is that? What value? What profit?"

With a great sigh he put down his fork. "That was delicious." His satisfaction felt to me like an accolade.

"You're only describing human nature." I took his plate.

"Is that what keeps us on a level with the amoeba, my dear, and makes us worth about as much individual affection? Come now! We allow ourselves to be ruled by every brutish, greedy instinct, not by what is significantly human in our nature! Our imagination is our greatest gift. It gives us our moral sensibility." He looked away through the dining-room window at the glittering domes of Gautier House and in the light the lines of his face were suddenly emphasised.

I had no wish ever to quarrel with him again. The previous argument, we were agreed, had cost us both too much. But I had to say what I thought. "I was once told the moment I mentioned morality was the moment I'd crossed the line into lunacy," I said. "I suppose we must agree to understand things differently."

For once he had forgotten his usual courtesy. I don't think he heard me. "Wasn't all this damage avoidable?" he murmured. "Weren't there ways in which cities could have grown up as we grew up, century adding to century, style to style, wisdom to wisdom? Isn't there something seriously wrong with the cycle we're in? Isn't there some way out?"

I made to reply but he shook his head, his hands on the table. "I saw her again, you know, several times after the birth. How beautiful she was! How much beauty she showed me! It's like an amplification, my dear, of every sense!

A discovery of new senses. An understanding that we don't need to discard anything as long as we continue to learn from it. It isn't frightening what she showed me. It's perfectly familiar once you begin to see. It's like looking at the quintessential versions of our ordinary realities. Trees, animals—they're there, in essence. You begin to discover all that. The fundamental geometry's identified. Well, you've seen this new math, haven't you?"

He seemed so vulnerable at that moment that for once I wasn't frank. I was unconvinced by what I judged as hippy physics made possible only by the new creative powers of computers. I didn't offer him an argument.

"You can't help but hope that it's what death is like," he said. "You become an angel."

He got up and returned slowly to his dusty study, beckoning me to look out with him into the twilight gathering around the trees where crows croaked their mutual reassurances through the darkening air. He glanced only once towards the old elm then turned his head away sharply. "You'll think this unlikely, I know, but we first came together physically at midnight under a full moon as bright and thin and yellow as honesty in a dark blue sky. I looked at the moon through those strong black branches the moment before we touched. The joy of our union was indescribable. It was a confirmation of my faith. I made a mistake going back into public life. What good did it do for anyone, my dear?"

"We all made too many easy assumptions," I said. "It wasn't your fault."

"I discovered sentimental solutions and comforted myself with them. Those comforts I turned to material profit. They became lies. And I lost her, my dear." He made a small, anguished gesture. "I'm still waiting for her to come back."

He was scarcely aware of me. I felt I had intruded upon a private moment and suggested that I had tired him and should leave. Looking at me in surprise but without dispute he came towards me, remarking in particular on the saffron sauce. "I can't tell you how much it meant to me, my dear, in every way."

I promised to return the following Wednesday and cook. He licked his pink lips in comic anticipation and seemed genuinely delighted by the prospect. "Yum, yum." He embraced me suddenly with his frail body, his sweet face staring blindly into mine.

I had found his last revelations disturbing and my tendency was to dismiss them perhaps as an early sign of his senility. I even considered putting off my promised visit, but was already planning the next lunch when three days later I took a call from Mrs. Arthur Begg who kept an eye on him and had my number. The Clapham Antichrist had died in his sleep. She had found him at noon with his head raised upon his massive pillows, the light from the open window falling on his face. She enthused over his wonderful expression in death.

The Opium General (1982)

"The Opium General" was originally published in *The Opium General and Other Stories* (Harrap) in 1984.

A rarity in the Moorcock canon, being a wholly non-fantastical story, it shares a great deal in common, thematically, with "A Dead Singer."

The Opium General

THEY HAD LIVED in a kind of besieged darkness for several weeks. At first she had welcomed the sense of solitude after the phone was cut off. They ignored the front door unless friends knew the secret knock. It was almost security, behind the blinds. From his ugly anxiety Charlie had calmed for a while but had soon grown morose and accusatory. There were too many creditors. The basement flat turned into a prison he was afraid to leave. When she had arrived three years ago it had seemed a treasure house; now she saw it merely as a record of his unrealised dreams: his half-read books, his comics, his toys, his synthesisers no longer stimulated him yet he refused to get rid of a single broken model Spitfire. They were tokens of his former substance, of a glorious past. When she suggested they go for a walk he said: "Too many people know me in Notting Hill." He meant the customers he had burned, taking money for drugs he never delivered, and the important dealers he had never paid. He tried to form a unity of his many frustrations: a general pattern, a calculated plot against him. A friend was murdered in a quarrel over sulphate at a house in Talbot Road. He decided the knife had been meant for him. "I've made too many enemies." This was his self-pitying phase.

She steered him as best she could away from paranoia. She was frightened by overt instability, but had learned to feel relaxed so long as the signs were unadmitted, buried. In response to her nervousness he pulled himself together in the only way he knew: the appropriate image. He said it was time for a stiff upper-lip, for holding the thin red line. She was perfectly satisfied, her sympathy for him was restored and she had been able to keep going. He became like Leslie Howard in an old war film. She tried to find somebody who could help him. This awful uncertainty stopped him doing his best. If he got clear, got a bit of money, they could start afresh. He wanted to write a novel: in Inverness, he thought, where he had worked in an hotel. Once away she could calm him down, get him to be his old self. But there remained the suspicion he might still choose madness as his escape. His friends said he habitually got himself into mental hospitals where he need feel no personal responsibility. He said, though, that it was chemical.

"Nobody's after you, Charlie, really." She had spent hours trying to win round all the big dealers. She went to see some of them on her own. They assured her with dismissive disgust that they had written off his debts and forgotten about him but would never do business with him again. The landlord was trying to serve them with a summons for almost a year's unpaid rent and had been unnecessarily rude the last time she had appealed to him. She blamed herself. She had longed for a return of the euphoria of their first weeks together. There had been plenty of money then, or at least credit. She had deliberately shut out the voice of her own common sense. In her drugged passivity she let him convince her something concrete would come of his elaborate fantasies; she lent her own considerable manipulative powers to his, telling his bank-manager of all the record-companies who were after his work, of the planned tour, of the ex-agent who owed him a fortune. This lifted him briefly and he became the tall handsome red-headed insouciant she had first met. "Partners in bullshit," he said cheerfully. "You should be on the stage, Ellie. You can be a star in my next road-show." It had been his apparent good-humoured carelessness in the face of trouble which made him seem so attractive to her three years ago when she left home to live here. She had not realised nobody in the music business would work with him any more, not even on sessions, because he got so loony. It was nerves, she knew, but he could be so rude to her, to everybody, and make a terrible impression. At the very last guest spot he had done, in Dingwalls, the roadies deliberately sabotaged his sound because he had been so overbearing. As Jimmy had told her gravely later: "Ye canna afford to get up the roadies' noses, Ellie. They can make or break a set." Jimmy had been Charlie's partner in their first psychedelic group, but had split the third time Charlie put himself in the bin. It was a bad sign, Jimmy told her, when Charlie started wearing his "army suit," as he had done to the Dingwalls gig.

Over the past two weeks Charlie had worn his uniform all the time. It seemed to make him feel better. "Look out for snipers, Algy," he warned her when she went shopping. He kept the shutters of the front-room windows closed, lay in bed all day and stayed up at night rolling himself cigarettes and fiddling with his little Casio synthesiser. He needed R&R, he said. When, through tiredness, she had snapped at him not to be so silly, playing at soldiers, he turned away from her sorrowfully: a military martyr, a decent Englishman forced into the dirty business of war. "This isn't fun for any of us." His father had been a regular sergeant in the Royal Artillery and had always wanted Charlie to go to Sandhurst. His parents were in Africa now, running a Bulawayo grocery shop. He frequently addressed her as sergeant-major. Creditors became "the enemy"; he needed more troops, reinforcements, fresh supplies. "What about a cup of coffee, s'a'rnt-major?" and she would have to get up to make him one. His old friends found the rôle familiar. They didn't help by playing up to it. "How's the general?" they would ask. He got out his military prints, his badges, his model soldiers, his aircraft charts. They were on every wall and surface now. He read Biggles books and old copies of *The Eagle*.

His last phone call had been to Gordon in Camden. "'Morning to you, field marshal. Spot of bother at this end. Pinned down under fire. Troops needing supplies. What can you get to us?" Gordon, his main coke-supplier, told him to fuck himself. "The chap's gone over to the enemy." Charlie was almost crying. "Turned yellow. Made of the wrong bally stuff." She pushed her long pale hair away from her little oval face and begged him to talk normally. "Nobody's going to take you seriously if you put on a funny voice."

"Can't think what you mean, old thing." He straightened his black beret on his cropped head. He had always been vain but now he spent fifty per cent of his waking time in front of the mirror. "Don't tell me you're crackin', too." He rode his motorbike to Brixton and came back with cash, claiming he had been cheated on the price. "We're going to have transport and logistics problems for a bit, s'a'rnt-major. But we'll get by somehow, eh? Darkest before the dawn and so on." She had just begun to warm to his courage when he gloomily added: "But I suppose you'll go AWOL next. One simply can't get the quality of front-line chap." All his other girlfriends had finally been unable to take him. She swore she was not the same. She made him a cup of tea and told him to go to bed and rest: her own universal remedy. It always seemed to work for her. Dimly she recognised his desperate reaching for certainties and order, yet his "general" was slowly wearing her down. She asked her mother to come to stay with her for a couple of days. "You should be on your own, love," said her mother. She was discomfited by Charlie's rôle. "Get yourself a little place. A job."

Ellie spread her short fingers on the table and stared at them. She was numb all over. He had made her senses flare like a firework; now she felt spent. She looked dreadful, said her mother. She was too thin, she was wearing too much make-up and perfume. Charlie liked it she said. "He's not doing you any good, love. The state of you!" All this in a murmur, while Charlie napped in the next room.

"I can't let him down now." Ellie polished her nails. "Everybody owes him money." But she knew she was both too frightened to leave and felt obscurely that she had given him more than his due, that he owed her for something. There was nobody else to support her; she was worn out. It was up to him. She would get him on his feet again, then he would in turn help her.

"You'd be better off at home," said her mother doubtfully. "Dad's a lot calmer than he used to be." Her father hated Charlie. The peculiar thing was they were very much alike in a lot of ways. Her father looked back with nostalgia to wartime and his Tank Regiment.

She and her mother went up to Tesco's together. The Portobello Road was crowded as usual, full of black women with prams and shopping bags, Pakistani women in saris, clutching at the hands of two or three kids, old hippies in big miserable coats, Irish drunks, gypsies, a smattering of middle-class women from the other side of Ladbroke Grove. Her mother hated the street; she wanted them to move somewhere more respectable. They pushed the cart round the supermarket. Her mother paid for the groceries. "At least you've got your basics for a bit," she said. She was a tiny, harassed woman with a face permanently masked, an ear permanently deaf to anything but the most conventional statements. "Bring Charlie to Worthing for a couple of weeks. It'll do you both good." But Charlie knew, as well as anyone, that he and Ellie's dad would be at loggerheads within a day. "Got to stay at HQ" he said. "Position could improve any moment." He was trying to write new lyrics for Jimmy's band, but they kept coming out the same as those they'd done together ten years before, about war and nuclear bombs and cosmic soldiers. Her mother returned to Worthing with a set, melancholy face; her shoulders rounded from thirty years of dogged timidity. Ellie noticed her own shoulders were becoming hunched, too. She made an effort to straighten them and then heard in her mind Charlie (or was it her dad?) saying "back straight, stomach in" and she let herself slump again. This self-defeating defiance was the only kind she dared allow herself. Her long hair (which Charlie insisted she keep) dragged her head to the ground.

That night he burned all his lyrics. "Top Secret documents," he called them. When she begged him to stop, saying somebody would buy them surely, he rounded on her. "If you're so into money, why don't you go out and earn some?" She was afraid to leave him to his own devices. He might do anything while she was away. He'd have a new girlfriend in five minutes. He couldn't stand being alone. She had thought him sensitive and vulnerable when he courted her. They met in a pub near the Music Machine. He seemed so interested in her, at once charmingly bold, shy and attentive. He made her laugh. She had mothered him a bit, she supposed. She would have done anything for him. Could that have been a mistake?

"You've got to find out what you want," said her sluttish friend Joan, who lived with an ex-biker. "Be independent." Joan worked at the health-food shop and was into feminism. "Don't let any fucking feller mess you around. Be your own woman." But Joan was bisexual and had her eye on Ellie. Her objectivity couldn't be trusted. Joan was having trouble with her old man yet she didn't seem about to split.

"I don't know who I am." Ellie stared at the Victorian screen Charlie had bought her. It had pictures of Lancers and Guardsmen varnished brownish yellow. "I was reading. We all define ourselves through other people, don't we?"

"Not as much as you do, dearie," said Joan. "What about a holiday? I'm thinking of staying at this cottage in Wales next month. We could both do with a break away from blokes."

Ellie said she'd think about it. She now spent most of her time in the kitchen looking out at the tiny overgrown yard. She made up lists in her mind: lists of things they could sell, lists of outfits she could buy, lists of places she would like to visit, lists of people who might be able to help Charlie. She had a list of their debts in a drawer somewhere. She considered a list of musicians and A&R men they knew. But these days all Charlie had that people wanted was dope contacts. And nobody would let him have as much as a joint on credit any more. It was disgusting. People kept in touch because you could help them score. The minute you weren't useful, they dropped you. Charlie wouldn't let her say this, though. He said it was her fault. She turned friends against him. "Why don't you fuck off, too? You've had everything I've got." But when she began to pack (knowing she could not leave) he told her he needed her. She was all he had left. He was sorry for being a bastard.

"I think I'm bad luck for you." Really she meant something else which she was too afraid to let into her consciousness. He was weak and selfish. She had stood by him through everything. But possibly he was right to blame her. She had let herself be entranced by his wit, his smiling mouth, his lean, nervous body so graceful in repose, so awkward when he tried to impress. She should have brought him down to earth sooner. She had known it was going wrong, but had believed something must turn up to save them. "Can't we go away?" she asked him early one afternoon. The room was in semi-darkness. Sun fell on the polished pine of the table between them; a single beam from the crack in the shutters. "What about that mate of yours in Tangier?" She picked unconsciously at the brocade chair left by his ex-wife. She felt she had retreated behind a wall which was her body, painted, shaved, perfumed: a lie of sexuality and compliance. She had lost all desire.

"And have the enemy seize the flat while we're there? You've got to remember, sergeant-major, that possession is nine-tenths of the law." He lay in his red Windsor rocker. He wore nothing but army gear, with a big belt round his waist, a sure sign of his insecurity. He drew his reproduction Luger from its holster and checked its action with profound authority. She stared at the reddish hair on his thick wrists, at the flaking spots on his fingers which resembled the early stages of a disease. His large, flat cheekbones seemed inflamed; there were huge bags under his eyes. He was almost forty. He was fighting off mortality as ferociously as he fought off what he called "the mundane world." She continued in an abstracted way to feel sorry for him. She still thought, occasionally, of Leslie Howard in the trenches. "Then couldn't we spend a few days on Vince's houseboat?"

"Vince has retreated to Shropshire. A non-pukkah wallah," he said sardonically. He and Vince had often played Indian army officers. "His old lady's given him murder. Shouldn't have taken her aboard. Women always let you down in a crunch." He glanced away.

She was grateful for the flush of anger which pushed her to her feet and carried her into the kitchen. "You ungrateful bastard. You should have kept your bloody dick in your trousers then, shouldn't you!" She became afraid, but it was not the old immediate terror of a blow, it was a sort of dull expectation of pain. She was seized with contempt for her own dreadful judgement. She sighed, waiting for him to respond in anger. She turned. He looked miserably at his Luger and reholstered it. He stood up, plucking at his khaki creases, patting at his webbing. He straightened his beret in front of the mirror, clearing his throat. He was pale. "What about organising some tiffin, sergeant-major?"

"I'll go out and get the bread." She took the Scottish pound note from the tin on the mantelpiece.

"Don't be long. The enemy could attack at any time." For a second he looked genuinely frightened. He was spitting a little when he spoke. His hair needed washing. He was normally so fussy about his appearance but he hadn't bathed properly in days. She had not dared say anything.

She went up the basement steps. Powys Square was noisy with children playing Cowboys and Indians. They exasperated her. She was twenty-five and felt hundreds of years older than them, than Charlie, than her mum and dad. Perhaps I'm growing up, she thought as she turned into Portobello Road and stopped outside the baker's. She stared at the loaves, pretending to choose. She looked at the golden bread and inhaled the sweet warmth; she looked at her reflection in the glass. She wore her tailored skirt, silk blouse, stockings, lacy bra and panties. He usually liked her to be feminine, but sometimes preferred her as a tomboy. "It's the poofter in me." She wasn't sure what she should be wearing now. A uniform like his? But it would be a lie. She looked at herself again. It was all a lie. Then she turned away from the baker's and walked on, past stalls of fruit, past stalls of avocados and Savoys, tomatoes and oranges, to the pawn shop where two weeks ago she had given up her last treasures. She paid individual attention to each electronic watch and every antique ring in the window and saw nothing she wanted. She crossed the road. Finch's pub was still open. Black men lounged in the street drinking from bottles, engaged in conventional badinage; she hoped nobody would recognise her. She went down Elgin Crescent, past the newsagent where she owed money, into the cherry- and apple-blossom of the residential streets. The blossom rose around her high heels like a sudden tide. Its colour, pink and white, almost blinded her. She breathed heavily. The scent came as if through a filter, no longer consoling. Feeling faint she sat on a low wall outside somebody's big house, her shopping bag and purse in her left hand, her right hand stroking mechanically at the rough concrete, desperate for sensation. Ordinary feeling was all she wanted. She could not imagine where it had gone. An ordinary life. She saw her own romanticism as a rotting tooth capped with gold. Her jaw ached. She looked upwards through the blossom at the blue sky in which sharply defined white clouds moved very slowly towards the sun, like cut-outs on a stage. She became afraid, wanting to turn back: she must get the bread before the scene ended and the day became grey again. But she needed this peace so badly. She grew self-conscious as a swarthy youth in a cheap black velvet suit went by whistling to himself. With only a little effort she could have made him attractive, but she no longer had the energy. Panic made her heart beat. Charlie could go over the top any minute. He might stack all the furniture near the doors and windows, as he had done once, or decide to rewire his equipment (he was useless at practical jobs) and be throwing a fit, breaking things, blaming her because a fuse had blown. Or he might be out in the street trying to get a reaction from a neighbour, baiting them, insulting them, trying to charm them. Or he might be at the Princess Alexandra, looking for somebody who would trust him with the money for a gram of coke or half-a-g of smack and stay put until closing time when he promised to return: restoring his ego, as he sometimes did, with a con-trick. If so he could be in real trouble. Everyone said he'd been lucky so far. She forgot the bread and hurried back.

The children were still yelling and squealing as she turned into the square in time to see him walking away round the opposite corner of the building. He was dressed in his combat beret, his flying jacket, his army boots, his sunglasses. He had his toy Luger and his sheath-knife on his belt. She forced herself to control her impulse to run after him. Trembling, she went down the steps of the basement, put her key in his front door, turned it, stepped inside. The whole of the front room was in confusion, as if he had been searching for something. The wicker chair had been turned over. The bamboo table was askew. As she straightened it (for she was automatically neat) she saw a note. He had used a model jeep as a weight. She screwed the note up. She went into the kitchen and put the kettle on. Waiting for the kettle to boil she flattened the paper on the draining board:

> *1400 hrs. Duty calls. Instructions from HQ to proceed at once to battle-zone. Will contact at duration of hostilities. Trust nobody. Hold the fort.*
>
> *—BOLTON, C-in-C, Sector Six.*

Her legs shook as she crossed back to the teapot. Within three or four days he would probably be in a police-station or a mental hospital. He would opt to become a voluntary patient. He had surrendered.

Her whole body shook now, with relief, with a sense of her own failure. He had won, after all. He could always win. She returned to the front door and slowly secured the bolts at top and bottom. She pushed back the shutters. Carefully she made herself a cup of tea and sat at the table with her chin in her hand staring through the bars of the basement window. The tea grew cold, but she continued to sip at it. She was out of the contest. She awaited her fate.

Behold the Man (1966)

"Behold the Man" first appeared in *New Worlds* No. 166 (Moorcock-edited), in September 1966. The story went on to win the following year's coveted Nebula Award for Best Novella, and courted a great deal of controversy along the way.

Moorcock expanded "Behold the Man" to novel-length in 1969, but it is presented here pretty much as it appeared in *New Worlds*.

BEHOLD THE MAN

He has no material power as the god-emperors had; he has only a following of desert people and fishermen. They tell him he is a god; he believes them. The followers of Alexander said: "He is unconquerable, therefore he is a god." The followers of this man do not think at all; he was their act of spontaneous creation. Now he leads them, this madman called Jesus of Nazareth.

And he spoke, saying unto them: Yeah verily I was *Karl Glogauer and now I am Jesus the Messiah, the Christ.*

And it was so.

1

THE TIME MACHINE was a sphere full of milky fluid in which the traveller floated, enclosed in a rubber suit, breathing through a mask attached to a hose leading to the wall of the machine. The sphere cracked as it landed and the fluid spilled into the dust and was soaked up. Instinctively, Glogauer curled himself into a ball as the level of the liquid fell and he sank to the yielding plastic of the sphere's inner lining. The instruments, cryptographic, unconventional, were still and silent. The sphere shifted and rolled as the last of the liquid dripped from the great gash in its side.

Momentarily, Glogauer's eyes opened and closed, then his mouth stretched in a kind of yawn and his tongue fluttered and he uttered a groan that turned into an ululation.

He heard himself. *The Voice of Tongues*, he thought. The language of the unconscious. But he could not guess what he was saying.

His body became numb and he shivered. His passage through time had not been easy and even the thick fluid had not wholly protected him, though it had doubtless saved his life. Some ribs were certainly broken. Painfully, he straightened his arms and legs and began to crawl over the slippery plastic towards the crack in the machine. He could see harsh sunlight, a sky like shimmering steel. He pulled himself halfway through the crack, closing his eyes as the full strength of the sunlight struck them. He lost consciousness.

Christmas term, 1949. He was nine years old, born two years after his father had reached England from Austria.

The other children were screaming with laughter in the gravel of the playground. The game had begun earnestly enough and somewhat nervously Karl had joined in in the same spirit. Now he was crying.

"Let me *down*! Please, Mervyn, stop it!"

They had tied him with his arms spread-eagled against the wire-netting of the playground fence. It bulged outwards under his weight and one of the posts threatened to come loose. Mervyn Williams, the boy who had proposed the game, began to shake the post so that Karl was swung heavily back and forth on the netting.

"Stop it!"

He saw that his cries only encouraged them and he clenched his teeth, becoming silent.

He slumped, pretending unconsciousness; the school ties they had used as bonds cut into his wrists. He heard the children's voices drop.

"Is he all right?" Molly Turner was whispering.

"He's only kidding," Williams replied uncertainly.

He felt them untying him, their fingers fumbling with the knots.

Deliberately, he sagged, then fell to his knees, grazing them on the gravel, and dropped face down to the ground.

Distantly, for he was half-convinced by his own deception, he heard their worried voices.

Williams shook him. "Wake up, Karl. Stop mucking about."

He stayed where he was, losing his sense of time until he heard Mr. Matson's voice over the general babble.

"What on Earth were you doing, Williams?"

"It was a play, sir, about Jesus. Karl was being Jesus. We tied him to the fence. It was his idea, sir. It was only a game, sir."

Karl's body was stiff, but he managed to stay still, breathing shallowly.

"He's not a strong boy like you, Williams. You should have known better."

"I'm sorry, sir. I'm really sorry." Williams sounded as if he were crying.

Karl felt himself lifted; felt the triumph...

He was being carried along. His head and side were so painful that he felt sick. He had had no chance to discover where exactly the time machine had brought him, but, turning his head now, he could see by the way the man on his right was dressed that he was at least in the Middle East.

He had meant to land in the year 29 A.D. in the wilderness beyond Jerusalem, near Bethlehem. Were they taking him to Jerusalem now?

He was on a stretcher that was apparently made of animal skins; this indicated that he was probably in the past, at any rate. Two men were carrying the stretcher on their shoulders. Others walked on both sides. There was a smell of sweat and animal fat and a musty smell he could not identify. They were walking towards a line of hills in the distance.

He winced as the stretcher lurched and the pain in his side increased. For the second time he passed out.

He woke up briefly, hearing voices. They were speaking what was evidently some form of Aramaic. It was night, perhaps, for it seemed very dark. They were no longer moving. There was straw beneath him. He was relieved. He slept.

In those days came John the Baptist preaching in the wilderness of Judaea, And saying, Repent ye: for the kingdom of heaven is at hand. For this is he that was spoken of by the prophet Esaias, saying, The voice of one crying in the wilderness, Prepare ye the way of the Lord, make his paths straight. And the same John had his raiment of camel's hair, and a leathern girdle about his loins; and his meat was locusts and wild honey. Then went out to him Jerusalem, and all Judaea, and all the region round about Jordan, And were baptised of him in Jordan, confessing their sins.

(Matthew 3: 1–6)

They were washing him. He felt the cold water running over his naked body. They had managed to strip off his protective suit. There were now thick layers of cloth against his ribs on the right, and bands of leather bound them to him.

He felt very weak now, and hot, but there was less pain.

He was in a building—or perhaps a cave; it was too gloomy to tell—lying on a heap of straw that was saturated by the water. Above him, two men continued to sluice water down on him from their earthenware pots. They were stern-faced, heavily bearded men, in cotton robes.

He wondered if he could form a sentence they might understand. His knowledge of written Aramaic was good, but he was not sure of certain pronunciations.

He cleared his throat. "Where—be—this—place?"

They frowned, shaking their heads and lowering their water jars.

"I—seek— a—Nazarene—Jesus..."

"Nazarene. Jesus." One of the men repeated the words, but they did not seem to mean anything to him. He shrugged.

The other, however, only repeated the word Nazarene, speaking it slowly as if it had some special significance for him. He muttered a few words to the other man and went towards the entrance of the room.

Karl Glogauer continued to try to say something the remaining man would understand.

"What—year—doth—the Roman Emperor—sit—in Rome?"

It was a confusing question to ask, he realised. He knew Christ had been crucified in the fifteenth year of Tiberius's reign, and that was why he had asked the question. He tried to phrase it better.

"How many—year—doth Tiberius rule?"

"Tiberius?" The man frowned.

Glogauer's ear was adjusting to the accent now and he tried to simulate it better. "Tiberius. The emperor of the Romans. How many years has he ruled?"

"How many?" The man shook his head. "I know not."

At least Glogauer had managed to make himself understood.

"Where is this place?" he asked.

"It is the wilderness beyond Machaerus," the man replied. "Know you not that?"

Machaerus lay to the south-east of Jerusalem, on the other side of the Dead Sea. There was no doubt that he was in the past and that the period was sometime in the reign of Tiberius, for the man had recognised the name easily enough.

His companion was now returning, bringing with him a huge fellow with heavily muscled hairy arms and a great barrel chest. He carried a big staff in one hand. He was dressed in animal skins and was well over six feet tall. His black, curly hair was long and he had a black, bushy beard that covered the upper half of his chest. He moved like an animal and his large, piercing brown eyes looked reflectively at Glogauer.

When he spoke, it was in a deep voice, but too rapidly for Glogauer to follow. It was Glogauer's turn to shake his head.

The big man squatted down beside him. "Who art thou?"

Glogauer paused. He had not planned to be found in this way. He had intended to disguise himself as a traveller from Syria, hoping that the local accents would be different enough to explain his own unfamiliarity with the language. He decided that it was best to stick to this story and hope for the best.

"I am from the north," he said.

"Not from Egypt?" the big man asked. It was as if he had expected Glogauer to be from there. Glogauer decided that if this was what the big man thought, he might just as well agree to it.

"I came out of Egypt two years since," he said.

The big man nodded, apparently satisfied. "So you are a magus from Egypt. That is what we thought. And your name is Jesus, and you are the Nazarene."

"I *seek* Jesus, the Nazarene," Glogauer said.

"Then what is your name?" The man seemed disappointed.

Glogauer could not give his own name. It would sound too strange to them. On impulse, he gave his father's first name. "Emmanuel," he said.

The man nodded, again satisfied. "Emmanuel."

Glogauer realised belatedly that the choice of name had been an unfortunate one in the circumstances, for Emmanuel meant in Hebrew "God with us" and doubtless had a mystic significance for his questioner.

"And what is your name?" he asked.

The man straightened up, looking broodingly down on Glogauer. "You do not know me? You have not heard of John, called the Baptist?"

Glogauer tried to hide his surprise, but evidently John the Baptist saw that his name was familiar. He nodded his shaggy head. "You do know of me, I see. Well, magus, now I must decide, eh?"

"What must you decide?" Glogauer asked nervously.

"If you be the friend of the prophecies or the false one we have been warned against by Adonai. The Romans would deliver me into the hands of mine enemies, the children of Herod."

"Why is that?"

"You must know why, for I speak against the Romans who enslave Judaea, and I speak against the unlawful things that Herod does, and I prophesy the time when all those who are not righteous shall be destroyed and Adonai's kingdom will be restored on Earth as the old prophets said it would be. I say to the people 'Be ready for that day when ye shall take up the sword to do Adonai's will.' The unrighteous know that they will perish on this day, and they would destroy me."

Despite the intensity of his words, John's tone was matter-of-fact. There was no hint of insanity or fanaticism in his face or bearing. He sounded most of all like an Anglican vicar reading a sermon whose meaning for him had lost its edge.

The essence of what he said, Karl Glogauer realised, was that he was arousing the people to throw out the Romans and their puppet Herod and establish a more "righteous" régime. The attributing of this plan to "Adonai" (one of the spoken names of Jahweh and meaning The Lord) seemed, as many scholars had guessed in the twentieth century, a means of giving the plan extra weight. In a world where politics and religion, even in the West, were inextricably bound together, it was necessary to ascribe a supernatural origin to the plan.

Indeed, Glogauer thought, it was more than likely that John believed his idea had been inspired by God, for the Greeks on the other side of the Mediterranean had not yet stopped arguing about the origins of inspiration—whether it originated in a man's head or was placed there by the gods. That

John accepted him as an Egyptian magician of some kind did not surprise Glogauer particularly, either. The circumstances of his arrival must have seemed extraordinarily miraculous and at the same time acceptable, particularly to a sect like the Essenes who practised self-mortification and starvation and must be quite used to seeing visions in this hot wilderness. There was no doubt now that these people were the neurotic Essenes, whose ritual washing—baptism—and self-deprivation, coupled with the almost paranoiac mysticism that led them to invent secret languages and the like, was a sure indication of their mentally unbalanced condition. All this occurred to Glogauer the psychiatrist manqué, but Glogauer the man was torn between the poles of extreme rationalism and the desire to be convinced by the mysticism itself.

"I must meditate," John said, turning towards the cave entrance. "I must pray. You will remain here until guidance is sent to me."

He left the cave, striding rapidly away.

Glogauer sank back on the wet straw. He was without doubt in a limestone cave, and the atmosphere in the cave was surprisingly humid. It must be very hot outside. He felt drowsy.

2

Five years in the past. Nearly two thousand in the future. Lying in the hot, sweaty bed with Monica. Once again, another attempt to make normal love had metamorphosed into the performance of minor aberrations which seemed to satisfy her better than anything else.

Their real courtship and fulfilment was yet to come. As usual, it would be verbal. As usual, it would find its climax in argumentative anger.

"I suppose you're going to tell me you're not satisfied again." She accepted the lighted cigarette he handed to her in the darkness.

"I'm all right," he said.

There was silence for a while as they smoked.

Eventually, and in spite of knowing what the result would be if he did so, he found himself talking.

"It's ironic, isn't it?" he began.

He waited for her reply. She would delay for a little while yet.

"What is?" she said at last.

"All this. You spend all day trying to help sexual neurotics to become normal. You spend your nights doing what they do."

"Not to the same extent. You know it's all a matter of degree."

"So you say."

He turned his head and looked at her face in the starlight from the window. She was a gaunt-featured redhead, with the calm, professional seducer's voice of the psychiatric social worker that she was. It was a voice that was soft, reasonable and insincere. Only occasionally, when she became particularly agitated, did her voice begin to indicate her real character. Her features never seemed to be in repose, even when she slept. Her eyes were forever wary, her movements rarely spontaneous. Every inch of her was protected, which was probably why she got so little pleasure from ordinary love-making.

"You just can't let yourself go, can you?" he said.

"Oh, shut up, Karl. Have a look at yourself if you're looking for a neurotic mess."

Both were amateur psychiatrists—she a psychiatric social worker, he merely a reader, a dabbler, though he had done a year's study some time ago when he had planned to become a psychiatrist. They used the terminology of psychiatry freely. They felt happier if they could name something.

He rolled away from her, groping for the ashtray on the bedside table, catching a glance of himself in the dressing-table mirror. He was a sallow, intense, moody Jewish bookseller, with a head full of images and unresolved obsessions, a body full of emotions. He always lost these arguments with Monica. Verbally, she was the dominant one. This kind of exchange often seemed to him more perverse than their love-making, where usually at least his rôle was masculine. Essentially, he realised, he was passive, masochistic, indecisive. Even his anger, which came frequently, was impotent. Monica was ten years older than he was, ten years more bitter. As an individual, of course, she had far more dynamism than he had; but as a psychiatric social worker she had had just as many failures. She plugged on, becoming increasingly cynical on the surface but still, perhaps, hoping for a few spectacular successes with patients. They tried to do too much, that was the trouble, he thought. The priests in the confessional supplied a panacea; the psychiatrists tried to cure, and most of the time they failed. But at least they tried, he thought, and then wondered if that was, after all, a virtue.

"I did look at myself," he said.

Was she sleeping? He turned. Her wary eyes were still open, looking out of the window.

"I did look at myself," he repeated. "The way Jung did. 'How can I help those persons if I am myself a fugitive and perhaps also suffer from the *morbus sacer* of a neurosis?' That's what Jung asked himself..."

"That old sensationalist. That old rationaliser of his own mysticism. No wonder you never became a psychiatrist."

"I wouldn't have been any good. It was nothing to do with Jung..."

"Don't take it out on me..."

"You've told me yourself that you feel the same—you think it's useless..."

"After a hard week's work, I might say that. Give me another fag."

He opened the packet on the bedside table and put two cigarettes in his mouth, lighting them and handing one to her.

Almost abstractedly, he noticed that the tension was increasing. The argument was, as ever, pointless. But it was not the argument that was the important thing; it was simply the expression of the essential relationship. He wondered if that was in any way important, either.

"You're not telling the truth." He realised that there was no stopping now that the ritual was in full swing.

"I'm telling the practical truth. I've no compulsion to give up my work. I've no wish to be a failure..."

"Failure? You're more melodramatic than I am."

"You're too earnest, Karl. You want to get out of yourself a bit."

He sneered. "If I were you, I'd give up my work, Monica. You're no more suited for it than I was."

She shrugged. "You're a petty bastard."

"I'm not jealous of you, if that's what you think. You'll never understand what I'm looking for."

Her laugh was artificial, brittle. "Modern man in search of a soul, eh? Modern man in search of a crutch, I'd say. And you can take that any way you like."

"We're destroying the myths that make the world go round."

"Now you say 'And what are we putting in their place?' You're stale and stupid, Karl. You've never looked rationally at anything—including yourself."

"What of it? You say the myth is unimportant."

"The reality that creates it is important."

"Jung knew that the myth can also create the reality."

"Which shows what a muddled old fool he was."

He stretched his legs. In doing so, he touched hers and he recoiled. He scratched his head. She still lay there smoking, but she was smiling now.

"Come on," she said. "Let's have some stuff about Christ."

He said nothing. She handed him the stub of her cigarette and he put it in the ashtray. He looked at his watch. It was two o'clock in the morning.

"Why do we do it?" he said.

"Because we must." She put her hand to the back of his head and pulled it towards her breast. "What else can we do?"

> *We Protestants must sooner or later face this question: Are we to understand the "imitation of Christ" in the sense that we should copy his life and, if I may use the expression, ape his stigmata; or in the deeper sense that we are to live our own proper lives as truly as he lived his in all its implications? It is no easy matter to live a life that is modelled on Christ's, but it is unspeakably harder to live one's own life as truly as Christ lived his. Anyone who did this would ... be misjudged, derided, tortured and crucified ... A neurosis is a dissociation of personality.*
>
> (Jung: *Modern Man in Search of a Soul*)

For a month, John the Baptist was away and Glogauer lived with the Essenes, finding it surprisingly easy, as his ribs mended, to join in their daily life. The Essenes' township consisted of a mixture of single-storey houses, built of limestone and clay brick, and the caves that were to be found on both sides of the shallow valley. The Essenes shared their goods in common and this particular sect had wives, though many Essenes led completely monastic lives. The Essenes were also pacifists, refusing to own or to make weapons—yet this sect plainly tolerated the warlike Baptist. Perhaps their hatred of the Romans overcame their principles. Perhaps they were not sure of John's entire intention. Whatever the reason for their toleration, there was little doubt that John the Baptist was virtually their leader.

The life of the Essenes consisted of ritual bathing three times a day, of prayer and of work. The work was not difficult. Sometimes Glogauer guided a plough pulled by two other members of the sect; sometimes he looked after the goats that were allowed to graze on the hillsides. It was a peaceful, ordered life, and even the unhealthy aspects were so much a matter of routine that Glogauer hardly noticed them for anything else after a while.

Tending the goats, he would lie on a hilltop, looking out over the wilderness which was not a desert, but rocky scrubland sufficient to feed animals like goats or sheep. The scrubland was broken by low-lying bushes and a few small trees growing along the banks of the river that doubtless ran into the Dead Sea. It was uneven ground. In outline, it had the appearance of a stormy lake, frozen and turned yellow and brown. Beyond the Dead Sea lay Jerusalem. Obviously Christ had not entered the city for the last time yet. John the Baptist would have to die before that happened.

The Essenes' way of life was comfortable enough, for all its simplicity. They had given him a goatskin loincloth and a staff and, except for the fact that he was watched by day and night, he appeared to be accepted as a kind of lay member of the sect.

Sometimes they questioned him casually about his chariot—the time machine they intended soon to bring in from the desert—and he told them that it had borne him from Egypt to Syria and then to here. They accepted the miracle calmly. As he had suspected, they were used to miracles.

The Essenes had seen stranger things than his time machine. They had seen men walk on water and angels descend to and from heaven; they had heard the voice of God and his archangels as well as the tempting voice of Satan and his minions. They wrote all these things down in their vellum scrolls. They were merely a record of the supernatural as their other scrolls were records of their daily lives and of the news that travelling members of their sect brought to them.

They lived constantly in the presence of God and spoke to God and were answered by God when they had sufficiently mortified their flesh and starved themselves and chanted their prayers beneath the blazing sun of Judaea.

Karl Glogauer grew his hair long and let his beard come unchecked. He mortified his flesh and starved himself and chanted his prayers beneath the sun, as they did. But he rarely heard God and only once thought he saw an archangel with wings of fire.

In spite of his willingness to experience the Essenes' hallucinations, Glogauer was disappointed, but he was surprised that he felt so well considering all the self-inflicted hardships he had to undergo, and he also felt relaxed in the company of these men and women who were undoubtedly insane. Perhaps it was because their insanity was not so very different from his own that after a while he stopped wondering about it.

John the Baptist returned one evening, striding over the hills followed by twenty or so of his closest disciples. Glogauer saw him as he prepared to drive the goats into their cave for the night. He waited for John to get closer.

The Baptist's face was grim, but his expression softened as he saw Glogauer. He smiled and grasped him by the upper arm in the Roman fashion.

"Well, Emmanuel, you are our friend, as I thought you were. Sent by Adonai to help us accomplish his will. You shall baptise me on the morrow, to show all the people that He is with us."

Glogauer was tired. He had eaten very little and had spent most of the day in the sun, tending the goats. He yawned, finding it hard to reply. However, he was relieved. John had plainly been in Jerusalem trying to discover if the Romans had sent him as a spy. John now seemed reassured and trusted him.

He was worried, however, by the Baptist's faith in his powers.

"John," he began. "I'm no seer..."

The Baptist's face clouded for a moment, then he laughed awkwardly. "Say nothing. Eat with me tonight. I have wild honey and locusts."

Glogauer had not yet eaten this food, which was the staple of travellers who did not carry provisions but lived off the food they could find on the journey. Some regarded it as a delicacy.

He tried it later, as he sat in John's house. There were only two rooms in the house. One was for eating in, the other for sleeping in. The honey-and-locusts was too sweet for his taste, but it was a welcome change from barley or goat-meat.

He sat cross-legged, opposite John the Baptist, who ate with relish. Night had fallen. From outside came low murmurs and the moans and cries of those at prayer.

Glogauer dipped another locust into the bowl of honey that rested between them. "Do you plan to lead the people of Judaea in revolt against the Romans?" he asked.

The Baptist seemed disturbed by the direct question. It was the first of its nature that Glogauer had put to him.

"If it be Adonai's will," he said, not looking up as he leaned towards the bowl of honey.

"The Romans know this?"

"I do not know, Emmanuel, but Herod the incestuous has doubtless told them I speak against the unrighteous."

"Yet the Romans do not arrest you."

"Pilate dare not—not since the petition was sent to the Emperor Tiberius."

"Petition?"

"Aye, the one that Herod and the Pharisees signed when Pilate the procurator did place votive shields in the palace at Jerusalem and seek to violate the Temple. Tiberius rebuked Pilate and since then, though he still hates the Jews, the procurator is more careful in his treatment of us."

"Tell me, John, do you know how long Tiberius has ruled in Rome?" He had not had the chance to ask that question again until now.

"Fourteen years."

It was 28 A.D.; something less than a year before the crucifixion would take place, and his time machine was smashed.

Now John the Baptist planned armed rebellion against the occupying Romans, but, if the Gospels were to be believed, would soon be decapitated by Herod. Certainly no large-scale rebellion had taken place at this time. Even those who claimed that the entry of Jesus and his disciples into Jerusalem and the invasion of the Temple were plainly the actions of armed rebels had found no records to suggest that John had led a similar revolt.

Glogauer had come to like the Baptist very much. The man was plainly a hardened revolutionary who had been planning revolt against the Romans for years and had slowly been building up enough followers to make the attempt successful. He reminded Glogauer strongly of the resistance leaders of the Second World War. He had a similar toughness and understanding of the realities of his position. He knew that he would only have one chance to smash the cohorts garrisoned in the country. If the revolt became protracted, Rome would have ample time to send more troops to Jerusalem.

"When do you think Adonai intends to destroy the unrighteous through your agency?" Glogauer said tactfully.

John glanced at him with some amusement. He smiled. "The Passover is a time when the people are restless and resent the strangers most," he said.

"When is the next Passover?"

"Not for many months."

"How can I help you?"

"You are a magus."

"I can work no miracles."

John wiped the honey from his beard. "I cannot believe that, Emmanuel. The manner of your coming was miraculous. The Essenes did not know if you were a devil or a messenger from Adonai."

"I am neither."

"Why do you confuse me, Emmanuel? I know that you are Adonai's messenger. You are the sign that the Essenes sought. The time is almost ready. The kingdom of heaven shall soon be established on Earth. Come with me. Tell the people that you speak with Adonai's voice. Work mighty miracles."

"Your power is waning, is that it?" Glogauer looked sharply at John. "You need me to renew your rebels' hopes?"

"You speak like a Roman, with such lack of subtlety." John got up angrily. Evidently, like the Essenes he lived with, he preferred less direct conversation. There was a practical reason for this, Glogauer realised, in that John and his men feared betrayal all the time. Even the Essenes' records were partially written in cipher, with one innocent-seeming word or phrase meaning something else entirely.

"I am sorry, John. But tell me if I am right." Glogauer spoke softly.

"Are you not a magus, coming in that chariot from nowhere?" The Baptist waved his hands and shrugged his shoulders. "My men saw you! They saw the shining thing take shape in air, crack and let you enter out of it. Is that not magical? The clothing you wore—was that earthly raiment? The talismans within the chariot—did they not speak of powerful magic? The prophet said that a magus would come from Egypt and be called Emmanuel. So it is written in the Book of Micah! Is none of these things true?"

"Most of them. But there are explanations—" He broke off, unable to think of the nearest word to "rational." "I am an ordinary man, like you. I have no power to work miracles! I am just a man!"

John glowered. "You mean you refuse to help us?"

"I'm grateful to you and the Essenes. You saved my life almost certainly. If I can repay that..."

John nodded his head deliberately. "You can repay it, Emmanuel."

"How?"

"Be the great magus I need. Let me present you to all those who become impatient and would turn away from Adonai's will. Let me tell them the manner of your coming to us. Then you can say that all is Adonai's will and that they must prepare to accomplish it."

John stared at him intensely. "Will you, Emmanuel?"

"For your sake, John. And in turn, will you send men to bring my chariot here as soon as possible? I wish to see if it may be mended."

"I will."

Glogauer felt exhilarated. He began to laugh. The Baptist looked at him with slight bewilderment. Then he began to join in.

Glogauer laughed on. History would not mention it, but he, with John the Baptist, would prepare the way for Christ.

Christ was not born yet. Perhaps Glogauer knew it, one year before the crucifixion.

> *And the Word was made flesh, and dwelt among us (and we beheld his glory, the glory as of the only begotten of the Father) full of grace and truth. John bare witness of him, and cried, saying, This was he of whom I spake, He that cometh after me is preferred before me; for he was before me.*
>
> (John 1: 14–15)

Even when he had first met Monica they had had long arguments. His father had not then died and left him the money to buy the Occult Bookshop in Great Russell Street, opposite the British Museum. He was doing all sorts of temporary work and his spirits were very low. At that time Monica had seemed a great help, a great guide through the mental darkness engulfing him. They had both lived close to Holland Park and went there for walks almost every Sunday of the summer of 1962. At twenty-two, he was already obsessed with Jung's strange brand of Christian mysticism. She, who despised Jung, had soon begun to denigrate all his ideas. She never really convinced him. But, after a while, she had succeeded in confusing him. It would be another six months before they went to bed together.

It was uncomfortably hot.

They sat in the shade of the cafeteria, watching a distant cricket match. Nearer to them, two girls and a boy sat on the grass, drinking orange squash from plastic cups. One of the girls had a guitar across her lap and she set the cup down and began to play, singing a folksong in a high, gentle voice. Glogauer tried to listen to the words. As a student, he had always liked traditional folk music.

"Christianity is dead." Monica sipped her tea. "Religion is dying. God was killed in 1945."

"There may yet be a resurrection," he said.

"Let us hope not. Religion was the creation of fear. Knowledge destroys fear. Without fear, religion can't survive."

"You think there's no fear about, these days?"

"Not the same kind, Karl."

"Haven't you ever considered the *idea* of Christ?" he asked her, changing his tack. "What that means to Christians?"

"The idea of the tractor means as much to a Marxist," she replied.

"But what came first? The idea or the actuality of Christ?"

She shrugged. "The actuality, if it matters. Jesus was a Jewish troublemaker organising a revolt against the Romans. He was crucified for his pains. That's all we know and all we need to know."

"A great religion couldn't have begun so simply."

"When people need one, they'll make a great religion out of the most unlikely beginnings."

"That's my point, Monica." He gesticulated at her and she drew away slightly. "The *idea* preceded the *actuality* of Christ."

"Oh, Karl, don't go on. The actuality of *Jesus* preceded the idea of *Christ.*"

A couple walked past, glancing at them as they argued.

Monica noticed them and fell silent. She got up and he rose as well, but she shook her head. "I'm going home, Karl. You stay here. I'll see you in a few days."

He watched her walk down the wide path towards the park gates.

The next day, when he got home from work, he found a letter. She must have written it after she had left him and posted it the same day.

Dear Karl,

Conversation doesn't seem to have much effect on you, you know. It's as if you listen to the tone of the voice, the rhythm of the words, without ever hearing what is trying to be communicated. You're a bit like a sensitive animal who can't understand what's being said to it, but can tell if the person talking is pleased or angry and so on. That's why I'm writing to you—to try to get my idea across. You respond too emotionally when we're together.

You make the mistake of considering Christianity as something that developed over the course of a few years, from the death of Jesus to the time the Gospels were written. But Christianity wasn't new. Only the name was new. Christianity was merely a stage in the meeting, cross-fertilisation metamorphosis of Western logic and Eastern mysticism. Look how the religion itself changed over the centuries, re-interpreting itself to meet changing times. Christianity is just a new name for a conglomeration of old myths and philosophies. All the Gospels do is retell the sun myth and garble some of the ideas from the Greeks and Romans. Even in the second century, Jewish scholars were showing it up for the mishmash it was! They pointed out the strong similarities between the various sun myths and the Christ myth. The miracles didn't happen—they were invented later, borrowed from here and there.

Remember the old Victorians who used to say that Plato was really a Christian because he anticipated Christian thought? Christian thought! Christianity was a vehicle for ideas in circulation for centuries before Christ. Was Marcus Aurelius a Christian? He was writing in the direct tradition of Western philosophy. That's why Christianity caught on in Europe and not in the East! You should have been a theologian with your bias, not a psychiatrist. The same goes for your friend Jung.

Try to clear your head of all this morbid nonsense and you'll be a lot better at your job.

Yours,
Monica.

He screwed the letter up and threw it away. Later that evening he was tempted to look at it again, but he resisted the temptation.

3

John stood up to his waist in the river. Most of the Essenes stood on the banks watching him. Glogauer looked down at him.

"I cannot, John. It is not for me to do it."

The Baptist muttered, "You must."

Glogauer shivered as he lowered himself into the river beside the Baptist. He felt light-headed. He stood there trembling, unable to move.

His foot slipped on the rocks of the river and John reached out and gripped his arm, steadying him.

In the clear sky, the sun was at zenith, beating down on his unprotected head.

"Emmanuel!" John cried suddenly. "The spirit of Adonai is within you!"

Glogauer still found it hard to speak. He shook his head slightly. It was aching and he could hardly see. Today he was having his first migraine attack since he had come here. He wanted to vomit. John's voice sounded distant.

He swayed in the water.

As he began to fall toward the Baptist, the whole scene around him shimmered. He felt John catch him and heard himself say desperately: "John, baptise *me*!" And then there was water in his mouth and throat and he was coughing.

John's voice was crying something. Whatever the words were, they drew a response from the people on both banks. The roaring in his ears increased, its quality changing. He thrashed in the water, then felt himself lifted to his feet.

The Essenes were swaying in unison, every face lifted upward towards the glaring sun.

Glogauer began to vomit into the water, stumbling as John's hands gripped his arms painfully and guided him up the bank.

A peculiar, rhythmic humming came from the mouths of the Essenes as they swayed; it rose as they swayed to one side, fell as they swayed to the other.

Glogauer covered his ears as John released him. He was still retching, but it was dry now, and worse than before.

He began to stagger away, barely keeping his balance, running, with his ears still covered; running over the rocky scrubland; running as the sun throbbed in the sky and its heat pounded at his head; running away.

But John forbade him, saying, I have need to be baptised of thee, and comest thou to me? And Jesus answering said unto him, Suffer it to be so now: for thus it becometh us to fulfil all righteousness. Then he suffered him. And Jesus, when he was baptised, went up straightway out of the water: and, lo, the heavens were opened unto him, and he saw the Spirit of God descending like a dove, and lighting upon him: And lo a voice from heaven, saying, This is my beloved Son, in whom I am well pleased.

(Matthew 3: 14–17)

He had been fifteen, doing well at the grammar school. He had read in the newspapers about the Teddy Boy gangs that roamed South London, but the odd youth he had seen in pseudo-Edwardian clothes had seemed harmless and stupid enough.

He had gone to the pictures in Brixton Hill and decided to walk home to Streatham because he had spent most of the bus money on an ice cream. They came out of the cinema at the same time. He hardly noticed them as they followed him down the hill.

Then, quite suddenly, they had surrounded him. Pale, mean-faced boys, most of them a year or two older than he was. He realised that he knew two of them vaguely. They were at the big council school in the same street as the grammar school. They used the same football ground.

"Hello," he said weakly.

"Hello, son," said the oldest Teddy Boy. He was chewing gum, standing with one knee bent, grinning at him. "Where you going, then?"

"Home."

"Heouwm," said the biggest one, imitating his accent. "What are you going to do when you get there?"

"Go to bed." Karl tried to get through the ring, but they wouldn't let him. They pressed him back into a shop doorway. Beyond them, cars droned by on the main road. The street was brightly lit, with street-lamps and neon from the shops. Several people passed, but none of them stopped. Karl began to feel panic.

"Got no homework to do, son?" said the boy next to the leader. He was redheaded and freckled and his eyes were a hard grey.

"Want to fight one of us?" another boy asked. It was one of the boys he knew.

"No. I don't fight. Let me go."

"You scared, son?" said the leader, grinning. Ostentatiously, he pulled a streamer of gum from his mouth and then replaced it. He began chewing again.

"No. Why should I want to fight you?"

"You reckon you're better than us, is that it, son?"

"No." He was beginning to tremble. Tears were coming into his eyes. " 'Course not."

" 'Course not, son."

He moved forward again, but they pushed him back into the doorway.

"You're the bloke with the kraut name, ain't you?" said the other boy he knew. "Glow-worm or somethink."

"Glogauer. Let me go."

"Won't your mummy like it if you're back late?"

"More a yid name than a kraut name."

"You a yid, son?"

"He looks like a yid."

"You a yid, son?"

"You a Jewish boy, son?"

"You a yid, son?"

"Shut up!" Karl screamed. He pushed into them. One of them punched him in the stomach. He grunted with pain. Another pushed him and he staggered.

People were still hurrying by on the pavement. They glanced at the group as they went past. One man stopped, but his wife pulled him on. "Just some kids larking about," she said.

"Get his trousers down," one of the boys suggested with a laugh. "That'll prove it."

Karl pushed through them and this time they didn't resist. He began to run down the hill.

"Give him a start," he heard one of the boys say.

He ran on.

They began to follow him, laughing.

They did not catch up with him by the time he turned into the avenue where he lived. He reached the house and ran along the dark passage beside it. He opened the back door. His step-mother was in the kitchen.

"What's the matter with you?" she said.

She was a tall, thin woman, nervous and hysterical. Her dark hair was untidy.

He went past her into the breakfast-room.

"What's the matter, Karl?" she called. Her voice was high-pitched.

"Nothing," he said.

He didn't want a scene.

It was cold when he woke up. The false dawn was grey and he could see nothing but barren country in all directions. He could not remember a great deal about the previous day, except that he had run a long way.

Dew had gathered on his loincloth. He wet his lips and rubbed the skin over his face. As he always did after a migraine attack he felt weak and completely drained. Looking down at his naked body, he noticed how skinny he had become. Life with the Essenes had caused that, of course.

He wondered why he had panicked so much when John had asked him to baptise him. Was it simply honesty—something in him which resisted deceiving the Essenes into thinking he was a prophet of some kind? It was hard to know.

He wrapped the goatskin about his hips and tied it tightly just above his left thigh. He supposed he had better try to get back to the camp and find John and apologise, see if he could make amends.

The time machine was there now, too. They had dragged it there, using only rawhide ropes.

If a good blacksmith could be found, or some other metal-worker, there was just a chance that it could be repaired. The journey back would be dangerous.

He wondered if he ought to go back right away, or try to shift to a time nearer to the actual crucifixion. He had not gone back specifically to witness the crucifixion, but to get the mood of Jerusalem during the Feast of the Passover, when Jesus was supposed to have entered the city. Monica had thought Jesus had stormed the city with an armed band. She had said that all the evidence pointed to that. All the evidence of one sort did point to it, but he could not accept the evidence. There was more to it, he was sure. If only he could meet Jesus. John had apparently never heard of him, though he had told Glogauer that there was a prophecy that the Messiah would be a Nazarene. There were many prophecies, and many of them conflicted.

He began to walk back in the general direction of the Essene camp. He could not have come so far. He would soon recognise the hills where they had their caves.

Soon it was very hot and the ground more barren. The air wavered before his eyes. The feeling of exhaustion with which he had awakened increased. His mouth was dry and his legs were weak. He was hungry and there was nothing to eat. There was no sign of the range of hills where the Essenes had their camp.

There was one hill, about two miles away to the south. He decided to make for it. From there he would probably be able to get his bearings, perhaps even see a township where they would give him food.

The sandy soil turned to floating dust around him as his feet disturbed it. A few primitive shrubs clung to the ground and jutting rocks tripped him.

He was bleeding and bruised by the time he began, painfully, to clamber up the hillside.

The journey to the summit (which was much further away than he had originally judged) was difficult. He would slide on the loose stones of the hillside, falling on his face, bracing his torn hands and feet to stop himself from sliding down to the bottom, clinging to tufts of grass and lichen that grew here and there, embracing larger projections of rock when he could, resting frequently, his mind and body both numb with pain and weariness.

He sweated beneath the sun. The dust stuck to the moisture on his half-naked body, caking him from head to foot. The goatskin was in shreds.

The barren world reeled around him, sky somehow merging with land, yellow rock with white clouds. Nothing seemed still.

He reached the summit and lay there gasping. Everything had become unreal.

He heard Monica's voice, thought he glanced her for a moment from the corner of his eye.

Don't be melodramatic, Karl...

She had said that many times. His own voice replied now.

I'm born out of my time, Monica. This age of reason has no place for me. It will kill me in the end.

Her voice replied.

Guilt and fear and your own masochism. You could be a brilliant psychiatrist, but you've given in to all your own neuroses so completely...

"Shut up!"

He rolled over on his back. The sun blazed down on his tattered body.

"Shut up!"

The whole Christian syndrome, Karl. You'll become a Catholic convert next, I shouldn't doubt. Where's your strength of mind?

"Shut up! Go away, Monica."

Fear shapes your thoughts. You're not searching for a soul or even a meaning for life. You're searching for comforts.

"Leave me alone, Monica!"

His grimy hands covered his ears. His hair and beard were matted with dust. Blood had congealed on the minor wounds that were now on every part of his body. Above, the sun seemed to pound in unison with his heartbeats.

You're going downhill, Karl, don't you realise that? Downhill. Pull yourself together. You're not entirely incapable of rational thought...

"Oh, Monica! Shut up!"

His voice was harsh and cracked. A few ravens circled the sky above him now. He heard them calling back at him in a voice not unlike his own.

God died in 1945...

"It isn't 1945—it's 28 A.D. God is alive!"

How you can bother to wonder about an obvious syncretistic religion like Christianity—Rabbinic Judaism, Stoic ethics, Greek mystery cults. Oriental ritual...

"It doesn't matter!"

Not to you in your present state of mind.

"I need God!"

That's what it boils down to, doesn't it? Okay, Karl, carve your own crutches. Just think what you could have been if you'd have come to terms with yourself...

Glogauer pulled his ruined body to its feet and stood on the summit of the hill and screamed.

The ravens were startled. They wheeled in the sky and flew away.

The sky was darkening now.

> *Then was Jesus led up of the Spirit into the wilderness to be tempted of the devil. And when he had fasted forty days and forty nights, he was afterward an hungered.*
>
> (Matthew 4: 1–2)

4

The madman came stumbling into the town. His feet stirred the dust and made it dance and dogs barked around him as he walked mechanically, his head turned upwards to face the sun, his arms limp at his sides, his lips moving.

To the townspeople, the words they heard were in no familiar language; yet they were uttered with such intensity and conviction that God himself might be using this emaciated, naked creature as his spokesman.

They wondered where the madman had come from.

The white town consisted primarily of double- and single-storeyed houses of stone and clay-brick, built around a marketplace that was fronted by an ancient, simple synagogue outside which old men sat and talked, dressed in dark robes. The town was prosperous and clean, thriving on Roman commerce. Only one or two beggars were in the streets and these were well-fed. The streets followed the rise and fall of the hillside on which they were built. They were winding streets, shady and peaceful; country streets. There was a smell of newly cut timber everywhere in the air, and the sound of carpentry, for the town was chiefly famous for its skilled carpenters. It lay on the edge of the Plain of Jezreel, close to the trade route between Damascus and Egypt, and waggons were always leaving it, laden with the work of the town's craftsmen. The town was called Nazareth.

The madman had found it by asking every traveller he saw where it was. He had passed through other towns—Philadelphia, Gerasa, Pella and Scythopolis, following the Roman roads—asking the same question in his outlandish accent. "Where lies Nazareth?"

Some had given him food on the way. Some had asked for his blessing and he had laid hands on them, speaking in that strange tongue. Some had pelted him with stones and driven him away.

He had crossed the Jordan by the Roman viaduct and continued northwards towards Nazareth.

There had been no difficulty in finding the town, but it had been difficult for him to force himself towards it. He had lost a great deal of blood and had eaten very little on the journey. He would walk until he collapsed and lie there until he could go on, or, as had happened increasingly, until someone found him and had given him a little sour wine or bread to revive him.

Once some Roman legionaries had stopped and with brusque kindness asked him if he had any relatives they could take him to. They had addressed him in pidgin-Aramaic and had been surprised when he replied in a strangely accented Latin that was purer than the language they spoke themselves.

They asked him if he was a rabbi or a scholar. He told them he was neither. The officer of the legionaries had offered him some dried meat and wine. The men were part of a patrol that passed this way once a month. They were stocky, brown-faced men, with hard, clean-shaven faces. They were dressed in stained leather kilts and breastplates and sandals, and had iron helmets on their heads, scabbarded short swords at their hips. Even as they stood around him in the evening sunlight they did not seem relaxed. The officer, softer-voiced than his men but otherwise much like them save that he wore a metal breastplate and a long cloak, asked the madman what his name was.

For a moment the madman had paused, his mouth opening and closing, as if he could not remember what he was called.

"Karl," he said at length, doubtfully. It was more a suggestion than a statement.

"Sounds almost like a Roman name," said one of the legionaries.

"Are you a citizen?" the officer asked.

But the madman's mind was wandering, evidently. He looked away from them, muttering to himself.

All at once, he looked back at them and said: "Nazareth?"

"That way." The officer pointed down the road that cut between the hills. "Are you a Jew?"

This seemed to startle the madman. He sprang to his feet and tried to push through the soldiers. They let him through, laughing. He was a harmless madman.

They watched him run down the road.

"One of their prophets, perhaps," said the officer, walking towards his horse. The country was full of them. Every other man you met claimed to be spreading the message of their god. They didn't make much trouble and religion seemed to keep their minds off rebellion. We should be grateful, thought the officer.

His men were still laughing.

They began to march down the road in the opposite direction to the one the madman had taken.

Now the madman was in Nazareth and the townspeople looked at him with curiosity and more than a little suspicion as he staggered into the market square. He could be a wandering prophet or he could be possessed by devils. It was often hard to tell. The rabbis would know.

As he passed the knots of people standing by the merchants' stalls, they fell silent until he had gone by. Women pulled their heavy woollen shawls about their well-fed bodies and men tucked in their cotton robes so that he would not touch them. Normally their instinct would have been to have taxed him with his business in the town, but there was an intensity about his gaze, a quickness and vitality about his face, in spite of his emaciated appearance, that made them treat him with some respect and they kept their distance.

When he reached the centre of the marketplace, he stopped and looked around him. He seemed slow to notice the people. He blinked and licked his lips.

A woman passed, eyeing him warily. He spoke to her, his voice soft, the words carefully formed. "Is this Nazareth?"

"It is." She nodded and increased her pace.

A man was crossing the square. He was dressed in a woollen robe of red-and-brown stripes. There was a red skullcap on his curly, black hair. His face was plump and cheerful. The madman walked across the man's path and stopped him. "I seek a carpenter."

"There are many carpenters in Nazareth. The town is famous for its carpenters. I am a carpenter myself. Can I help you?" The man's voice was good-humoured, patronising.

"Do you know a carpenter called Joseph? A descendant of David. He has a wife called Mary and several children. One is named Jesus."

The cheerful man screwed his face into a mock frown and scratched the back of his neck. "I know more than one Joseph. There is one poor fellow in yonder street." He pointed. "He has a wife called Mary. Try there. You should soon find him. Look for a man who never laughs."

The madman looked in the direction in which the man pointed. As soon as he saw the street, he seemed to forget everything else and strode towards it.

In the narrow street he entered, the smell of cut timber was even stronger. He walked ankle-deep in wood-shavings. From every building came the thud of hammers, the scrape of saws. There were planks of all sizes resting against the pale, shaded walls of the houses and there was hardly room to pass between them. Many of the carpenters had their benches just outside their doors. They were carving bowls, operating simple lathes, shaping wood into everything imaginable. They looked up as the madman entered the street and approached one old carpenter in a leather apron who sat at his bench carving a figurine. The man had grey hair and seemed short-sighted. He peered up at the madman.

"What do you want?"

"I seek a carpenter called Joseph. He has a wife—Mary."

The old man gestured with his hand that held the half-completed figurine.

"Two houses along on the other side of the street."

The house the madman came to had very few planks leaning against it, and the quality of the timber seemed poorer than the other wood he had seen. The bench near the entrance was warped on one side and the man who sat hunched over it repairing a stool seemed misshapen also. He straightened up as the madman touched his shoulder. His face was lined and pouched with misery. His eyes were tired and his thin beard had premature streaks of grey. He coughed slightly, perhaps in surprise at being disturbed.

"Are you Joseph?" asked the madman.

"I've no money."

"I want nothing—just to ask a few questions."

"I'm Joseph. Why do you want to know?"

"Have you a son?"

"Several, and daughters, too."

"Your wife is called Mary? You are of David's line."

The man waved his hand impatiently. "Yes, for what good either has done me…"

"I wish to meet one of your sons. Jesus. Can you tell me where he is?"

"That good-for-nothing. What has he done now?"

"Where is he?"

Joseph's eyes became more calculating as he stared at the madman. "Are you a seer of some kind? Have you come to cure my son?"

"I am a prophet of sorts. I can foretell the future."

Joseph got up with a sigh. "You can see him. Come." He led the madman through the gateway into the cramped courtyard of the house. It was crowded with pieces of wood, broken furniture and implements, rotting sacks of shavings. They entered the darkened house. In the first room—evidently a kitchen—a woman stood by a large clay stove. She was tall and bulging with fat. Her long, black hair was unbound and greasy, falling over large, lustrous eyes that still had the heat of sensuality. She looked the madman over.

"There's no food for beggars," she grunted. "He eats enough as it is." She gestured with a wooden spoon at a small figure sitting in the shadow of a corner. The figure shifted as she spoke.

"He seeks our Jesus," said Joseph to the woman. "Perhaps he comes to ease our burden."

The woman gave the madman a sidelong look and shrugged. She licked her red lips with a fat tongue. "Jesus!"

The figure in the corner stood up.

"That's him," said the woman with a certain satisfaction.

The madman frowned, shaking his head rapidly. "No."

The figure was misshapen. It had a pronounced hunched back and a cast in its left eye. The face was vacant and foolish. There was a little spittle on the lips. It giggled as its name was repeated. It took a crooked step forward. "Jesus," it said. The word was slurred and thick. "Jesus."

"That's all he can say." The woman sneered. "He's always been like that."

"God's judgement," said Joseph bitterly.

"What is wrong with him?" There was a pathetic, desperate note in the madman's voice.

"He's always been like that." The woman turned back to the stove. "You can have him if you want him. Addled inside and outside. I was carrying him when my parents married me off to that half-man..."

"You shameless—" Joseph stopped as his wife glared at him. He turned to the madman. "What's your business with our son?"

"I wished to talk to him. I..."

"He's no oracle—no seer—we used to think he might be. There are still people in Nazareth who come to him to cure them or tell their fortunes, but he only giggles at them and speaks his name over and over again..."

"Are—you sure—there is not—something about him—you have not noticed?"

"Sure!" Mary snorted sardonically. "We need money badly enough. If he had any magical powers, we'd know."

Jesus giggled again and limped away into another room.

"It is impossible," the madman murmured. Could history itself have changed? Could he be in some other dimension of time where Christ had never been?

Joseph appeared to notice the look of agony in the madman's eyes.

"What is it?" he said. "What do you see? You said you foretold the future. Tell us how we will fare?"

"Not *now*," said the prophet, turning away. "Not *now*."

He ran from the house and down the street with its smell of planed oak, cedar and cypress. He ran back to the marketplace and stopped, looking wildly about him. He saw the synagogue directly ahead of him. He began to walk towards it.

The man he had spoken to earlier was still in the marketplace, buying cooking pots to give to his daughter as a wedding gift. He nodded towards the strange man as he entered the synagogue. "He's a relative of Joseph the carpenter," he told the man beside him. "A prophet, I shouldn't wonder."

The madman, the prophet, Karl Glogauer, the time-traveller, the neurotic psychiatrist manqué, the searcher for meaning, the masochist, the man with a death-wish and the messiah-complex, the anachronism, made his way into the synagogue gasping for breath. He had seen the man he had sought. He had seen Jesus, the son of Joseph and Mary. He had seen a man he recognised without any doubt as a congenital imbecile.

"All men have a messiah-complex, Karl," Monica had said.

The memories were less complete now. His sense of time and identity was becoming confused.

"There were dozens of messiahs in Galilee at the time. That Jesus should have been the one to carry the myth and the philosophy was a coincidence of history..."

"There must have been more to it than that, Monica."

Every Tuesday in the room above the Occult Bookshop, the Jungian discussion group would meet for purposes of group analysis and therapy. Glogauer had not organised the group, but he had willingly lent his premises to it and had joined it eagerly. It was a great relief to talk with like-minded people once a week. One of his reasons for buying the Occult Bookshop was so that he would meet interesting people like those who attended the Jungian discussion group.

An obsession with Jung brought them together, but everyone had special obsessions of their own. Mrs. Rita Blenn charted the courses of flying saucers, though it was not clear if she believed in them or not. Hugh Joyce believed that all Jungian archetypes derived from the original race of Atlanteans who had perished millennia before. Alan Cheddar, the youngest of the group, was interested in Indian mysticism, and Sandra Peterson, the organiser, was a great witchcraft specialist. James Headington was interested in time. He was the group's pride; he was Sir James Headington, wartime inventor, very rich and with all sorts of decorations for his contribution to the Allied victory. He had had the reputation of being a great improviser during the War, but after it he had become something of an embarrassment to the War Office. He was a crank, they thought, and what was worse, he aired his crankiness in public.

Every so often, Sir James would tell the other members of the group about his time machine. They humoured him. Most of them were liable to exaggerate their own experiences connected with their different interests.

One Tuesday evening, after everyone else had left, Headington told Glogauer that his machine was ready.

"I can't believe it," Glogauer said truthfully.

"You're the first person I've told."

"Why me?"

"I don't know. I like you—and the shop."

"You haven't told the government."

Headington had chuckled. "Why should I? Not until I've tested it fully, anyway. Serves them right for putting me out to pasture."

"You don't know it works?"

"I'm sure it does. Would you like to see it?"

"A time machine." Glogauer smiled weakly.

"Come and see it."

"Why me?"

"I thought you might be interested. I know you don't hold with the orthodox view of science..."

Glogauer felt sorry for him.

"Come and see," said Headington.

He went out to Banbury the next day. The same day he left 1976 and arrived in 28 A.D.

The synagogue was cool and quiet with a subtle scent of incense. The rabbis guided him into the courtyard. They, like the townspeople, did not know what to make of him, but they were sure it was not a devil that possessed him. It was their custom to give shelter to the roaming prophets who were now everywhere in Galilee, though this one was stranger than the rest. His face was immobile and his body was stiff, and there were tears running down his dirty cheeks. They had never seen such agony in a man's eyes before.

"Science can say how, but it never asks why," he had told Monica. "It can't answer."

"Who wants to know?" she'd replied.

"I do."

"Well, you'll never find out, will you?"

"Sit down, my son," said the rabbi. "What do you wish to ask of us?"

"Where is Christ?" he said. "Where is Christ?"

They did not understand the language.

"Is it Greek?" asked one, but another shook his head.

Kyrios: The Lord.

Adonai: The Lord.

Where was the Lord?

He frowned, looking vaguely about him.

"I must rest," he said in their language.

"Where are you from?"

He could not think what to answer.

"Where are you from?" a rabbi repeated.

"*Ha-Olam Hab-Bah...*" he murmured at length.

They looked at one another. "*Ha-Olam Hab-Bah*," they said. *Ha-Olam Hab-Bah; Ha-Olam Haz-Zeh*: The world to come and the world that is.

"Do you bring us a message?" said one of the rabbis. They were used to prophets, certainly, but none like this one. "A message?"

"I do not know," said the prophet hoarsely. "I must rest. I am hungry."

"Come. We will give you food and a place to sleep."

He could only eat a little of the rich food and the bed with its straw-stuffed mattress was too soft for him. He was not used to it.

He slept badly, shouting as he dreamed, and, outside the room, the rabbis listened, but could understand little of what he said.

Karl Glogauer stayed in the synagogue for several weeks. He would spend most of his time reading in the library, searching through the long scrolls for some answer to his dilemma. The words of the Testaments, in many cases capable of a dozen interpretations, only confused him further. There was nothing to grasp, nothing to tell him what had gone wrong.

The rabbis kept their distance for the most part. They had accepted him as a holy man. They were proud to have him in their synagogue. They were sure that he was one of the special chosen of God and they waited patiently for him to speak to them.

But the prophet said little, muttering only to himself in snatches of their own language and snatches of the incomprehensible language he often used, even when he addressed them directly.

In Nazareth, the townsfolk talked of little else but the mysterious prophet in the synagogue, but the rabbis would not answer their questions. They would tell the people to go about their business, that there were things they were not yet meant to know. In this way, as priests had always done, they avoided questions they could not answer while at the same time appearing to have much more knowledge than they actually possessed.

Then, one sabbath, he appeared in the public part of the synagogue and took his place with the others who had come to worship.

The man who was reading from the scroll on his left stumbled over the words, glancing at the prophet from the corner of his eye.

The prophet sat and listened, his expression remote.

The Chief Rabbi looked uncertainly at him, then signed that the scroll should be passed to the prophet. This was done hesitantly by a boy who placed the scroll into the prophet's hands.

The prophet looked at the words for a long time and then began to read. The prophet read without comprehending at first what he read. It was the book of Esaias.

> *The Spirit of the Lord is upon me, because he hath anointed me to preach the gospel to the poor; he hath sent me to heal the brokenhearted, to preach deliverance to the captives, and recovering of sight to the blind, to set at liberty them that are bruised, to preach the acceptable year of the Lord. And he closed the book, and gave it again to the minister, and sat down. And the eyes of all of them that were in the synagogue were fastened on him.*
>
> (Luke 4: 18–20)

5

They followed him now, as he walked away from Nazareth towards the Lake of Galilee. He was dressed in the white linen robe they had given him and though they thought he led them, they, in fact, drove him before them.

"He is our messiah," they said to those that enquired. And there were already rumours of miracles.

When he saw the sick, he pitied them and tried to do what he could because they expected something of him. Many he could do nothing for, but others, obviously in psychosomatic conditions, he could help. They believed in his power more strongly than they believed in their sickness. So he cured them.

When he came to Capernaum, some fifty people followed him into the streets of the city. It was already known that he was in some way associated with John the Baptist, who enjoyed huge prestige in Galilee and had been declared a true prophet by many Pharisees. Yet this man had a power greater, in some ways, than John's. He was not the orator that the Baptist was, but he had worked miracles.

Capernaum was a sprawling town beside the crystal lake of Galilee, its houses separated by large market gardens. Fishing boats were moored at the white quayside, as well as trading ships that plied the lakeside towns. Though the green hills came down from all sides to the lake, Capernaum itself was built on flat ground, sheltered by the hills. It was a quiet town and, like most others in Galilee, had a large population of gentiles. Greek, Roman and Egyptian traders walked its streets and many had made permanent homes there. There was a prosperous middle class of merchants, artisans and ship-owners, as well as doctors, lawyers and scholars, for Capernaum was on the borders of the provinces of Galilee, Trachonitis and Syria, and though a comparatively small town was a useful junction for trade and travel.

The strange, mad prophet in his swirling linen robes, followed by the heterogeneous crowd that was primarily composed of poor folk but also could be seen to contain men of some distinction, swept into Capernaum. The news spread that this man really could foretell the future, that he had already predicted the arrest of John by Herod Antipas and soon after Herod had imprisoned the Baptist at Peraea. He did not make the predictions in general terms, using vague words the way other prophets did. He spoke of things that were to happen in the near future and he spoke of them in detail.

None knew his name. He was simply the prophet from Nazareth, or the Nazarene. Some said he was a relative, perhaps the son, of a carpenter in Nazareth, but this could be because the written words for "son of a carpenter" and "magus" were almost the same and the confusion had come about in that way. There was even a very faint rumour that his name was Jesus. The name had been used once or twice, but when they asked him if that was, indeed, his name, he denied it or else, in his abstracted way, refused to answer at all.

His actual preaching tended to lack the fire of John's. This man spoke gently, rather vaguely, and smiled often. He spoke of God in a strange way, too, and he appeared to be connected, as John was, with the Essenes, for he preached against the accumulation of personal wealth and spoke of mankind as a brotherhood, as they did.

But it was the miracles that they watched for as he was guided to the graceful synagogue of Capernaum. No prophet before him had healed the sick and seemed to understand the troubles that people rarely spoke of. It was his sympathy that they responded to, rather than the words he spoke.

For the first time in his life, Karl Glogauer had forgotten about Karl Glogauer. For the first time in his life he was doing what he had always sought to do as a psychiatrist.

But it was not his life. He was bringing a myth to life—a generation before that myth would be born. He was completing a certain kind of psychic circuit. He was not changing history, but he was giving history more substance.

He could not bear to think that Jesus had been nothing more than a myth. It was in his power to make Jesus a physical reality rather than the creation of a process of mythogenesis.

So he spoke in the synagogues and he spoke of a gentler God than most of them had heard of, and where he could remember them, he told them parables.

And gradually the need to justify what he was doing faded and his sense of identity grew increasingly more tenuous and was replaced by a different sense of identity, where he gave greater and greater substance to the rôle he had chosen. It was an archetypal rôle. It was a rôle to appeal to a disciple of Jung. It was a rôle that went beyond a mere imitation. It was a rôle that he must now play out to the very last grand detail. Karl Glogauer had discovered the reality he had been seeking.

> *And in the synagogue there was a man, which had a spirit of an unclean devil, and cried out with a loud voice, saying, Let us alone; what have we to do with thee, thou Jesus of Nazareth? art thou come to destroy us? I know thee who thou art; the Holy One of God. And Jesus rebuked him, saying, Hold thy peace, and come out of him. And when the devil had thrown him in the midst, he came out of him, and hurt him not. And they were all amazed, and*

spake among themselves, saying, What a word is this! for with authority and power he commandeth the unclean spirits, and they come out. And the fame of him went out into every place of the country round about.

(Luke 4: 33–37)

"Mass hallucination. Miracles, flying saucers, ghosts, it's all the same," Monica had said.

"Very likely," he had replied. "But why did they see them?"

"Because they wanted to."

"Why did they want to?"

"Because they were afraid."

"You think that's all there is to it?"

"Isn't it enough?"

When he left Capernaum for the first time, many more people accompanied him. It had become impractical to stay in the town, for the business of the town had been brought almost to a standstill by the crowds that sought to see him work his simple miracles.

He spoke to them in the spaces beyond the towns. He talked with intelligent, literate men who appeared to have something in common with him. Some of them were the owners of fishing fleets—Simon, James and John among them. Another was a doctor, another a civil servant who had first heard him speak in Capernaum.

"There must be twelve," he said to them one day. "There must be a zodiac."

He was not careful in what he said. Many of his ideas were strange. Many of the things he talked about were unfamiliar to them. Some Pharisees thought he blasphemed.

One day he met a man he recognised as an Essene from the colony near Machaerus.

"John would speak with you," said the Essene.

"Is John not dead yet?" he asked the man.

"He is confined at Peraea. I would think Herod is too frightened to kill him. He lets John walk about within the walls and gardens of the palace, lets him speak with his men, but John fears that Herod will find the courage soon to have him stoned or decapitated. He needs your help."

"How can I help him? He is to die. There is no hope for him."

The Essene looked uncomprehendingly into the mad eyes of the prophet.

"But, master, there is no one else who can help him."

"I have done all that he wished me to do," said the prophet. "I have healed the sick and preached to the poor."

"I did not know he wished this. Now he needs help, master. You could save his life."

The prophet had drawn the Essene away from the crowd.

"His life cannot be saved."

"But if it is not, the unrighteous will prosper and the kingdom of heaven will not be restored."

"His life cannot be saved."

"Is it God's will?"

"If I am God, then it is God's will."

Hopelessly, the Essene turned and began to walk away from the crowd.

John the Baptist would have to die. Glogauer had no wish to change history, only to strengthen it.

He moved on, with his following, through Galilee. He had selected his twelve educated men, and the rest who followed him were still primarily poor people. To them he offered their only hope of fortune. Many were those who had been ready to follow John against the Romans, but now John was imprisoned. Perhaps this man would lead them in revolt, to loot the riches of Jerusalem and Jericho and Caesarea. Tired and hungry, their eyes glazed by the burning sun, they followed the man in the white robe. They needed to hope and they found reasons for their hope. They saw him work greater miracles.

Once he preached to them from a boat, as was often his custom, and as he walked back to the shore through the shallows, it seemed to them that he walked over the water.

All through Galilee in the autumn they wandered, hearing from everyone the news of John's beheading. Despair at the Baptist's death turned to renewed hope in this new prophet who had known him.

In Caesarea they were driven from the city by Roman guards used to the wildmen with their prophecies who roamed the country.

They were banned from other cities as the prophet's fame grew. Not only the Roman authorities, but the Jewish ones as well seemed unwilling to tolerate the new prophet as they had tolerated John. The political climate was changing.

It became hard to find food. They lived on what they could find, hungering like starved animals.

He taught them how to pretend to eat and take their minds off their hunger.

Karl Glogauer, witch-doctor, psychiatrist, hypnotist, messiah.

Sometimes his conviction in his chosen rôle wavered and those that followed him would be disturbed when he contradicted himself. Often, now, they called him the name they had heard, Jesus the Nazarene. Most of the time he did not stop them from using the name, but at others he became angry and cried a peculiar, guttural name.

"Karl Glogauer! Karl Glogauer!"

And they said, Behold, he speaks with the voice of Adonai.

"Call me not by that name!" he would shout, and they would become disturbed and leave him by himself until his anger had subsided.

When the weather changed and the winter came, they went back to Capernaum, which had become a stronghold of his followers.

In Capernaum he waited the winter through, making prophecies.

Many of these prophecies concerned himself and the fate of those that followed him.

> *Then charged he his disciples that they should tell no man that he was Jesus the Christ. From that time forth began Jesus to shew unto his disciples, how that he must go unto Jerusalem, and suffer many things of the elders and chief priests and scribes, and be killed, and be raised again the third day.*
>
> (Matthew 16: 20–21)

They were watching television at her flat. Monica was eating an apple. It was between six and seven on a warm Sunday evening. Monica gestured at the screen with her half-eaten apple.

"Look at that nonsense," she said. "You can't honestly tell me it means anything to you."

The programme was a religious one, about a pop-opera in a Hampstead Church. The opera told the story of the crucifixion.

"Pop-groups in the pulpit," she said. "What a comedown."

He didn't reply. The programme seemed obscene to him, in an obscure way. He couldn't argue with her.

"God's corpse is really beginning to rot now," she jeered. "Whew! The stink!"

"Turn it off, then," he said quietly.

"What's the pop-group called? The Maggots?"

"Very funny. I'll turn it off, shall I?"

"No, I want to watch. It's funny."

"Oh, turn it off!"

"Imitation of Christ!" she snorted. "It's a bloody caricature."

A negro singer, who was playing Christ and singing flat to a banal accompaniment, began to drone out lifeless lyrics about the brotherhood of man.

"If he sounded like that, no wonder they nailed him up," said Monica.

He reached forward and switched the picture off.

"I was enjoying it." She spoke with mock disappointment. "It was a lovely swan-song."

Later, she said with a trace of affection that worried him, "You old fogey. What a pity. You could have been John Wesley or Calvin or someone. You can't be a messiah these days, not in your terms. There's nobody to listen."

6

The prophet was living in the house of a man called Simon, though the prophet preferred to call him Peter. Simon was grateful to the prophet because he had cured his wife of a complaint which she had suffered from for some time. It had been a mysterious complaint, but the prophet had cured her almost effortlessly.

There were a great many strangers in Capernaum at that time, many of them coming to see the prophet. Simon warned the prophet that some were known agents of the Romans or the Pharisees. The Pharisees had not, on the whole, been antipathetic towards the prophet, though they distrusted the talk of miracles that they heard. However, the whole political atmosphere was disturbed and the Roman occupation troops, from Pilate, through his officers, down to the troops themselves, were tense, expecting an outbreak but unable to see any tangible signs that one was coming.

Pilate himself hoped for trouble on a large scale. It would prove to Tiberius that the emperor had been too lenient with the Jews over the matter of the votive shields. Pilate would be vindicated and his power over the Jews increased. At present he was on bad terms with all the Tetrarchs of the provinces—particularly the unstable Herod Antipas who had seemed at one time his only supporter. Aside from the political situation, his own domestic situation was upset in that his neurotic wife was having her nightmares again and was demanding far more attention from him than he could afford to give her.

There might be a possibility, he thought, of provoking an incident, but he would have to be careful that Tiberius never learned of it. This new prophet might provide a focus, but so far the man had done nothing against the laws of either the Jews or the Romans. There was no law that forbade a man to claim he was a messiah, as some said this one had done, and he was hardly inciting the people to revolt—rather the contrary.

Looking through the window of his chamber, with a view of the minarets and spires of Jerusalem, Pilate considered the information his spies had brought him.

Soon after the festival that the Romans called Saturnalia, the prophet and his followers left Capernaum again and began to travel through the country.

There were fewer miracles now that the hot weather had passed, but his prophecies were eagerly asked. He warned them of all the mistakes that would be made in the future, and of all the crimes that would be committed in his name.

Through Galilee he wandered, and through Samaria, following the good Roman roads towards Jerusalem.

The time of the Passover was coming close now.

In Jerusalem, the Roman officials discussed the coming festival. It was always a time of the worst disturbances. There had been riots before during the Feast of the Passover, and doubtless there would be trouble of some kind this year, too.

Pilate spoke to the Pharisees, asking for their co-operation. The Pharisees said they would do what they could, but they could not help it if the people acted foolishly.

Scowling, Pilate dismissed them.

His agents brought him reports from all over the territory. Some of the reports mentioned the new prophet, but said that he was harmless.

Pilate thought privately that he might be harmless now, but if he reached Jerusalem during the Passover, he might not be so harmless.

Two weeks before the Feast of the Passover, the prophet reached the town of

Bethany near Jerusalem. Some of his Galilean followers had friends in Bethany and these friends were more than willing to shelter the man they had heard of from other pilgrims on their way to Jerusalem and the Great Temple.

The reason they had come to Bethany was that the prophet had become disturbed at the number of the people following him.

"There are too many," he had said to Simon. "Too many, Peter."

Glogauer's face was haggard now. His eyes were set deeper into their sockets and he said little.

Sometimes he would look around him vaguely, as if unsure where he was.

News came to the house in Bethany that Roman agents had been making enquiries about him. It did not seem to disturb him. On the contrary, he nodded thoughtfully, as if satisfied.

Once he walked with two of his followers across country to look at Jerusalem. The bright yellow walls of the city looked splendid in the afternoon light. The towers and tall buildings, many of them decorated in mosaic reds, blues and yellows, could be seen from several miles away.

The prophet turned back towards Bethany.

"When shall we go into Jerusalem?" one of his followers asked him.

"Not yet," said Glogauer. His shoulders were hunched and he grasped his chest with his arms and hands as if cold.

Two days before the Feast of the Passover in Jerusalem, the prophet took his men towards the Mount of Olives and a suburb of Jerusalem that was built on its side and called Bethphage.

"Get me a donkey," he told them. "A colt. I must fulfil the prophecy now."

"Then all will know you are the Messiah," said Andrew.

"Yes."

Glogauer sighed. He felt afraid again, but this time it was not physical fear. It was the fear of an actor who was about to make his final, most dramatic scene and who was not sure he could do it well.

There was cold sweat on Glogauer's upper lip. He wiped it off.

In the poor light he peered at the men around him. He was still uncertain of some of their names. He was not interested in their names, particularly, only in their number. There were ten here. The other two were looking for the donkey.

They stood on the grassy slope of the Mount of Olives, looking towards Jerusalem and the Great Temple which lay below. There was a light, warm breeze blowing.

"Judas?" said Glogauer enquiringly.

There was one called Judas.

"Yes, master," he said. He was tall and good-looking, with curly red hair and neurotic intelligent eyes. Glogauer believed he was an epileptic.

Glogauer looked thoughtfully at Judas Iscariot. "I will want you to help me later," he said, "when we have entered Jerusalem."

"How, master?"

"You must take a message to the Romans."

"The Romans?" Iscariot looked troubled. "Why?"

"It must be the Romans. It can't be the Jews—they would use a stake or an axe. I'll tell you more when the time comes."

The sky was dark now, and the stars were out over the Mount of Olives. It had become cold. Glogauer shivered.

Rejoice greatly O daughter of Zion,
Shout, O daughter of Jerusalem:
Behold, thy King cometh unto thee!
He is just and having salvation;
Lowly and riding upon an ass,
And upon a colt, the foal of an ass.
(Zechariah 9: 9)

"*Osha'na! Osha'na! Osha'na!*"

As Glogauer rode the donkey into the city, his followers ran ahead, throwing down palm branches. On both sides of the street were crowds, forewarned by the followers of his coming. Now the new prophet could be seen to be fulfilling the prophecies of the ancient prophets and many believed that he had come to lead them against the Romans. Even now, possibly, he was on his way to Pilate's house to confront the procurator.

"*Osha'na! Osha'na!*"

Glogauer looked around distractedly. The back of the donkey, though softened by the coats of his followers, was uncomfortable. He swayed and clung to the beast's mane. He heard the words, but could not make them out clearly.

"*Osha'na! Osha'na!*"

It sounded like "hosanna" at first, before he realised that they were shouting the Aramaic for "Free us."

"Free us! Free us!"

John had planned to rise in arms against the Romans this Passover. Many had expected to take part in the rebellion.

They believed that he was taking John's place as a rebel leader.

"No," he muttered at them as he looked around at their expectant faces. "No, I am the Messiah. I cannot free you. I can't..."

They did not hear him above their own shouts.

Karl Glogauer entered Christ. Christ entered Jerusalem. The story was approaching its climax.

"*Osha'na!*"

It was not in the story. He could not help them.

> *Verily, verily, I say unto you, that one of you shall betray me. Then the disciples looked one on another, doubting of whom he spake. Now there was leaning on Jesus' bosom one of his disciples, whom Jesus loved. Simon Peter therefore beckoned to him, that he should ask who it should be of whom he spake. He then lying on Jesus' breast saith unto him, Lord, who is it? Jesus answered, He it is, to whom I shall give a sop, when I have dipped it. And when he had dipped the sop, he gave it to Judas Iscariot, the son of Simon. And after the sop Satan entered into him. Then said Jesus unto him, That thou doest, do quickly.*
>
> (John 13: 21–27)

Judas Iscariot frowned with some uncertainty as he left the room and went out into the crowded street, making his way towards the governor's palace. Doubtless he was to perform a part in a plan to deceive the Romans and have the people rise up in Jesus' defence, but he thought the scheme foolhardy. The mood amongst the jostling men, women and children in the streets was tense. Many more Roman soldiers than usual patrolled the city.

Pilate was a stout man. His face was self-indulgent and his eyes were hard and shallow. He looked disdainfully at the Jew.

"We do not pay informers whose information is proved to be false," he warned.

"I do not seek money, lord," said Judas, feigning the ingratiating manner that the Romans seemed to expect of the Jews. "I am a loyal subject of the emperor."

"Who is this rebel?"

"Jesus of Nazareth, lord. He entered the city today..."

"I know. I saw him. But I heard he preached of peace and obeying the law."

"To deceive you, lord."

Pilate frowned. It was likely. It smacked of the kind of deceit he had grown to anticipate in these soft-spoken people.

"Have you proof?"

"I am one of his lieutenants, lord. I will testify to his guilt."

Pilate pursed his heavy lips. He could not afford to offend the Pharisees at this moment. They had given him enough trouble. Caiaphas, in particular, would be quick to cry "injustice" if he arrested the man.

"He claims to be the rightful king of the Jews, the descendant of David," said Judas, repeating what his master had told him to say.

"Does he?" Pilate looked thoughtfully out of the window.

"As for the Pharisees, lord..."

"What of them?"

"The Pharisees distrust him. They would see him dead. He speaks against them."

Pilate nodded. His eyes were hooded as he considered this information. The Pharisees might hate the madman, but they would be quick to make political capital out of his arrest.

"The Pharisees want him arrested," Judas continued. "The people flock to listen to the prophet and today many of them rioted in the Temple in his name."

"Is this true?"

"It is true, lord." It was true. Some half a dozen people had attacked the money-changers in the Temple and tried to rob them. When they had been arrested, they had said they had been carrying out the will of the Nazarene.

"I cannot make the arrest," Pilate said musingly. The situation in Jerusalem was already dangerous, but if they were to arrest this "king," they might find that they precipitated a revolt. Tiberius would blame him, not the Jews. The Pharisees must be won over. They must make the arrest. "Wait here," he said to Judas. "I will send a message to Caiaphas."

And they came to a place which was named Gethsemane: and he saith to his disciples. Sit ye here, while I shall pray. And he taketh with him Peter and James and John, and began to be sore amazed, and to be very heavy;

And saith unto them, My soul is exceeding sorrowful unto death: tarry ye here, and watch.

(Mark 14: 32–34)

Glogauer could see the mob approaching now. For the first time since Nazareth he felt physically weak and exhausted. They were going to kill him. He had to die; he accepted that, but he was afraid of the pain that was to come. He sat down on the ground of the hillside, watching the torches as they came closer.

"The ideal of martyrdom only ever existed in the minds of a few ascetics," Monica had said. *"Otherwise it was morbid masochism, an easy way to forgo ordinary responsibility, a method of keeping repressed people under control..."*

"It isn't as simple as that..."

"It is, Karl."

He could show Monica now. His regret was that she was unlikely ever to know. He had meant to write everything down and put it into the time machine and hope that it would be recovered. It was strange. He was not a religious man in the usual sense. He was an agnostic. It was not conviction that had led him to defend religion against Monica's cynical contempt for it; it was rather *lack* of conviction in the ideal in which she had set her own faith, the ideal of science as a solver of all problems. He could not share her faith and there was nothing else but religion, though he could not believe in the kind of God of Christianity. The God seen as a mystical force of the mysteries of Christianity and other great religions had not been personal enough for him. His rational mind had told him that God did not exist in any personal form. His unconscious had told him that faith in science was not enough.

"Science is basically opposed to religion," Monica had once said harshly. *"No matter how many Jesuits get together and rationalise their views of science, the fact remains that religion cannot accept the fundamental attitudes of science and it is implicit to science to attack the fundamental principles of religion. The only area in which there is no difference and need be no war is in the ultimate assumption. One may or may not assume there is a supernatural being called God. But as soon as one begins to defend one's assumption, there must be strife."*

"You're talking about organised religion..."

"I'm talking about religion as opposed to a belief. Who needs the ritual of

religion when we have the far superior ritual of science to replace it? Religion is a reasonable substitute for knowledge. But there is no longer any need for substitutes, Karl. Science offers a sounder basis on which to formulate systems of thought and ethics. We don't need the carrot of heaven and the big stick of hell any more when science can show the consequences of actions and men can judge easily for themselves whether those actions are right or wrong."

"I can't accept it."

"That's because you're sick. I'm sick, too, but at least I can see the promise of health."

"I can only see the threat of death..."

As they had agreed, Judas kissed him on the cheek and the mixed force of Temple guards and Roman soldiers surrounded him.

To the Romans he said, with some difficulty, "I am the King of the Jews." To the Pharisees' servants he said: "I am the messiah who has come to destroy your masters." Now he was committed and the final ritual was to begin.

7

It was an untidy trial, an arbitrary mixture of Roman and Jewish law which did not altogether satisfy anyone. The object was accomplished after several conferences between Pontius Pilate and Caiaphas and three attempts to bend and merge their separate legal systems in order to fit the expediencies of the situation. Both needed a scapegoat for their different purposes and so at last the result was achieved and the madman convicted, on the one hand of rebellion against Rome and on the other of heresy.

A peculiar feature of the trial was that the witnesses were all followers of the man and yet had seemed eager to see him convicted.

The Pharisees agreed that the Roman method of execution would fit the time and the situation best in this case and it was decided to crucify him. The man had prestige, however, so that it would be necessary to use some of the tried Roman methods of humiliation in order to make him into a pathetic and ludicrous figure in the eyes of the pilgrims. Pilate assured the Pharisees that he would see to it, but he made sure that they signed documents that gave their approval to his actions.

And the soldiers led him away into the hall, called Praetorium; and they call together the whole band. And they clothed him with purple, and platted a crown of thorns, and put it about his head, And began to salute him, Hail, King of the Jews! And they smote him on the head with a reed, and did spit upon him, and bowing their knees worshipped him. And when they had mocked him, they took off the purple from him, and put his own clothes on him, and led him out to crucify him.

(Mark 15: 16–20)

His brain was clouded now, by pain and by the ritual of humiliation; by his having completely given himself up to his rôle.

He was too weak to bear the heavy wooden cross and he walked behind it as it was dragged towards Golgotha by a Cyrenian whom the Romans had press-ganged for the purpose.

As he staggered through the crowded, silent streets, watched by those who had thought he would lead them against the Roman overlords, his eyes filled with tears so that his sight was blurred and he occasionally staggered off the road and was nudged back onto it by one of the Roman guards.

"You are too emotional, Karl. Why don't you use that brain of yours and pull yourself together..."

He remembered the words, but it was difficult to remember who had said them or who Karl was.

The road that led up the side of the hill was stony and he slipped sometimes, remembering another hill he had climbed long ago. It seemed to him that he had been a child, but the memory merged with others and it was impossible to tell.

He was breathing heavily and with some difficulty. The pain of the thorns in his head was barely felt, but his whole body seemed to throb in unison with his heartbeat. It was like a drum.

It was evening. The sun was setting. He fell on his face, cutting his head on a sharp stone, just as he reached the top of the hill. He fainted.

And they bring him unto the place Golgotha, which is being interpreted The place of a skull. And they gave him to drink wine mingled with myrrh: but he received it not.

(Mark 15: 22–23)

He knocked the cup aside. The soldier shrugged and reached out for one of his arms. Another soldier already held the other arm.

As he recovered consciousness Glogauer began to tremble violently. He felt the pain intensely as the ropes bit into the flesh of his wrists and ankles. He struggled.

He felt something cold placed against his palm. Although it only covered a small area in the centre of his hand it seemed very heavy. He heard a sound that also was in rhythm with his heartbeats. He turned his head to look at the hand.

The large iron peg was being driven into his hand by a soldier swinging a mallet, as he lay on the cross which was at this moment horizontal on the ground. He watched, wondering why there was no pain. The soldier swung the mallet higher as the peg met the resistance of the wood. Twice he missed the peg and struck Glogauer's fingers.

Glogauer looked to the other side and saw that the second soldier was also hammering in a peg. Evidently he missed the peg a great many times because the fingers of the hand were bloody and crushed.

The first soldier finished hammering in his peg and turned his attention to the feet. Glogauer felt the iron slide through his flesh, heard it hammered home.

Using a pulley, they began to haul the cross into a vertical position. Glogauer noticed that he was alone. There were no others being crucified that day.

He got a clear view of the lights of Jerusalem below him. There was still a little light in the sky but not much. Soon it would be completely dark. There was a small crowd looking on. One of the women reminded him of Monica. He called to her.

"Monica?"

But his voice was cracked and the word was a whisper. The woman did not look up.

He felt his body dragging at the nails which supported it. He thought he felt a twinge of pain in his left hand. He seemed to be bleeding very heavily.

It was odd, he reflected, that it should be him hanging here. He supposed that it was the event he had originally come to witness. There was little doubt, really. Everything had gone perfectly.

The pain in his left hand increased.

He glanced down at the Roman guards who were playing dice at the foot of his cross. They seemed absorbed in their game. He could not see the markings of the dice from this distance.

He sighed. The movement of his chest seemed to throw extra strain on his hands. The pain was quite bad now. He winced and tried somehow to ease himself back against the wood.

The pain began to spread through his body. He gritted his teeth. It was dreadful. He gasped and shouted. He writhed.

There was no longer any light in the sky. Heavy clouds obscured stars and moon.

From below came whispered voices.

"Let me down," he called. "Oh, please let me down!"

The pain filled him. He slumped forward, but nobody released him.

A little while later he raised his head. The movement caused a return of the agony and again he began to writhe on the cross.

"Let me down. Please. Please stop it!"

Every part of his flesh, every muscle and tendon and bone of him, was filled with an almost impossible degree of pain.

He knew he would not survive until the next day as he had thought he might. He had not realised the extent of his pain.

> *And at the ninth hour Jesus cried with a loud voice, saying, "Eloi, Eloi, lama sabachthani?" which is, being interpreted, My God, my God, why hast thou forsaken me?*
>
> (Mark 15: 34)

Glogauer coughed. It was a dry, barely heard sound. The soldiers below the cross heard it because the night was now so quiet.

"It's funny," one said. "Yesterday they were worshipping him. Today they seemed to want us to kill him—even the ones who were closest to him."

"I'll be glad when we get out of this country," said another.

He heard Monica's voice again. "It's weakness and fear, Karl, that's driven you to this. Martyrdom is a conceit. Can't you see that?"

Weakness and fear.

He coughed once more and the pain returned, but it was duller now.

Just before he died he began to talk again, muttering the words until his breath was gone. "It's a lie. It's a lie. It's a lie."

Later, after his body was stolen by the servants of some doctors who believed it to have special properties, there were rumours that he had not died. But the corpse was already rotting in the doctors' dissecting rooms and would soon be destroyed.

A Winter Admiral (1994)

"A Winter Admiral" first appeared in the *Daily Telegraph* in March 1994.

A wholly non-fantastical story, it introduces another of the many and disparate members of the Family von Bek, one Marjorie Begg.

A

Winter Admiral

After lunch she woke up, thinking the rustling from the pantry must be a foraging mouse brought out of hibernation by the unusual warmth. She smiled. She never minded a mouse or two for company and she had secured anything she would not want them to touch.

No, she really didn't mind the mice at all. Their forebears had been in these parts longer than hers and had quite as much right to the territory. More of them, after all, had bled and died for home and hearth. They had earned their tranquillity. Her London cats were perfectly happy to enjoy a life of peaceful co-existence.

"We're a family." She yawned and stretched. "We probably smell pretty much the same by now." She took up the brass poker and opened the fire door of the stove. "One big happy family, us and the mice and the spiders."

After a few moments the noise from the pantry stopped. She was surprised it did not resume. She poked down the burning logs, added two more from her little pile, closed the door and adjusted the vents. That would keep in nicely.

As she leaned back in her chair she heard the sound again. She got up slowly to lift the latch and peer in. Through the outside pantry window, sunlight laced the bars of dust and brightened her shelves. She looked on the floor for droppings. Amongst her cat-litter bags, her indoor gardening tools, her electrical bits and pieces, there was nothing eaten and no sign of a mouse.

Today it was even warm in the pantry. She checked a couple of jars of pickles. It didn't do for them to heat up. They seemed all right. This particular pantry had mostly canned things. She only ever needed to shop once a week.

She closed the door again. She was vaguely ill at ease. She hated anything odd going on in her house. Sometimes she lost perspective. The best way to get rid of the feeling was to take a walk. Since the sun was so bright today, she would put on her coat and stroll up the lane for a bit.

It was one of those pleasant February days which deceives you into believing spring has arrived. A cruel promise, really, she thought. This weather would be gone soon enough. Make the best of it, she said to herself. She would leave the radio playing, put a light on in case it grew dark before she was back, and promise herself *The Charlie Chester Show*, a cup of tea and a scone when she got home. She lifted the heavy iron kettle, another part of her inheritance, and put it on the hob. She set her big, brown teapot on the brass trivet.

The scent of lavender struck her as she opened her coat cupboard. She had just re-lined the shelves and drawers. Lavender reminded her of her first childhood home.

"We're a long way from Mitcham now," she told the cats as she took her tweed overcoat off the hanger. Her Aunt Becky had lived here until her last months in the nursing home. Becky had inherited Crow Cottage from the famous Great Aunt Begg. As far as Marjorie Begg could tell, the place had been inhabited by generations of retired single ladies, almost in trust, for centuries.

Mrs. Begg would leave Crow Cottage to her own niece, Clare, who looked after Jessie, her half-sister. A chronic invalid, Jessie must soon die, she was so full of rancour.

A story in a Cotswold book said this had once been known as Crone's Cottage. She was amused by the idea of ending her days as the local crone. She would have to learn to cackle. The crone was a recognised figure in any English rural community, after all. She wondered if it were merely coincidence that made Rab, the village idiot, her handyman. He worshipped her. She would do anything for him. He was like a bewildered child since his wife had thrown him out: she could make more in benefits than he made in wages. He had seemed reconciled to the injustice: "I was never much of an earner." That apologetic grin was his response to most disappointment. It probably hadn't been fitting for a village idiot to be married, any more than a crone. Yet who had washed and embroidered the idiot's smocks in the old days?

She had been told Rab had lost his digs and was living wild in Wilson's abandoned farm buildings on the other side of the wood.

Before she opened her front door she thought she heard the rustling again. The sound was familiar, but not mice. Some folded cellophane unravelling as the cupboard warmed up? The cottage had never been cosier.

She closed the door behind her, walking up the stone path under her brown tangle of honeysuckle and through the gate to the rough farm lane. Between the tall, woven hedges she kept out of the shade as much as she could. She relished the air, the winter scents, the busy finches, sparrows, tits and yellowhammers. A chattering robin objected to her passing and a couple of wrens fussed at her. She clicked her tongue, imitating their angry little voices. The broad meadows lay across the brow of the hills like shawls, their dark-brown furrows laced with melting frost, bright as crystal. Birds flocked everywhere, to celebrate this unexpected ease in the winter's grey.

Her favourites were the crows and magpies. Such old, alien birds. So wise. Closer to the dinosaurs and inheriting an unfathomable memory. Was that why people took against them? She had learned early that intelligence was no better admired in a bird than in a woman. The thought of her father made her shudder, even out here on this wide, unthreatening Cotswold hillside, and she felt suddenly lost, helpless, the cottage no longer her home. Even the steeple on the village church, rising beyond the elms, seemed completely inaccessible. She hated the fear more than she hated the man who had infected her with it—as thoroughly as if he had infected her with a disease. She blamed herself. What good was hatred? He had died wretchedly, of exposure, in Hammersmith, between his pub and his flat, a few hundred yards away.

Crow Cottage, with its slender evergreens and lattice of willow boughs, was as safe and welcoming as always when she turned back into her lane. As the sun fell it was growing colder, but she paused for a moment. The cottage, with its thatch and its chimney, its walls and its hedges, was a picture. She loved it. It welcomed her, even now, with so little colour in the garden.

She returned slowly, enjoying the day, and stepped back over her hearth, into her dream of security, her stove and her cats and her rattling kettle. She was in good time for *Sing Something Simple* and would be eating her scones by the time Charlie Chester came on. She had never felt the need for a television here, though she had been a slave to it in Streatham. Jack had liked his sport.

He had been doing his pools when he died.

When she came back to the flat that night, Jack was in the hall, stretched out with his head on his arm. She knew he was dead, but she gave him what she hoped was the kiss of life, repeatedly blowing her warm breath through his cold lips until she got up to phone for the ambulance. She kept kissing him, kept pouring her breath into him, but was weeping almost uncontrollably when they arrived.

He wouldn't have known anything, love, they consoled her.

No consolation at all to Jack! He had hated not knowing things. She had never anticipated the anguish that came with the loss of him, which had lasted until she moved to Crow Cottage. She had written to Clare. By some miracle, the cottage had cured her of her painful grief and brought unexpected reconciliation.

It was almost dark.

Against the sprawling black branches of the old elms, the starlings curled in ranks towards the horizon, while out of sight in the tall wood the crows began to call, bird to bird, family to family. The setting sun had given the few clouds a powdering of terracotta and the air was suddenly a Mediterranean blue behind them. Everything was so vivid and hurrying so fast, as if to greet the end of the world.

She went to draw the back curtains and saw the sunset over the flooded fields fifteen miles away, spreading its bloody light into the water. She almost gasped at the sudden beauty of it.

Then she heard the rustling again. Before the light failed altogether, she was determined to discover the cause. It would be awful to start getting fancies after dark.

As she unlatched the pantry door something rose from the floor and settled against the window. She shivered, but did not retreat.

She looked carefully. Then, to her surprise: "Oh, it's a butterfly!"

The butterfly began to beat again upon the window. She reached to cup it in her hands, to calm it. "Poor thing."

It was a newborn Red Admiral, its orange, red and black markings vibrant as summer. "Poor thing." It had no others of its kind.

For a few seconds the butterfly continued to flutter, and then was still. She widened her hands to look in. She watched its perfect, questing antennae, its extraordinary legs, she could almost smell it. A small miracle, she thought, to make a glorious day complete.

An unexpected sadness filled her as she stared at the butterfly. She carried it to the door, pushed the latch with her cupped hands, and walked into the twilight. When she reached the gate she opened her hands again, gently, to relish the vivacious delicacy of the creature. Mrs. Begg sighed, and with a sudden, graceful movement lifted her open palms to let the Admiral taste the air.

In two or three wingbeats the butterfly was up, a spot of busy, brilliant colour streaming towards the east and the cold horizon.

As it gained height, it veered, its wings courageous against the freshening wind.

Shielding her eyes, Mrs. Begg watched the Admiral turn and fly over the thatch, to be absorbed in the setting sun.

It was far too cold now to be standing there. She went inside and shut the door. The cats still slept in front of the stove. With the pot holder she picked up the kettle, pouring lively water over the tea. Then she went to close her pantry door.

"I really couldn't bear it," she said. "I couldn't bear to watch it die."

London Bone (1997)

Another, much more up-to-date story from *New Worlds* now, appearing in the most recent issue, No. 222 (White Wolf), edited by David Garnett in 1997.

Earlier in this collection, in "Lunching with the Antichrist," much was made of the wrongdoings of one Barbican Begg. There were plans for a whole novel to be named after him, but that project transformed itself throughout the '90s, eventually appearing in 2000 as *King of the City*, a fast-and-furious, at times almost stream-of-consciousness first-person-narrative rail against the preceding two decades' Thatcherite/Conservative-led excesses and abuses of power.

"London Bone" was in many ways a precursor to *King of the City*, sharing much of that book's rapid-fire prose style.

LONDON BONE

For Ronnie Scott

I

MY NAME IS Raymond Gold and I'm a well-known dealer. I was born too many years ago in Upper Street, Islington. Everybody reckons me in the London markets and I have a good reputation in Manchester and the provinces. I have bought and sold, been the middleman, an agent, an art representative, a professional mentor, a tour guide, a spiritual bridge-builder. These days I call myself a cultural speculator.

But, you won't like it, the more familiar word for my profession, as I practised it until recently, is *scalper*. This kind of language is just another way of isolating the small businessman and making what he does seem sleazy while the stockbroker dealing in millions is supposed to be legitimate. But I don't need to convince anyone today that there's no sodding justice.

"Scalping" is risky. What you do is invest in tickets on spec and hope to make a timely sale when the market for them hits zenith. Any kind of ticket, really, but mostly shows. I've never seen anything offensive about getting the maximum possible profit out of an American matron with more money than sense who's anxious to report home with the right items ticked off the *been-to* list. We've all seen them rushing about in their overpriced limos and mini-buses, pretending to be individuals: **Thursday: Changing-of-the-Guard, Harrods, Planet Hollywood, Royal Academy, Tea-at-the-Ritz,** *Cats*. It's a sort of tribal dance they are compelled to perform. If they don't perform it, they feel inadequate. **Saturday: Tower of London, Bucket of Blood, Jack-the-Ripper talk, Sherlock Holmes Pub, Sherlock Holmes tour, Madame Tussauds, Covent Garden Cream Tea,** ***Dogs***. These are people so traumatised by contact with strangers that their only security lies in these rituals, these well-blazed trails and familiar chants. It's my job to smooth their paths, to make them exclaim how pretty and wonderful and elegant and *magical* it all is. The street people aren't a problem. They're just so many charming Dick Van Dykes.

Americans need bullshit the way koala bears need eucalyptus leaves. They've become totally addicted to it. They get so much of it back home that they can't survive without it. It's your duty to help them get their regular fixes while they travel. And when they make it back after three weeks on alien shores, their friends, of course, are always glad of some foreign bullshit for a change.

Even if you sell a show ticket to a real enthusiast, who has already been forty-nine times and is so familiar to the cast they see him in the street and think he's a relative, who are you hurting? Andros Loud Website, Lady Hatchet's loyal laureate, who achieved rank and wealth by celebrating the lighter side of the moral vacuum? He would surely applaud my enterprise in the buccaneering spirit of the free market. Venture capitalism at its bravest. Well, he'd applaud me if he had time these days from his railings against fate, his horrible understanding of the true nature of his coming obscurity. But that's partly what my story's about.

I have to say in my own favour that I'm not merely a speculator or, if you like, exploiter. I'm also a patron. For many years, not just recently, a niagara of dosh has flowed out of my pocket and into the real arts faster than a cat up a Frenchman. Whole orchestras and famous soloists have been brought to the Wigmore Hall on the money they get from me. But I couldn't have afforded this if it wasn't for the definitely iffy *Miss Saigon* (a triumph of well-oiled machinery over dodgy morality) or the unbelievably decrepit *Good Rockin' Tonite* (in which the living dead jive in the aisles), nor, of course, that first great theatrical triumph of the new millennium, *Schindler: The Musical*. Make 'em weep, Uncle Walt!

So who is helping most to support the arts? You, me, the lottery?

I had another reputation, of course, which some saw as a second profession. I was one of the last great London characters. I was always on late-night telly, lit from below, and Iain Sinclair couldn't write a paragraph without dropping my name at least once. I'm a quintessential Londoner, I am. I'm a Cockney gentleman.

I read Israel Zangwill and Gerald Kersh and Alexander Baron. I can tell you the best books of Pett Ridge and Arthur Morrison. I know Pratface Charlie, Driff and Martin Stone, Bernie Michaud and the even more legendary Gerry and Pat Goldstein. They're all historians, archaeologists, revenants. There isn't another culture-dealer in London, oldster or child, who doesn't at some time come to me for an opinion. Even now, when I'm as popular as a pig at a Putney wedding and people hold their noses and dive into traffic rather than have to say hello to me, they still need me for that.

I've known all the famous Londoners or known someone else who did. I can tell stories of long-dead gangsters who made the Krays seem like Amnesty International. Bare-knuckle boxing. Fighting the Fascists in the East End. Gun-battles with the police all over Stepney in the 1900s. The terrifying girl gangsters of Whitechapel. Barricading the Old Bill in his own barracks down in Notting Dale.

I can tell you where all the music halls were and what was sung in them. And why. I can tell Marie Lloyd stories and Max Miller stories that are fresh and sharp and bawdy as the day they happened, because their wit and experience came out of the market streets of London. The same streets. The same markets. The same family names. London is markets. Markets are London.

I'm a Londoner through and through. I know Mr. Gog personally. I know Ma Gog even more personally. During the day I can walk anywhere from Bow to Bayswater faster than any taxi. I love the markets. Brick Lane. Church Street. Portobello. You won't find me on a bike with my bum in the air on a winter's afternoon. I walk or drive. Nothing in between. I wear a camel-hair in winter and a Barraclough's in summer. You know what would happen to a coat like that on a bike.

I love the theatre. I like modern dance, very good movies and ambitious international contemporary music. I like poetry, prose, painting and the decorative arts. I like the lot, the very best that London's got, the whole bloody casserole. I gobble it all up and bang on my bowl for more. Let timid greenbelters creep in at weekends and sink themselves in the West End's familiar deodorised shit if they want to. That's not my city. That's a tourist set. It's what I live off. What all of us show-people live off. It's the old, familiar circus. The big rotate.

We're selling what everybody recognises. What makes them feel safe and certain and sure of every single moment in the city. Nothing to worry about in jolly old London. We sell charm and colour by the yard. Whole word factories turn out new rhyming slang and saucy street characters are trained on council grants. Don't frighten the horses. Licensed pearlies pause for a photo opportunity in the dockside Secure Zones. Without all that cheap scenery, without our myths and magical skills, without our whorish good cheer and instincts for trade—any kind of trade—we probably wouldn't have a living city.

As it is, the real city I live in has more creative energy per square inch at work at any given moment than anywhere else on the planet. But you'd never know it from a stroll up the Strand. It's almost all in those lively little side-streets the English-speaking tourists can't help feeling a bit nervous about and that the French adore.

If you use music for comfortable escape you'd probably find more satisfying and cheaper relief in a massage parlour than at the umpteenth revival of *The Sound of Music*. I'd tell that to any hesitant punter who's not too sure. Check out the phone boxes for the ladies, I'd say, or you can go to the half-price ticket-booth in Leicester Square and pick up a ticket that'll deliver real value—Ibsen or Shakespeare, Shaw or Churchill. Certainly you can fork out three hundred sheets for a fifty-sheet ticket that in a justly ordered world wouldn't be worth two pee and have your ears salved and your cradle rocked for two hours. Don't worry, I'd tell them, I make no judgements. Some hardworking whore profits, whatever you decide. So who's the cynic?

I went on one of those tours when my friends Dave and Di from Bury came down for the Festival of London in 2001 and it's amazing, the crap they tell people. They put sex, violence and money into every story. They know fuck-all. They soup everything up. It's *Sun*-reader history. Even the Beefeaters at the Tower. Poppinsland. All that old English duff.

It makes you glad to get back to Soho.

Not so long ago you would usually find me in the Princess Louise, Berwick Street, at lunchtime, a few doors down from the Chinese chippy and just across from Mrs. White's trim stall in Berwick Market. It's only a narrow door and is fairly easy to miss. It has one bottle-glass window onto the street. This is a public house that has not altered since the 1940s when it was very popular with Dylan Thomas, Mervyn Peake, Ruthven Todd, Henry Treece and a miscellaneous bunch of other Welsh adventurers who threatened for a while to take over English poetry from the Irish.

It's a shit pub, so dark and smoky you can hardly find your glass in front of your face, but the look of it keeps the tourists out. It's used by all the culture pros—from arty types with backpacks, who do specialised walking tours, to famous gallery owners and top museum management—and by the heavy-metal bikers. We all get on a treat. We are mutually dependent in our continuing resistance to invasion or change, to the preservation of the best and most vital aspects of our culture. We leave the bikers alone because they protect us from the tourists, who might recognise us and make us put on our masks in a hurry. They leave us alone because the police won't want to bother a bunch of well-connected middle-class wankers like us. It is a wonderful example of mutuality. In the back rooms, thanks to some freaky acoustics, you can talk easily above the music and hardly know it's there.

Over the years there have been some famous friendships and unions struck between the two groups. My own lady wife was known as Karla the She-Goat in an earlier incarnation and had the most exquisite and elaborate tattoos I ever saw. She was a wonderful wife and would have made a perfect mother. She died on the A1, on the other side of Watford Gap. She had just found out she was pregnant and was making her last sentimental run. It did me in for marriage for a while. And urban romance.

I first heard about London Bone in the Princess Lou when Claire Rood, that elegant old dyke from the Barbican, who'd tipped me off about my new tailor, pulled my ear to her mouth and asked me in words of solid gin and garlic to look out for some for her, darling. None of the usual faces seemed to know about it. A couple of top-level museum people knew a bit, but it was soon obvious they were hoping I'd fill them in on the details. I showed them a confident length of cuff. I told them to keep in touch.

I did my Friday walk, starting in the horrible pre-dawn chill of the Portobello Road where some youth tried to sell me a bit of scrimshawed reconstitute as "the real old Bone." I warmed myself in the showrooms of elegant Kensington and Chelsea dealers telling outrageous stories of deals, profits and crashes until they grew uncomfortable and wanted to talk about me and I got the message and left.

I wound up that evening in the urinal of The Dragoons in Meard Alley, swapping long-time-no-sees with my boyhood friend Bernie Michaud who begins immediately by telling me he's got a bit of business I might be interested in. And since it's Bernie Michaud telling me about it I listen. Bernie never deliberately spread a rumour in his life but he's always known how to make the best of one. This is kosher, he thinks. It has a bit of a glow. It smells like a winner. A long-distance runner. He is telling me out of friendship, but I'm not really interested. I'm trying to find out about London Bone.

"I'm not talking drugs, Ray, you know that. And it's not bent." Bernie's little pale face is serious. He takes a thoughtful sip of his whisky. "It is, admittedly, a commodity."

I wasn't interested. I hadn't dealt in goods for years. "Services only, Bernie," I said. "Remember. It's my rule. Who wants to get stuck paying rent on a warehouse full of yesterday's faves? I'm still trying to move those *Glenda Sings Michael Jackson* sides Pratface talked me into."

"What about investment?" he says. "This is the real business, Ray, believe me."

So I heard him out. It wouldn't be the first time Bernie had brought me back a nice profit on some deal I'd helped him bankroll and I was all right at the time. I'd just made the better part of a month's turnover on a package of theatreland's most profitable stinkers brokered for a party of filthy-rich New Muscovites who thought Chekhov was something you did with your lottery numbers.

As they absorbed the quintessence of Euro-ersatz, guaranteed to offer, as its high emotional moment, a long, relentless bowel movement, I would be converting their hard roubles back into Beluga.

It's a turning world, the world of the international free market, and everything's wonderful and cute and pretty and *magical* so long as you keep your place on the carousel. It's not good if it stops. And it's worse if you get thrown off altogether. Pray to Mammon that you never have to seek the help of an organisation that calls you a 'client.' That puts you outside the fairground for ever. No more rides. No more fun. No more life.

Bernie only did quality art, so I knew I could trust that side of his judgement, but what was it? A new batch of Raphaels turned up in a Willesden attic? Andy Warhol's lost landscapes found at the Pheasantry?

"There's American collectors frenzied for this stuff," murmurs Bernie through a haze of Sons of the Wind, Motorchair and Montecristo fumes. "And if it's decorated they go through the roof. All the big Swiss guys are looking for it. Freddy K. in Cairo has a Saudi buyer who tops any price. Rose Sarkissian in Agadir represents three French collectors. It's never catalogued. It's all word of mouth. And it's already turning over millions. There's one inferior piece in New York and none at all in Paris. The pieces in Zurich are probably all fakes."

This made me feel that I was losing touch. I still didn't know what he was getting at.

"Listen," I say, "before we go any further, let's talk about this London Bone."

"You're a fly one, Ray," he says. "How did you suss it?"

"Tell me what you know," I say. "And then I'll fill you in."

We went out of the pub, bought some fish and chips at the Chinese and then walked up Berwick Street and round to his little club in D'Arblay Street where we sat down in his office and closed the door. The place stank of cat-pee. He doted on his Persians. They were all out in the club at the moment, being petted by the patrons.

"First," he says, "I don't have to tell you, Ray, that this is strictly double-schtum and I will kill you if a syllable gets out."

"Naturally," I said.

"Have you ever seen any of this Bone?" he asked. He went to his cupboard and found some vinegar and salt. "Or better still handled it?"

"No," I said. "Not unless it's fake scrimshaw."

"This stuff's got a depth to it you've never dreamed about. A lustre. You can tell it's the real thing as soon as you see it. Not just the shapes or the decoration, but the quality of it. It's like it's got a soul. You could come close, but you could never fake it. Like amber, for instance. That's why the big collectors are after it. It's authentic, it's newly discovered and it's rare."

"What bone is it?"

"Mastodon. Some people still call it mammoth ivory, but I haven't seen any actual ivory. It could be dinosaur. I don't know. Anyway, this bone is *better* than ivory. It's in weird shapes, probably fragments off some really big animal."

"And where's it coming from?"

"The heavy clay of good old London," says Bernie. "A fortune at our feet, Ray. And my people know where to dig."

2

I had to be straight with Bernie. Until I saw a piece of the stuff in my own hand and got an idea about it for myself, I couldn't do anything. The only time in my life I'd gone for a gold brick I'd bought it out of respect for the genius running the scam. He deserved what I gave him. Which was a bit less than he was hoping for. Rather than be conned, I would rather throw the money away. I'm like that with everything.

I had my instincts, I told Bernie. I had to go with them. He understood completely and we parted on good terms.

If the famous Lloyd Webber meltdown of '03 had happened a few months earlier or later I would never have thought again about going into the Bone business, but I was done in by one of those sudden changes of public taste that made the George M. Cohan crash of '31 seem like a run of *The Mousetrap*.

Sentimental fascism went out the window. Liberal-humanist contemporary relevance, artistic aspiration, intellectual and moral substance and all that stuff was somehow in demand. It was *better* than the '60s. It was one of those splendid moments when the public pulls itself together and tries to grow up. Jones's *Rhyme of the Flying Bomb* song-cycle made a glorious comeback. *American Angels* returned with even more punch.

And Sondheim became a quality brand name. If it wasn't by Sondheim or based on a tune Sondheim used to hum in the shower, the punters didn't want to know. Overnight, the public's product loyalty had changed. And I must admit it had changed for the better. But my investments were in *Cats*, and *Dogs* (Lord Webber's last desperate attempt to squeeze from Thurber what he'd sucked from Eliot), *Duce!* and *Starlight Excess*, all of which were now taking a walk down *Sunset Boulevard*. I couldn't even get a regular-price ticket for myself at *Sunday in the Park*, *Assassins* or *Follies*. *Into the Woods* was solid for eighteen months ahead. I saw *Passion* from the wings and *Sweeney Todd* from the gods. *Five Guys Named Moe* crumbled to dust. *Phantom* closed. Its author claimed sabotage.

"Quality will out, Ray," says Bernie next time I see him at the Lou. "You've got to grant the public that. You just have to give it time."

"Fuck the public," I said, with some feeling. "They're just nostalgic for quality at the moment. Next year it'll be something else. Meanwhile I'm bloody ruined. You couldn't drum a couple of oncers on my entire stock. Even my E.N.O. side-bets have died. Covent Garden's a disaster. The weather in Milan didn't help. That's where Cecilia Bartoli caught her cold. I was lucky to be offered half-price for the Rossinis without her. And I know what I'd do if I could get a varda at bloody Simon Rattle."

"So you won't be able to come in on the Bone deal?" said Bernie, returning to his own main point of interest.

"I said I was ruined," I told him, "not wiped out."

"Well, I got something to show you now, anyway," says Bernie.

We went back to his place.

He put it in my hand as if it were a nugget of plutonium: a knuckle of dark, golden Bone, split off from a larger piece, covered with tiny pictures.

"The engravings are always on that kind of Bone," he said. "There are other kinds that don't have drawings, maybe from a later date. It's the work of the first Londoners, I suppose, when it was still a swamp. About the time your Phoenician ancestors started getting into the up-river woad-trade. I don't know the significance, of course."

The Bone itself was hard to analyse because of the mixture of chemicals that had created it and some of it had fused, suggesting prehistoric upheavals of some kind. The drawings were extremely primitive. Any bored person with a sharp object and minimum talent could have done them at any time in history. The larger, weirder-looking Bones had no engravings.

Stick-people pursued other stick-people endlessly across the fragment. The work was unremarkable. The beauty really was in the tawny ivory colour of the Bone itself. It glowed with a wealth of shades and drew you hypnotically into its depths. I imagined the huge animal of which this fragment had once been an active part. I saw the bellowing trunk, the vast ears, the glinting tusks succumbing suddenly to whatever had engulfed her. I saw her body swaying, her tail lashing as she trumpeted her defiance of her inevitable death. And now men sought her remains as treasure. It was a very romantic image and of course it would become my most sincere sales pitch.

"That's six million dollars you're holding there," said Bernie. "Minimum."

Bernie had caught me at the right time and I had to admit I was convinced. Back in his office he sketched out the agreement. We would go in on a fifty-fifty basis, funding the guys who would do the actual digging, who knew where the Bonefields were and who would tell us as soon as we showed serious interest. We would finance all the work, pay them an upfront earnest and then load by load in agreed increments. Bernie and I would split the net profit fifty-fifty. There were all kinds of clauses and provisions covering the various problems we foresaw and then we had a deal.

The archaeologists came round to my little place in Dolphin Square. They were a scruffy bunch of students from the University of Norbury who had discovered the Bone deposits on a run-of-the-mill field trip in a demolished Southwark housing estate and knew only that there might be a market for them. Recent cuts to their grants had made them desperate. Some lefty had come up with a law out of the Magna Carta or somewhere saying public land couldn't be sold to private developers and so there was a court case disputing the council's right to sell the estate to Livingstone International, which also put a stop to the planned rebuilding. So we had indefinite time to work.

The stoodies were grateful for our expertise, as well as our cash. I was happy enough with the situation. It was one I felt we could easily control. Middle-class burbnerds get greedy the same as anyone else, but they respond well to reason. I told them for a start-off that all the Bone had to come in to us. If any of it leaked onto the market by other means, we'd risk losing our prices and that would mean the scheme was over. "Terminated," I said significantly. Since we had reputations as well as investments to protect there would also be recriminations. That was all I had to say. Since those V-serials kids think we're Krays and Mad Frankie Frasers just because we like to look smart and talk properly.

We were fairly sure we weren't doing anything obviously criminal. The stuff wasn't treasure trove. It had to be cleared before proper foundations could be poured. Quite evidently L.I. didn't think it was worth paying security staff to shuft the site. We didn't know if digging shafts and tunnels was even trespass, but we knew we had a few weeks before someone started asking about us and by then we hoped to have the whole bloody mastodon out of the deep clay and nicely earning for us. The selling would take the real skill and that was my job. It was going to have to be played sharper than South African diamonds.

After that neither Bernie nor I had anything to do with the dig. We rented a guarded lock-up in Clapham and paid the kids every time they brought in a substantial load of Bone. It was incredible stuff. Bernie thought that chemical action, some of it relatively recent, had caused the phenomenon. "Like chalk, you know. You hardly find it anywhere. Just a few places in England, France, China and Texas." The kids reported that there was more than one kind of animal down there, but that all the Bone had the same rich appearance. They had constructed a new tunnel, with a hidden entrance, so that even if the building site was blocked to them, they could still get at the Bone. It seemed to be a huge field, but most of the Bone was at roughly the same depth. Much of it had fused and had to be chipped out. They had found no end to it so far and they had tunnelled through more than half an acre of the dense, dark clay.

Meanwhile I was in Amsterdam and Rio, Paris and Vienna and New York and Sydney. I was in Tokyo and Seoul and Hong Kong. I was in Riyadh, Cairo and Baghdad. I was in Kampala and New Benin, everywhere there were major punters. I racked up so many free air-miles in a couple of months that they were automatically jumping me to first class. But I achieved what I wanted. Nobody bought London Bone without checking with me. I was the acknowledged expert. The prime source, the best in the business. If you want Bone, said the art world, you want Gold.

The Serious Fraud Squad became interested in Bone for a while, but they had been assuming we were faking it and gave up when it was obviously not rubbish.

Neither Bernie nor I expected it to last any longer than it did. By the time our first phase of selling was over we were turning over so much dough it was silly and the kids were getting tired and were worrying about exploring some of their wildest dreams. There was almost nothing left, they said. So we closed down the operation, moved our warehouses a couple of times and then let the Bone sit there to make us some money while everyone wondered why it had dried up.

And at that moment, inevitably, and late as ever, the newspapers caught on to the story. There was a brief late-night TV piece. A few supplements talked about it in their arts pages. This led to some news stories and eventually it went to the tabloids and the Bone became anything you liked, from the remains of Martians to a new kind of nuclear waste. Anyone who saw the real stuff was convinced but everyone had a theory about it. The real exclusive market was finished. We kept schtum. We were gearing up for the second phase. We got as far away from our stash as possible.

Of course, a few faces tracked me down, but I denied any knowledge of the Bone. I was a middleman, I said. I just had good contacts. Half-a-dozen people claimed to know where the Bone came from. Of course they talked to the papers. I sat back in satisfied security, watching the mud swirl over our tracks. Another couple of months and we'd be even safer than the house I'd bought in Hampstead overlooking the Heath. It had a rather forlorn garden the size of Kilburn, which needed a lot of nurturing. That suited me. I was ready to retire to the country and a big indoor swimming pool.

By the time a close version of the true story came out, from one of the stoodies who'd lost all his share in a lottery syndicate, it was just one of many. It sounded too dull. I told newspaper reporters that while I would love to have been involved in such a lucrative scheme, my money came from theatre tickets. Meanwhile, Bernie and I thought of our warehouse and said nothing.

Now the stuff was getting into the culture. It was chic. *Puncher* used it in their ads. It was called Mammoth Bone by the media. There was a common story about how a herd had wandered into the swampy river and drowned in the mud. Lots of pictures dusted off from the Natural History Museum. Experts explained the colour, the depths, the markings, the beauty. Models sported a Bone motif.

Our second phase was to put a fair number of inferior fragments on the market and see how the public responded. That would help us find our popular price—the most a customer would pay. We were looking for a few good millionaires.

Frankly, as I told my partner, I was more than ready to get rid of the lot. But Bernie counselled me to patience. We had a plan and it made sense to stick to it.

The trade continued to run well for a while. As the sole source of the stuff, we could pretty much control everything. Then one Sunday lunchtime I met Bernie at the Six Jolly Dragoons in Meard Alley, Soho. He had something to show me, he said. He didn't even glance around. He put it on the bar in plain daylight. A small piece of Bone with the remains of decorations still on it.

"What about it?" I said.

"It's not ours," he said.

My first thought was that the stoodies had opened up the field again. That they had lied to us when they said it had run out.

"No," said Bernie, "it's not even the same colour. It's the same stuff—but different shades. Gerry Goldstein lent it to me."

"Where did he get it?"

"He was offered it," Bernie said.

We didn't bother to speculate where it had come from. But we did have rather a lot of our Bone to shift quickly. Against my will, I made another world tour and sold mostly to other dealers this time. It was a standard second-wave operation but run rather faster than was wise. We definitely missed the crest.

However, before deliveries were in and cheques were cashed, Jack Merrywidow, the fighting MP for Brookgate and East Holborn, gets up in the House of Commons on telly one afternoon and asks if Prime Minister Bland or any of his dope-dazed Cabinet understand that human remains, taken from the hallowed burial grounds of London, are being sold by the piece in the international marketplace? Mr. Bland makes a plummy joke enjoyed at Mr. Merrywidow's expense and sits down. But Jack won't give up. They're suddenly on telly. It's *The Struggle of Parliament* time. Jack's had the Bone examined by experts. It's human. Undoubtedly human. The strange shapes are caused by limbs melting together in soil heavy with lime. Chemical reactions, he says. We have—he raises his eyes to the camera—been mining mass graves.

A shock to all those who still long for the years of common decency. Someone, says Jack, is selling more than our heritage. Hasn't free-market capitalism got a little bit out of touch when we start selling the arms, legs and skulls of our forebears? The torsos and shoulder-blades of our honourable dead? What did we used to call people who did that? When was the government going to stop this trade in corpses?

It's denied.

It's proved.

It looks like trade is about to slump.

I think of framing the cheques as a reminder of the vagaries of fate and give up any idea of popping the question to my old muse Little Trudi, who is back on the market, having been dumped by her corporate suit in a fit, he's told her, of self-disgust after seeing *The Tolstoy Investment* with Eddie Izzard. Bernie, I tell my partner, the Bone business is down the drain. We might as well bin the stuff we've stockpiled.

Then, two days later the TV news reports a vast public interest in London Bone. Some lordly old queen with four names comes on the evening news to say how by owning a piece of Bone, you own London's true history. You become a curator of some ancient ancestor. He's clearly got a vested interest in the stuff. It's the hottest tourist item since Jack-the-Ripper razors and O.J. gloves. More people want to buy it than ever.

The only trouble is, I don't deal in dead people. It is, in fact, where I have always drawn the line. Even Pratface Charlie wouldn't sell his great-great-grandmother's elbow to some overweight Jap in a deerstalker and a kilt. I'm faced with a genuine moral dilemma.

I make a decision. I make a promise to myself. I can't go back on that. I go down to the Italian chippy in Fortess Road, stoke up on nourishing ritual grease (cod roe, chips and mushy peas, bread and butter and tea, syrup pudding), then heave my out-of-shape, but mentally prepared, body up onto

Parliament Hill to roll myself a big wacky-baccy fag and let my subconscious think the problem through.

When I emerge from my reverie, I have looked out over the whole misty London panorama and considered the city's complex history. I have thought about the number of dead buried there since, say, the time of Boudicca, and what they mean to the soil we build on, the food we still grow here and the air we breathe. We are recycling our ancestors all the time, one way or another. We are sucking them in and shitting them out. We're eating them. We're drinking them. We're coughing them up. The dead don't rest. Bits of them are permanently at work. So what am I doing wrong?

This thought is comforting until my moral sense, sharpening itself up after a long rest, kicks in with—But what's different here is you're flogging the stuff to people who take it home with them. Back to Wisconsin and California and Peking. You take it out of circulation. You're dissipating the deep fabric of the city. You're unravelling something. Like, the real infrastructure, the spiritual and physical bones of an ancient settlement…

On Kite Hill I suddenly realise that those bones are in some way the deep lifestuff of London.

It grows dark over the towers and roofs of the metropolis. I sit on my bench and roll myself a further joint. I watch the silver rising from the river, the deep golden glow of the distant lights, the plush of the foliage, and as I watch it seems to shred before my eyes, like a rotten curtain. Even the traffic noise grows fainter. Is the city sick? Is she expiring? Somehow it seems there's a little less breath in the old girl. I blame myself. And Bernie. And those kids.

There and then, on the spot, I renounce all further interest in the Bone trade. If nobody else will take the relics back, then I will.

There's no resolve purer than the determination you draw from a really good reefer.

3

So now there isn't a tourist in any London market or antique arcade who isn't searching out Bone. They know it isn't cheap. They know they have to pay. And pay they do. Through the nose. And half of what they buy is crap or fakes. This is a question of status, not authenticity. As long as we say it's good, they can say it's good. We give it a provenance, a story, something to colour the tale to the folks back home. We're honest dealers. We sell only the authentic stuff. Still they get conned. But still they look. Still they buy.

Jealous Mancunians and Brummies long for a history old enough to provide them with Bone. A few of the early settlements, like Chester and York, start turning up something like it, but it's not the same. Jim Morrison's remains disappear from Père-Lachaise. They might be someone else's bones, anyway. Rumour is they were KFC bones. The Revolutionary death-pits fail to deliver the goods. The French are furious. They accuse the British of gross materialism and poor taste. Oscar Wilde disappears. George Eliot. Winston Churchill. You name them. For a few months there is a grotesque trade in the remains of the famous. But the fashion has no intrinsic substance and fizzles out. Anyone could have seen it wouldn't run.

Bone has the image, because Bone really is beautiful.

Too many people are yearning for that Bone. The real stuff. It genuinely hurts me to disappoint them. Circumstances alter cases. Against my better judgement I continue in the business. I bend my principles, just for the duration. We have as much turnover as we had selling to the Swiss gnomes. It's the latest item on the *been-to* list. "You *have* to bring me back some London Bone, Ethel, or I'll never forgive you!" It starts to appear in the American luxury catalogues.

But by now there are ratsniffers everywhere—from Trade and Industry, from the National Trust, from the Heritage Corp, from half a dozen South London councils, from the Special Branch, from the C.I.D., the Inland Revenue and both the Funny and the Serious Fraud Squads.

Any busybody who ever wanted to put his head under someone else's bed is having a wonderful time. Having failed dramatically with the STOP THIS DISGUSTING TRADE approach, the tabloids switch to offering bits of Bone as prizes in circulation boosters. I sell a newspaper consortium a Tesco's plastic bagful for two-and-a-half mill via a go-between. Bernie and I are getting almost frighteningly rich. I open some bank accounts offshore and I become an important anonymous shareholder in the Queen Elizabeth Hall when it's privatised.

It doesn't take long for the experts to come up with an analysis. Most of the Bone has been down there since the seventeenth century and earlier. They are the sites of the old plague pits where, legend had it, still-living people were thrown in with the dead. For a while it must have seemed like Auschwitz-on-Thames. The chemical action of lime, partial burning, London clay and decaying flesh, together with the broadening spread of the London water-table, thanks to various engineering works over the last century, letting untreated sewage into the mix, had created our unique London Bone. As for the decorations, that, it was opined, was the work of the pit guards, working on earlier bones found on the same site.

"Blood, shit and bone," says Bernie. "It's what makes the world go round. That and money, of course."

"And love," I add. I'm doing all right these days. It's true what they say about a Roller. Little Trudi has enthusiastically rediscovered my attractions. She has her eye on a ring. I raise my glass. "And love, Bernie."

"Fuck that," says Bernie. "Not in my experience." He's buying Paul McCartney's old place in Wamering and having it converted for Persians. He has, it is true, also bought his wife her dream house. She doesn't seem to mind it's on the island of Las Cascadas about six miles off the coast of Morocco. She's at last agreed to divorce him. Apart from his mother, she's the only woman he ever had anything to do with and he isn't, he says, planning to try another. The only females he wants in his house in future come with a pedigree a mile long, have all their shots and can be bought at Harrods.

4

I expect you heard what happened. The private Bonefields, which contractors were discovering all over South and West London, actually contained public bones. They were part of our national inheritance. They had living relatives. And stones, some of them. So it became a political and a moral issue. The Church got involved. The airwaves were crowded with concerned clergy. There was the problem of the self-named bone-miners. Kids, inspired by our leaders' rhetoric and aspiring to imitate those great captains of free enterprise they had been taught to admire, were turning over ordinary graveyards, which they'd already stripped of their saleable masonry, and digging up somewhat fresher stiffs than was seemly.

A bit too fresh. It was pointless. The Bone took centuries to get seasoned and so far nobody had been able to fake the process. A few of the older graveyards had small deposits of Bone in them. Brompton Cemetery had a surprising amount, for instance, and so did Highgate. This attracted prospectors. They used shovels mainly, but sometimes low explosives. The area around Karl Marx's monument looked like they'd refought the Russian Civil War over it. The barbed wire put in after the event hadn't helped. And, as usual, the public paid to clean up after private enterprise. Nobody in their right mind got buried any more. Cremation became very popular. The borough councils and their financial managers were happy because more valuable real estate wasn't being occupied by a non-consumer.

It didn't matter how many security guards were posted or, by one extreme authority, landmines, the teenies left no grave unturned. Bone was still a profitable item, even though the market had settled down since we started. They dug up Bernie's mother. They dug up my cousin Leonard. There wasn't a Londoner who didn't have some intimate unexpectedly back above ground. Every night you saw it on telly.

It had caught the public imagination. The media had never made much of the desecrated graveyards, the chiselled-off angels' heads and the uprooted headstones on sale in King's Road and the Boulevard St. Michel since the 1970s. These had been the targets of first-generation grave-robbers. Then there had seemed nothing left to steal. Even they had baulked at doing the corpses. Besides, there wasn't a market. This second generation was making up for lost time, turning over the soil faster than an earthworm on E.

The news shots became clichés. The heaped earth, the headstone, the smashed coffin, the hint of the contents, the leader of the Opposition coming on to say how all this has happened since his mirror image got elected. The councils argued that they should be given the authority to deal with the problem. They owned the graveyards. And also, they reasoned, the Bonefields. The profits from those fields should rightly go into the public purse. They could help pay for the Health Service. "Let the dead," went their favourite slogan, "pay for the living for a change."

What the local politicians actually meant was that they hoped to claim the land in the name of the public and then make the usual profits privatising it. There was a principle at stake. They had to ensure their friends and not outsiders got the benefit.

The High Court eventually gave the judgement to the public, which really meant turning it over to some of the most rapacious borough councils in our history. A decade or so earlier, that Charlie Peace of elected bodies, the Westminster City Council, had tried to sell their old graveyards to new developers. This current judgement allowed all councils at last to maximise their assets from what was, after all, dead land, completely unable to pay for itself, and therefore a natural target for privatisation. The feeding frenzy began. It was the closest thing to mass cannibalism I've ever seen.

We had opened a fronter in Old Sweden Street and had a couple of halfway presentable slags from Bernie's club taking the calls and answering enquiries. We were straight up about it. We called it *The City Bone Exchange*. The bloke who decorated it and did the sign specialised in giving offices that long-established look. He'd created most of those old-fashioned West End hotels you'd never heard of until 1999. "If it's got a Scottish name," he used to say, "it's one of mine. Americans love the skirl of the pipes, but they trust a bit of brass and varnish best."

Our place was almost all brass and varnish. And it worked a treat. The Ritz and the Savoy sent us their best potential buyers. Incredibly exclusive private hotels gave us taxi-loads of bland-faced American boy-men, reeking of health and beauty products, bellowing their credentials to the wind, rich matrons eager for anyone's approval, massive Germans with aggressive cackles, stern orientals glaring at us, daring us to cheat them. They bought. And they bought. And they bought.

The snoopers kept on snooping but there wasn't really much to find out. Livingstone International took an aggressive interest in us for a while, but what could they do? We weren't up to anything illegal just selling the stuff and nobody could identify what—if anything—had been nicked anyway. I still had my misgivings. They weren't anything but superstitions, really. It did seem sometimes that for every layer of false antiquity, for every act of Disneyfication, an inch or two of our real foundations crumbled. You knew what happened when you did that to a house. Sooner or later you got trouble. Sooner or later you had no house.

We had more than our share of private detectives for a while. They always pretended to be customers and they always looked wrong, even to our girls.

Livingstone International had definitely made a connection. I think they'd found our mine and guessed what a windfall they'd lost. They didn't seem at one with themselves over the matter. They even made veiled threats. There was some swagger came in to talk about violence but they were spotties who'd got all their language off old '90s TV shows. So we sweated it out and the girls took most of the heat. Those girls really didn't know anything. They were magnificently ignorant. They had tellies with chips that switch channels as soon as they detect a news or information programme.

I've always had a rule. If you're caught by the same wave twice, get out of the water.

While I didn't blame myself for not anticipating the Great Andrew Lloyd Webber Slump, I think I should have guessed what would happen next. The tolerance of the public for bullshit had become decidedly and aggressively negative. It was like the Bone had set new standards of public aspiration as well as beauty. My dad used to say that about the Blitz. Classical music enjoyed a huge success during the Second World War. Everybody grew up at once. The Bone had made it happen again. It was a bit frightening to those of us who had always relied on a nice, passive, gullible, greedy punter for an income.

The bitter fights that had developed over graveyard and Bonefield rights and boundaries, the eagerness with which some borough councils exploited their new resource, the unseemly trade in what was, after all, human remains, the corporate involvement, the incredible profits, the hypocrisies and politics around the Bone brought us the outspoken disgust of Europe. We were used to that. In fact, we tended to cultivate it. But that wasn't the problem.

The problem was that our *own* public had had enough.

When the elections came round, the voters systematically booted out anyone who had supported the Bone trade. It was like the sudden rise of the anti-slavery vote in Lincoln's America. They demanded an end to the commerce in London Bone. They got the Boneshops closed down. They got work on the Bonefields stopped. They got their graveyards and monuments protected and cleaned up. They got a city that started cultivating peace and security as if it was a cash crop. Which maybe it was. But it hurt me.

It was the end of my easy money, of course. I'll admit I was glad it was stopping. It felt like they were slowing entropy, restoring the past. The quality of life improved. I began to think about letting a few rooms for company.

The mood of the country swung so far into disapproval of the Bone trade that I almost began to fear for my life. Road and anti-abortion activists switched their attention to Bone merchants. Hampstead was full of screaming lefties convinced they owned the moral high-ground just because they'd paid off their enormous mortgages. Trudi, after three months, applied for a divorce, arguing that she had not known my business when she married me. She said she was disgusted. She said I'd been living on blood-money. The courts awarded her more than half of what I'd made, but it didn't matter any more. My investments were such that I couldn't stop earning. Economically, I was a small oil-producing nation. I had my own international dialling code. It was horrible in a way. Unless I tried very hard, it looked like I could never be ruined again. There was no justice.

I met Bernie in the King Lyar in Old Sweden Street, a few doors down from our burned-out office. I told him what I planned to do and he shrugged.

"We both knew it was dodgy," he told me. "It was dodgy all along, even when we thought it was mastodons. What it feels like to me, Ray, is—it feels like a sort of a massive transformation of the *zeitgeist*—you know, like Virginia Woolf said about the day human nature changed—something happens slowly and you're not aware of it. Everything seems normal. Then you wake up one morning and—bingo!—it's Nazi Germany or Bolshevik Russia or Thatcherite England or the Golden Age—and all the rôles have changed."

"Maybe it was the Bone that did it," I said. "Maybe it was a symbol everyone needed to rally round. You know. A focus."

"Maybe," he said. "Let me know when you're doing it. I'll give you a hand."

About a week later we got the van backed up to the warehouse loading bay. It was three o'clock in the morning and I was chilled to the marrow. Working in silence we transferred every scrap of Bone to the van. Then we drove back to Hampstead through a freezing rain.

I don't know why we did it the way we did it. There would have been easier solutions, I suppose. But behind the high walls of my big back garden, under the old trees and etiolated rhododendrons, we dug a pit and filled it with the glowing remains of the ancient dead.

The stuff was almost phosphorescent as we chucked the big lumps of clay back onto it. It glowed a rich amber and that faint rosemary smell came off it. I can still smell it to this day when I go in there. My soft fruit is out of this world. The whole garden's doing wonderfully now.

In fact London's doing wonderfully. We seem to be back on form. There's still a bit of a Bone trade, of course, but it's marginal.

Every so often I'm tempted to take a spade and turn over the earth again, to look at the fortune I'm hiding there. To look at the beauty of it. The strange amber glow never fades and sometimes I think the decoration on the Bone is an important message I should perhaps try to decipher.

I'm still a very rich man. Not justly so, but there it is. And, of course, I'm about as popular with the public as Percy the Paedophile. Gold the Bone King? I might as well be Gold the Graverobber. I don't go down to Soho much. When I do make it to a show or something I try to disguise myself a bit. I don't see anything of Bernie any more and I heard two of the stoodies topped themselves.

I do my best to make amends. I'm circulating my profits as fast as I can. Talent's flooding into London from everywhere, making a powerful mix. They say they haven't known a buzz like it since 1967. I'm a reliable investor in great new shows. Every year I back the Iggy Pop Awards, the most prestigious in the business. But not everybody will take my money. I am regularly reviled. That's why some organisations receive anonymous donations. They would refuse them if they knew they were from me.

I've had the extremes of good and bad luck riding this particular switch in the *zeitgeist* and the only time I'm happy is when I wake up in the morning and I've forgotten who I am. It seems I share a common disgust for myself.

A few dubious customers, however, think I owe them something.

Another bloke, who used to be very rich before he made some frenetic investments after his career went down the drain, called me the other day. He knew of my interest in the theatre, that I had invested in several West End hits. He thought I'd be interested in his idea. He wanted to revive his first success, *Rebecca's Incredibly Far Out Well* or something, which he described as a powerful religious rock opera guaranteed to capture the new nostalgia market. The times, he told me, they were a-changin'. His show, he continued, was full of raw old-fashioned R&B energy. Just the sort of authentic sound to attract the new no-nonsense youngsters. Wasn't it cool that Madonna wanted to do the title rôle? And Bob Geldof would play the Spirit of the Well. *Rock and roll, man! It's all in the staging, man! Remember the boat in* Phantom*? I can make it look better than real. On stage, man, that well is W.E.T. WET! Rock and roll!* I could see that little wizened fist punching the air in a parody of the vitality he craved and whose source had always eluded him.

I had to tell him it was a non-starter. I'd turned over a new leaf, I said. I was taking my ethics seriously.

These days I only deal in living talent.

Colour (1991)

"Colour" first appeared in *New Worlds* No. 217 (Gollancz), edited by David Garnett in 1991, and was very much inspired by Moorcock's interest in chaos theory and fractal geometry, which he has since likened to his own concept of myriad layers of the "multiverse" permeating his work.

The story—revised and expanded—went on to form the opening part of *Blood: A Southern Fantasy* (1995), but is presented here pretty much as it appeared in *New Worlds.*

For John Fogerty

The very nature of our dreams is changing. We have deconstructed the universe and are refusing to rebuild it. This is our madness and our glory. Now we can again begin the true course of our explorations, without preconceptions or agendas.

—Lobkowitz

1 A Victim of the Game

The heat of the New Orleans night pressed against the window like an urgent lover. Jack Karaquazian stood sleepless, naked, staring out into the sweating darkness as if he might see at last some tangible horror which he could confront and even hope to conquer.

"Tomorrow," he told his handsome friend Sam Oakenhurst, "I shall take the *Star* up to Natchez and from there make my way to McClellan by way of the Trace. Will you come?"

(The vision of a sunlit bayou, recollection of an extraordinarily rich perfume, the wealth of the earth. He remembered the yellow-billed herons standing in the shadows, moving their heads to regard him with thoughtful eyes before returning their respect to the water; the grey ibises, seeming to sit in judgement of the others; the delicate egrets congregating on the old logs and branches; a cloud of monarch butterflies, black and orange, diaphanous, settling over the pale reeds and, in the dark green waters, a movement might have been copperhead or alligator, or even a pike. In that moment of silence before the invisible insects began a fresh song, her eyes were humorous, enquiring. She had worked for a while, she said, as a chanteuse at the Fallen Angel on Bourbon Street.)

Sam Oakenhurst understood the invitation to be a courtesy. "I think not, Jack. My luck has been running pretty badly lately and travelling ain't likely to improve it much." Wiping his ebony fingers against his undershirt, he delicately picked an ace from the baize of his folding table.

For a moment the overhead fan, fuelled by some mysterious power, stirred the cards. Pausing, Mr. Oakenhurst regarded this phenomenon with considerable satisfaction, as if his deepest faith had been confirmed. "Besides, I got me all the mung I need right now." And he patted his belt, full of hard guineas—better than muscle.

"It looked for a moment as if our energy had come back." Mr. Karaquazian got onto his bed and sat there undecided whether to try sleeping or to talk. "I'm also planning to give the game a rest. I swear it will be a while before I play at the Terminal." They both smiled.

"You still looking to California, Jack?" Mr. Oakenhurst stroked down a card. "And the Free States?"

"Well, maybe eventually." Jack Karaquazian offered his attention back to the darkness while a small, dry, controlled cough shook his body. He cursed softly and vigorously and went to pour himself a careful drink from the whiskey on the table.

"You should do it," said Mr. Oakenhurst. "Nobody knows who you are any more."

"I left some unfinished business between Starkville and McClellan." Quietly satisfied by this temporary victory over his disease, the gambler drew in a heavy breath. "Anywhere's better than this, Sam. I'll go in the morning. As soon as they sound the up-boat siren."

Putting down the remaining cards, his partner rose to cross, through sluggish shadows, the unpolished floor and, beneath the fluttering swampcone on the wall, pry up one of the boards. He removed a packet of money and divided it into two without counting it. "There's your share of Texas. Brother Ignatius and I agreed, if only one of us got back, you'd have half."

Jack Karaquazian accepted the bills and slipped them into a pocket of the black silk jacket which hung over the other chair on top of his pants, his linen and brocaded vest. "It's rightfully all yours, Sam, and I'll remember that. Who knows how our luck will run? But it'll be a sad year down here, I think, win or lose." Mr. Karaquazian found it difficult to express most emotions; for too long his trade had depended on hiding them. Yet he was able to lay a pale, fraternal hand on his friend's shoulder, a gesture which meant a great deal more to both than any amount of conversation. His eyes, half-hidden behind long lashes, became gentle for a moment.

Both men blinked when, suddenly, the darkness outside was ripped by a burst of fire, of flickering arsenical greens and yellows, of vivid scarlet sparks. The *mechanish* squealed and wailed as if in torment, while other metallic lungs uttered loud, suppressed groans occasionally interrupted by an aggressive bellow, a shriek of despair from xylonite vocal cords, or a deeper, more threatening klaxon as the steel militia, their bodies identified by bubbling globules of burning, dirty orange plastic, gouting black smoke, roamed the narrow streets in search of flesh—human or otherwise—which had defied the city's intolerable curfew. Mr. Karaquazian never slept well in New Orleans. The fundamental character of the authority appalled him.

2 Two of a Kind

At dawn, as the last of the garishly decorated, popishly baroque *mechanish* blundered over the cobbles of the rue Dauphine, spreading their unwholesome ichor behind them, Jack Karaquazian carried his carpetbag to the quayside, joining other men and women making haste to board *L'Étoile d'Memphes*, anxious to leave the oppressive terrors of a quarter where the colour-greedy *machinoix*, that brutal aristocracy, allowed only their engines the freedom of the streets.

Compared to the conscious barbarism of the machines, the riverboat's cream filigree gothic was in spare good taste, and Mr. Karaquazian ascended the gangplank with his first-class ticket in his hand, briefly wishing he were going all the way to the capital, where at least some attempt was made to maintain old standards. But duty—according to Jack Karaquazian's idiosyncratic morality, and the way in which he identified an abiding obsession—had to be served. He had sworn to himself that he must perform a particular task and obtain certain information before he could permit himself any relief, any company other than Colinda Dovero's.

He followed an obsequious steward along a familiar colonnaded deck to the handsomely carved door of the stateroom he favoured when in funds. By way of thanks for a generous tip, he was offered a knowing leer and the murmured intelligence that a high-class snowfrail was travelling in the adjoining suite. Mr. Karaquazian rewarded this with a scowl and a sharp oath so that the steward left before, as he clearly feared, the tip was snatched back from his fingers. Shaking his head at the irredeemable vulgarity of the white race, Mr. Karaquazian unpacked his own luggage. The boat shuddered suddenly as she began to taste her steam, her paddle-wheel stirring the dark waters of the Mississippi. Compared to the big ocean-going schoomer on which, long ago, the gambler had crossed from Alexandria, the *Étoile* was comfortingly reliable and responsive. For him she belonged to an era when time had been measured by chronometers rather than degrees of deliquescence.

He was reminded, against his guard, of the first day he had met the adventuress, Colinda Dovero, who had been occupying those same adjoining quarters and following the same calling as himself.

(Dancing defiantly with her on deck in the summer night amongst the mosquito lamps to the tune of an accordion, a fiddle, a dobro and a bass guitar, while the Second Officer, Mr. Pitre, sang "Poor Hobo" in a sweet baritone... *O, pauvre hobo, mon petit pierrot, ah, foolish hope, my grief, mon coeur... Ai-ee, no longer, no longer Houston, but our passion she never resolves. Allons dansez! Allons dansez!* The old traditional elegies; the pain of inconstancy. *La musique, ma tristesse...* They were dancing, they were told in turn, with a sort of death. But the oracles whom the fashion favoured in those days, and who swarmed the same boats as Karaquazian and his kind, were of proven inaccuracy. Even had they not been, Karaquazian and Mrs. Dovero could have done nothing else than what they did, for theirs was at that time an ungovernable chemistry...)

As it happened, the white woman kept entirely to her stateroom and all Karaquazian knew of her existence was an occasional overheard word to her stewardess. Seemingly, her need for solitude matched his own. He spent the better part of the first forty-eight hours sleeping, his nightmares as troubled as his memories. When he woke up, he could never be sure whether he had been dreaming or remembering, but he was almost certain he had shouted out at least once. Horrified by the thought of what he might reveal, he dosed himself with laudanum until only his snores disturbed the darkness. Yet he continued to dream.

Her name, she had said, was West African or Irish in origin, she was not sure. They had met for the second time in the Terminal Café on the stablest edge of the Biloxi Fault. The café's sharply defined walls constantly jumped and mirrored, expanding space, contracting it, slowing time, frantically dancing in and out of a thousand mirror matrixes; its neon sign (*LAST HEAT ON THE BEACH*), usually lavender and cerise, drawing power directly from the howling chaos a few feet away, between the white sand and the blue ocean, where all the unlikely geometries of the multiverse, all the terrible wild colours, that maelstrom of uninterpretable choices, were displayed in a smooth, perfect circle which the engineers had sliced through the core of all-time and all-space, its rim edged by a rainbow ribbon of vanilla-scented crystal. Usually, the Terminal Café occupied roughly the area of space filled by the old pier, which itself had been absorbed by the vortex during the early moments of an experiment intended to bore into the very marrow of ultra-reality and extract all the energy the planet needed.

The operation had been aborted twenty-two seconds after it began.

Since then, adventurers of many persuasions and motives had made the sidestep through the oddly coloured flames of the Fault into that inferno of a billion perishing space-time continua, drawn down into a maw which sucked to nothingness the substance of whole races and civilisations, whole planetary systems, whole histories, while Earth and sun bobbed in some awkward and perhaps temporary semi-parasitical relationship between the feeding and the food; their position in this indecipherable matrix being generally considered a fluke. (Or perhaps the planet was the actual medium of this destruction, as untouched by it as the knife which cuts the throat of the Easter lamb.)

Even the least fanciful of theorists agreed that they might have accelerated or at least were witnesses to a universal destruction. They believed the engineers had drilled through unguessable dimensions, damaging something which had until now regulated the rate of entropy to which human senses had, over millions of years, evolved. With that control damaged and the rate accelerating to infinity, their perceptions were no longer adequate to the psychic environment.

The multiverse raced perhaps towards the creation of a new sequence of realities, perhaps towards some cold and singular conformity; perhaps towards unbridled Chaos, the end of all consciousness. This last was what drew certain people to the edge of the Fault, their fascination taking them step by relentless step to the brink, there to be consumed.

On a dance floor swept by peculiar silhouettes and shifts of light, Boudreaux Ramsadeen, who had brought his café here by rail from Meridian, encouraged the zee-band to play on while he guided his tiny partners in their Cajun steps. These professional dancers travelled from all over Arcadia to join him. Their hands on their swaying hips, their delicate feet performing figures as subtly intricate as the Terminal's own dimensions, they danced to some other tune than the band's.

Boudreaux's neanderthal brows were drawn together in an expression of seraphic concentration as, keeping all his great bulk on his poised left foot, describing graceful steps with his right, he moved his partners with remarkable tenderness and delicacy.

(Jack Karaquazian deals seven hands of poker, fingering the sensors of his *kayplay* with deliberate slowness. Only here, on the whole planet, is there a reservoir of energy deep enough to run every machine, synthetic reasoner, or cybe in the world, but not transmittable beyond the Terminal's peculiar boundaries. Only those with an incurable addiction to the past's electronic luxuries come here, and they are all gamblers of some description. Weird light saturates the table; the light of hell. He is waiting for his passion, his muse.)

Colinda Dovero and Jack Karaquazian had met again across the blue, flat sheen of a *mentasense* and linked into the wildest, riskiest game of Slick Image anyone had ever witnessed, let alone joined. When they came out of it, Dovero was eight guineas up out of a betting range which had made psychic bids most seasoned players never cared to imagine. It had caused Boudreaux Ramsadeen to rouse himself from his mood of ugly tolerance and insist thereafter on a stakes ceiling that would protect the metaphysical integrity of his establishment. Some of the spectators had developed peculiar psychopathic obsessions, while others had merely become subject to chronic vomiting. Dovero and Karaquazian had, however, gone into spacelessness together and did not properly emerge for nine variations, while the walls expanded and turned at odd angles and the colours saturated and amplified all subtleties of sensation. There is no keener experience, they say, than the act of love during a matrix shift at the Terminal Café.

"That buzz? It's self-knowledge," she told the Egyptian, holding him tight as they floated in the calm between one bizarre reality and another.

"No disrespect, Jack," she had added.

3 Il Fait Chaud

Karaquazian found her again a year later on the *Princesse du Natchez*. He recognised, through her veil, her honey-coloured almond eyes. She was, she said, now ready for him. They turned their stateroom into marvellous joint quarters. Her reason for parting had been a matter of private business. That business, she warned him, was not entirely resolved but he was grateful for even a hint of a future. The old Confederate autonomies were lucky if their matrixes were only threadbare. They were collapsing. There were constant minor reality meltdowns now and yet there was nothing to be done but continue as if continuation were possible. Soon the Mississippi might become one of the few geographical constants. "When we start to go," he said, "I want to be on the river."

"Maybe chaos is already our natural condition," she had teased. She was always terrifyingly playful in the face of annihilation, whereas he found it difficult even to confront the idea. She still had a considerable amount of hope in reserve.

They began to travel as brother and sister. A month after they had established this relationship, there was some question of her arrest for fraud when two well-uniformed cool boys had stepped aboard at New Auschwitz on the Arkansas side as the boat was casting off and suddenly they had no authority. In midstream they made threats. They insisted on entering the ballroom where she and the Egyptian were occupied. And then Karaquazian had suffered watching her raise promising eyes to the captain who saluted, asked if she had everything she needed, ordered the boys to disembark at Greenville, and said that he might stop by later to make sure she was properly comfortable. She had told him she would greatly appreciate the attention and returned to the floor, where a lanky zee-band bounced out the old favourites. With an unsisterly flirt of her hands, she had offered herself back to her pseudo-brother.

Jack Karaquazian had felt almost sour, though gentleman enough to hide it, while he took charge of the unpleasant feelings experienced by her cynical use of a sensuality he had thought, for the present at least, his preserve. Yet that sensuality was in no way diminished by its knowing employment, and his loyalty to her remained based upon profound respect—a type of love he would cheerfully have described as feminine, and through which he experienced some slight understanding of the extraordinary individual she was. He relished her lust for freedom, her optimism, her insistence on her own right to exist beyond the destruction of their universe, her willingness to achieve some form of immortality in any terms and at any cost. She thrilled him precisely because she disturbed him. He had not known such deep excitement since his last two-and-a-half weeks before leaving Egypt and his first three weeks in America; and never because of a woman. Until then, Mr. Karaquazian had enjoyed profound emotion only for the arts of gaming and his Faith. His many liaisons, while frequently affectionate, had never been allowed to interfere with his abiding passion. At first he had been shocked by the realisation that he was more fascinated by Colinda Dovero than he had ever been by the intellectual strategies of the Terminal's ranks of Grand Turks.

The mind which had concentrated on gambling and its attendant skills, upon self-defence and physical fitness, upon self-control, now devoted itself almost wholly to her. He was obsessed with her thoughts, her motives, her background, her story, the effect which her reality had upon his own. He was no longer the self-possessed individual he had been before he met her; and, when they had made love again that first night, he had been ready to fall in with any scheme which kept them together. Eventually, after the New Auschwitz incident, he had made some attempt to rescue his old notion of himself, but when she revealed her business had to do with a potential colour strike valuable beyond any modern hopes, he had immediately agreed to go with her to help establish the claim. In return, she promised him a percentage of the proceeds. He committed himself to her in spite of his not quite believing anything she told him. She had been working the boats for some while now, raising money to fund the expedition, ready to call it quits as soon as her luck turned bad. Since Memphis, her luck had run steadily down. This could also be why she had been so happy to seek an ally in him. The appearance of the cool boys had alarmed her: as if that evening had been the first time she had suffered any form of accusation. Besides, she told him, with the money he had they could now easily meet the top price for the land, which was only swamp anyway. She would pay the fees and expenses. There would be no trouble raising funds once the strike was claimed.

At Chickasaw, they had left the boat and set off up the Trace together.

She had laughed as she looked back at the levee and the *Princesse* outlined against the cold sky. "I have made an enemy, I think, of that captain." He was touched by what he perceived as her wish to reassure him of her constancy. But in Carthage, they had been drawn into a flat game, which had developed around a random hot-spot no bigger than a penny, and played until the spot faded. When the debts were paid, they were down to a couple of guineas between them and had gambled their emergency batteries. At this point, superstition overwhelmed them and each had seen sudden bad luck in the other.

Jack Karaquazian regretted their parting almost immediately and would have returned to her, but by the time he heard of her again she was already lost to Peabody, the planter. It had been Peabody that time who had sent his cool boys after her. She wrote once to Mr. Karaquazian, in care of the Terminal. She said she was taking a rest but would be in touch.

Meanwhile Mr. Karaquazian had a run of luck at the Terminal which, had he not cheated against himself and put the winnings back into circulation, would have brought a halt to all serious gambling for a while. Jack Karaquazian now played with his back to the Fault. The sight of that mighty appetite, that insatiable mystery, distracted him these days. He was impatient for her signal.

4 La Pointe à Pain

Sometimes Jack Karaquazian missed the ancient, exquisite colours of the Egyptian evening, where shades of yellow, red and purple touched the warm stone of magnificent ruins, flooded the desert and brought deep shadows, as black and sharp as flint, upon that richly faded landscape, one subtle tint blending into the other, one stone with the next, supernaturally married and near to their final gentle merging, in the last, sweet centuries of their material state. Here, on the old *Étoile*, he remembered the glories of his youth, before they drilled the Fault, and he found some consolation, if not satisfaction, in bringing back a time when he had not known much in the way of self-discipline, had gloried in his talents. When he had seemed free.

Once again, he strove to patch together some sort of consistent memory of when they had followed the map into the cypress swamp; of times when he had failed to reach the swamp. He had a sense of making progress up the

Trace after he had disembarked, but he had probably never reached McClellan and had never seen the Stains again. How much of this repetition was actual experience? How much was dream?

Recently, the semi-mutable nature of the matrix meant that such questions had become increasingly common. Jack Karaquazian had countless memories of beginning this journey to join her and progressing so far (usually no closer than Vicksburg) before his recollections became uncertain, and the images isolated, giving no clue to any particular context. Now, however, he felt as if he were being carried by some wise momentum allowing his unconscious to steer a path through the million psychic turnings and culs-de-sac this environment provided. It seemed to him that his obsession with the woman, his insane association of her with his Luck, his Muse, was actually supplying the force needed to propel him back to the reality he longed to find. She was his goal, but she was also his reason.

5 Les Veuves des la Coulee

They had met for the third time while she was still with Peabody, the brute said to own half Tennessee and to possess the mortgages on the other half. Peabody's red stone fortress lay outside Memphis. He was notorious for the cruel way in which his plantation whites were treated, but his influence among the eight states of the Confederacy meant he would inevitably be next Governor General, with the power of life and death over all but the best-protected *machinoix* or guild neutrals, like Jack Karaquazian and Colinda Dovero. "I am working for him," she admitted. "As a kind of ambassador. You know how squeamish people are about dealing with the North. They lose face even by looking directly at a whitey. But I find them no different, in the main. A little feckless. Social conditioning." She did not hold with genetic theories of race. She had chatted in this manner at a public occasion where, by coincidence, they were both guests.

"You are his property, I think," Mr. Karaquazian had murmured without rancour. But she had shaken her head.

Whether she had become addicted to Peabody's power or was merely deeply fascinated by it, Mr. Karaquazian never knew. For his own part, he had taken less and less pleasure in the liaison that followed while still holding profound feelings for her. Then she had come to his room one evening when he was in

Memphis and she in town with Peabody, who attended some bond auction at the big hotel, and told him that she deeply desired to stay with him, but they must be so rich they would never lose their whole roll again. Mr. Karaquazian thought she was ending their affair on a graceful note. Then she produced a creased read-out which showed colour sightings in the depths of Mississippi near the Tombigbee not far from Starkville. This was the first evidence she had ever offered him, and he believed now that she was trying to demonstrate that she trusted him, that she was telling the truth. She had intercepted the report before it reached Peabody. The airship pilot who sent it had crashed in flames a day later. "This time we go straight to it."

She had pushed him back against his cot, sniffing at his neck, licking him. Then, with sudden honesty, she told him that, through her Tarot racing, she was into Peabody for almost a million guineas, and he was going to make her go North permanently to pay him back by setting up deals with the white bosses of the so-called Insurgent Republics. "Peabody's insults are getting bad enough. Imagine suffering worse from a white man."

Within two weeks, they had repeated their journey up the Trace, got as far as McClellan, and taken a pirogue into the Streams, following, as best they could, the grey contours of the aerial map, heading towards a cypress swamp. It had been fall then, too, with the leaves turning; the tree-filled landscapes of browns, golds, reds and greens reflected in the cooling sheen of the water. The swamp still kept its heat during the day.

"We are the same," he had suggested to her, to explain their love. "We have the same sense of boredom."

"No, Jack, we have the same habits. But I arrived at mine through fear. I had to learn a courage that for you was simply an inheritance." She had described her anxieties. "It occasionally feels like the victory of some ancient winter."

The waterways were full of birds which always betrayed their approach. No humans came here at this time of year, but any hunters would assume them to be hunting, too. Beautiful as it was, the country was forbidding and with no trace of Indians, a sure sign that the area was considered dangerous, doubtless because of the snakes.

She foresaw a world rapidly passing from contention to warfare; from warfare to brute struggle, from that to insensate matter, and from that to nothingness. "This is the reality offered as our future," she said. They determined they would, if only through their mutual love, resist such a future.

They had grown comfortable with one another, and when they camped at night they would remind themselves of their story, piecing it back into some sort of whole, restoring to themselves the extraordinary intensity of their long relationship. By this means, and the warmth of their sexuality, they raised a rough barrier against encroaching Chaos.

6 Mon Coeur et Mon Amour

It had been twilight, with the cedars turning black and silver, a cool mist forming on the water, when they had reached the lagoon marked on the map, poling the dugout through the shallows, breaking dark gashes in the weedy surface, the mud sucking and sighing at the pole. Each movement tired Mr. Karaquazian too much, threatening to leave him with no energy in reserve, so they chose a fairly open spot, where snakes might not find them, and, placing a variety of sonic and visual beacons, settled down to sleep. They would have slept longer had not the novelty and potential danger of their situation excited their lusts.

In the morning, sitting with the canvas folded back and the tree-studded water roseate from the emerging sun, the mist becoming golden, the white ibises and herons flapping softly amongst the glowing autumn foliage, Jack Karaquazian and Colinda Dovero breakfasted on their well-planned supplies, studying their map before continuing deeper into the beauty of that unwelcoming swamp. Then, at about noon, with a cold blue-grey sky reflected in the still surface of a broad, shallow pond, they found colour—one large Stain spread over an area almost five feet in circumference, and two smaller Stains, about a foot across, almost identical to those noted by the pilot.

From a distance, the Stains appeared to rest upon the surface of the water, but as Mr. Karaquazian poled the boat closer, they saw that they had in fact penetrated deeply into the muddy bottom of the pond. The gold Stains formed a kind of membrane over the openings, effectively sealing them, and yet it was impossible to tell if the colour were solid or a kind of dense, utterly stable gas.

"Somebody drilled here years ago and then, I don't know why, thought better of it." Colinda looked curiously at the Stains, mistaking them for capped bores. "Yet it must be of first quality. Near pure."

Jack Karaquazian was disappointed by what he understood to be a note of greed in her voice, but he smiled. "There was a time colour had to come out perfect," he said. "This must have been drilled before Biloxi—or around the same time."

"Now they're too scared, most of them, to drill at all!" Shivering, she peered over the side of the boat, expecting to see her image in the big Stain, and instead was surprised, almost shocked.

Watching her simply for the pleasure it gave him, Jack Karaquazian was curious and moved his own body to look down. The Stain had a strangely solid, unreflective depth, like a gigantic ingot of gold hammered deep into the reality of the planet.

Both were now aware of a striking abnormality, yet neither wanted to believe anything but some simpler truth, and they entered into an unspoken bond of silence on the matter. "We must go to Jackson and make the purchase," he said. "Then we must look for some expert engineering help. Another partner, even."

"This will get me clear of Peabody," she murmured, her eyes still upon the Stain, "and that's all I care about."

"He'll know you double-crossed him as soon as you begin to work this."

She shrugged.

At her own insistence she had remained with the claim while he went back to Jackson to buy the land and, when this was finalised, buy a prospecting licence without which they would not be able to file, such were Mississippi's bureaucratic subtleties; but when he returned to the cypress swamp, she and the pirogue were gone. Only the Stains remained as evidence of their experience. Enquiring frantically in McClellan, he heard of a woman being caught wild and naked in the swamp and becoming the common possession of the brothers Berger and their father, Ox, until they tired of her. It was said she could no longer speak any human language but communicated in barks and grunts like a hog. It was possible that the Bergers had drowned her in the swamp before continuing on up towards Tupelo where they had property.

7 Valse de Coeur Casser

Convinced of their kidnapping and assault upon Colinda Dovero, of their responsibility for her insanity and possibly her death, Jack Karaquazian was only an hour behind the Bergers on the Trace when they stopped to rest at the Breed Papoose. The *mendala* tavern just outside Belgrade in Chickasaw Territory was the last before Mississippi jurisdiction started again. It served refreshments as rough and new as its own timbers.

A ramshackle, unpainted shed set off the road in a clearing of slender firs and birches, its only colour was its sign, the crude representation of a baby, black on its right side, white on its left, and wearing Indian feathers. Usually Jack Karaquazian avoided such places, for the stakes were either too low or too high, and a game usually ended in some predictable brutality. Dismounting in the misty woods, Mr. Karaquazian took firm control of his fury and slept for a little while before rising and leading his horse to the hitching post. A cold instrument of justice, the Egyptian entered the tavern, a mean, unclean room where even the sawdust on the floor was filthy beyond recognition. His weapon displayed in an obvious threat, he walked slowly up to the *mendala*-sodden bar and ordered a Fröm.

The two Bergers and their huge sire were drinking at the bar with every sign of relaxed amiability, like creatures content in the knowledge that they had no natural enemies. They were honestly surprised as Jack Karaquazian spoke to them, his voice hardly raised, yet cutting through the other conversations like a Mason knife.

"Ladies are not so damned plentiful in this territory we can afford to give offence to one of them," Mr. Karaquazian had said, his eyes narrowing slightly, his body still as a hawk. "And as for hitting one or cursing one or having occasion to offer harm to one, or even murdering one, well, gentlemen, that looks pretty crazy to me. Or if it isn't craziness, then it's dumb cowardice. And there's nobody in this here tavern thinks a whole lot of a coward, I believe. And even less, I'd guess, of three damned cowards."

At this scarcely disguised challenge, the majority of the Breed Papoose's customers turned into discreet shadows until only Mr. Karaquazian, in his dusty silks and linen, and the Bergers, still in their travelling kaftans, their round Ugandan faces bright with sweat, were left confronting one another along the line of the plank bar. Mr. Karaquazian made no movement until the Bergers fixed upon a variety of impulsive actions.

The Egyptian did not draw as Japh Berger ran for the darkness of the backdoor convenience, neither did his hand begin to move as Ach Berger flung himself towards the cover of an overturned bench. It was only as Pa Ox, still mildly puzzled, pulled up the huge Vickers 9 on its swivel holster that Mr. Karaquazian's right hand moved with superhuman speed to draw and level the delicate silver stem of a pre-rip Sony, cauterising the older Berger's gun-hand and causing his terrible weapon to crash upon stained, warped boards—to slice away the bench around the shivering Ach, who pulled back withering fingers with a yelp, and to send a slender beam of lilac carcinogens to ensure that Japh would never again take quite the same pleasure in his private pursuits. Then the gambler had replaced the Sony in its holster and signalled, with a certain embarrassment, for a drink.

From the darkness, Ach Berger said: "Can I go now, mister?"

Without turning, Karaquazian raised his voice a fraction. "I hope in future you'll pay attention to better advice than your pa's, boy." He looked directly into the face of the wounded Ox who turned, holding the already healing stump of his wrist, to make for the door, leaving the Vickers and the four parts of his hand in the sawdust.

"I never would have thought that Sony was anything but a woman's weapon," said the barkeep admiringly.

"Oh, you can be sure of that." Jack Karaquazian lifted a glass in cryptic salute.

8 Les Flemmes d'Enfer

It had been perhaps a month later, still in the Territory, that Mr. Karaquazian had met a man who had seen the Bergers with the mad woman in Aberdeen a week before Jack Karaquazian had caught up with them.

The man told Mr. Karaquazian that Ox Berger had paid for the woman's board at an hotel in Aberdeen. Berger had made sure a doctor was found and a woman hired to look after her "until her folks came looking for her." The man had spoken, in quiet wonder, of her utter madness, the exquisite beauty of her face, the peculiar cast of her eyes.

"Ox told me she had looked the same since they'd found her, wading waist-deep in the swamp." From Aberdeen, he heard, she had been taken back to New Auschwitz by Peabody's people. In Memphis, Mr. Karaquazian learned she had gone North. He settled in Memphis for a while, perhaps hoping she would return and seek him out.

He was in a state of profound shock.

Jack Karaquazian refused to discuss or publicly affirm any religion. His faith in God did not permit it. He believed that when faith became religion it inevitably turned into politics. He was firmly determined to have as little to do with politics as possible. In general conversation he was prepared to admit that politics provided excellent distraction and consolation to those who needed them, but such comfort was usually bought at too high a price. Privately, he held a quiet certainty in the manifest power of Good and Evil. The former he personified simply as the Deity; the latter he called the Old Hunter, and imagined this creature stalking the world in search of souls. He had always congratulated himself on the skill with which he avoided the Old Hunter's traps and enticements, but now he understood that he had been made to betray himself through what he valued most: his honour. He was disgusted and astonished at how his most treasured virtues had destroyed his self-esteem and robbed him of everything but his uncommon luck at cards.

She did not write. Eventually, he took the *Étoile* down to Baton Rouge and from there rode the omnus towards the coast, by way of McComb and Wiggins. It was easy to find Biloxi. The sky was a fury of purple and black for thirty miles around, but above the Fault was a patch of perfect pale blue, there since the destruction began. Even as continua collided and became merely elemental, you could always find the Terminal Café, flickering in and out of a thousand subtly altering realities, pulsing, expanding, contracting, pushing unlikely angles through the after-images of its own shadows, making unique each outline of each ordinary piece of furniture and equipment, and yet never fully affected by that furious vortex above which the solar system bobbed, as it were, like a cork at the centre of the maelstrom. They were not entirely invulnerable to the effects of Chaos, that pit of non-consciousness. There were the hot-spots, the time-shifts, the perceptual problems, the energy drains, the odd geographies. Heavy snow had fallen over the Delta one winter, a general cooling, a coruscation, while the following summer, most agreed, was perfectly normal. And yet there remained always that sense of borrowed time. She had seen the winter as an omen for the future. "We have no right to survive this catastrophe," she had said. "Yet we must try, surely." He had recognised a faith as strong as his own.

Boudreaux Ramsadeen brought in a new band, electrok addicts from somewhere in Tennessee where they had found a hot-spot and brained in until it went dry. They had been famous in those half-remembered years before the Fault, and they played with extraordinary vigour and pleasure, so that Boudreaux's strange, limping dance took on increasingly complex figures and his partners, thrilled at the brute's exquisite grace and gentleness, threw their bodies into rapturous invention, stepping in and out of the zigzagging after-images, sometimes dancing with twin selves, their heads flung back and the colours of hell reflected in their duplicated eyes. And Boudreaux cried with the joy of it, while Jack Karaquazian, on the raised game floor, where the window looked directly out into the Fault, took no notice. Here, at his favourite flat game, his fingers playing a ten-dimensional pseudo-universe like an old familiar deck, the Egyptian still presented his back to that voracious fault. Its colours swirling in a kind of glee, it swallowed galaxies while Mr. Karaquazian gave himself to old habits. But he was never unconscious.

Mr. Karaquazian remained in the limbo of the Terminal Café. Up in Memphis, he heard, bloody rivalries and broken treaties would inevitably end in the Confederacy's absolute collapse, unless some sort of alliance was made with the reluctant Free States. Either way, wars must begin. Colinda Dovero's vision of the future had been clearer than most of the oracles'.

Mr. Karaquazian had left Egypt because of civil war. Now he refused to move on or even discuss the situation. He kept his back to the Fault because he had come to believe it was the antithesis of God, a manifestation of the Old Hunter. Yet, unlike most of his fellow gamblers, he still hoped for some chance of reconciliation with his Deity. His faith had grown more painful but was not diminished by his constant outrage at his own obscene arrogance, which had led him to ruin innocent men. Yet something of that arrogance remained, and he believed he would not find any reconciliation until he had rid himself of it. He knew of no way to confront and redeem his action. To seek out the Bergers, to offer them his remorse, would merely compound his crime, shift the moral burden and, what was more, further insult them. He remembered the mild astonishment in Ox's eyes. At last he understood the man's expression as Ox sought to defend himself against one whom he guessed must be a psychopath blood looking for a coup.

Sam Oakenhurst wondered, in the words of a new song he had heard, if they were not "killing time for eternity." Maybe, one by one, they would get bored enough with the game and stroll casually down into the mouth of hell, to suffer whatever punishment, pleasure or annihilation was their fate. But Mr. Karaquazian became impatient with this, and Sam apologised. "I'm growing sentimental, I guess."

Mr. Oakenhurst and Brother Ignatius had borrowed two of his systems for the big Texas game. They had acted out of good will, attempting to re-involve him in the things which had once pleased him. Mr. Oakenhurst had told of an illegal acoustic school in New Orleans. Only a few people still had those old cruel skills. "Why don't you meet me down there, Jack, when I get back from Texas?"

"They're treacherous dudes, those *machinoix*—outlaws or otherwise."

"What's the difference, Jack? It'll make a change for you."

So, after a few more hands and a little more time on the edge of eternity, he had joined Mr. Oakenhurst in New Orleans. Brother Ignatius was gone, taken out in some freak pi-jump on the way home, his horse with him. Mr. Karaquazian discovered the *machinoix* to be players more interested in remorseful nostalgia and the pain than the game itself. It had been ugly money, but easy, and their fellow players, far from resenting losses, grew steadily more friendly, courting their company between games, offering to display their most intimate scarifications.

Jack Karaquazian had wondered, chiefly because of the terror he sensed resonating between them, if the *machinoix* might allow him a means of salvation, if only through some petty martyrdom. He had nothing but a dim notion of conventional theologies, but the *machinoix* spoke often of journeying into the shadowlands, by which he eventually realised they meant an afterlife. It was one of their fundamental beliefs. Swearing he was not addicted, Sam Oakenhurst was able, amiably, to accept their strangeness and continue to win their guineas, but Mr. Karaquazian became nervous, not finding the dangers in any way stimulating.

When his luck had turned, Mr. Karaquazian had been secretly relieved. He had remained in the city only to honour his commitment to his partner. He felt it might be time to try the Trace again. He felt she might be calling him.

9 Louisiana Two-Step

"The world was always a mysterious dream to me," she had told him. "But now it is an incomprehensible nightmare. Was it like this for those Jews, do you think?"

"Which Jews?" He had never had much interest in anthropology.

She had continued speaking, probably to herself, as she stood on the balcony of the hotel in Gatlinburg and watched the aftershocks of some passing skirmish billow over the horizon: "Those folk, those Anglo-Saxons, had no special comfort in dying. Not for them the zealotry of the Viking or the Moor. They paraded their iron and their horses and they made compacts with those they conquered or who threatened them. They offered a return to a Roman Golden Age, a notion of universal justice. And they gradually prevailed until Chaos was driven into darkness and ancient memory. Even the Normans could not reverse what the Anglo-Saxons achieved. But with that achievement, Jack, also vanished a certain wild vivacity. What the Christians came to call 'pagan.'" She had sighed and kissed his hands, looking away at the flickering ginger moon. "Do you long for those times, Jack? That pagan dream?"

Mr. Karaquazian thought it astonishing that anyone had managed to create a kind of order out of ungovernable Chaos. And that, though he would never say so, was his reason for believing in God and also, because logic would have it, the Old Hunter. "Total consciousness must, I suppose, suggest total anti-consciousness—and all that lies between."

She told him then of her own belief. If the Fault were manifest Evil, then somewhere there must be an equivalent manifestation of Good. She loved life with a positive relish, which he enjoyed vicariously and which in turn restored to him sensibilities long since atrophied.

When he left the steamboat at Greenville, Mr. Karaquazian bought himself a sturdy riding horse and made his way steadily up the Trace, determined to admire and relish the beauty of it, as if for the first time. Once again, many of the trees had already dropped their leaves.

Through their skeletons, a faint pink-gold wash in the pearly sky showed the position of the sun. Against this cold, soft light, the details of the trees were emphasised, giving each twig a character of its own. Jack Karaquazian kept his mind on these wonders and pleasures, moving day by day towards McClellan and the silver cypress swamp, the gold Stains. In the sharp, new air he felt a strength that he had not known, even before his act of infamy. Perhaps it was a hint of redemption. Of his several previous attempts to return, he had no clear recollections; but this time, though he anticipated forgetfulness, as it were, he was more confident of his momentum. In his proud heart, his sinner's heart, he saw Colinda Dovero as the means of his salvation. She alone would give him a choice which might redeem him in his eyes, if not in God's. She was still his Luck. She would be back at her Stains, he thought, maybe working her claim, a rich machine-baron herself by now and unsettled by his arrival; but once united, he knew they could be parted only by an act of uncalled-for courage, perhaps something like a martyrdom. He felt she was offering him, at last, a destiny.

Mr. Karaquazian rode up on the red-gold Trace, between the tall, dense trees of the Mississippi woods, crossing the Broken and New rivers, following the joyfully foaming Pearl for a while until he was in Chocktaw country, where he paid his toll in *piles noires* to an unsmiling Indian who had not seen, he said, a good horse in a long time. He spoke of an outrage, an automobile which had come by a few days ago, driven by a woman with auburn hair. He pointed. The deep tyre tracks were still visible. Mr. Karaquazian began to follow them, guessing that Colinda Dovero had left them for him. At what enormous cost? It seemed she must already be tapping the Stains. Such power would be worth almost anything when war eventually came. He could feel the disintegration in the air. Soon these people would be mirroring the metaphysical destruction by falling upon and devouring their fellows. Yet, through their self-betrayal, he thought, Colinda Dovero might survive and even prosper, at least for a while.

He arrived in McClellan expecting to find change, enrichment from the colour strike. But the town remained the pleasant, unaltered place he had known, her maze of old railroad tracks crossing and recrossing at dozens of intersections, from the pre-Biloxi days when the meat plants had made her rich, her people friendly and easy, her whites respectful yet dignified.

Jack Karaquazian spent the night at the Henry Clay Hotel and was disappointed to find no one in the tidy little main street (now a far cry from its glory) who had heard of activity out around the Streams. Only a fool, he was told, would go into that cypress swamp at any time of year, least of all during a true season. Consoling himself with the faint hope that she might have kept her workings a secret, Mr. Karaquazian rented himself a pirogue, gave an eager kiddikin a guinea to take care of his horse, and set off into the Streams, needing no map, no memory—merely his will and the unreasoning certainty that she was drawing him to her.

10 Sugar Bee

"I had been dying all my life, Jack," she had said. "I decided I wanted to live. I'm giving it my best shot. If we are here as the result of an accident, let us take advantage of that!"

The swamp fog obscured all detail. There was the sharp sound of the water as he paddled the pirogue; the rustle of a wing, a muffled rush, a faint shadow moving amongst the trunks. Jack Karaquazian began to wonder if he were not in limbo, moving from one matrix to another. Would those outlines remain the outlines of trees and vines? Would they crystallise, perhaps, or become massive cliffs of basalt and obsidian? There was sometimes a clue in the nature of the echoes. He whistled a snatch of "Grand Mamou." The old dance tune helped his spirits. He believed he must still be in the same reality.

"Human love, Jack, is our only weapon against Chaos. And yet, consistently, we reject its responsibilities in favour of some more abstract and therefore less effective notion."

Suddenly, through the agitated grey, as if in confirmation of his instinct, a dozen ibises winged low beneath the branches of the cypresses and cedars, as silvery as bass, so that Mr. Karaquazian in his scarlet travelling cloak felt an intruder on all that exquisite paleness.

When at last the sun began to wash across the west and the mist was touched with the subtle colours of the tea-rose, warming and dissipating to reveal the tawny browns and dark greens it had been hiding, he grew more certain that this time, inevitably, he and Colinda Dovero must reunite. He was half prepared to see the baroque brass and diamonds of the legendary Prosers, milking the Stains for his sweetheart's security, but only herons disturbed the covering of leaves upon the water; only ducks and perpetua geese shouted and bickered into the cold air, the rapid flutter of their wings bearing eery resemblance to a *mechanish* engine. The cypress swamp was avoided by men, was genuinely timeless, perhaps the only place on Earth completely unaffected by the Biloxi error.

Why would such changelessness be feared?

Or had fundamental change already occurred? Something too complex and delicate for the human brain to comprehend, just as it could not really accept the experience of more than one matrix. Jack Karaquazian, contented by the swamp's familiarity, did not wish to challenge its character. Instead, he drew further strength from it so that when, close to twilight, he saw the apparently ramshackle cabin, its blackened logs and planks two storeys high, riveted together by old salt and grit cans that still advertised the virtues of their ancient brands, and perched low in the fork of two great silvery cypress branches overhanging the water and the smallest of the Stains, he knew at once that she had never truly left her claim; that in some way she had always been here, waiting for him.

For a few seconds, Jack Karaquazian allowed himself the anguish of regret and self-accusation, then he threw back his cloak, cupped his hands around his mouth, and with his white breath pouring into the air, called out:

"Colinda!"

And from within her fortress, her nest, she replied:

"Jack."

She was leaning out over the verandah of woven branches, her almond eyes the colour of honey, bright with tears and hope; an understanding that this time, perhaps for the first time, he had actually made it back to her. He was no longer a ghost. When she spoke to him, however, her language was incomprehensible; seemingly a cacophony, without melody or sense. Terrible yelps and groans burst out of her perfect lips. He could scarcely bear to listen. *Is this*, he wondered, *how we first perceive the language of angels?*

The creosoted timbers lay in odd marriage to the pale branches which cradled them. Flitting with urgent joy, from verandah to branch and from branch to makeshift ladder, she was a tawny spirit.

Naked, yet unaffected by the evening chill, she reached the landing she had made. The planks, firmly moored by four oddly plaited ropes tied into the branches, rolled and bounced under her tiny bare feet.

"Jack, my *pauvre hobo*!" It was as if she could only remember the language through snatches of song, as a child does. "*Ma pauvre pierrot.*" She smiled in delight.

He stepped from the pirogue to the landing. They embraced, scarlet engulfing dark gold. It was the resolution he had so often prayed for; but without redemption. For now it was even clearer to him that the mistake he had made at the Breed Papoose had never been an honest one. He also knew that she need never discover this; and what was left of the hypocrite in him called to him to forget the past as irredeemable. And when she sensed his tension, a hesitation, she asked in halting speech if he had brought bad news, if he no longer loved her, if he faltered. She had waited for him a long time, she said, relinquishing all she had gained so that she might be united with him, to take him with her, to show him what she had discovered in the Stain.

She drew him up to her cabin. It looked as if it had been here for centuries. It seemed in places to have grown into or from the living tree. Inside it was full of magpie luxury—plush and brass and gold-plated candelabra, mirrors and crystals and flowing *muralos*. There was a little power from the Stains, she said, but not much. She had brought everything in the car long ago. She took him onto the verandah and, through the semi-darkness, pointed out the burgundy carcass of an antique Oldsmobile.

"I thought..." But he was unable either to express the emotion he felt or to comprehend the sickening temporal shifts which had almost separated them for ever. It was as if dream and reality had at last resolved, but at the wrong moment. "Some men took you to Aberdeen."

"They were kind." Her speech was still thick.

"So I understand."

"But mistaken. I had returned to find you. I went into the Stain while you were gone. When I tried to seek you out, I had forgotten how to speak or wear clothes. I got back here easily. It's never hard for me."

"Very hard for me." He embraced her again, kissed her.

"This is what I longed for." She studied his dark green eyes, his smooth brown skin, the contours of his face, his disciplined body. "Waiting in this place has not been easy, with the world so close. But I came back for you, Jack. I believe the Stain is not a sign of colour but a kind of counter-effect to the Fault. It leads into a cosmos of wonderful stability. Not stasis, they say, but with a slower rate of entropy. What they once called a lower chaos factor, when I studied physics. I met a woman whom I think we would call 'the Rose' in our language. She is half-human, half-flower, like all her race. And she was my mentor as she could be yours. And we could have children, Jack. It's an extraordinary adventure. So many ways of learning to see and so much time for it. Time for consideration, time to create justice. Here, Jack, all the time is going. You know that." She sensed some unexpected resistance in him. She touched his cheek. "Jack, we are on the edge of chaos here. We must eventually be consumed by what we created. But we also created a way out. What you always talked about. What you yearned for. You know."

"Yes, I know." Perhaps she was really describing heaven. He made an awkward gesture. "Through there?" He indicated, in the gathering darkness, the pale wash of the nearest Stain.

"The big one only." She became enthusiastic, her uncertainties fading before the vividness of her remembered experience. "We have responsibilities. We have duties there. But they are performed naturally, clearly from self-interest. There's understanding and charity there, Jack. The logic is what you used to talk about. What you thought you had dreamed. Where chance no longer rules unchecked. It's a heavenly place, Jack. The Rose will accept us both. She'll guide us. We can go there now, if you like. You must want to go, *mon chéri, mon chéri*." But now, as she looked at him, at the way he stood, at the way he stared, unblinking, down into the swamp, she hesitated. She took his hand and gripped it. "You want to go. It isn't boring, Jack. It's as real as here. But they have a future, a precedent. We have neither."

"I would like to find such a place." He checked the spasm in his chest and was apologetic. "But I might not be ready, *ma fancy*."

She held tight to his gambler's hand, wondering if she had misjudged its strength. "You would rather spend your last days at a table in the Terminal Café, waiting for the inevitable moment of oblivion?"

"I would rather journey with you," he said, "to paradise or anywhere you wished, Colinda. But paradise will accept you, *mon honey*. Perhaps I have not yet earned my place there."

She preferred to believe he joked with her. "We will leave it until the morning." She stroked his blue-black hair, believing him too tired to think. "There is no such thing as earning. It's always luck, Jack. It was luck we found the Stains. It's luck that brought us together. Brought us our love. Our love brought us back together. It is a long, valuable life they offer us, *bon papillon*. Full of hope and peace. Take your chance, Jack. As you always did."

He shook his head. "But some of us, my love, have earning natures. I made a foolish play. I am ashamed."

"No regrets, Jack. You can leave it all behind. This is luck. Our luck. What is it in you, Jack, this new misery?" She imagined another woman.

He could not tell her. He wanted the night with her. He wanted a memory. And her own passion for him conquered her curiosity, her trepidation, yet there was a desperate quality to her love-making which neither she nor he had ever wished to sense again. Addressing this, she was optimistic: "This will all go once we enter the Stain. Doesn't it seem like heaven, Jack?"

"Near enough," he admitted. A part of him, a bitter part of him, wished that he had never made this journey, that he had never left the game behind; for the game, even at its most dangerous, was better than this scarcely bearable pain. "Oh, my heart!"

For the rest of the night he savoured every second of his torment, and yet in the morning he knew that he was not by this means to gain release from his pride. It seemed that his self-esteem, his stern wall against the truth, crumbled in unison with the world's collapse; he saw for himself nothing but an eternity of anguished regret.

"Come." She moved towards sadness as she led him down through the branches and the timbers to his own pirogue. She refused to believe she had waited only for this.

He let her row them out into the pastel brightness of the lagoon until they floated above the big gold Stain, peering through that purity of colour as if they might actually glimpse the paradise she had described.

"Your clothes will go away." She was as gentle as a Louisiana April. "You needn't worry about that."

She slipped over the side and, with a peculiar lifting motion, moved under the membrane to hang against the density of the gold, smiling up to him to demonstrate that there was nothing to fear, as beautiful as she could ever be, as perfect as the colour. And then she had re-emerged in the shallow water, amongst the lilies and the weeds and the sodden leaves. "Come, Jack. You must not hurt me further, sweetheart. We will go now. But if you stay I shall not return." Horrified by what she understood as his cowardice, she fell back against the Stain, staring up at the grey-silver branches of the big trees, watching the morning sun touch the rising mist, refusing to look at Jack Karaquazian while he wept for his failures, for his inability to seize this moment, for all his shame, his unforgotten dreams; at his unguessable loss.

She spoke from the water. "It wasn't anything that happened to me there that turned me crazy. It was the journey here did that. It's sane down there, Jack."

"No place for a gambler, then," he said, and laughed suddenly. "What is this compensatory heaven? What proof is there that it is real? The only reason for its existence appears to be a moral one!"

"It's a balance," she said. "Nature offers balances."

"That was always a human illusion. Look at Biloxi. There's the reality. I'm not ready."

"This isn't worthy of you, Jack." She was frightened now, perhaps doubting everything.

"I'm not your Jack," he told her. "Not any longer. I can't come yet. You go on, *ma chérie*. I'll join you if I can. I'll follow you. But not yet."

She put her fingers on the edge of the boat. She spoke with soft urgency. "It's hard for me, Jack. I love you. You're growing old here." She reached up her arms, the silver water falling upon his clothes, as if to drag him with her. She gripped his long fingers. It was his hands, she had said, that had first attracted her. "You're growing old here, Jack."

"Not old enough." He pulled away. He began to cough. He lost control of the spasm. Suddenly drops of his blood mingled with the water, fell upon the Stain. She cupped some in her hand and then, as if carrying a treasure, she slipped back into the colour, folding herself down until she had merged with it entirely.

By the time he had recovered himself, there was only a voice, an unintelligible shriek, a rapidly fading bellow, as if she had made one last plea for him to follow.

"And not man enough either, I guess." He had watched the rest of his blood until it mingled invisibly with the water.

11 Pourquoi m'Aimes-tu Pas?

He remained in her tree-cabin above the Stain for as long as the food she had stored lasted. She had prepared the place so that he might wait for her if she were absent. He forced himself to live there, praying that through this particular agony he might confront and perhaps even find a means of lifting his burden. But pain was not enough. He began to suspect that pain was not even worth pursuing.

More than once he returned to the big Stain and sat in the pirogue, looking down, trying to find some excuse, some rationale which would allow him this chance of paradise. But he could not. All he had left to him was a partial truth. He felt that if he lost that, he lost all hope of grace. Eventually he abandoned the cabin and the colour and made his way up the Trace to Nashville, where he played an endless succession of reckless games until at last, as fighting broke out in the streets between rival guilds of musician-assassins, he managed to get on a military train to Memphis before the worst of the devastation. At the Peabody Hotel in Memphis, he bathed and smoked a cigar and, through familiar luxuries, sought to evade the memories of the colour swamp. He took the *Étoile* down to Natchez, well ahead of the holocaust, and then there was nowhere to go but the Terminal Café, where he could sit and watch Boudreaux Ramsadeen perform his idiosyncratic measures on the dance floor, his women partners flocking like delicate birds about a graceful bull. As their little feet stepped in and around the uncertain outlines of an infinite number of walls, floors, ceilings and roofs, expertly holding their metaphysical balance even as they grinned and whooped to the remorseless melodies of the fiddles, accordion and tambourines, Jack Karaquazian would come to sense that only when he lost interest in his own damaged self-esteem would he begin to know hope of release.

Then, unexpectedly, like a visitation, Ox Berger, a prosthesis better than the original on his arm, sought Mr. Karaquazian out at the main table and stood looking at him across the flat board, its dimensions roiling, shimmering and cross-flashing within the depths of its singular machinery, and said, with calm respect, "I believe you owe me a game, sir."

Jack Karaquazian looked as if a coughing fit would take control of him, but he straightened up, his eyes and muscles sharply delineated against a paling skin, and said with courtesy, almost with warmth, "I believe I do, sir."

And they played the long forms, sign for sign, commitment to commitment, formula for formula; the great classic flat-game schemes, the logic and counter-logic of a ten-dimensional matrix, rivalrous metaphysics, a quasi-infinity held in a metre-long box in which they dabbled minds and fingers and ordered the fate of millions, claimed responsibility for the creation, the maintenance and the sacrifice of whole semi-real races and civilisations, not to mention individuals, some of whom formed cryptic dependencies on an actuality they would never directly enjoy. And Ox Berger played with grace, with irony and skill which, lacking the experience and recklessness of Jack Karaquazian's style, could not in the end win, but showed the mettle of the player.

As he wove his famous "Faust" web, which only Colinda Dovero had ever been able to identify and counter, Jack Karaquazian developed a dawning respect for the big farmer who had chosen never to exploit a talent as great as the gambler's own. And in sharing this with his opponent, Ox Berger achieved a profound act of forgiveness, for he released Mr. Karaquazian from his burden of self-disgust and let him imagine, instead, the actual character of the man he had wronged and so understand the true nature of his sin. Jack Karaquazian was able to confront and repent, in dignified humility, his lie for what it had truly been.

When the game was over (by mutual concession) the two men stood together on the edge of the Fault, watching the riotous death of universes, and Mr. Karaquazian wondered now if all he lacked was courage, if perhaps the only way back to her was by way of the chaos which seduced him with its mighty and elaborate violence. But then, as he stared into that university of dissolution, he knew that in losing his pride he had not, after all, lost his soul, and just as he knew that pride would never earn him the right to paradise, so, he judged, there was no road to heaven by way of hell. And he thanked Ox Berger for his game and his charity. Now he planned, when he was ready, to make a final try at the Trace, though he could not be sure that his will alone, without hers, would be sufficient to get him through a second time. Even should he succeed, he would have to find a way through the Stain without her guidance. Mr. Karaquazian shook hands with his opponent. By providing this peculiar intimacy, this significant respect, Ox Berger had done Mr. Karaquazian the favour not only of forgiving him, but of helping him to forgive himself.

The gambler wished the map of the Stain were his to pass on, but he knew that it had to be sought for and only then would the lucky ones find it. As for Ox Berger, he had satisfied his own conscience and required nothing else of Jack Karaquazian. "When you take your journey, sir, I hope you find the strength to sustain yourself."

"Thanks to you, sir," says Jack Karaquazian.

The olive intensity of his features framed by the threatening madness of the Biloxi Fault, its vast walls of seething colour rising and falling, the Egyptian plays with anyone, black, white, red or yellow, who wants his kind of game. And the wilder he plays, the more he wins. Clever as a jackal, he lets his slender hands, his woman's hands, weave and flow within the ten dimensions of his favourite flat game, and he is always happy to raise the psychic stakes. Yet there is no despair in him.

Only his familiar agony remains, the old pain of frustrated love, sharper than ever, for now he understands how he failed Colinda Dovero and how he wounded her. And he knows that she will never again seek him out at the Terminal Café.

"You're looking better, Jack." Sam Oakenhurst has recovered from the *machinoix*'s torments. "Your old self."

Jack Karaquazian deals seven hands of poker. In his skin is the reflection of a million dying cultures given up to the pit long before their time; in his green eyes is a new kind of courtesy. Coolly amiable in his silk and linen, his raven hair straight to his shoulders, his back firmly set against the howling triumph of Satan, he is content in the speculation that, for a few of his fellow souls at least, there may be some chance of paradise.

"I'm feeling it, Sam," he says.

Thanks to Garth Brooks, Doug Kershaw, all the artists on Swallow Records, Ville Platte, LA; and friends in Atlanta, New Orleans, Houston, West Point MS, Hattiesburg MS, Oxford MS and Oxford U.K., where this was written. Special thanks to Ed Kramer, Mustafa al-Bayoumi and Brother Willie Love…

My Experiences in the Third World War (1979/'80)

The following sequence comprises three of the four stories written by Moorcock that are set in (and around the run-up to) a third World War.

"Crossing into Cambodia," the most acclaimed of these, was first to be written but actually forms the last part in the series. It was originally published in 1979, in an anthology, *Twenty Houses of the Zodiac* (New English Library), edited by Maxim Jakubowski.

"Going to Canada," and "Leaving Pasadena" formed prequels to "Crossing..." and were originally published in *My Experiences in the Third World War* (Savoy Books) in 1980.

A further prequel, "Casablanca," written some years later, does not appear here but was originally published in *Casablanca* (Gollancz) in 1989. The full quartet has since been known collectively as Some Reminiscences of the Third World War.

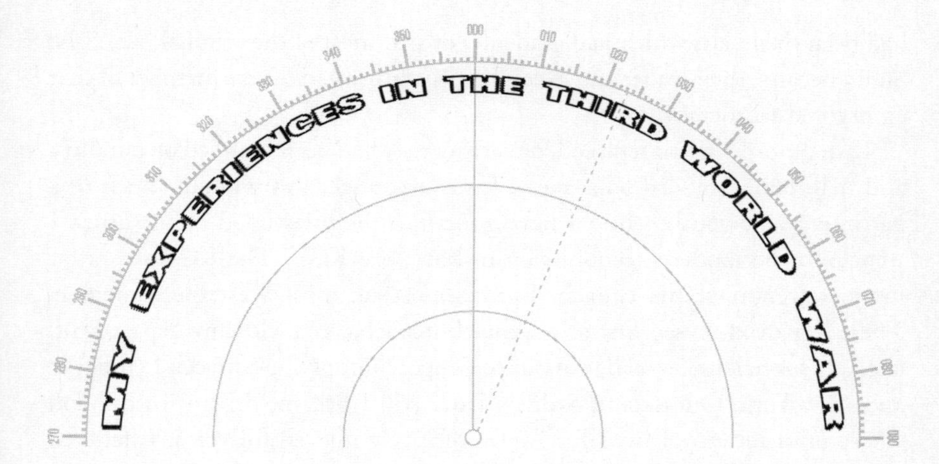

Going to Canada

I WAS ORDERED TO Canada; that pie-dish of privilege and broken promises: to Toronto. My chief was uncomprehending when I showed disappointment. "Canada! Everybody wants to go there."

"I have stayed in Toronto before," I told him.

He knew. He became suspicious, so I said that I had been joking. I chuckled to confirm this. His old, Great Russian face, moulded by the imposition of a dozen conflicting tyrannies, made a little mad smile. "You are to look up Belko, an émigré. He is the only Belko in the phone book."

"Very well, Victor Andreyevitch." I accepted the colourful paper wallet of tickets and money. This supply was an unusual one. My "front" normally allowed me to be self-supporting. I work as an antique-dealer in the Portobello Road.

"Belko knows why you are meeting him. He will tell you what you have to know. It concerns some American planes, I gather."

I shook hands and descended the green-carpeted stairs into the rain of East London.

During our Civil War many pretended to be Bolsheviks in order to terrorise local communities. After the war these people had continued as commissars. It had been their class which had gradually ousted most of the original Marxists. Stalin became their leader and exemplar. My father had been a member of that embryonic aristocracy.

Like the order it had replaced, our aristocracy had been founded on banditry and maintained by orthodox piety. I was a younger son without much of a patrimony. Previously I might have gone into the priesthood or the army. I went into the modern combination of both, the KGB. The KGB was a far more conventional and congenial profession than most Westerners imagine. There I enjoyed myself first as a minor bureaucrat in a Moscow department, later as a special officer on one of our passenger ships plying between Leningrad and New York, Odessa and Sydney. Later still I became a plant in London where until recently I lived for twelve relatively uneventful years. I flattered myself that my background and character suited me to the rôle of a seedy near-alcoholic dealer in old furniture and over-priced bric-a-brac. It was believed that I was a Polish expatriate and indeed I had taken the name and British passport of just such an émigré; he had returned voluntarily to Poland on a whim and had sold his old identity to us in a perfectly amiable arrangement. We eased his way with the Cracow authorities who granted him new papers and found him a flat and a job.

In spite of changing régimes my own life had remained relatively untroubled. My name in London was Tomas Dubrowski. For my private amusement I preferred the name of Tom Conrad. It was this name, in '30s "modern" lettering, which adorned my shop. I paid taxes, VAT, and owned a TV licence. Although I had no particular desire to maintain my part for ever, I enjoyed it for its complete lack of anxiety and the corresponding sense of security it gave me. Now that I was to return briefly to the real world, I should have to seek a fresh *context.*

A Russian citizen requires a *context,* because his conditioning makes him a permanent child. Anything will do. Therefore the *context* is often simple slavery. Even I, of Jewish Ukrainian extraction (through my grandmother), need that sense of boundaries. It is probably no coincidence that Kropotkin, founder of modern anarchism, was a Russian: his defiant views are directly opposed to our needs, which are on the whole of an authoritarian nature.

My father had been a naval petty officer. Later he became "commissar" of a small town in Belorussia. He had eleven other deserting sailors with him when he had arrived in early 1918. They represented themselves as Bolsheviks. He had worn a leather jacket with two Mauser pistols in his belt and he had rarely taken off his sailor's peaked cap. Somehow the civil war did not touch the town much, so the gang made the most of its time.

My father took five young girls from the local gymnasium for himself and gave the rest to his men. He instructed the girls in every debauchery. When the civil war ended and it became obvious who had won, my father did not do away with the girls (as he might well have—it was common practice) but made them read to him from the works of Marx and Engels, from Lenin's writings, *Pravda* and *Izvestia* until he and they were all familiar with the new dogma. Then he formed his thugs into the nucleus of the local Party, sent four of the girls (now fully fledged Komsomol leaders) back to the gymnasium as teachers and married Vera Vladimirovna, my mother.

In time he was praised for his example to the community and was awarded a medal by the State. During the famines of the next few years he and my mother were never hungry. During the purges they never seemed to be in danger. They had two children, a boy and a girl.

In 1936 my father went off on Party business and in 1938 I was born. The young writer who begat me was subsequently sent to a camp and died. I had long considered myself the secret guardian of his blood. My father was in most respects a realist. He preferred to accept me as his own rather than risk the scandal of his name being associated with that of the writer. My older sister was killed in the War. My older brother became a hero during the Siege of Stalingrad. He ran a large power-plant near Smolensk on the Dnieper. He was a self-satisfied, right-thinking man.

"A little pain," my mother used to say to her friends, "makes good girls of us all."

My father trained his girls to kiss his feet, his legs, his private parts, his arse. My mother was more wholehearted at this than her rivals, which is how he came to pick her as his wife. Again, she behaved in a Russian way. She was dutiful in all things, but, when his authority was absent, she became irresponsible. The Russian soul is a masochist's wounds. It is a frightening, self-indulgent, monumentally sentimental relinquishing of individual responsibility: it is schizophrenic. More than elsewhere, personal suffering is equated with virtue.

My grandmother was apparently raped by a young Jew and my mother was the result. The Jew was killed shortly afterwards, in a general pogrom resulting from the affair. That was in Ekaterinaslav province in the last years of the nineteenth century. My grandmother never would say for certain that it had been rape. I remember her winking at me when the word was mentioned. My great-uncle, the surviving brother of the dead man, told me that after the Revolution some Red Cossacks came to his shtetl. He was mortally afraid, of course, and would have done anything to stay alive. A Cossack named Konkoff billeted himself in my great-uncle's house. My great-uncle was mindless with terror, grovelling before the Cossack, ready to lick the soles off his boots at the first demand. Instead, Konkoff had laughed at him, offered him some rations, pulled him upright, patted him on the back and called him "comrade." My great-uncle realised that the Revolution had actually changed things. He was no longer a detested animal. He had become a Cossack's pet Jew.

In Russia, in those days before the present war, there had been a resurgence of Nationalism, encouraged by the State. Because of the absence of real democratic power, many had turned (as they did under Tsarism) to Pan-Slavism. A direct consequence of this movement was anti-Semitism, also blessed unofficially by the State, and a spirit amongst our élite which, while not so unequivocally anti-Semitic, was reminiscent of the Black Hundreds or the Legion of the Archangel Michael, the early twentieth-century pogromists. It was obvious that the State equated radicalism with intellectual Jewish trouble-makers. The State therefore encouraged—through the simple prejudices of its cunning but not considerably intelligent leaders—a movement in no way dissimilar to that which had followed the troubles of 1905, when Jewish socialists had been scapegoats for everything. Stalin had eliminated virtually the entire Jewish element of the Party, of course, by 1935.

When I was young it had been fashionable to scoff at the trappings of Nationalism—at folk costumes, at peasant blouses and so on. Outside of cultural exhibitions and performances these things were a sign of old-fashioned romanticism. They were not considered progressive. When I returned to Russia briefly in 1980 young people were walking the streets looking as if they had stepped out of a performance of *Prince Igor*. Even some of the younger leaders would on occasions be photographed in Cossack costume. Anti-Semitic books and paintings, even songs, received official patronage. The authoritarian republic had at last, in sixty years, managed to resemble in detail the autocracy it had replaced. Soon there would be no clear differences save that poverty and sickness had been abolished in the Slavic regions of the Union.

These benefits had been gained by relinquishing dignity and liberty, and the nobler forms of idealism which had given the early Revolution its rhetoric and its impetus. There were no longer any private arts. Everything had been sacrificed to formalised ceremonies similar to Church ritual or other primitive affirmations of superstition. The Soviet Union had codified and sanctified this terrifying impulse of human beings to shout reassuring lies to one another while standing with eyes tight shut on the brink of a chasm of reality. The State pretended that it was impossible (or at very least immoral) for such a chasm to exist. Soviet bureaucracy, too, formalised human failing and gave it shape and respectability; it did not merely accept this failing: it exalted it. I was as conditioned as anyone to believe that our lobotomising methods of ordering the human condition were the most sensible. I had found all these aspects of Soviet life comforting and reassuring. I did not have the character necessary for the enjoyment of personal freedom.

Like the Celts, Russians have no ethical system as such, merely a philosophy of life based firmly on the dignity of pain, on fear of the unknown and suspicion of anything we cannot at once recognise. That is why Bolshevism was so attractive an ideology to many peasants who identified it with a benevolently modified Church and Monarchy and for a time believed that Lenin intended to restore the Tsar to his throne; it is why it was so quickly adapted to Russian needs and Russian methods. I do not disapprove of the government of the Soviet Union. I accept it as a necessity. In 1930, as a result of the bourgeois Revolution headed by Kerenski, and the Revolution initiated by the bourgeois Lenin, women and children were starving to death all over Russia. Stalin was at heart an Orthodox peasant. He and other Orthodox peasants saved Russia from the monster released upon the nation by foolish, middle-class idealists. In doing so he punished the Communists who had brought about the disaster; the intellectuals and fanatics who were truly to blame for our misfortunes.

Stalin took on the great burden and responsibilities of a Tsar and all his ministers. Stalin knew that History would revile him and that his followers would become cynical and cruel. He countered their cynicism and cruelty with the only weapon he was able to use: terror. He became mad. He was himself not a cynic. He made factories efficient. He gave us our industry, our education, our health service. He made homes clean and sanitary. He killed millions for the sake of all those other millions who would otherwise have perished. He made it possible for us to round, eventually, on Hitler and drive him back to Germany. He returned to us the security of our Empire. And when he died we destroyed his memory. He knew that we would and I believe that he understood that this would have to happen. He was a realist; but he possessed an Orthodox conscience and his conscience made him mad. I am a realist happily born of an age which countered and adapted Christianity and that is doubtless what continues to make me such a good and reliable employee of the Russian State.

Because of the increasingly strict controls applied to those who wished to travel to and from Canada, it was necessary for me to go to my doctor for a medical certificate. I used a fashionable private doctor in South Kensington who was quick to prescribe the drugs I required. In his waiting-room I found three young women wearing the elaborate and violent make-up and costume then favoured by the British demimonde. They were whispering together in a peculiar way common only to whores and nuns, full of sudden shifts of volume and tone and oblique reference, glances and gestures, so I only heard snatches of their conversation.

"I was doing this job, you know—straight... At the club. He said he wanted me to work for him—you know—so I said I wouldn't—he said to go out with him—but I wouldn't—he was a funny guy, you know—he gave me this—" A bandaged arm was held up. It was a soft arm in a soft dress. "He had a bottle, you know—they called the cops—they're prosecuting—his lawyer phoned me and offered me thirty thousand to settle out of court..."

"Settle," advised one of the other girls.

"I would," said the second.

"But my lawyer says we can get fifty."

"Settle for thirty."

"He gave me seventeen stitches." All this was relayed in a neutral, almost self-satisfied tone. "What you doing here, anyway?"

"I just came with her," said the prettiest. "It's about her pills."

"I came to get my slimming pills changed. Those others make me feel really sick, you know."

"What! Durophets?"

"Yeah. They make me feel terrible."

"What you going to ask him for? Terranin?"

"They're what I use," said her friend.

"They're much better," agreed the wounded whore. "You're looking different," she told the girl's friend. "I wouldn't have recognised you. You're looking terrible."

They all laughed.

"Did you know what happened to Mary?" She put her mouth close to the girl's ear and began to whisper rapidly.

The doctor's receptionist opened the door. "You can go in now, Miss Williams."

"... all over the bed," finished Miss Williams, rising and following the receptionist.

When she had gone the other two began to discuss her in a disinterested fashion, as if they followed some unconscious habit. Neither, it emerged, believed that thirty thousand pounds had been offered. "More like three," said one. They, too, were not at all outraged by the event. Most whores are frightened of any demonstration of passion, which is why they choose masters who treat them coldly. I had for a short while been in charge of a whore-house in Greece and had learned how to deal with the girls who were conditioned to confuse love with fear. If they were afraid of their master they thought they loved him. Because they were not afraid of their clients they could not love them and in the main felt contempt for them. But it was self-contempt they actually felt. I remembered with some dismay the single-mindedness of such girls who pursued persecution and exploitation as an anodyne, as their customers often pursued sexual sensation; who learned to purchase the favours of their employers with the very money they received from the hire of their own bodies. My spell as a whore-master had been the only time I had tasted direct power and it had taken every ounce of self-discipline to administer; it was a relief to become what I now was.

Miss Williams rejoined her friends. "I'm going to have it photographed this afternoon," she told them, pulling down her sleeve.

The two girls went in to the doctor. They came out. All three left together.

I was next in the surgery. The doctor smiled at me. "More trouble?"

I shook my head.

"The penicillin worked?"

"Yes."

"It's funny, that. Acts like a shot on you, won't touch me. Well, what's the trouble?" He spoke rapidly in a high-pitched voice. He was a Jew.

"None. I just need a certificate to say I'm not suffering from anything a Canadian's likely to catch."

He laughed. "That depends on you, doesn't it?" He was already reaching for his pad of forms. "Canada, eh? Lucky you."

He filled in the form swiftly and handed it to me. "Going for long?"

"I don't think so," I said.

"Business?"

"Believe it or not, we're buying our antiques from North America these days." It was true.

"No! Really?" He was amused. He stood up as I stood up. He leaned across his desk to shake hands. "Well, good luck. Enjoy yourself."

"I will."

I left his surgery and began to walk up Kensington Church Street, passing the three girls who were waiting on the kerb for a taxi. One of them looked very much like the girl who had given me the disease. I wondered if she would recognise me as I went by. But she was too deep in conversation to notice, even though I walked to within an inch or two of her shoulder, close enough to identify her heavy perfume.

The morning of the day I was due to take the overnight plane from Gatwick (it was a budget flight) I read the news of a border clash between China and India, but I did not give it too much attention. The Russo-Indian Pact had been signed the previous year, in Simla, and I believed that the Chinese would take the pact seriously. By the afternoon the radio news reported Moscow's warnings to Peking. When I left for Gatwick on the train from Victoria, I bought an evening paper. I had begun to consider the possibility of war between Russia and China. The evening news was vague and told me no more than had the radio news. On the plane, which took off on schedule, I watched a Walt Disney film about two teenage girls who seemed to be twins.

I reached Toronto at eleven o'clock in the evening, local time, took a taxi to a downtown hotel and turned on the television to discover that Confederation troops and tanks were invading China while Indian forces, with some British and American divisions already stationed there, were moving towards the Chinese border. A newsflash brought the information that both CIS and EC countries had lent their support to India and that China and her allies were expected to capitulate very soon.

Early the next day I found myself in a pleasant suburban street of tall, Victorian wooden houses, birch-trees and maples and soft lawns, ringing the bell of my contact, Mr. Belko. An angry girl, a pudgy seventeen, came to the door. She was wearing a blue dressing gown.

"Mr. Belko is expecting me," I told her.

She was triumphant. "Mr. Belko left an hour ago."

"Where did he go? Would you mind?"

"To the airport. Hadn't you heard? It's World War Three!"

For a moment I was amused by the inevitability of her remark; the assumption, moreover, of the inevitable event.

"You look beat," she said. "Are you a diplomat?"

"Not really."

She grew to feeling guilty. "Come in and have some coffee."

"I accept. Thank you."

Her mother was at breakfast in the large, modern kitchen. "Dubrowski," I said, removing my hat. "I am so sorry..."

"Vassily's left. Janet told you?"

"Yes." I unbuttoned my overcoat. Janet took it. I thanked her. I sat down at the table. I was brought a cup of that Western coffee which smells so good but does not taste of anything. I drank it.

"Was it important?" asked Janet's mother.

"Well..."

"To do with the crisis?"

I was not sure. I waved a palm.

"Well," said Janet's mother, "you're lucky to be here, that's all I can say."

"You think there will be a full-scale war?" I accepted sugar from the young girl's hands.

"Let them fight it out," said Janet's mother. "Get it over with."

"It will involve Canada."

Janet's mother buttered some toast. "Not directly."

"Are you Ukrainian, too?" said Janet.

"Too?"

"We're Ukrainians." Janet sat down beside me. I became aware of her warmth. "Or at least momma and poppa are."

I looked at the woman in the housecoat with her dyed red hair, her make-up, her American way of slouching against the table. I wondered if I were not enduring some kind of complicated test.

"I came over in 1947," said Janet's mother. "From England. We'd been deported during the German occupation and when the allies arrived we managed to get to England. Fedya was born here. Are you Ukrainian?"

I began to laugh a little. It was a feeble titter, but it was the first spontaneous expression of emotion I had had in years. "Yes," I said. "I am."

"We haven't really stayed in touch much," said Janet's mother, "with the Community here, you know. Janet's been to some meetings. She sees more of the old people than we do. She's a Nationalist, aren't you, dear?"

"Convinced," said Janet.

"Canadian," I asked, "or Ukrainian?" I was genuinely confused.

Janet took this well. She put youthful fingers on my sleeve. "Both," she said.

When I returned to my hotel I found a note telling me to go to our embassy. At the embassy I was ordered to fly direct to Moscow on the next Aeroflot flight. There I would be briefed about my new rôle. By the time I reached Moscow, Allied troops were already withdrawing from China and an agreement was being negotiated in the United Nations. I was given a Ukrainian passport and told to return to London.

My brief stay in Moscow had made me homesick. I would have been grateful for a holiday in the country for a week or two. I have yet to have my dream fulfilled. A month after I got back, the real War broke and I, in common with so many others, began to taste the euphoria of Armageddon.

Leaving Pasadena

I was asked by the woman why I had no pity. She sat on the floor, her elbow resting upon a couch, her head in her hand. She had not wept. Her anguish had tempered her eyes: they glittered with unvoiced needs. I could not touch her. I could not insult her with my compassion. I told her that pity was an inappropriate emotion. Our world was burning and there was no time for anything but rapid action. Africa and Australia were already gone. The clouds and the contamination were a matter of anxiety to those who survived. She told me, in slow, over-controlled syllables, that she was probably dying. She needed love, she said. I told her she should find someone, therefore, whose needs matched her own. My first loyalty was to my unit. I could not reach my hand to her. Any gesture would have been cruel.

The other two women came into the room. One had my bag. "You still don't know where you're going?" said the blonde, Julia. Her fashionably garish cosmetics appeared to give her face the lustre and texture of porcelain.

I turned my back and walked into the hallway. "Not yet."

Julia said: "I'll try to look after her."

As I got to the front door of the apartment, the brown-haired woman, Honour, said: "You pious bastard." She wore no make-up. Her face was as pale as Julia's.

I accepted her accusation. I had at that moment nothing left but piety and I would not dignify it with words. I nodded, shook hands with them both. I heard her mumbling some despairing question from the room, then I had walked down the white steps of the Pasadena condominium, crossed the courtyard with its silenced fountain, its poised cherubs, brilliant in the sun, and entered the car which had been sent to collect me. I was leaving California. That was all I had been told.

My chief had a rented house in Long Beach, near the marina. We drove to it through avenues of gigantic palms until we reached the almost deserted freeway. Vehicles kept well apart, considering the others warily. Only government people had official driving permits; anyone else could be psychotic or a criminal.

Long Beach was still populated. There were even people sailing their yachts into the harbour. The Pacific threat seemed to bother the people only as much as they had been bothered by the threat of earthquakes. The houses were low and calm, divided by shrubs and trees, with neat grass. I saw a man riding a pony across his lawn. He waved sardonically at the car. Groups of women stared at the limousine with expressions of contempt. We found my chief's house. The chauffeur went to tell him we were there. He came out immediately.

As he stopped to join me, the chief said: "You look bad. You should sleep more."

I told him, dutifully, about the woman. He was sympathetic. "There's a war on. It's how it is in war." Naturally, I agreed with him. "We are fighting for their good, after all," he added.

We drove to a military airfield. Both Soviet and U.S. planes were there. We went immediately to our Ilyushin, and had scarcely settled in the uncomfortable seats before we took off.

My chief handed me a passport. It had my real name and a recent photograph. "You're officially with the liaison staff, at last," he said. "It means you can report either to the Americans or to us. Nothing will be kept back. Matters are too urgent now." I expressed appropriate surprise.

I looked down on Los Angeles; its beaches, its fantasies. It was like setting aside a favourite story as a child. We headed inland over mountains, going east.

"The Third World War has already been fought," said my chief, "in the third world, as the Americans call it. Why else would they call it that? This is actually the Fifth World War."

"What was the Fourth?" I asked.

"It was fought in the country of the soul."

I laughed. I had forgotten his sentimentality. "Who won?"

"Nobody. It merely prepared us for this."

There were clouds beneath us. It seemed to become calm as the altitude encouraged deafness. I could hardly hear his next remark: "It has sharpened our wits and deadened our emotional responses. War is a great relief, eh? A completely false sense of objectivity. The strain to remain grown-up is too much for most of us."

It was familiar stuff from him. I unfastened my seat-belt and walked clumsily along the plane to where a Cossack sergeant served at a small bar. I ordered some of the Finnish vodka we had recently acquired. I drank the glass down and returned to my place. Four high-ranking officers in tropical uniforms were arguing in the seats behind me. One of them was of the opinion that we should begin full-scale rocket attacks on major Chinese cities. The others were for caution. The bombing had, after all, been stopped. Most of the civilised countries were still unharmed.

My chief began coughing. It was that dry noise usually associated with smoke inhalation. He recovered himself and in answer to my concerned expression told me that he was probably getting a cold. "We should be in Washington soon. All this travelling about is bad for the constitution." He shrugged. "But life is never easy. Even in wartime."

An official car met us at the airport. It bore the arms of the President. We passed the monstrous neo-classical buildings which celebrated that naïve eighteenth-century rationalism we all now regretted and from which we seemed to be suffering at present. We arrived at a modern block of government offices. In the elevator my chief told me not to show surprise at whatever we discussed. He believed that we were thought to know more than we had actually been told.

A bland, smooth-faced man in a light-coloured suit introduced himself as Mansfield and offered us deep, black chairs. He asked us about our journey, about California, and told us of the people living along the West Coast. "People learn to identify their homes with their security. When something like this happens... Well, we all know about the Jews refusing to leave Germany."

"Your newspapers contradict themselves," said my chief. He smiled. "They say there is little to fear."

"True." Mansfield offered us Lucky Strike cigarettes which we accepted. My chief coughed a little before he took a light.

"We think you'll have more success in Venezuela." Mansfield returned the lighter to his desk. "They are suspicious of our motives, naturally."

"And not of ours?" My chief continued to smile.

"They could believe your arguments better. They are not too sure if the alliance will maintain itself. You might be able to persuade them."

"Possibly."

"They can't stay neutral much longer."

"Why not?"

"Because someone will attack them."

"Then perhaps we should wait until that happens. It would be easier to liberate them, eh?"

"We need their oil. This freeze of theirs is pointless. It does nobody any good."

"And why do you want us to go?"

"The Russians?"

"No." My chief waved a hand at me. "Us."

"We have to contact their intelligence first. After that the politicians can sort things out."

"You've made arrangements?"

"Yes. It was thought best not to meet in Caracas. You'll go to Maracaibo. It's where the oil is, anyway. Most of their oil people want to sell. We're not certain of the attitudes you'll find, but we understand that there is a lot of pressure from that side."

"You have material for us?"

Mansfield lifted a folder from his desk and showed it to us.

Although my chief seemed to be taking the meeting seriously, I began to wonder at the vagueness of its content. I suspected that our going to Maracaibo would have no effect at all. We were going because it was something to do.

I resisted an urge, when we reached our hotel in Maracaibo, to telephone the woman and ask how she was. It would do her no good, I decided, for her to hear from me. I knew that, in other circumstances, I would have loved her. She had done me several favours in the course of my work, so I was also grateful to her. The sense of gratitude was the only indulgence I allowed myself.

My chief walked through the connecting door into my room. He rubbed his eyebrows. "I have a meeting with a member of their intelligence. A colonel. But it is to be a one-to-one thing. You're free to do what you like this evening. I have the name of a house."

"Thank you." I wrote down the address he gave me.

"It will do you good," he said. He was sympathetic. "And one of us might as well enjoy the pleasures of the town. I hear the whores are of a high quality."

"I am much obliged to you." I would go, I thought, only because I had no wish to stay in my room the whole time. His giving me leave confirmed my suspicion that there was no real reason for us being in Maracaibo.

The town, with its skyscrapers and remnants of Spanish-style architecture, was well-lit and relatively clean. I had once been told that "Venezuela is the future." They had been experimenting with different energy sources, using their oil income to develop systems which would not be much dependent on oil. But Maracaibo seemed very little different, save that the lake itself, full of machinery and rigging, occasionally gave off mysterious puffs of flame which would illuminate buildings and create uncertain shadows. There was a stink of oil about the place. As I walked, local map in hand, to the address my chief had given me I saw one of their airships, built by a British firm at Cardington, sail into the darkness beyond the city. Venezuela had been perhaps the last country to associate romance with practical engineering.

I reached the house. It was large and fairly luxurious. The décor was comfortable and lush in the manner of some of the more grandiose family restaurants I had visited in Pasadena. There was a pianist playing similar music to his American counterpart. There was a bar. I sat down and ordered a Scotch. I was approached by a pretty hostess who wore a blonde wig. Her skin was dark and her smile was wide and seemed genuine. In English she said that she thought she had seen me there before. I told her that this was only my second visit to Maracaibo. She asked if I were Swedish. I said that I was Russian. She kissed me and said that she loved Russian people, that they knew how to enjoy themselves. "Lots of vodka," she said. But I was drinking Scotch; was I an émigré? I said, from habit, that I was. Her name was Anna. Her father, she said, had been born in South London. Did I know London? Very well, I said. I had lived there for some years. Anna wondered if Brixton were like Maracaibo. I said there were some similarities. We look for familiarity in the most unlikely circumstances before we accept what is strange to us. It is as true of travellers as it is of lovers.

Anna brought a girl for me. She had fine black hair tied back from her face; a white dress with a great deal of lace. She looked about sixteen. Her make-up was subtle. She pretended to be shy. I found her appealing. Her name was Maria, she told me. She spoke excellent English with an American accent. I bought her a drink, expecting to go to her room, but she said she would like to take me home, if that suited me. I decided against caution. She led me outside and we drove in a taxi to a street of what seemed to be quiet, middle-class apartment buildings. We climbed two flights of stairs. She opened a well-polished wooden door with her key and we entered an apartment full of quality furniture in subdued good taste. I began to suspect I had been picked up by a schoolgirl and that this was her parents' home. But the way she moved in it, getting me another Scotch, switching on the overhead fan, taking my jacket, convinced me that she was the mistress of the place. Moreover, I knew that she was actually older than sixteen; that she cultivated the appearance of a teenager. I began to experience a reluctance to go to bed with her. Against my will I remembered the woman in Pasadena. I forced myself towards that belief that all women were, after all, the same, that it satisfied them to give themselves up to a man. The whore, at least, would make money from her instincts. The woman in Pasadena came by nothing but pain. We went into the bedroom and undressed. In the large and comfortable white bed I eventually confessed that I was in no haste to make love to her. I had been unable to adjust my mood. I asked her why she had shaved her pubic hair. She said that it increased her own pleasure and besides many men found it irresistible. She began to tell me her story. She had been, she said, in love with the man who introduced her to prostitution. Evidently she was still obsessed by him, because it required no great expression of interest from me for her to tell me the whole story. It was familiar enough. What she said, of course, was couched in the usual sort of sentimentality and romanticism. She mentioned love a great deal and her knowledge that, although he did not say so, he really loved her and cared for her and it was only right, because she loved him, that he should be allowed to be the way he was. He had many other girls, including, I gathered, a wife. Initially Maria had, in the manner of despairing women, attempted to make of herself an improved piece of capital: she had dyed her hair, shaved her pubis, painted her face and nails. The girl-whore is always highly valued wherever one goes in the world. I gathered that while the man had appreciated the gesture he had told her that he intended to continue seeing other women. All this was depressing, for I was never particularly interested in economics. I found myself moralising a trifle. I told her that maturity and self-possession were in the end more attractive qualities to me. They guaranteed me a certain kind of freedom based on mutually accepted responsibility. She did not understand a word, of course. I added that a woman's attempts to use a man as her context were thoroughly understood by me. I had my loyalties. But, like most men, I was not able to be either a woman's nation or her cause. Maria made some attempt to rouse me and then fell back. She said that it was her bad luck to pick up a bore. She had thought I would be interesting. She added that she did not feel she could charge me much. I was amused. I got up and telephoned the hotel. The chief had not yet returned. I said that I would stay longer in that case. She said that she would enjoy my company, but I would have to be more entertaining. Eventually I achieved a reasonable state of mind and made love to her. She was soft, yielding and foul-mouthed. She was able to bring me to a more than satisfactory orgasm. As I left, she insisted that I telephone her the next day if I could. I agreed that I would if it were at all possible.

My chief was jovial when we breakfasted together in his room. "We have at least a week here," he said. "There are subtleties. These people are worse than the Arabs."

I reported the girl. He shrugged. "You have nothing to reveal. Even if it is some kind of strategy, they would be wasting their time."

I had the impression that he had brought me here on holiday. In the outside world, the news was not good. A bomb had landed somewhere in India and no one was absolutely certain where it had come from. No major city had been hit. This was not acceptable warfare, said my chief. War was supposed to cut down on ambiguities.

I telephoned the girl from the breakfast table. I arranged to see her for lunch.

We ate in a smart restaurant at the top of a modern tower. There was mist on the lake and Maracaibo was covered in pale gold light. She wore a red suit with a matching hat. She was gentle and obviously amused by what she saw as my stiffness. She had a way of making me relax. Naturally, I resisted falling too much under her spell.

After lunch, she took us to a quay. Several men in tattered nautical clothes called to her. She spoke to one of them and then we had climbed down into a small, elegant motor-boat. She started the engine, took the wheel, and we rode out into the mist.

I asked her what her man thought of all this. She became gay. "He doesn't care."

"But you are making no money."

"It's not really like that," she said. "He's kind, you know. Or can be."

The whole episode had the character of a lull in a singularly bad storm. I could not entirely rid my mind of the knowledge of the woman in Pasadena, but I could think of no better way of spending my time. Maria steered the boat inexpertly past a series of oil derricks which stood in the water like stranded and decapitated giraffes. A breeze began to part the mist. I had the impression of distant mountains.

She stopped the engine and we embraced. She suggested that we fuck. "It's always been an ambition of mine," she said.

I did my best, but the boat was uncomfortable and my body was too tired. I eventually brought her to orgasm with my mouth. She seemed more than contented. After a while she got up and returned to the wheel. "You look happier," she said. "So do you," I replied. I was hard put not to feel affection for her. But that sense of affection did me no good because it recalled the woman in Pasadena. I began to tell her a joke about the War. Some Chinese commandos had entered what they thought was Indian territory and completely destroyed one of their own bases. She became serious. "Will the War reach Venezuela?"

"Almost certainly," I said. "Unless a few people come to their senses. But there has been no true catharsis yet."

She asked me what I meant. I said: "No orgasm, eh?"

"My God," she said.

On the quay, we agreed to meet at the same spot that evening. "I want to show you the lake at night." She looked up suddenly and pointed. There was a soft sound of engines. It was another airship, white and painted with the Venezuelan military colours. Reassessed technology was to have been the salvation of the world. Now this country would be lucky if it escaped complete destruction. I said nothing of this to Maria.

When I was first ordered to work abroad I felt I was going into exile. The territory was unfamiliar, offering dangers I could not anticipate. I saw Maria to her taxi and walked back to my hotel. For some reason I was reminded, perhaps by a sign or a face on the street, of the strange suburb-ghetto of Watts, where everyone lived better than almost anyone in the Soviet Union. It had amused me to go there. They had food stamps: the young have never known a breadline. One had hoped to match America. Before the War, we were only a short distance behind on the road to discontented capitalism. Beyond that was anarchy, which cannot appeal to me, although I know it was supposed to have been our goal.

I bought a Polish-language newspaper. It was over a week old and I could barely understand the references. The newspaper was published in New York. But I enjoyed the feel of the print. I read it as I lay in my bath. My chief telephoned. He sounded drunk. It occurred to me that he, too, believed himself to be on vacation. He told me that I was free for the evening.

Maria had two friends with her when I arrived at the quay. They were both some years older than she and wore the sort of heavy '40s make-up which had been fashionable a few years previously in the West. Their cotton dresses, one pink and one yellow, followed the same style, as did their hair. They wore very strong perfume and looked like versions of Rita Hayworth. They were far more self-conscious than Maria. She said they spoke little English and apologised for bringing them along. Her explanation was vague, consisting mainly of shrugs and raised brows. I made no objection. I was content to enjoy the close presence of so much femininity.

Once again, Maria drove us out into the twilight. The water seemed to brighten as it became blacker. The two older women sat together behind Maria and myself. They produced some Mexican Tequila and passed the bottle. Soon we were all fairly drunk. When Maria stopped the boat in the middle of the lake again, we all rolled together in one another's arms. I realised that this was part of Maria's plan. Another fantasy she wished to experience. I allowed the women to have their way with me, although I was not of much use to them. It gave me considerable pleasure to watch them making love. Maria took no part in this, but observed and directed, giggling the whole time. The unreality was disarming. The situation was no stranger than the situation in the world at large. It seemed that I moved from one dream to another and that this dream, given the cheerfulness of everyone involved, was preferable to the rest. I knew now that Maria felt safe with me, because I controlled my emotions so thoroughly and because I was a stranger. I knew that I was proving of help to her and this made me happy. I thought of warning her that in seeking catharsis through her sexuality she could lose touch with the source of her feelings, lose her lovers, lose her bearings, but it did not seem to matter. With the War threatening to become more widespread our futures were all so thoroughly in doubt that we might as well enjoy what we could of the present.

Several days and nights passed. Each time we met, Maria would propose another sexual escapade and I would agree. My own curiosity was satisfied, as was my impulse to believe myself of use to someone. My chief continued to be drunk and wave me on, even when I reported exactly what was happening. As I grew to know her better I believed that she was desperately anxious to become a woman, to escape the form of security in which she now found herself. Her need for instantaneous maturity, her greedy reaching for experience, however painful, was in itself childish. She had indulged herself and been indulged for so long that her means of achieving liberty were crude and often graceless. And yet liberty, maturity might gradually come to her, earned through trauma and that feminine willingness to find fulfilment in despair. There was no doubt that her activities, her attitudes, disguised a considerable amount of despair and emotional confusion. I wondered if I were not exploiting her, even though superficially she seemed to be exploiting me. We were, I determined, merely making reasonable use of one another's time. And in the meanwhile, I recalled, there was the figure of her protector, Ramirez. He presumably knew what was happening, just as my chief knew. I began to feel a certain fondness for him, a certain gratitude. I told Maria that I should like to meet him. This did not appeal to her, but she said she would let him know what I had said. I told her that I would let her know when I was leaving, so that the meeting, if it occurred, could be on my last night. I also warned her that I might be forced to leave suddenly. She said that she had guessed this. On one level, I realised, I was asking her to give up the only power she had. I made some drunken remarks about people who surround themselves with ambiguity in order to maintain their course. They are eventually trapped by the conditions they have created, become confused and begin to question almost every aspect of their own judgement. I felt a certain amount of self-disgust after this statement. I had no business offering Maria a moral education. But political habits are hard to lose.

Puzzled, she told me that she thought Ramirez meant security for her. Yet she knew that she had no desire to marry him. She would not be happy if, tomorrow, he came to her and offered her his all. We laughed together at this. Women marry for security, I remarked, while men often marry merely for the promise of regular sex. The man is inclined to keep his side of the marriage bargain because it is fairly clear. But the woman, having no idea of what the bargain was, is baffled when the man complains.

"Are all marriages like that?" she asked. She had doubtless had many customers who had verified this. I said no, not all. I knew of several very satisfactory marriages. By and large, however, in countries where political or religious orthodoxy held sway, sexual relationships became extremely confused. Again I had lost her. I became bored with my own simplifications. As we made love, I found myself desperately yearning for the woman in Pasadena.

Maria began to speak more and more of Ramirez. I was now a confessor. From what she said I formed an opinion of him. He was tight-fisted but had made his caution and lack of generosity into a creed so that it sometimes seemed he was expressing self-discipline and neutrality, whereas he was actually indulging himself absolutely. As a result he had begun to fail in business (her flat was threatened), partly through an inability to risk capital, partly through the loss of nerve which comes when security is equated with material goods and well-being. His was a typical dilemma of the middle class, but she had no way of knowing that since she had spent most of her life in a working-class or bohemian environment. This materialism extended into his sex-life, as is so frequently the case: he hoped to get something for nothing if he could (his life was a series of deals) but expected a good return on any expenditure. He was attractive, boyish and emotionally somewhat naïve. These qualities appealed, needless to say, to many women, not all of them childless. He was easily understood and fairly easy to manipulate. Moreover, the woman had some sense of control over the relationship, for such men can also be, on certain levels, highly impressionable: they are nearly all ego. However, his inability, ultimately, to accept responsibility either for himself or others made him a frustrating partner and his relationships were inclined to deteriorate after a period in which some reform had been attempted on him and he had become resentful. We are changed only by circumstance, never by will alone. She had, for her part, she said, accepted him gladly for what he was. He was better than most, and more interesting. He was not a fool. Neither am I, I found myself saying. She shook her head. "No. You are a big fool. It is why I'm fond of you." I was astonished.

News came from my chief early that morning that we were due to return to the United States the next day. I saw Maria for lunch and said that I should like to see Ramirez. She made me swear that I was leaving and then arranged to meet later at the quay.

From the quayside we went to a nearby bar. It was an ordinary place, dark and a little seamy. Maria knew many of the regulars, particularly the women, whom she kissed. Ramirez arrived. He wore a good suit of dark blue cloth and I was surprised that he was bearded and had spectacles. He shook hands. His flesh was a little soft and his grasp feminine. He said that he was not sure why he had come, except "I can resist no request from Maria." We had several strong drinks. We took the motor-boat out into the lake. It was a warm night. He removed his jacket but not his waistcoat and asked me if I sniffed cocaine. I said that I did. As he prepared the drug on a small hand-mirror he informed me that he was Maria's master and allowed her sometimes, as in this case, to play with other men: I should go away now or I might find myself the subject of either blackmail or violence. I was amused when I realised that Maria was deceiving him. I decided to play her game as best I could. I told him that I had run whores in Greece and that I knew he did not possess the character of a true ponce. He was not insulted. We took the cocaine. It was of the best quality. I complimented him. "You understand me, however," he said. I did not reply until we returned to the harbour. When we were out of the boat and standing together, Maria on my right, Ramirez beside the open door of his car, I threatened him with death. I told him that I was an agent of the KGB. He became nervous, made no comment, got into his car and left. Maria, on the way home, was disturbed. She asked me what she was going to do. I told her that she was free to take a number of choices. She said she needed money. I gave her some. We stayed together in her flat through the rest of that night and in the morning drove the boat onto the lake again. When Maracaibo disappeared and we seemed alone in the middle of the still, blue water, she took out a small packet of cocaine and, steadying her thin body against a seat, carefully cut two lines on her compact mirror. I took the first, through an American ten dollar bill. She paused before sniffing half the line into one nostril, half into the other. She smiled at me, weary and intimate. "Well?"

"You'll go back to Ramirez?"

"Not if I can stay at an hotel."

"And if you stay at an hotel?"

"I can earn some money. Could you help me get to America?"

"At present? You're safer here."

"But could you?"

"Only on terms I do not wish to make. I repeat, you're better off here."

"Really?"

"Believe me."

Her dark eyes looked away into the lake. "The future is no better than the past."

I guessed that within a week she would be back with Ramirez; within a year she would be free of him. I started the engine and headed towards the reality of the rigs and refineries. I told Maria that I knew she would survive, if there were any luck in the world at all. She had none of that self-involved sexuality which contains in it a peculiar coldness: the more it is indulged, the more the coldness grows. One meets libertines whose lives are devoted to sex and yet who have gradually lost any sexual generosity. Certain women are the same. They cease to celebrate and come more and more to control. It is the inevitable progress of rationalised romance, as I knew well.

In the hotel my chief notified me suddenly that he was dying. He wanted me, eventually, to go to Kiev as liaison officer with a Cossack regiment. "I think it's the best I can offer you," he said. He added that his will-power had failed him. I asked him if he were suffering from radiation poisoning. He said that he was. He would be returning to Long Beach for a short while, but I could stay in Washington if I wished. I would be allowed some leave. I could not begin to guess at the manipulation and persuasion he had exerted in order to gain us both so much time, but I was grateful to him and indicated as much. I had decided, I said, to return to Pasadena.

"Good," he said. "We can take the same plane."

I decided not to telephone ahead but went directly from Burbank airport to Pasadena. Los Angeles was quieter than ever, though there was now some evidence of desertion and vandalism. Most of the cars on the freeways were police vehicles. As I drove my rented Toyota towards the richer suburbs I was stopped twice and had my papers checked. Now, in the current situation, it had become an advantage in America to possess a Soviet passport and KGB identification.

I drove off the freeway onto South Orange. The wide, palm-shaded streets seemed without texture or density after Maracaibo. A thin dream. Pasadena was a geometrical kindergarten vision of security. Only downtown, amongst the bricks and stones of the original settlement, and at the railroad station, was there a sense of complexity at all, and that was the complexity of any small American rural town. I yearned for Europe, for London and its mysterious, claustrophobic streets.

I parked in the communal garages, took my bag from the back seat and walked along the neat crazy-paving to the end block of the condominium. Like so much Los Angeles building it was less than ten years old and beginning to show signs of decay beneath the glaring white glaze. I walked up the steps, glad of the shade, and rang the bell on the right of the double doors. I stopped and picked up a folded newspaper, surprised that there were still deliveries. Julia's voice came from the other side of the doors. I said who it was. She seemed delighted. "You came back. This is wonderful. She's been in a bad way." I felt as if, unknowingly, I had reaffirmed Julia's faith in the entire human race. Some of us have such a terrible desire for a decent world that we will clutch at the tiniest strand of evidence for its existence and reject all other proof to the contrary. Julia looked tired. Her hair was disordered.

I unbuttoned my light raincoat and handed it to her. I pushed my suitcase under a small table which sat against the wall of the entrance hall.

"Honour went back to Flagstaff," said Julia. She looked rueful. "Just as well. She didn't think a lot of you."

"I enjoyed her candour," I said.

The woman knew I had arrived but she continued to sit at the easel we had erected together in the large front room. Light fell on a half-finished landscape, on her thinning, ash-blonde hair, on her pastel skin. She was more delicate, more beautiful, yet still I checked myself against the sensation of love for her.

"Why are you here?" She spoke in a low voice. She began to turn, resisting hope, looking at me as if I might wound her afresh. "The War isn't over."

I gestured with the newspaper. "Apparently not."

"This is too much," she said.

I told her that I had decided to take a leave. Nobody but my chief knew where I was and he had made up some story about my need to go underground with a group of radical pacifists.

"Your people won't believe that."

"Our structure is so rigid it can be resisted only by the most audacious means," I said, "and then often very successfully. It is probably one of the few advantages of orthodoxy."

"You're full of bullshit, as ever," she said. "You can't do what you did to me a second time. I'd kill myself."

I moved close to her so that my chest was on a level with her lovely head. We did not embrace. She did not look as grey or as drawn as she had when she had first been given confirmation of her illness. As she looked up at me I was impressed with her gentle beauty. She was at once noble and pathetic. Her eyes began to fill with tears. One fell. She apologised. I told her there was no need. I touched her shoulder, her cheek. She began to speak my name several times, holding tightly to my hand.

"You don't look well," she said. "You were afraid you would go crazy, weren't you?"

"I am not going to go mad," I told her. "I often wish that I could. This state of control is a kind of madness, isn't it? Perhaps more profoundly insane than any other kind. But it has none of the appeal of irresponsibility, of giving up any sense of others, which the classic lunatic experiences." I laughed. "So it has no advantages."

"What about your duty?"

"To the War?"

"Or your cause, or whatever."

"Excellent excuses."

"What's more important?"

I drew a breath. "I don't know. Affection?"

"You've changed your mind. Your rationale. Your logic."

"I had to simplify."

"Now?"

"I am defeated. I can no longer maintain it. Things remain as perplexing as ever."

"What are you saying?"

I shrugged. "Love conquers all?"

"Not you!" She shook her head.

"I do not know," I said, "what the truth is. It has been my duty to lie and to counter lies. Duty allows this, demands it. The only other truth for me is the truth of my feelings, my cravings, and senses. Anything else is hypocrisy, self-deception. At best it is a sentimental rationale. We are all moved by self-interest."

"But sometimes self-interest takes on a broader form," she said. "And that is when we become human. Why are you here?"

"To see you. To be with you."

"We'll lie down," she said. "We'll go to bed."

The bed was very large. The place had belonged to her parents. Now they were in Iowa where they believed themselves to be safer. We undressed and I took her in my arms. We kissed. Her body was warm and still strong. We did not make love, but talked, as we always had. I told her that I did not know the meaning of love and that what had brought me back to her was a sense that the alternatives were less tolerable to me. I told her that a mixture of sentimentality and power politics had been the nearest substitute for love I had been able to afford in my circumstances. Altruism was a luxury. She said that she believed it a necessity. Without altruism there was no virtue in human existence, therefore if one rejected it one also rejected the only rationale for the race's continuation. Could that be why I was now on leave from the War?

I praised her for her fine fundamentalism and said that I regretted my inability to live according to such principles. She told me that it was not difficult: one did not take extra responsibility—one relinquished power and in doing that one also relinquished guilt. The very idea, I told her humorously, was terrifying to the Russian soul. Without guilt there was no movement at all! She shook her head at what she called my cynicism, my self-contempt. I said that I preferred to think I had my own measure.

I got out of bed and went into the hall. From my bag I took a pendant I had bought for her in Maracaibo. I came back and presented it to her. She looked at it and thanked me bleakly. She set it aside. "You'll never be free, then?" she said. "I believe not," I said. It was too late for that.

She rose and put on a robe, walking with her hands folded beneath her breasts into the room she used as a studio. "Love and art wither without freedom." She stared at a half-finished portrait stacked against the wall. I seemed much older in the picture. "I suppose so," I said. But I was in the business of politics which, by definition, was opposed both to lovers and to artists. They were factors which always would over-complicate the game and cause enormous frustrations in those of us who preferred, by temperament, to simplify the world as much as possible.

"You've always found my reasoning stupidly romantic, haven't you?" she said. She discredited my intelligence, I said. We lived in a world of power and manipulation. Currently political decisions (I took her hand) decided if we should live or die—if we should love or create art. My realism, I said, was limited to the situation; hers was appropriate to her life as an artist and as an individual who must continue to hope. "But I am dying," she said. "I have no need for hope." She smiled as she completed the sentence. She turned away with a shrug which had much of her old gaiety in it. She ran her hands over the frames of the canvases. "I wish my life to have had some point, of course."

I could not answer her, yet suddenly I was lost in her again, as I had been during the early days of our affair. I went towards her and I embraced her. I kissed her. She recognised my emotion at once. She responded. There was a great generosity in her, a kindness. I could not at the moment bear to think of its leaving the world. But I should have a memory of it, I thought.

I told her that I admired her tendency to ascribe altruistic motives to me, to all other people. But most of us were far too selfish. We had to survive in a cynical world. She said that she had to believe in self-sufficiency and altruism was the only way by which we could, with any meaning, survive at all. One had to keep one's eye on the world as it was and somehow learn to trust oneself to maintain tolerance and hope. I said her courage was greater than mine. She acknowledged this. She said that a woman found it necessary to discover courage if she were to make any sense of her life as an individual. "But you pursued me," I said gently. "I love you," she said. "I want you for myself and will do everything I can to keep you."

"I cannot change."

"I would not wish it."

"You have won me."

"Well," she said, "I have won something of you and for the time being am content. Have I won it honourably, do you think? Did you return simply out of pity?"

"I was drawn here, to you. I have no reservations."

"You don't feel trapped?"

"On the contrary."

"You'll stay here?"

"Until you die."

"It might be—I might ask you to kill me when the worst begins."

"I know."

"Could you?"

"I suspect you were attracted to me because you knew that I could."

She became relieved. The tension between us vanished completely. She smiled at me and took my hand again: in love with her executioner.

Crossing into Cambodia

In homage to Isaac Babel, 1894–1941?

1

I approached and Savitsky, Commander of the Sixth Division, got up. As usual I was impressed by his gigantic, perfect body. Yet he seemed unconscious either of his power or of his elegance. Although not obliged to do so, I almost saluted him. He stretched an arm towards me. I put the papers into his gloved hand. "These were the last messages we received," I said. The loose sleeve of his Cossack cherkesska slipped back to reveal a battle-strengthened forearm, brown and glowing. I compared his skin to my own. For all that I had ridden with the Sixth for five months, I was still pale; still possessed, I thought, of an intellectual's hands. Evening light fell through the jungle foliage and a few parrots shrieked their last goodnight. Mosquitoes were gathering in the shadows, whirling in tight-woven patterns, like a frightened mob. The jungle smelled of rot. Yakovlev, somewhere, began to play a sad accordion tune.

The Vietnamese spy we had caught spoke calmly from the other side of Savitsky's camp-table. "I think I should like to be away from here before nightfall. Will you keep your word, sir, if I tell you what I know?"

Savitsky looked back and I saw the prisoner for the first time (though his presence was of course well known to the camp). His wrists and ankles were pinned to the ground with bayonets but he was otherwise unhurt.

Savitsky drew in his breath and continued to study the documents I had brought him. Our radio was now useless. "He seems to be confirming what these say." He tapped the second sheet. "An attack tonight."

The temple on the other side of the clearing came to life within. Pale light rippled on greenish, half-ruined stonework. Some of our men must have lit a fire there. I heard noises of delight and some complaints from the women who had been with the spy. One began to shout in that peculiar, irritating high-pitched half-wail they all use when they are trying to appeal to us. For a moment Savitsky and I had a bond in our disgust. I felt flattered. Savitsky made an impatient gesture, as if of embarrassment. He turned his handsome face and looked gravely down at the peasant. "Does it matter to you? You've lost a great deal of blood."

"I do not think I am dying."

Savitsky nodded. He was economical in everything, even his cruelties. He had been prepared to tear the man apart with horses, but he knew that he would tire two already overworked beasts. He picked up his cap from the camp-table and put it thoughtfully on his head. From the deserted huts came the smell of our horses as the wind reversed its direction. I drew my borrowed burka about me. I was the only one in our unit to bother to wear it, for I felt the cold as soon as the sun was down.

"Will you show me on the map where they intend to ambush us?"

"Yes," said the peasant. "Then you can send a man to spy on their camp. He will confirm what I say."

I stood to one side while these two professionals conducted their business. Savitsky strode over to the spy and very quickly, like a man plucking a hen, drew the bayonets out and threw them on the ground. With some gentleness, he helped the peasant to his feet and sat him down in the leather campaign chair he had carried with him on our long ride from Danang, where we had disembarked off the troop-ship which had brought us from Vladivostok.

"I'll get some rags to stop him bleeding," I said.

"Good idea," confirmed Savitsky. "We don't want the stuff all over the maps. You'd better be in on this, anyway."

As the liaison officer, it was my duty to know what was happening. That is why I am able to tell this story. My whole inclination was to return to my billet where two miserable ancients cowered and sang at me whenever I entered or left but where at least I had a small barrier between me and the casual day-to-day terrors of the campaign. But, illiterate and obtuse though these horsemen were, they had accurate instincts and could tell immediately if I betrayed any sign of fear. Perhaps, I thought, it is because they are all so used to disguising their own fears. Yet bravery was a habit with them and I yearned to catch it. I had ridden with them in more than a dozen encounters, helping to drive the Cambodians back into their own country. Each time I had seen men and horses blown to pieces, torn apart, burned alive. I had come to exist on the smell of blood and gunpowder as if it were a substitute for air and food—I identified it with the smell of Life itself—yet I had still failed to achieve that strangely passive sense of inner calm my comrades all, to a greater or lesser degree, displayed.

Only in action did they seem possessed in any way by the outer world, although they still worked with efficient ferocity, killing as quickly as possible with lance, sabre or carbine and, with ghastly humanity, never leaving a wounded man of their own or the enemy's without his throat cut or a bullet in his brain. I was thankful that these, my traditional foes, were now allies for I could not have resisted them had they turned against me.

I bound the peasant's slender wrists and ankles. He was like a child. He said: "I knew there were no arteries cut." I nodded at him. "You're the political officer, aren't you?" He spoke almost sympathetically.

"Liaison," I said.

He was satisfied by my reply, as if I had confirmed his opinion. He added: "I suppose it's the leather coat. Almost a uniform."

I smiled. "A sign of class difference, you think?"

His eyes were suddenly drowned with pain and he staggered, but recovered to finish what he had evidently planned to say: "You Russians are natural bourgeoisie. It's not your fault. It's your turn."

Savitsky was too tired to respond with anything more than a small smile. I felt that he agreed with the peasant and that these two excluded me, felt superior to me. I knew anger, then. Tightening the last rag on his left wrist, I made the spy wince. Satisfied that my honour was avenged I cast an eye over the map. "Here we are," I said. We were on the very edge of Cambodia. A small river, easily forded, formed the border. We had heard it just before we had entered this village. Scouts confirmed that it lay no more than half a verst to the west. The stream on the far side of the village, behind the temple, was a tributary.

"You give your word you won't kill me," said the Vietnamese.

"Yes," said Savitsky. He was beyond joking. We all were. It had been ages since any of us had been anything but direct with one another, save for the conventional jests which were merely part of the general noise of the squadron, like the jangling of harness. And he was beyond lying, except where it was absolutely necessary. His threats were as unqualified as his promises.

"They are here." The spy indicated a town. He began to shiver. He was wearing only torn shorts. "And some of them are here, because they think you might use the bridge rather than the ford."

"And the attacking force for tonight?"

"Based here." A point on our side of the river.

Savitsky shouted. "Pavlichenko."

From the Division Commander's own tent, young Pavlichenko, capless, with ruffled fair hair and a look of restrained disappointment, emerged. "Comrade?"

"Get a horse and ride with this man for half an hour the way we came today. Ride as fast as you can, then leave him and return to camp."

Pavlichenko ran towards the huts where the horses were stabled. Savitsky had believed the spy and was not bothering to check his information. "We can't attack them," he murmured. "We'll have to wait until they come to us. It's better." The flap of Savitsky's tent was now open. I glanced through and to my surprise saw a Eurasian girl of about fourteen. She had her feet in a bucket of water. She smiled at me. I looked away.

Savitsky said: "He's washing her for me. Pavlichenko's an expert."

"My wife and daughters?" said the spy.

"They'll have to remain now. What can I do?" Savitsky shrugged in the direction of the temple. "You should have spoken earlier."

The Vietnamese accepted this and, when Pavlichenko returned with the horse, leading it and running as if he wished to get the job over with in the fastest possible time, he allowed the young Cossack to lift him onto the saddle.

"Take your rifle," Savitsky told Pavlichenko. "We're expecting an attack."

Pavlichenko dashed for his own tent, the small one close to Savitsky's. The horse, as thoroughly trained as the men who rode him, stood awkwardly but quietly beneath his nervous load. The spy clutched the saddle pommel, the mane, his bare feet angled towards the mount's neck. He stared ahead of him into the night. His wife and daughter had stopped their appalling wailing but I thought I could hear the occasional feminine grunt from the temple. The flames had become more animated. His other daughter, her feet still in the bucket, held her arms tightly under her chest and her curious eyes looked without rancour at her father, then at the Division Commander, then, finally, at me. Savitsky spoke. "You're the intellectual. She doesn't know Russian. Tell her that her father will be safe. She can join him tomorrow."

"My Vietnamese might not be up to that."

"Use English or French, then." He began to tidy his maps, calling over Kreshenko, who was in charge of the guard.

I entered the tent and was shocked by her little smile. She had a peculiar smell to her—like old tea and cooked rice. I knew my Vietnamese was too limited so I asked her if she spoke French. She was of the wrong generation. "Amerikanski," she told me. I relayed Savitsky's message. She said: "So I am the price of the old bastard's freedom."

"Not at all." I reassured her. "He told us what we wanted. It was just bad luck for you that he used you three for cover."

She laughed. "Nuts! It was me got him to do it. With my sister. Tao's boyfriend works for the Cambodians." She added: "They seemed to be winning at the time."

Savitsky entered the tent and zipped it up from the bottom. He used a single, graceful movement. For all that he was bone-weary, he moved with the unconscious fluidity of an acrobat. He lit one of his foul-smelling papyrosi and sat heavily on the camp-bed beside the girl.

"She speaks English," I said. "She's a half-caste. Look."

He loosened his collar. "Could you ask her if she's clean, comrade?"

"I doubt it," I said. I repeated what she had told me.

He nodded. "Well, ask her if she'll be a good girl and use her mouth. I just want to get on with it. I expect she does, too."

I relayed the D.C.'s message.

"I'll bite his cock off if I get the chance," said the girl.

Outside in the night the horse began to move away. I explained what she had said.

"I wonder, comrade," Savitsky said, "if you would oblige me by holding the lady's head." He began to undo the belt of his trousers, pulling up his elaborately embroidered shirt.

The girl's feet became noisy in the water and the bucket overturned. In my leather jacket, my burka, with my automatic pistol at her right ear, I restrained the girl until Savitsky had finished with her. He began to take off his boots. "Would you care for her, yourself?"

I shook my head and escorted the girl from the tent. She was walking in that familiar stiff way women have after they have been raped. I asked her if she was hungry. She agreed that she was. I took her to my billet. The old couple found some more rice and I watched her eat it.

Later that night she moved towards me from where she had been lying more or less at my feet. I thought I was being attacked and shot her in the stomach. Knowing what my comrades would think of me if I tried to keep her alive (it would be a matter of hours) I shot her in the head to put her out of her misery.

As luck would have it, these shots woke the camp and when the Khmer soldiers attacked a few moments later we were ready for them and killed a great many before the rest ran back into the jungle. Most of these soldiers were younger than the girl.

In the morning, to save any embarrassment, the remaining women were chased out of the camp in the direction taken by the patriarch. The old couple had disappeared and I assumed that they would not return or, if they did, that they would bury the girl, so I left her where I had shot her. A silver ring she wore would compensate them for their trouble. There was very little food remaining in the village, but what there was we ate for our breakfast or packed into our saddle-bags. Then, mounting up, we followed the almost preternaturally handsome Savitsky back into the jungle, heading for the river.

2

When our scout did not return after we had heard a long burst of machine-gun fire, we guessed that he had found at least part of the enemy ambush and that the spy had not lied to us, so we decided to cross the river at a less convenient spot where, with luck, no enemy would be waiting.

The river was swift but had none of the force of Russian rivers and Pavlichenko was sent across with a rope which he tied to a tree-trunk. Then we entered the water and began to swim our horses across. Those who had lost the canvas covers for their carbines kept them high in the air, holding the rope with one hand and guiding their horses with legs and with reins which they gripped in their teeth. I was more or less in the middle, with half the division behind me and half beginning to assemble on dry land on the other side, when Cambodian aircraft sighted us and began an attack dive. The aircraft were in poor repair, borrowed from half a dozen other countries, and their guns, aiming equipment and, I suspect, their pilots were in worse condition, but they killed seven of our men as we let go of the ropes, slipped out of our saddles, and swam beside our horses, making for the far bank, while those still on dry land behind us went to cover where they could. A couple of machine-gun carts were turned on the attacking planes, but these were of little use. The peculiar assortment of weapons used against us—tracers, two rockets, a few napalm canisters which struck the water and sank (only one opened and burned but the mixture was quickly carried off by the current) and then they were flying back to base somewhere in Cambodia's interior—indicated that they had very little conventional armament left. This was true of most of the participants at this stage, which is why our cavalry had proved so effective. But they had bought some time for their ground-troops who were now coming in.

In virtual silence, any shouts drowned by the rushing of the river, we crossed to the enemy bank and set up a defensive position, using the machine-gun carts which were last to come across on ropes. The Cambodians hit us from two sides—moving in from their original ambush positions—but we were able to return their fire effectively, even using the anti-tank weapons and the mortar which, hitherto, we had tended to consider useless weight. They used arrows, blow-darts, automatic rifles, pistols and a flame-thrower which only worked for a few seconds and did us no harm. The Cossacks were not happy with this sort of warfare and as soon as there was a lull we had mounted up, packed the gear in the carts, and with sabres drawn were howling into the Khmer Stalinists (as we had been instructed to term them). Leaving them scattered and useless, we found a bit of concrete road along which we could gallop for a while. We slowed to a trot and then to a walk. The pavement was pot-holed and only slightly less dangerous than the jungle floor. The jungle was behind us now and seemed to have been a screen hiding the devastation ahead. The landscape was virtually flat, as if it had been bombed clean of contours, with a few broken buildings, the occasional blackened tree, and ash drifted across the road, coming sometimes up to our horses' knees. The ash was stirred by a light wind. We had witnessed scenes like it before, but never on such a scale. The almost colourless nature of the landscape was emphasised by the unrelieved brilliance of the blue sky overhead. The sun had become very hot.

Once we saw two tanks on the horizon, but they did not challenge us. We continued until early afternoon when we came to the remains of some sort of modern power installation and we made camp in the shelter of its walls. The ash got into our food and we drank more of our water than was sensible. We were all covered in the grey stuff by this time.

"We're like corpses," said Savitsky. He resembled an heroic statue of the sort which used to be in almost every public square in the Soviet Union. "Where are we going to find anything to eat in this?"

"It's like the end of the world," I said.

"Have you tried the radio again?"

I shook my head. "It isn't worth it. Napalm eats through wiring faster than it eats through you."

He accepted this and with a naked finger began to clean off the inner rims of the goggles he (like most of us) wore as protection against sun, rain and dust. "I could do with some orders," he said.

"We were instructed to move into the enemy's territory. That's what we're doing."

"Where, we were told, we would link up with American and Australian mounted units. Those fools can't ride. I don't know why they ever thought of putting them on horses. Cowboys!"

I saw no point in repeating an already stale argument. It was true, however, that the Western cavalry divisions found it hard to match our efficient savagery. I had been amused, too, when they had married us briefly with a couple of Mongolian squadrons. The Mongols had not ridden to war in decades and had become something of a laughing stock with their ancient enemies, the Cossacks. Savitsky believed that we were the last great horsemen. Actually, he did not include me; for I was a very poor rider and not a Cossack, anyway. He thought it was our destiny to survive the War and begin a new and braver civilisation: "Free from the influence of women and Jews." He recalled the great days of the Zaporozhian Sech, from which women had been forbidden. Even amongst the Sixth he was regarded as something of a conservative. He continued to be admired more than his opinions.

When the men had watered our horses and replaced the water bags in the cart, Savitsky and I spread the map on a piece of concrete and found our position with the help of the compass and sextant (there were no signs or landmarks). "I wonder what has happened to Angkor," I said. It was where we were supposed to meet other units, including the Canadians to whom, in the months to come, I was to be attached (I was to discover later that they had been in our rear all along).

"You think it's like this?" Savitsky gestured. His noble eyes began to frown. "I mean, comrade, would you say it was worth our while making for Angkor now?"

"We have our orders," I said. "We've no choice. We're expected."

Savitsky blew dust from his mouth and scratched his head. "There's about half our division left. We could do with reinforcements. Mind you, I'm glad we can see a bit of sky at last." We had all felt claustrophobic in the jungle.

"What is it, anyway, this Angkor? Their capital?" he asked me.

"Their Stalingrad, maybe."

Savitsky understood. "Oh, it has an importance to their morale. It's not strategic?"

"I haven't been told about its strategic value."

Savitsky, as usual, withdrew into his diplomatic silence, indicating that he did not believe me and thought that I had been instructed to secrecy. "We'd best push on," he said. "We've a long way to go, eh?"

After we had mounted up, Savitsky and I rode side by side for a while, along the remains of the concrete road. We were some way ahead of the long column, with its riders, its baggage-waggons, and its Makhno-style machine-gun carts. We were sitting targets for any planes and, because there was no cover, Savitsky and his men casually ignored the danger. I had learned not to show my nervousness but I was not at that moment sure how well hidden it was.

"We are the only vital force in Cambodia," said the Division Commander with a beatific smile. "Everything else is dead. How these yellow bastards must hate one another." He was impressed, perhaps admiring.

"Who's to say?" I ventured. "We don't know who else has been fighting. There isn't a nation now that's not in the War."

"And not one that's not on its last legs. Even Switzerland." Savitsky gave a superior snort. "But what an inheritance for us!"

I became convinced that, quietly, he was going insane.

3

We came across an armoured car in a hollow, just off the road. One of our scouts had heard the crew's moans. As Savitsky and I rode up, the scout was covering the uniformed Khmers with his carbine, but they were too far gone to offer us any harm.

"What's wrong with 'em?" Savitsky asked the scout.

The scout did not know. "Disease," he said. "Or starvation. They're not wounded."

We got off our horses and slid down into the crater. The car was undamaged. It appeared to have rolled gently into the dust and become stuck. I slipped into the driving seat and tried to start the engine, but it was dead. Savitsky had kicked one of the wriggling Khmers in the genitals but the man did not seem to notice the pain much, though he clutched himself, almost as if he entered into the spirit of a ritual. Savitsky was saying "Soldiers. Soldiers," over and over again. It was one of the few Vietnamese words he knew. He pointed in different directions, looking with disgust on the worn-out men. "You'd better question them," he said to me.

They understood my English, but refused to speak it. I tried them in French. "What happened to your machine?"

The man Savitsky had kicked continued to lie on his face, his arms stretched along the ashy ground towards us. I felt he wanted to touch us: to steal our vitality. I felt sick as I put the heel of my boot on his hand. One of his comrades said: "There's no secret to it. We ran out of essence." He pointed to the armoured car. "We ran out of essence."

"You're a long way from your base."

"Our base is gone. There's no essence anywhere."

I believed him and told Savitsky who was only too ready to accept this simple explanation.

As usual, I was expected to dispatch the prisoners. I reached for my holster, but Savitsky, with rare sympathy, stayed my movement. "Go and see what's in that can," he said, pointing. As I waded towards the punctured metal, three shots came from the Division Commander's revolver. I wondered at his mercy. Continuing with this small farce, I looked at the can, held it up, shook it, and threw it back into the dust. "Empty," I said.

Savitsky was climbing the crater towards his horse. As I scrambled behind him he said: "It's the Devil's world. Do you think we should give ourselves up to him?"

I was astonished by this unusual cynicism.

He got into his saddle. Unconsciously, he assumed the pose, often seen in films and pictures, of the noble revolutionary horseman—his head lifted, his palm shielding his eyes as he peered towards the west.

"We seem to have wound up killing Tatars again," he said with a smile as I got clumsily onto my horse. "Do you believe in all this history, comrade?"

"I've always considered the theory of precedent absolutely infantile," I said.

"What's that?"

I began to explain, but he was already spurring forward, shouting to his men.

4

On the third day we had passed through the ash-desert and our horses could at last crop at some grass on the crest of a line of low hills which looked down on glinting, misty paddy-fields. Savitsky, his field-glasses to his eyes, was relieved. "A village," he said. "Thank god. We'll be able to get some provisions."

"And some exercise," said Pavlichenko behind him. The boy laughed, pushing his cap back on his head and wiping grimy sweat from his brow. "Shall I go down there, comrade?" Savitsky agreed, telling Pavlichenko to take two others with him. We watched the Cossacks ride down the hill and begin cautiously to wade their horses through the young rice. The sky possessed a greenish tinge here, as if it reflected the fields. It looked like the Black Sea lagoons at midsummer. A smell of foliage, almost shocking in its unfamiliarity, floated up to us. Savitsky was intent on watching the movements of his men, who had unslung their carbines and dismounted as they reached the village. With reins looped on their arms they moved slowly in, firing a few experimental rounds at the huts. One of them took a dummy grenade from his saddle-bag and threw it into a nearby doorway. Peasants, already starving to the point of death it seemed, ran out. The young Cossacks ignored them, looking for soldiers. When they were satisfied that the village was clear of traps, they waved us in. The peasants began to gather together at the centre of the village. Evidently they were used to this sort of operation.

While our men made their thorough search I was again called upon to perform my duty and question the inhabitants. These, it emerged, were almost all intellectuals, part of an old Khmer Rouge re-education programme (virtually a sentence of death by forced labour). It was easier to speak to them but harder to understand their complicated answers. In the end I gave up and, made impatient by the whining appeals of the wretches, ignored them. They knew nothing of use to us. Our men were disappointed in their expectations. There were only old people in the village. In the end they took the least aged of the women off and had them in what had once been some sort of administration hut. I wondered at their energy. It occurred to me that this was something they expected of one another and that they would lose face if they did not perform the necessary actions. Eventually, when we had eaten what we could find, I returned to questioning two of the old men. They were at least antagonistic to the Cambodian troops and were glad to tell us anything they could. However, it seemed there had been no large movements in the area. The occasional plane or helicopter had gone over a few days earlier. These were probably part of the flight which had attacked us at the river. I asked if they had any news of Angkor, but there was no radio here and they expected us to know more than they did. I pointed towards the purple hills on the other side of the valley. "What's over there?"

They told me that as far as they knew it was another valley, similar to this but larger. The hills looked steeper and were wooded. It would be a difficult climb for us unless there was a road. I got out the map. There was a road indicated. I pointed to it. One of the old men nodded. Yes, he thought that road was still there, for it led, eventually, to this village. He showed me where the path was. It was rutted where, some time earlier, heavy vehicles had been driven along it. It disappeared into dark, green, twittering jungle. All the jungle meant to me now was mosquitoes and a certain amount of cover from attacking planes.

Careless of leeches and insects, the best part of the division was taking the chance of a bath in the stream which fed the paddy-fields. I could not bring myself to strip in the company of these healthy men. I decided to remain dirty until I had the chance of some sort of privacy.

"I want the men to rest," said Savitsky. "Have you any objection to our camping here for the rest of today and tonight?"

"It's a good idea," I said. I sought out a hut, evicted the occupants, and went almost immediately to sleep.

In the morning I was awakened by a trooper who brought me a metal mug full of the most delicately scented tea. I was astonished and accepted it with some amusement. "There's loads of it here," he said. "It's all they've got!"

I sipped the tea. I was still in my uniform, with the burka on the ground beneath me and my leather jacket folded for a pillow. The hut was completely bare. I was used to noticing a few personal possessions and began to wonder if they had hidden their stuff when they had seen us coming. Then I remembered that they were from the towns and had been brought here forcibly. Perhaps now, I thought, the War would pass them by and they would know peace, even happiness, for a bit. I was scratching my ear and stretching when Savitsky came in, looking grim. "We've found a damned burial ground," he said. "Hundreds of bodies in a pit. I think they must be the original inhabitants. And one or two soldiers—at least, they were in uniform."

"You want me to ask what they are?"

"No! I just want to get away. God knows what they've been doing to one another. They're a filthy race. All grovelling and secret killing. They've no guts."

"No soldiers, either," I said. "Not really. They've been preyed on by bandits for centuries. Bandits are pretty nearly the only sort of soldiers they've ever known. So the ones who want to be soldiers emulate them. Those who don't want to be soldiers treat the ones who do as they've always treated bandits. They are conciliatory until they get a chance to turn the tables."

He was impressed by this. He rubbed at a freshly shaven chin. He looked years younger, though he still had the monumental appearance of a god. "Thieves, you mean. They have the mentality of thieves, their soldiers?"

"Aren't the Cossacks thieves?"

"That's foraging." He was not angry. Very little I said could ever anger him because he had no respect for my opinions. I was the necessary political officer, his only link with the higher, distant authority of the Kremlin, but he did not have to respect my ideas any more than he respected those which came to him from Moscow. What he respected there was the power and the fact that in some way Russia was mystically represented in our leaders. "We leave in ten minutes," he said.

I noticed that Pavlichenko had polished his boots for him.

By that afternoon, after we had crossed the entire valley on an excellent dirt road through the jungle and had reached the top of the next range of hills, I had a pain in my stomach. Savitsky noticed me holding my hands against my groin and said laconically, "I wish the doctor hadn't been killed. Do you think it's typhus?" Naturally, it was what I had suspected.

"I think it's just the tea and the rice and the other stuff. Maybe mixing with all the dust we've swallowed."

He looked paler than usual. "I've got it, too. So have half the others. Oh, shit!"

It was hard to tell, in that jungle at that time of day, if you had a fever. I decided to put the problem out of my mind as much as possible until sunset when it would become cooler.

The road began to show signs of damage and by the time we were over the hill and looking down on the other side we were confronting scenery if anything more desolate than that which we had passed through on the previous three days. It was a grey desert, scarred by the broken road and bomb-craters. Beyond this and coming towards us was a wall of dark dust; unmistakably an army on the move. Savitsky automatically relaxed in his saddle and turned back to see our men moving slowly up the wooded hill. "I think they must be heading this way." Savitsky cocked his head to one side. "What's that?"

It was a distant shriek. Then a whole squadron of planes was coming in low. We could see their crudely painted Khmer Rouge markings, their battered fuselages. The men began to scatter off the road, but the planes ignored us. They went zooming by, seeming to be fleeing rather than attacking. I looked at the sky, but nothing followed them.

We took our field-glasses from their cases and adjusted them. In the dust I saw a mass of barefoot infantry bearing rifles with fixed bayonets. There were also trucks, a few tanks, some private cars, bicycles, motorbikes, ox-carts, hand-carts, civilians with bundles. It was an orgy of defeated soldiers and refugees.

"I think we've missed the action." Savitsky was furious. "We were beaten to it, eh? And by Australians, probably!"

My impulse to shrug was checked. "Damn!" I said a little weakly.

This caused Savitsky to laugh at me. "You're relieved. Admit it!"

I knew that I dare not share his laughter, lest it become hysterical and turn to tears, so I missed a moment of possible comradeship. "What shall we do?" I asked. "Go round them?"

"It would be easy enough to go through them. Finish them off. It would stop them destroying this valley, at least." He did not, by his tone, much care.

The men were assembling behind us. Savitsky informed them of the nature of the rabble ahead of us. He put his field-glasses to his eyes again and said to me: "Infantry, too. Quite a lot. Coming on faster."

I looked. The barefoot soldiers were apparently pushing their way through the refugees to get ahead of them.

"Maybe the planes radioed back," said Savitsky. "Well, it's something to fight."

"I think we should go round," I said. "We should save our strength. We don't know what's waiting for us at Angkor."

"It's miles away yet."

"Our instructions were to avoid any conflict we could," I reminded him.

He sighed. "This is Satan's own country." He was about to give the order which would comply with my suggestion when, from the direction of Angkor

Wat, the sky burst into white fire. The horses reared and whinnied. Some of our men yelled and flung their arms over their eyes. We were all temporarily blinded. Then the dust below seemed to grow denser and denser. We watched in fascination as the dark wall became taller, rushing upon us and howling like a million dying voices. We were struck by the ash and forced onto our knees, then onto our bellies, yanking our frightened horses down with us as best we could. The stuff stung my face and hands and even those parts of my body protected by heavy clothing. Larger pieces of stone rattled against my goggles.

When the wind had passed and we began to stand erect, the sky was still very bright. I was astonished that my field-glasses were intact. I put them up to my burning eyes and peered through swirling ash at the Cambodians. The army was running along the road towards us, as terrified animals flee a forest fire. I knew now what the planes had been escaping. Our Cossacks were in some confusion, but were already regrouping, shouting amongst themselves. A number of horses were still shying and whickering but by and large we were all calm again.

"Well, comrade," said Savitsky with a sort of mad satisfaction, "what do we do now? Wasn't that Angkor Wat, where we're supposed to meet our allies?"

I was silent. The mushroom cloud on the horizon was growing. It had the hazy outlines of a gigantic, spreading cedar tree, as if all at once that wasteland of ash had become promiscuously fertile. An aura of bloody red seemed to surround it, like a silhouette in the sunset. The strong, artificial wind was still blowing in our direction. I wiped dust from my goggles and lowered them back over my eyes. Savitsky gave the order for our men to mount. "Those bastards down there are in our way," he said. "We're going to charge them."

"What?" I could not believe him.

"When in doubt," he told me, "attack."

"You're not scared of the enemy," I said, "but there's the radiation."

"I don't know anything about radiation." He turned in his saddle to watch his men. When they were ready he drew his sabre. They imitated him. I had no sabre to draw.

I was horrified. I pulled my horse away from the road. "Division Commander Savitsky, we're duty-bound to conserve…"

"We're duty-bound to make for Angkor," he said. "And that's what we're doing." His perfect body poised itself in the saddle. He raised his sabre.

"It's not like ordinary dying," I began. But he gave the order to trot forward.

There was a rictus of terrifying glee on each mouth. The light from the sky was reflected in every eye.

I moved with them. I had become used to the security of numbers and I could not face their disapproval. But gradually they went ahead of me until I was in the rear. By this time we were almost at the bottom of the hill and cantering towards the mushroom cloud which was now shot through with all kinds of dark, swirling colours. It had become like a threatening hand, while the wind-borne ash stung our bodies and drew blood on the flanks of our mounts.

Yakovlev, just ahead of me, unstrapped his accordion and began to play some familiar Cossack battle-song. Soon they were all singing. Their pace gradually increased. The noise of the accordion died but their song was so loud now it seemed to fill the whole world. They reached full gallop, charging upon that appalling outline, the quintessential symbol of our doom, as their ancestors might have charged the very gates of hell. They were swift, dark shapes in the dust. The song became a savage, defiant roar.

My first impulse was to charge with them. But then I had turned my horse and was trotting back towards the valley and the border, praying that, if I ever got to safety, I would not be too badly contaminated.

Doves in the Circle (1997)

Like "The Opium General" and "A Winter Admiral," earlier in this collection, "Doves in the Circle" is another more or less non-fantastical story.

That said, it does mention the Kakatanawas, a native American tribe featured in *The Skrayling Tree*, a recent Elric book.

"Doves in the Circle" was originally published in 1997, in an anthology, *The Time Out Book of New York Short Stories* (Penguin), edited by Nicholas Royle.

Situated between Church Street and Broadway, several blocks from Houston Street, just below Canal Street, *Houston Circle* is entered via Houston Alley from the North, and *Lispenard, Walker* and *Franklin* Streets from the West. The only approach from the South and East is via *Courtland Alley.* Houston Circle was known as *Indian Circle* or *South Green* until about 1820. It was populated predominantly by Irish, English and, later, Jewish people and today has a poor reputation. The circle itself, forming a green, now an open market, had some claims to antiquity. Aboriginal settlements have occupied the spot for about five hundred years and early travellers report finding non-indigenous standing stones, remarkably like those erected by the Ancient Britons. The *Kakatanawas,* whom early explorers first encountered, spoke a distinctive Iroquois dialect and were of a high standard of civilisation. Captain Adriaen Block reported encountering the tribe in 1612. Their village was built around a stone circle "whych is their *Kirke.*" When, under the Dutch, Fort Amsterdam was established nearby, there was no attempt to move the tribe which seems to have become so quickly absorbed into the dominant culture that it took no part in the bloody Indian War of 1643–5 and had completely disappeared by 1680. Although of considerable architectural and historical interest, because of its location and reputation Houston Circle has not attracted redevelopment and its buildings, some of which date from the 18th century, are in poor repair. Today the Circle is best known for "The Three Sisters," which comprise the Catholic Church of *St. Mary the Widow* (one of Huntingdon Begg's earliest commissions), the Greek Orthodox Church of *St. Sophia* and the Orthodox Jewish Synagogue which stand side by side at the East end, close to *Doyle's Ale House*, built in 1780 and still in the same family. Next door to this is *Doyle's Hotel* (1879), whose tariff reflects its standards. Crossed by the Elevated Railway, which destroys the old village atmosphere, and generally neglected now, the Circle should be visited in daylight hours and in the company of other visitors. *Subway:* White Street IRT. *Elevated:* 6th Ave. El. at Church Street, *Streetcar:* B & 7th Ave., B'way & Church.

—*New York: A Traveller's Guide.* R. P. Downes,
Charles Kelly, London 1924

I

IF THERE IS such a thing as unearned innocence, then America has it, said Barry Quinn mysteriously lifting his straight glass to the flag and downing the last of Corny Doyle's passable porter. Oh, there you go again, says Corny, turning to a less contentious customer and grinning to show he saw several viewpoints. Brown as a tinker, he stood behind his glaring pumps in his white shirtsleeves, his skin glowing with the bar work, polishing up some silverware with all the habitual concentration of the rosary.

Everyone in the pub had an idea that Corny was out of sorts. They thought, perhaps, he would rather not have seen Father McQueeny there in his regular spot. These days the old priest carried an aura of desolation with him so that even when he joined a toast he seemed to address the dead. He had never been popular and his church had always chilled you but he had once enjoyed a certain authority in the parish. Now the Bishop had sent a new man down and McQueeny was evidently retired but wasn't admitting it. There'd always been more faith and Christian charity in Doyle's, Barry Quinn said, than could ever be found in that damned church. Apart from a few impenetrable writers in the architectural journals, no one had ever liked it. It was altogether too modern and Spanish-looking.

Sometimes, said Barry Quinn putting down his glass in the copper stand for a refill, there was so much good will in Doyle's Ale House he felt like he was taking his pleasure at the benign heart of the world. And who was to say that Houston Circle, with its profound history, the site of the oldest settlement on Manhattan, was not a centre of conscious grace and mystery like Camelot or Holy Island or Dublin, or possibly London? You could find all the inspiration you needed here. And you got an excellent confessional. Why freeze your bones talking to old McQueeny in the box when you might as well talk to him over in that booth. Should you want to.

The fact was that nobody wanted anything at all to do with the old horror. There were some funny rumours about him. Nobody was exactly sure what Father McQueeny had been caught doing, but it must have been bad enough for the Church to step in. And he'd had some sort of nasty secretive surgery. Mavis Byrne and her friends believed the Bishop made him have it. A popular rumour was that the Church castrated him for diddling little boys. He would not answer if you asked him. He was rarely asked. Most of the time people tended to forget he was there. Sometimes they talked about him in his hearing. He never objected.

She's crossed the road now, look. Corny pointed through the big, green-lettered window of the pub to where his daughter walked purposefully through the wrought-iron gates of what was nowadays called Houston Park on the maps and Houston Green by the realtors.

She's walking up the path. Straight as an arrow. He was proud of her. Her character was so different from his own. She had all her mother's virtues. But he was more afraid of Kate than he had ever been of his absconded spouse.

Will you look at that? Father McQueeny's bloody eyes stared with cold reminiscence over the rim of his glass. She is about to ask Mr. Terry a direct question.

He's bending an ear, says Barry Quinn, bothered by the priest's commentary, as if a fly interrupted him. He seems to be almost smiling. Look at her coaxing a bit of warmth out of that grim old mug. And at the same time she's getting the info she needs, like a bee taking pollen.

Father McQueeny runs his odd-coloured tongue around his lips and says, shrouded safe in his inaudibility, his invisibility: What a practical and down-to-earth little creature she is. She was always that. What a proper little madam, eh? She must have the truth, however dull. She will not allow us our speculations. She is going to ruin all our fancies!

His almost formless body undulates to the bar, settles over a stool and seems to coagulate on it. Without much hope of a quick response, he signals for a short and a pint. Unobserved by them, he consoles himself in the possession of some pathetic and unwholesome secret. He marvels at the depths of his own depravity, but now he believes it is his self-loathing which keeps him alive. And while he is alive, he cannot go to hell.

2

"Well," says Kate Doyle to Mr. Terry McLear, "I've been sent out and I beg your pardon but I am a kind of deputation from the whole Circle, or at least that part of it represented by my dad's customers, come to ask if what you're putting up is a platform on which you intend to sit, to make, it's supposed, a political statement of some kind? Or is it religious? Like a pole?"

And when she has finished her speech, she takes one step back from him. She folds her dark expectant hands before her on the apron of her uniform. There is a silence, emphasised by the distant, constant noise of the surrounding city. Framed by her bobbed black hair, her little pink oval face has that expression of sardonic good humour, that hint of self-mockery, which attracted his affection many years ago. She is the picture of determined patience, and she makes Mr. Terry smile.

"Is that what people are saying these days, is it? And they think I would sit up there in this weather?" He speaks the musical, old-fashioned convent-educated, precisely pronounced English he learned in Dublin. He'd rather die than make a contraction or split an infinitive. He glares up at the grey, Atlantic sky. Laughing helplessly at the image of himself on a pole he stretches hard-worn fingers towards her to show he means no mockery or rudeness to herself. His white hair rises in a halo. His big old head grows redder, his mouth rapidly opening and closing as his mirth engulfs him. He gasps. His pale blue eyes, too weak for such powerful emotions, water joyfully. Kate Doyle suspects a hint of senile dementia. She'll be sorry to see him lose his mind, it is such a good one, and so kind. He never really understood how often his company had saved her from despair.

Mr. Terry lifts the long thick dowel onto his sweat-shirted shoulder. "Would you care to give me a hand, Katey?"

She helps him steady it upright in the special hole he had prepared. The seasoned pine dowel is some four inches in diameter and eight feet tall. The hole is about two feet deep. Yesterday, from the big bar, they had all watched him pour in the concrete.

The shrubbery, trees and grass of the Circle nowadays wind neatly up to a little grass-grown central hillock. On this the City has placed two ornamental benches. Popular legend has it that an Indian chief rests underneath, together with his treasure.

When Mr. Terry was first seen measuring up the mound, they thought of the ancient redman. They had been certain, when he had started to dig, that McLear had wind of gold.

All Doyle's regulars had seized enthusiastically on this new topic. Corny Doyle was especially glad of it. Sales rose considerably when there was a bit of speculative stimulus amongst the customers, like a sensational murder or a political scandal or a sporting occasion.

Katey knew they would all be standing looking out now, watching her and waiting. They had promised to rescue her if he became unpleasant. Not that she expected anything like that. She was the only local that Mr. Terry would have anything to do with. He never would talk to most people. After his wife died he was barely civil if you wished him "good morning." His argument was that he had never enjoyed company much until he met her and now precious little other company satisfied him in comparison. Neither did he have anything to do with the Church. He'd distanced himself a bit from Katey when she started working with the Poor Clares. This was the first time she'd approached him in two years. She's grateful to them for making her come but sorry that it took the insistence of a bunch of feckless boozers to get her here.

"So," she says, "I'm glad I've cheered you up. And if that's all I've achieved, that's good enough for today, I'm sure. Can you tell me nothing about your pole?"

"I have a permit for it," he says. "All square and official." He pauses and watches the Sears delivery truck which has been droning round the Circle for the last fifteen minutes, seeking an exit. Slumped over his wheel, peering about for signs, the driver looks desperate.

"Nothing else?"

"Only that the pole is the start of it." He's enjoying himself. That heartens her.

"And you won't be doing some sort of black magic with the poor old Indian's bones?"

"Magic, maybe," he says, "but not a bit black, Katey. Just the opposite, you will see."

"Well, then," she says, "then I'll go back and tell them you're putting up a radio aerial."

"Tell them what you like," he says. "Whatever you like."

"If I don't tell them something, they'll be on at me to come out again," she says.

"You would not be unwelcome," he says, "or averse, I am sure, to a cup of tea." And gravely he tips that big head homeward, towards his brownstone basement on the far side of the Circle.

"Fine," she says, "but I'll come on my own when I do and not as a messenger. Good afternoon to you, Mr. Terry."

He lifts an invisible hat. "It was a great pleasure to talk with you again, Katey."

She's forgotten how that little smile of his so frequently cheers her up.

3

"Okay, Katey, so what's the story?" says Father McQueeny wearing his professional cheer like an old shroud, as ill-smelling and threadbare as his clerical black. The only life on him is his sweat, his winking veins. The best the regulars have for him these days is their pity, the occasional drink. He has no standing at all with the Church or the community. But, since Father Walsh died, that secret little smirk of his always chills her. Knowing that he can still frighten her is probably all that keeps the old shit alive. And since that knowledge actually informs the expression which causes her fear, she is directly feeding him what he wants. She has yet to work out a way to break the cycle. Years before, in her fiercest attempt, she almost succeeded.

To the others, the priest remains inaudible, invisible. "Did he come out with it, Katey?" says Corny Doyle, his black eyes and hair glinting like pitch, his near-fleshless body and head looking as artificially weathered as those shiny, smoked hams in Belladonna's. "Come on, Kate. There's real money riding on this now."

"He did not tell me," she says. She turns her back on Father McQueeny but she cannot control a shudder as she smiles from behind the bar where she has been helping out since Christmas, because of Bridget's pneumonia. She takes hold of the decorated china pump-handle and turns to her patient customer. "Two pints of Mooney's was it, Mr. Gold?"

"You're an angel," says Mr. Gold. "Well, Corny, the book, now how's it running?" He is such a plump, jolly man. You would never take him for a pawnbroker. And it must be admitted he is not a natural profiteer. Mr. Gold carries his pints carefully to the little table in the alcove, where Becky, his secretary, waits for him. Ageless, she is her own work of art. He dotes on her. If it wasn't for her he would be a ruined man. They'll be going out this evening. You can smell her perm and her Chantilly from here. A little less noise and you could probably hear her mascara flake.

"Radio aerial's still number one, Mr. Gold," says Katey. Her father's attention has gone elsewhere, to some fine moment of sport on the box. He shares his rowdy triumph with his fellow aficionados. He turns back to her, panting. "That was amazing," he says.

Kate Doyle calls him over with her finger. He knows better than to hesitate. "What?" he blusters. "What? There's nothing wrong with those glasses. I told you it's the dishwasher."

Her whisper is sharp as a needle in his wincing ear. She asks him why, after all she's spoken perfectly plainly to him, he is still letting that nasty old man into the pub?

"Oh, come on, Katey," he says, "where else can the poor devil go? He's a stranger in his own church these days."

"He deserves nothing less," she says. "And I'll remind you, Dad, of my original terms. I'm off for a walk now and you can run the bloody pub yourself."

"Oh, no!" He is mortified. He casts yearning eyes back towards the television. He looks like some benighted sinner in the picture books who has lost the salvation of Christ. "Don't do this to me, Kate."

"I might be back when he's gone," she says. "But I'm not making any promises."

Every so often she has to let him know he is going too far. Getting her father to work was a full-time job for her mother but she's not going to waste her own life on that non-starter. He's already lost the hotel next door to his debts. Most of the money Kate allows him goes in some form of gambling. Those customers who lend him money soon discover how she refuses to honour his IOUs. He's lucky these days to be able to coax an extra dollar or two out of the till, usually by short-changing a stranger.

"We'll lose business if you go, Kate," he hisses. "Why cut off your nose to spite your face?"

"I'll cut off *your* nose, you old fool, if you don't set it to that grindstone right now," she says. She hates sounding like her mother. Furiously, she snatches on her coat and scarf. "I'll be back when you get him out of here." She knows Father McQueeny's horrible eyes are still feeding off her through the pub's cultivated gloom.

"See you later, Katey, dear," her father trills as he places professional fingers on his bar and a smile falls across his face. "Now, then, Mrs. Byrne, a half of Guinness, is it, darling?"

4

The Circle was going up. There were all kinds of well-heeled people coming in. You could tell by the brass door-knockers and the window-boxes, the dark green paint. With the odd *boutique* and *croissanterie*, these were the traditional signs of gentrification. Taking down the last pylons of the ugly elevated had helped, along with the hippies who in the '60s and '70s had made such a success of the little park, which now had a playground and somewhere for the dogs to go. It was lovely in the summer.

It was quiet, too, since they had put in the one-way system. Now the only strange vehicles were those which thought they could still make a short cut and wound up whining round until, defeated, they left the way they had entered. You had to go up to Canal Street to get a cab. They wouldn't come any further than that. There were legends of drivers who had never returned.

This recent development had increased the sense of the Circle's uniqueness, a zone of relative tranquillity in one of the noisiest parts of New York City. Up to now they had been protected from a full-scale yuppie invasion by the nearby federal housing. Yet nobody from the projects had ever bothered the Circle. They thought of the place as their own, something they aspired to, something to protect. It was astonishing the affection local people felt for the place, especially the park, which was the best-kept in the city.

She was on her brisk way, of course, to take Mr. Terry McLear up on his invitation but she was not going there directly for all to see. Neither was she sure what she'd have to say to him when she saw him. She simply felt it was time they had one of their old chats.

Under a chilly sky, she walked quickly along the central path of the park. Eight paths led to the middle these days, like the arms of a compass, and there had been some talk of putting a sundial on the knoll, where Mr. Terry had now laid his discreet foundations. She paused to look at the smooth concrete of his deep, narrow hole. A flag, perhaps? Something that simple? But this was not a man to fly a flag at the best of times. And even the heaviest banner did not need so sturdy a pole. However, she was beginning to get a notion. A bit of a memory from a conversation of theirs a good few years ago now. Ah, she thought, it's about birds, I bet.

Certain some of her customers would still be watching her, she took the northern path and left the park to cross directly over to Houston Alley, where her uncle had his little toy-soldier shop where he painted everything himself and where, next door, the Italian shoe-repairer worked in his window. They would not be there much longer now that the real-estate people had christened the neighbourhood "Houston Village." Already the pub had had a sniff from Starbucks. Up at the far end of the alley the street looked busy. She thought about going back, but told herself she was a fool.

The traffic in Canal Street was unusually dense and a crew-cut girl in big boots had to help her when she almost fell into the street, shoved aside by some thrusting Wall Street stockman in a vast raincoat which might have sheltered half the Australian outback. She thought she recognised him as the boy who had moved in to Number 91 a few weeks ago and she had been about to say hello.

She was glad to get back into the quietness of the Circle, going round into Church Street and then through Walker Street which would bring her out only a couple of houses from Mr. Terry's place.

She was still a little shaken up but had collected herself by the time she reached the row of brownstones. Number 27 was in the middle and his flat was in the basement. She went carefully down the iron steps to his area. It was as smartly kept up as always, with the flower baskets properly stocked and his miniature greenhouse raising tomatoes in their gro-bags. And he was still neat and clean. No obvious slipping of standards, no signs of senile decay. She took hold of the old black lion knocker and rapped twice against the dented plate. That same vast echo came back, as if she stood at the door to infinity.

He was slow as Christmas unbolting it all and opening up. Then everything happened at once. Pulling back the door he embraced her and kicked it shut at the same time. The apartment was suddenly very silent. "Well," he said, "it has been such a long time. All my fault, too. I have had a chance to pull myself together and here I am."

"That sounds like a point for God for a change." She knew all the teachers had been anarchists or pagans or something equally silly in that school of his. She stared around at the familiar things, the copper and the oak and the big ornamental iron stove which once heated the whole building. "You're still dusting better than a woman. And polishing."

"She had high standards," he says. "I could not rise to them when she was alive, but now it seems only fair to try to live up to them. You would not believe what a slob I used to be."

"You never told me," she says.

"That is right. There is quite a bit I have not told you," he says.

"And us so close once," she says.

"We were good friends," he agreed. "The best of company. I am an idiot, Kate. But I do not think either of us realised I was in a sort of shock for years. I was afraid of our closeness, do you see? In the end."

"I believe I might have mentioned that." She went to put the kettle on. Filling it from his deep old-fashioned stone sink with its great brass faucets she carried it with both hands to the stove while he got out the teacakes and the toasting forks. He must have bought them only today from Van Beek's Bakery on Canal, the knowing old devil, and put them in the icebox. They were still almost warm. She fitted one to the fork. "It doesn't exactly take Sigmund Freud to work that out. But you made your decisions, Mr. Terry. And it is my general rule to abide by such decisions until the party involved decides to change. Which in my experience generally happens at the proper time."

"Oh, so you have had lots of these relationships, have you, Kate?" She laughed.

5

"I was sixteen when I first saw her. In the Circle there she was, coming out of Number 10, where the dry-cleaners is now. I said to myself, that is whom I am going to marry. And that was what I did. We used to sing quite a bit, duets together. She was a much better and sweeter singer than I, and she was smarter, as well." Mr. Terry looks into the fire and slowly turns his teacake against the glare. "What a little old snob I was in those days, thinking myself better than anyone, coming back from Dublin with an education. But she liked me anyway and was what I needed to take me down a peg or two. My father thought she was an angel. He spoke often of the grandchildren he would care for. But both he and she died before that event could become any sort of reality. And I grew very sorry for myself, Kate. In those first days, when we were having our chats, I was selfish."

"Oh, yes," she says, "but you were more than that. You couldn't help being more than that. That's one of the things hardest to realise about ourselves sometimes. Even in your morbid moments you often showed me how to get a grip on things. By example, you might say. You cannot help but be a good man, Mr. Terry. A protector, I think, rather than a predator."

"I do not know about that."

"But I do," she says.

"Anyway," he flips a teacake onto the warming plate, "we had no children and so the McLears have no heirs."

"It's a shame," she says, "but not a tragedy, surely?" For an instant it flashes through her head, Oh, no, he doesn't want me to have his bloody babies, does he?

"Not in any ordinary sense, I quite agree. But you see there is an inheritance that goes along with that. Something which must be remembered accurately and passed down by word of mouth. It is our family tradition and has been so for quite a time."

"My goodness," she says. "You're Brian Boru's rightful successor to the high throne of Erin, is that it?" With deft economy she butters their teacakes.

He takes some jelly from the dish and lays it lightly on top. "Oh, these are good, eh?"

When they are drinking their last possible cup of Assam he says very soberly: "Would you let me share this secret, Kate? I have no one else."

"Not a crime, is it, or something nasty?" she begs.

"Certainly not!" He falls silent. She can sense him withdrawing and laughs at his response. He sighs.

"Then get on with it," she says. "Give me a taste of it, for I'm a busy woman."

"The story does not involve the Irish much," he says. "Most of the Celts involved were from southern England, which was called Britannia in those days, by the Romans."

"Ancient history!" she cries. "How long, Mr. Terry, is your story?"

"Not very long," he says.

"Well," she says, "I will come back another time to hear it." She glances at her watch. "If I don't go now I'll miss my programme."

As he helps her on with her coat she says: "I have a very low tolerance for history. It is hard for me to see how most of it relates to the here and now."

"This will mean something to you, I think, Kate."

They exchange light kisses upon the cheek. There is a new warmth between them which she welcomes.

"Make it scones tomorrow," she says. "Those big juicy ones they do, with the raisins in them, and I will hear your secret. We'll have Darjeeling, too. I'll bring some if you don't have any."

"I have plenty," he says.

"Bye, bye for now," she says.

6

"All the goodness is in the marrow!" declares Mrs. Byrne, waving her bones at the other customers. "But these days the young people all turn their noses up at it."

"That's not the problem at all, Mavis. The plain truth is you're a bloody noisy eater," says Corny Doyle, backing up the other diners' complaints. "And you've had one too many now. You had better go home."

With her toothless mouth she sucks at her mutton.

"They don't know what they're missing, do they Mavis?" says Father McQueeny from where he sits panting in a booth.

"And you can fuck off, you old pervert." Mavis rises with dignity and sails towards the ladies'. She has her standards.

"Well, Kate, how's the weather out there?" says Father McQueeny.

"Oh, you are here at last, Kate. It seems Father McQueeny's been locked out of his digs." In other circumstances Corny's expression of pleading anxiety would be funny.

"That doesn't concern me," she says, coming down the stairs. "I just popped in for something. I have told you what I want, Dad." She is carrying her little bag.

He rushes after her, whispering and pleading. "What can I do?"

"I have told you what you can do."

She looks back into the shadows. She knows he is staring at her. Often she thinks it is not exactly him that she fears, only what is in him. What sense does that make? Does she fear his memories and secrets? Of course Father Walsh, her confessor, had heard what had happened and what she had done and she had been absolved. What was more, the Church, by some means of its own, had discovered at least part of the truth and taken steps to curb him. They had sent Father Declan down to St. Mary's. He was a tough old bugger but wholesome as they come. McQueeny was supposed to assist Declan who had found no use for him. However, since Father Walsh died, McQueeny revelled in their hideous secret, constantly hanging around the pub even before she started working there, haunting her, threatening to tell the world how he had come by his horrid surgery.

She is not particularly desperate about it. Sooner or later she knows her father will knuckle down and ban the old devil. It must be only a matter of time before the priest's liver kills him. She's never wished anyone dead in her life, save him, and her hatred of him is such that she fears for her own soul over it.

This time she goes directly across the park to Mr. Terry McLear's. It might look as if she plans to spend the night there but she does not care. Her true intention is to return eventually to her own flat in Delaware Court and wait until her father calls. She gives it twenty-four hours from the moment she stepped out of the pub.

But when she lifts the lion's head and lets it fall there is no reply. She waits. She climbs back up the steps. She looks into the park. She is about to go down again when an old chequer cab pulls up and out of its yellow-and-black depths comes Mr. Terry McLear with various bags and bundles. "Oh what luck!" he declares. "Just when I needed you, Kate."

She helps him get the stuff out of the cab and down into his den. He removes his coat. He opens the door into his workshop and switches on a light. "I was not expecting you back today."

"Circumstances gave me the opportunity." She squints at the bags. "Who is Happy the Hammer?"

"Look on the other side. It is Stadtler's Hardware. Their mascot. Just the last bits I needed."

"Is it a bird-house of some kind that you are building?" she asks.

"And so you are adding telepathy to your list of extraordinary qualities, are you, Katey?" He grins. "Did I ever mention this to you?"

"You might have done. Is it pigeons?"

"God bless you, Katey." He pulls a bunch of small dowels out of a bag and puts it on top of some bits of plywood. "I must have told you the story."

"Not much of a secret, then," she says.

"This is not the secret, though I suppose it has something to do with it. There used to be dovecotes here, Katey, years ago. And that is all I am building. Have you not noticed the little doves about?"

"I can't say I have."

"Little mourning doves," he says. "Brown and cream. Like a kind of delicate pigeon."

"Well," she says, "I suppose for the non-expert they'd be lost in the crowd."

"Maybe, but I think you would know them when I pointed them out. The City believes me, anyhow, and is anxious to have them back. And it is not costing them a penny. The whole thing is a matter of fifty dollars and a bit of time. An old-fashioned dovecote, Katey. There are lots of accounts of the dovecotes, when this was more or less an independent village."

"So you're building a little house for the doves," she says. "That will be nice for them."

"A little house, is it? More a bloody great hotel." Mr. Terry erupts with sudden pride. "Come on, Kate. I will take you back to look."

7

She admires him turning the wood this way and that against the whirling lathe he controls with a foot pedal.

"It is a wonderful smell," she says, "the smell of shavings." She peers with casual curiosity at his small, tightly organised workshop. Tools, timber, electrical bits and pieces, nails, screws and hooks are neatly stowed on racks and narrow shelves. She inspects the white-painted sides of the near-completed bird-house. In the room, it seems massive, almost large enough to hold a child. She runs her fingers over the neatly ridged openings, the perfect joints. Everything has been finished to the highest standard, as if for the most demanding human occupation. "When did they first put up the dovecotes?"

"Nobody knows. The Indians had them when the first explorers arrived from Holland and France. There are sketches of them in old books. Some accounts call the tribe that lived here 'the Dove Keepers.' The Iroquois respected them as equals and called them the Ga-geh-ta-o-no, the People of the Circle. But the phrase also means People of the Belt.

"The Talking Belts, the 'wampum' records of the Six Nations, are invested with mystical meanings. Perhaps our tribe were the Federation's record keepers. They were a handsome, wealthy, civilised people, apparently, who were happy to meet and trade with the newcomers. The famous Captain Block was their admirer and spoke of a large stone circle surrounding their dovecotes. He believed that these standing stones, which were remarkably like early European examples, enclosed their holy place and that the doves represented the spirit they worshipped.

"Other accounts mention the stones, but there is some suspicion that the writers simply repeated Block's observations. Occasionally modern construction work reveals some of the granite, alien rock driven into the native limestone like a knife, and there is a suspicion the rock was used as part of a later stockade. The only Jesuit records make no mention of the stones but concentrate on the remarkable similarity of Kakatanawa (as the Europeans called them) myths to early forms of Christianity."

"I have heard as much myself," she agrees, more interested than she expected. "What happened to the Indians?"

"Nothing dramatic. They were simply and painlessly absorbed, mainly through intermarriage and mostly with the Irish. It would not have been difficult for them, since they still had a considerable amount of blood in common. By 1720 this was a thriving little township, built around the green. It still had its dovecotes. The stones were gone, re-used in walls of all kinds. The Kakatanawa were living in ordinary houses and intermarrying. In those days it was not fashionable to claim native ancestry. But you see the Kakatanawa were hardly natives. They resembled many of the more advanced Iroquois peoples and spoke an Iroquois dialect, but their tradition had it that their ancestors came from the other side of the Atlantic."

"Where did you read all this?" she asks in some bewilderment.

"It is not conventionally recorded," he says. "But this is my secret."

And he told her of Trinovante Celts, part of the Boudicca uprising of 69 A.D., who had used all their wealth to buy an old Roman trading ship with the intention of escaping the emperor's cruel justice and sailing to Ireland. They were not navigators but good fortune eventually took them to these shores where they built a settlement. They chose Manhattan for the same reason as everyone else, because it commanded a good position on the river, had good harbours and could be easily defended.

They built their village inland and put a stockade around it, pretty much the same as the villages they had left behind. Then they sent the ship back with news and to fetch more settlers and supplies. They never heard of it again. The ship was in fact wrecked off Cornwall, probably somewhere near St. Ives, but there were survivors and the story remained alive amongst the Celts, even as they succumbed to Roman civilisation.

When, some hundreds of years later, the Roman legions were withdrawn and the Saxon pirates started bringing their families over, further bands of desperate Celts fled for Ireland and the land beyond, which they had named Hy Braseal. One other galley reached Manhattan and discovered a people more Senecan than Celtic.

This second wave of Celtic immigrants were the educated Christian stone-raisers, Romanised astronomers and mystics, who brought new wisdom to their distant cousins and were doubtless not generally welcomed for it. For whatever reasons, however, they were never attacked by other tribes. Even the stern Iroquois, the Romans of these parts, never threatened them, although they were nominally subject to Hiawatha's Federation. By the time the Dutch arrived, the dominant Iroquois culture had again absorbed the Celts, but they retained certain traditions, stories and a few artefacts. Most of these appear to have been sold amongst the Indians and travelled widely through the north-east. They gave rise to certain rumours of Celtic civilisations (notably the Welsh) established in America.

"But the Kakatanawa spoke with the same eloquence and wore the finery and fashions of the Federation. Their particular origin-legend was not remarkable. Other tribes had far more dramatic conceptions, involving spectacular miracles and wildly original plots. So nobody took much notice of us and so we have survived."

"Us?" says Kate Doyle. "We?"

"You," he says, "represent the third wave of Celtic settlement of the Circle during the nineteenth and twentieth centuries. And I represent the first and second. I am genuinely, Katey, and it is embarrassing to say so, the Last of the Kakatanawas. That was why my father looked forward to an heir, as did I. I suppose I was not up to the burden, or I would have married again."

"You'd be a fool to marry just for the sake of some old legend," she says. "A woman deserves more respect than that."

"I agree." He returns to his work. Now he's putting the fine little touches to the dowels, the decorations. It's a wonder to watch him.

"Do you have a feathered headdress and everything? A peace-pipe and a tomahawk?" Her mockery has hardly any scepticism in it.

"Go over to that box just there and take out what is in it," he says, concentrating on the wood.

She obeys him.

It is a little modern copper box with a Celtic motif in the lid. Inside is an old dull coin. She picks it up between wary fingers and fishes it out, turning it to try to read the faint letters of the inscription. "It's Constantine," she says. "A Roman coin."

"The first Christian Emperor. That coin has been in New York, in our family, Katey, since the sixth century. It is pure gold. It is what is left of our treasure."

"It must be worth a fortune," she says.

"Not much of one. The condition is poor, you see. And I am sworn never to reveal its provenance. But it is certainly worth a bit more than the gold alone. Anyway, that is it. It is yours, together with the secret."

"I don't want it," she says, "can't we bury it?"

"Secrets should not be buried," he said, "but kept."

"Well, speak for yourself," she says. "There are some secrets best buried."

While he worked on, she told him about Father McQueeny. He turned the wood more and more slowly as he listened. The priest's favourite joke that always made him laugh was "Little girls should be screwed and not heard." With her father's half-hearted compliance, the old wretch had enjoyed all his pleasures on her until one day when she was seventeen she had taken his penis in her mouth and, as she had planned, bitten down like a terrier. He had torn her hair out and almost broken her arm before he fainted.

"And I did not get all the way through. You would not believe how horrible it feels—like the worst sort of gristle in your mouth and all the blood and nasty crunching, slippery stuff. At first, at least, everything in you makes you want to stop. I was very sick afterwards, as you can imagine, and just able to dial 911 before I left him there. He almost died of losing so much blood. I hadn't expected it to spurt so hard. I almost drowned. I suppose if I had thought about it I should have anticipated that. And had a piece of string ready, or something. Anyway, it stopped his business. I was never reported. And I don't know how confessors get the news out, but the Church isn't taking any chances with him, so all he has now are his memories."

"Oh, dear," says Mr. Terry gravely. "Now there is a secret to share."

"It's the only one I have," she said. "It seemed fair to reciprocate."

8

Two days later, side by side, they stand looking up at his magnificent birdhouse, complete at last. He's studied romantic old plans from the turn of the century, so it has a touch or two of the Charles Rennie Mackintosh about it in its white austerity, its sweeping gables. There are seven fretworked entrances and eight beautifully turned perches, black as ebony, following the lines of the park's paths. He's positioned and prepared the cote exactly as instructed in Tiffany's *Modern Gardens* of 1892 and has laid his seed and corn carefully. At her request, and without much reluctance, he's buried the Roman coin in the pole's foundation. Now we must be patient, he says. And wait. As he speaks a whickering comes from above and a small dove, fawn and pale grey, settles for a moment upon the gleaming roof, then takes fright when she sees them.

"What a pretty thing. I will soon have to get back to my flat," she says. "My father will be going frantic by now. I put the machine on, but if I know him he'll be too proud to leave a message."

"Of course." He stoops to pick up a delicately coloured wing feather. It has a thousand shades of rose, beige, pink and grey. "I will be glad to come with you if you want anything done."

"I'll be all right," she says. But he falls in beside her.

As they turn their backs on the great bird-house three noisy mourning doves land on the perches as if they have been anticipating this moment for a hundred and fifty years. The sense of celebration, of relief, is so tangible it suffuses Kate Doyle and Mr. Terry McLear even as they walk away.

"This calls for a cup of coffee," says Mr. Terry McLear. "Shall we go to Belladonna's?"

They are smiling when Father McQueeny, evicted at last, comes labouring towards them along the path from the pub and pauses, suddenly gasping for his familiar fix, as if she has turned up in the nick of time to save his life.

"Good morning, Katey, dear." His eyes begin to fill with powerful memories. He speaks lovingly to her. "And Terry McLear, how are you?"

"Not bad thank you, Father," says Mr. Terry, looking him over.

"And when shall we be seeing you in church, Terry?" The priest is used to people coming back to the faith as their options begin to disappear.

"Oh, soon enough, Father, I hope. By the way, how is Mary's last supper doing? How is the little hot dog?" And he points.

It is a direct and fierce attack. Father McQueeny folds before it. "Oh, you swore!" he says to her.

She tries to speak but she cannot. Instead she finds herself laughing in the old wretch's face, watching him die, his secret, his sustenance lost for ever. He knows at once, of course, that his final power has gone. His cold eyes stare furiously into inevitable reality as his soul goes at last to the Devil. It will be no more than a day or two before they bury him.

"Well," says Katey, "we must be getting on."

"Goodbye, Father," says Mr. Terry McLear, putting his feather in his white hair and grinning like a fool.

When they look back the priest has disappeared, doubtless scuttling after some mirage of salvation. But the dovecote is alive with birds. It must have a dozen on it already, bobbing around in the little doorways, pecking up the seed.

They glance around with equanimity. You would think they had always been here. The distant noise of New York's traffic is muffled by their excited voices, as if old friends meeting after years. There is an air of approving recognition about their voices.

"They like the house. Now we must see if, when they have eaten the food, they will stay." Mr. Terry McLear links a proud arm with his companion. "I never expected it to happen so quickly. It was as if they were waiting to come home. It is a positive miracle."

Amused, she looks up at him. "Come on now, a grown man like you with tears in his eyes!

"After all, Mr. Terry." She takes his arm as they continue down the path towards Houston Alley. "You must never forget your honour as the Last of the Kakatanawas."

"You do not believe a word of it, do you, Kate?" he says.

"I do," she says. "Every word, in fact. It's just that I cannot fathom why you people went to so much trouble to keep it dark."

"Oh, you know all right, Kate," says Mr. Terry McLear, pausing to look back at the flocking doves. "Sometimes secrecy is our only means of holding on to what we value."

Whistling, she escorts him out of the Circle.

The Deep Fix (1964)

A similar preface to this one—for the first appearance of "The Deep Fix" in *Science Fantasy* No. 64, edited by John Carnell, in April 1964—said: "*This is one of those rare stories which requires reading a second time to fully appreciate the working of the author's plot. Let us say that none of the events depicted are what they really are—and leave it to you to work them out if you can.*"

Forty-four years later, I am not sure a lot has changed…

"The Deep Fix" was first published under the pseudonym James Colvin, a name adopted by Moorcock for some of his more experimental stories, often with less than conventional structures.

THE DEEP FIX

For William Burroughs, for obvious reasons

I

QUICKENING SOUNDS IN the early dusk. Beat of hearts, surge of blood.

Seward turned his head on the bed and looked towards the window. They were coming again. He raised his drug-wasted body and lowered his feet to the floor. He felt nausea sweep up and through him. Dizzily, he stumbled towards the window, parted the blind and stared out over the white ruins.

The sea splashed far away, down by the harbour, and the mob was again rushing through the broken streets towards the Research Lab. They were raggedly dressed and raggedly organised, their faces were thin and contorted with madness, but they were numerous.

Seward decided to activate the Towers once more. He walked shakily to the steel-lined room on his left. He reached out a grey, trembling hand and flicked down three switches on a bank of hundreds. Lights blinked on the board above the switches. Seward walked over to the monitor-computer and spoke to it. His voice was harsh, tired and cracking.

"GREEN 9/7—O Frequency. RED 8/5—B Frequency." He didn't bother with the other Towers. Two were enough to deal with the mob outside. Two wouldn't harm anybody too badly.

He walked back into the other room and parted the blind again. He saw the mob pause and look towards the roof where the Towers GREEN 9/7 and RED 8/5 were already beginning to spin. Once their gaze had been fixed on the Towers, they couldn't get it away. A few saw their companions look up and these automatically shut their eyes and dropped to the ground. But the others were now held completely rigid.

One by one, then many at a time, those who stared at the Towers began to jerk and thresh, eyes rolling, foaming at the mouth, screaming (he heard their screams faintly)—exhibiting every sign of an advanced epileptic fit.

Seward leaned against the wall feeling sick. Outside, those who'd escaped were crawling round and inching down the street on their bellies. Then, eyes averted from the Towers, they rose to their feet and began to run away through the ruins.

Saved again, he thought bitterly.

What was the point? Could he bring himself to go on activating the Towers every time? Wouldn't there come a day when he would let the mob get into the laboratory, search him out, kill him, smash his equipment? He deserved it, after all. The world was in ruins because of him, because of the Towers and the other hallucinomats which he'd perfected. The mob wanted its revenge. It was fair.

Yet, while he lived, there might be a way of saving something from the wreckage he had made of mankind's minds. The mobs were not seriously hurt by the Towers. It had been the other machines which had created the real damage. Machines like the Paramats, Schizomats, Engramoscopes, even Michelson's Stroboscope Type 8. A range of instruments which had been designed to help the world and had, instead, virtually destroyed civilisation.

The memory was all too clear. He wished it wasn't. Having lost track of time almost from the beginning of the disaster, he had no idea how long this had been going on. A year, maybe? His life had become divided into two sections: drug-stimulated working-period; exhausted, troubled, tranquillised sleeping-period. Sometimes, when the mobs saw the inactive Towers and charged towards the laboratory, he had to protect himself. He had learned to sense the coming of a mob. They never came individually. Mob hysteria had become the universal condition of mankind—for all except Seward who had created it.

Hallucinomatics, neural stimulators, mechanical psycho-simulatory devices, hallucinogenic drugs and machines, all had been developed to perfection at the Hampton Research Laboratory under the brilliant direction of Prof. Lee W. Seward (33), psychophysicist extraordinaire, one of the youngest pioneers in the field of hallucinogenic research.

Better for the world if he hadn't been, thought Seward wearily as he lowered his worn-out body into the chair and stared at the table full of notebooks and loose sheets of paper on which he'd been working ever since the result of Experiment Restoration.

Experiment Restoration. A fine name. Fine ideals to inspire it. Fine brains to make it. But something had gone wrong.

Originally developed to help in the work of curing mental disorders of all kinds, whether slight or extreme, the hallucinomats had been an extension on the old hallucinogenic drugs such as CO_2, Mescalin and Lysergic Acid derivatives. Their immediate ancestor was the stroboscope and machines like it. The stroboscope, spinning rapidly, flashing brightly coloured patterns into the eyes of a subject, often inducing epilepsy or a similar disorder; the research of Burroughs and his followers into the early types of crude hallucinomats, had all helped to contribute to a better understanding of mental disorders.

But, as research continued, so did the incidence of mental illness rise rapidly throughout the world.

The Hampton Research Laboratory and others like it were formed to combat that rise with what had hitherto been considered near-useless experiments in the field of Hallucinomatics. Seward, who had been stressing the potential importance of his chosen field since university, came into his own. He was made Director of the Hampton Lab.

People had earlier thought of Seward as a crank and of the hallucinomats as being at best toys and at worse "madness machines," irresponsibly created by a madman.

But psychiatrists specially trained to work with them had found them invaluable aids to their studies of mental disorders. It had become possible for a trained psychiatrist to induce in himself a temporary state of mental abnormality by use of these machines. Thus he was better able to understand and help his patients. By different methods—light, sound-waves, simulated brain-waves, and so on—the machines created the symptoms of dozens of basic abnormalities and thousands of permutations. They became an essential part of modern psychiatry.

The result: hundreds and hundreds of patients, hitherto virtually incurable, had been cured completely.

But the birth-rate was rising even faster than had been predicted in the middle part of the century. And mental illness rose faster than the birth-rate. Hundreds of cases could be cured. But there were millions to be cured. There was no mass-treatment for mental illness.

Not yet.

Work at the Hampton Research Lab became a frantic race to get ahead of the increase. Nobody slept much as, in the great big world outside, individual victims of mental illness turned into groups of—the world had only recently forgotten the old word and now remembered it again—*maniacs.*

An overcrowded, over-pressured world, living on its nerves, cracked up.

The majority of people, of course, did not succumb to total madness. But those who did became a terrible problem.

Governments, threatened by anarchy, were forced to re-institute the cruel, old laws in order to combat the threat. All over the world prisons, hospitals, mental homes, institutions of many kinds, all were turned into Bedlams. This hardly solved the problem. Soon, if the rise continued, the sane would be in a minority.

A dark tide of madness, far worse even than that which had swept Europe in the Middle Ages, threatened to submerge civilisation.

Work at the Hampton Research Laboratory speeded up and speeded up—and members of the team began to crack. Not all these cases were noticeable to the overworked men who remained sane. They were too busy with their frantic experiments.

Only Lee Seward and a small group of assistants kept going, making increasing use of stimulant-drugs and depressant-drugs to do so.

But, now that Seward thought back, they had not been sane, they had not remained cool and efficient any more than the others. They had seemed to, that was all. Perhaps the drugs had deceived them.

The fact was, they had panicked—though the signs of panic had been hidden, even to themselves, under the disciplined guise of sober thinking.

Their work on tranquillising machines had not kept up with their perfection of stimulatory devices. This was because they had had to study the reasons for mental abnormalities before they could begin to devise machines for curing them.

Soon, they decided, the whole world would be mad, well before they could perfect their tranquilomatic machines. They could see no way of speeding up this work any more.

Seward was the first to put it to his team. He remembered his words.

"Gentlemen, as you know, our work on hallucinomats for the actual *curing* of mental disorders is going too slowly. There is no sign of our perfecting such machines in the near future. I have an alternative proposal."

The alternative proposal had been Experiment Restoration. The title, now Seward thought about it, had been euphemistic. It should have been called Experiment Diversion. The existing hallucinomats would be set up throughout the world and used to induce *passive* disorders in the minds of the greater part of the human race. The co-operation of national governments and World Council was sought and given. The machines were set up secretly at key points all over the globe.

They began to "send" the depressive symptoms of various disorders. They worked. People became quiet and passive. A large number went into catatonic states. Others—a great many others, who were potentially inclined to melancholia, manic-depression, certain kinds of schizophrenia—committed suicide. Rivers became clogged with corpses, roads awash with the blood and flesh of those who'd thrown themselves in front of cars. Every time a plane or rocket was seen in the sky, people expected to see at least one body come falling from it. Often, whole cargoes of people were killed by the suicide of a captain, driver or pilot of a vehicle.

Even Seward had not suspected the extent of the potential suicides. He was shocked. So was his team.

So were the World Council and the national governments. They told Seward and his team to turn off their machines and reverse the damage they had done, as much as possible.

Seward had warned them of the possible result of doing this. He had been ignored. His machines had been confiscated and the World Council had put untrained or ill-trained operators on them. This was one of the last acts of the World Council. It was one of the last rational—however ill-judged—acts the world knew.

The real disaster had come about when the bungling operators that the World Council had chosen set the hallucinomats to send the full effects of the conditions they'd originally been designed to produce. The operators may have been fools—they were probably mad themselves to do what they did. Seward couldn't know. Most of them had been killed by bands of psychopathic murderers who killed their victims by the hundreds in weird and horrible rites which seemed to mirror those of prehistory—or those of the insane South American cultures before the Spaniards.

Chaos had come swiftly—the chaos that now existed.

Seward and his three remaining assistants had protected themselves the only way they could, by erecting the stroboscopic Towers on the roof of the laboratory building. This kept the mobs off. But it did not help their consciences. One by one Seward's assistants had committed suicide.

Only Seward, keeping himself alive on a series of ever-more-potent drugs, somehow retained his sanity. And, he thought ironically, this sanity was only comparative.

A hypodermic syringe lay on the table and beside it a small bottle marked M-A 19—Mescalin-Andrenol Nineteen—a drug hitherto only tested on animals, never on human beings. But all the other drugs he had used to keep himself going had either run out or now had poor effects. The M-A 19 was his last hope of being able to continue his work on the tranquilomats he needed to perfect and thus rectify his mistake in the only way he could.

As he reached for the bottle and the hypodermic, he thought coolly that, now he looked back, the whole world had been suffering from insanity well before he had even considered Experiment Restoration. The decision to make the experiment had been just another symptom of the world-disease. Something like it would have happened sooner or later, whether by natural or artificial means. It wasn't really his fault. He had been nothing much more than fate's tool.

But logic didn't help. In a way it *was* his fault. By now, with an efficient team, he might have been able to have constructed a few experimental tranquilomats, at least.

Now I've got to do it alone, he thought as he pulled up his trouser leg and sought a vein he could use in his clammy, grey flesh. He had long since given up dabbing the area with anaesthetic. He found a blue vein, depressed the plunger of the needle and sat back in his chair to await results.

2

They came suddenly and were drastic.

His brain and body exploded in a torrent of mingled ecstasy and pain which surged through him. Waves of pale light flickered. Rich darkness followed. He rode a ferris wheel of erupting sensations and emotions. He fell down a never-ending slope of obsidian rock surrounded by clouds of green, purple, yellow, black. The rock vanished, but he continued to fall.

Then there was the smell of disease and corruption in his nostrils, but even that passed and he was standing up.

World of phosphorescence drifting like golden spheres into black night. Green, blue, red explosions. Towers rotate slowly. Towers Advance. Towers Recede. Advance. Recede. Vanish.

Flickering world of phosphorescent tears falling into the timeless, spaceless wastes of Nowhere. World of Misery. World of Antagonism. World of Guilt. Guilt—guilt—guilt...

World of hateful wonder.

Heart throbbing, mind thudding, body shuddering as M-A 19 flowed up the infinity of the spine. Shot into back-brain, shot into mid-brain, shot into fore-brain.

EXPLOSION ALL CENTRES!

No-mind—No-body—No-where.

Dying waves of light danced out of his eyes and away through the dark world. Everything was dying. Cells, sinews, nerves, synapses—all crumbling. Tears of light, fading, fading.

Brilliant rockets streaking into the sky, exploding all together and sending their multicoloured globes of light—balls on an Xmas Tree—balls on a great tree—x-mass—drifting slowly earthwards.

Ahead of him was a tall, blocky building constructed of huge chunks of yellowed granite, like a fortress. Black mist swirled around it and across the bleak, horizonless nightscape.

This was no normal hallucinatory experience. Seward felt the ground under his feet, the warm air on his face, the half-familiar smells. He had no doubt that he had entered another world.

But where was it? How had he got here?

Who had brought him here?

The answer might lie in the fortress ahead. He began to walk towards it. Gravity seemed lighter, for he walked with greater ease than normal and was soon standing looking up at the huge green metallic door. He bunched his fist and rapped on it.

Echoes boomed through numerous corridors and were absorbed in the heart of the fortress.

Seward waited as the door was slowly opened.

A man who so closely resembled the Laughing Cavalier of the painting that he must have modelled his beard and clothes on it bowed slightly and said:

"Welcome home, Professor Seward. We've been expecting you."

The bizarrely dressed man stepped aside and allowed him to pass into a dark corridor.

"Expecting me," said Seward. "How?"

The Cavalier replied good-humouredly: "That's not for me to explain. Here we go—through this door and up this corridor." He opened the door and turned into another corridor and Seward followed him.

They opened innumerable doors and walked along innumerable corridors.

The complexities of the corridors seemed somehow familiar to Seward. He felt disturbed by them, but the possibility of an explanation overrode his qualms and he willingly followed the Laughing Cavalier deeper and deeper into the fortress, through the twists and turns until they arrived at a door which was probably very close to the centre of the fortress.

The Cavalier knocked confidently on the door, but spoke deferentially. "Professor Seward is here at last, sir."

A light, cultured voice said from the other side of the door: "Good. Send him in."

This door opened so slowly that it seemed to Seward that he was watching a film slowed down to a fraction of its proper speed. When it had opened sufficiently to let him enter, he went into the room beyond. The Cavalier didn't follow him.

It only occurred to him then that he might be in some kind of mental institution, which would explain the fortresslike nature of the building and the man dressed up like the Laughing Cavalier. But, if so, how had he got here—unless he had collapsed and order had been restored sufficiently for someone to have come and collected him. No, the idea was weak.

The room he entered was full of rich, dark colours. Satin screens and hangings obscured much of it. The ceiling was not visible. Neither was the source of the rather dim light. In the centre of the room stood a dais, raised perhaps a foot from the floor. On the dais was an old leather armchair.

In the armchair sat a naked man with a cool, blue skin.

He stood up as Seward entered. He smiled charmingly and stepped off the dais, advancing towards Seward with his right hand extended.

"Good to see you, old boy!" he said heartily.

Dazed, Seward clasped the offered hand and felt his whole arm tingle as if it had had a mild electric shock. The man's strange flesh was firm, but seemed to itch under Seward's palm.

The man was short—little over five feet tall. His eyebrows met in the centre and his shiny black hair grew to a widow's peak.

Also, he had no navel.

"I'm glad you could get here, Seward," he said, walking back to his dais and sitting in the armchair. He rested his head in one hand, his elbow on the arm of the chair.

Seward did not like to appear ungracious, but he was worried and mystified. "I don't know where this place is," he said. "I don't even know how I got here—unless…"

"Ah, yes—the drug. M-A 19, isn't it? That helped, doubtless. We've been trying to get in touch with you for ages, old boy."

"I've got work to do—back there," Seward said obsessionally. "I'm sorry, but I want to get back as soon as I can. What do you want?"

The Man Without A Navel sighed. "I'm sorry, too, Seward. But we can't let you go yet. There's something I'd like to ask you—a favour. That was why we were hoping you'd come."

"What's your problem?" Seward's sense of unreality, never very strong here, for in spite of the world's bizarre appearance it seemed familiar, was growing weaker. If he could help the man and get back to continue his research, he would.

"Well," smiled the Man Without A Navel, "it's really your problem as much as ours. You see," he shrugged diffidently, "we want your world destroyed."

"What!" Now something was clear, at last. This man and his kind did belong to another world—whether in space, time, or different dimensions—and they were enemies of Earth. "You can't expect me to help you do that!" He laughed. "You *are* joking."

The Man Without A Navel shook his head seriously. "Afraid not, old boy."

"That's why you want me here—you've seen the chaos in the world and you want to take advantage of it—you want me to be a—a fifth columnist."

"Ah, you remember the old term, eh? Yes, I suppose that is what I mean. I want you to be our agent. Those machines of yours could be modified to make those who are left turn against each other even more than at present. Eh?"

"You must be very stupid if you think I'll do that," Seward said tiredly. "I can't help you. I'm trying to help *them*." Was he trapped here for good? He said weakly: "You've got to let me go back."

"Not as easy as that, old boy. I—and my friends—want to enter your world, but we can't until you've pumped up your machines to such a pitch that the entire world is maddened and destroys itself, d'you see?"

"Certainly," exclaimed Seward. "But I'm having no part of it!"

Again the Man Without A Navel smiled, slowly. "You'll weaken soon enough, old boy."

"Don't be so sure," Seward said defiantly. "I've had plenty of chances of giving up—back there. I could have weakened. But I didn't."

"Ah, but you've forgotten the new factor, Seward."

"What's that?"

"The M-A 19."

"What do you mean?"

"You'll know soon enough."

"Look—I want to get out of this place. You can't keep me—there's no point—I won't agree to your plan. Where is this world, anyway?"

"Knowing that depends on you, old boy," the man's tone was mocking. "Entirely on you. A lot depends on you, Seward."

"I know."

The Man Without A Navel lifted his head and called: "Brother Sebastian, are you available?" He glanced back at Seward with an ironical smile. "Brother Sebastian may be of some help."

Seward saw the wall-hangings on the other side of the room move. Then, from behind a screen on which was painted a weird, surrealistic scene, a tall, cowled figure emerged, face in shadow, hands folded in sleeves. A monk.

"Yes, sir," said the monk in a cold, malicious voice.

"Brother Sebastian, Professor Seward here is not quite as ready to comply with our wishes as we had hoped. Can you influence him in any way?"

"Possibly, sir." Now the tone held a note of anticipation.

"Good. Professor Seward, will you go with Brother Sebastian?"

"No." Seward had thought the room contained only one door—the one he'd entered through. But now there was a chance of there being more doors—other than the one through which the cowled monk had come. The two men didn't seem to hear his negative reply. They remained where they were, not moving. "No," he said again, his voice rising. "What right have you to do this?"

"Rights? A strange question." The monk chuckled to himself. It was a sound like ice tumbling into a cold glass.

"Yes—rights. You must have some sort of organisation here. Therefore you must have a ruler—or government. I demand to be taken to someone in authority."

"But I am in authority here, old boy," purred the blue-skinned man. "And—in a sense—so are you. If you agreed with my suggestion, you could hold tremendous power. Tremendous."

"I don't want to discuss that again." Seward began to walk towards the wall-hangings. They merely watched him—the monk with his face in shadow—the Man Without A Navel with a supercilious smile on his thin lips. He walked around a screen, parted the hangings—and there they were on the other side. He went through the hangings. This was some carefully planned trick—an illusion—deliberately intended to confuse him. He was used to such methods, even though he didn't understand how they'd worked this one. He said: "Clever—but tricks of this kind won't make me weaken."

"What on Earth d'you mean, Seward, old man? Now, I wonder if you'll accompany Brother Sebastian here. I have an awful lot of work to catch up on."

"All right," Seward said. "All right, I will." Perhaps on the way to wherever the monk was going, he would find an opportunity to escape.

The monk turned and Seward followed him. He did not look at the Man Without A Navel as he passed his ridiculous dais, with its ridiculous leather armchair.

They passed through a narrow doorway behind a curtain and were once again in the complex series of passages. The tall monk—now he was close to him, Seward estimated his height at about six feet, seven inches—seemed to flow along in front of him. He began to dawdle. The monk didn't look back. Seward increased the distance between them. Still, the monk didn't appear to notice.

Seward turned and ran.

They had met nobody on their journey through the corridors. He hoped he could find a door leading out of the fortress before someone spotted him. There was no cry from behind him.

But as he ran, the passages got darker and darker until he was careering through pitch blackness, sweating, panting and beginning to panic. He kept blundering into damp walls and running on.

It was only much later that he began to realise he was running in a circle that was getting tighter and tighter until he was doing little more than spin round, like a top. He stopped, then.

These people evidently had more powers than he had suspected. Possibly they had some means of shifting the position of the corridor walls, following his movements by means of hidden TV cameras or something like them. Simply because there were no visible signs of an advanced technology didn't mean that they did not possess one. They obviously did. How else could they have got him from his own world to this?

He took a pace forward. Did he sense the walls drawing back? He wasn't sure. The whole thing reminded him vaguely of *The Pit and the Pendulum*.

He strode forward a number of paces and saw a light ahead of him. He walked towards it, turned into a dimly lit corridor.

The monk was waiting for him.

"We missed each other, Professor Seward. I see you managed to precede me." The monk's face was still invisible, secret in its cowl. As secret as his cold mocking, malevolent voice. "We are almost there, now," said the monk.

Seward stepped towards him, hoping to see his face, but it was impossible. The monk glided past him. "Follow me, please."

For the moment, until he could work out how the fortress worked, Seward decided to accompany the monk.

They came to a heavy, iron-studded door—quite unlike any of the other doors.

They walked into a low-ceilinged chamber. It was very hot. Smoke hung in the still air of the room. It poured from a glowing brazier at the extreme end. Two men stood by the brazier.

One of them was a thin man with a huge, bulging stomach over which his long, narrow hands were folded. He had a shaggy mane of dirty white hair, his cheeks were sunken and his nose extremely long and extremely pointed. He seemed toothless and his puckered lips were shaped in a senseless smile—like the smile of a madman Seward had once had to experiment on. He wore a stained white jacket buttoned over his grotesque paunch. On his legs were loose khaki trousers.

His companion was also thin, though lacking the stomach. He was taller and had the face of a mournful bloodhound, with sparse, highly greased, black hair that covered his bony head like a skullcap. He stared into the brazier, not looking up as Brother Sebastian led Seward into the room and closed the door.

The thin man with the stomach, however, pranced forward, his hands still clasped on his paunch, and bowed to them both.

"Work for us, Brother Sebastian?" he said, nodding at Seward.

"We require a straightforward 'Yes,'" Brother Sebastian said. "You have merely to ask the question 'Will You?' If he replies 'No' you are to continue. If he replies 'Yes,' you are to cease and inform me immediately."

"Very well, Brother. Rely on us."

"I hope I can." The monk chuckled again. "You are now in the charge of these men, professor. If you decide you want to help us, after all, you have only to say 'Yes.' Is that clear?"

Seward began to tremble with horror. He had suddenly realised what this place was.

"Now look here," he said. "You can't…"

He walked towards the monk who had turned and was opening the door. He grasped the man's shoulder. His hand seemed to clutch a delicate, birdlike structure. "Hey! I don't think you're a man at all. What *are* you?"

"A man or a mouse," chuckled the monk as the two grotesque creatures leapt forward suddenly and twisted Seward's arms behind him. Seward kicked back at them with his heels, squirmed in their grasp, but he might have been held by steel bands. He shouted incoherently at the monk as he shut the door behind him with a whisk of his habit.

The pair flung him onto the damp, hot stones of the floor. It smelled awful. He rolled over and sat up. They stood over him. The hound-faced man had his arms folded. The thin man with the stomach had his long hands on his paunch again. They seemed to rest there whenever he was not actually using them. It was the latter who smiled with his twisting, puckered lips, cocking his head to one side.

"What do *you* think, Mr. Morl?" he asked his companion.

"I don't know, Mr. Hand. After you." The hound-faced man spoke in a melancholy whisper.

"I would suggest Treatment H. Simple to operate, less work for us, a tried and trusty operation which works with most and will probably work with this gentleman."

Seward scrambled up and tried to push past them, making for the door. Again they seized him expertly and dragged him back. He felt the rough touch of rope on his wrists and the pain as a knot was tightened. He shouted, more in anger than agony, more in terror than either.

They were going to torture him. He knew it.

When they had tied his hands, they took the rope and tied his ankles. They twisted the rope up around his calves and under his legs. They made a halter of the rest and looped it over his neck so that he had to bend almost double if he was not to strangle.

Then they sat him on a chair.

Mr. Hand removed his hands from his paunch, reached up above Seward's head and turned on the tap.

The first drop of water fell directly on the centre of his head some five minutes later.

Twenty-seven drops of water later, Seward was raving and screaming. Yet every time he tried to jerk his head away, the halter threatened to strangle him and the jolly Mr. Hand and the mournful Mr. Morl were there to straighten him up again.

Thirty drops of water after that, Seward's brain began to throb and he opened his eyes to see that the chamber had vanished.

In its place was a huge comet, a fireball dominating the sky, rushing directly towards him. He backed away from it and there were no more ropes on his hands or feet. He was free.

He began to run. He leapt into the air and stayed there. He was swimming through the air.

Ecstasy ran up his spine like a flickering fire, touched his back-brain, touched his mid-brain, touched his fore-brain.

EXPLOSION ALL CENTRES!

He was standing one flower among many, in a bed of tall lupins and roses which waved in a gentle wind. He pulled his roots free and began to walk.

He walked into the Lab Control Room.

Everything was normal except that gravity seemed a little heavy. Everything was as he'd left it.

He saw that he had left the Towers rotating. He went into the room he used as a bedroom and workroom. He parted the blind and looked out into the night. There was a big, full moon hanging in the deep blue sky over the ruins of Hampton. He saw its light reflected in the faraway sea. A few bodies still lay prone near the lab. He went back into the Control Room and switched off the Towers.

Returning to the bedroom he looked at the card-table he had his notes on. They were undisturbed. Neatly, side by side near a large, tattered notebook, lay a half-full ampoule of M-A 19 and a hypodermic syringe. He picked up the ampoule and threw it in a corner. It did not break but rolled around on the floor for a few seconds.

He sat down.

His whole body ached.

He picked up a sheaf of his more recent notes. He wrote everything down that came into his head on the subject of tranquilomats; it helped him think better and made sure that his drugged mind and body did not hamper him as much as they might have done if he had simply relied on his memory.

He looked at his wrists. They carried the marks of the rope. Evidently the transition from the other world to his own involved leaving anything in the other world behind. He was glad. If he hadn't, he'd have had a hell of a job getting himself untied.

He tried hard to forget the questions flooding through his mind. Where had he been? Who were the people? What did they really want? How far could they keep a check on him? How did the M-A 19 work to aid his transport into the other world? Could they get at him here?

He decided they couldn't get at him, otherwise they might have tried earlier. Somehow it was the M-A 19 in his brain which allowed them to get hold of him. Well, that was simple—no more M-A 19.

With a feeling of relief, he forced himself to concentrate on his notes.

Out of the confusion, something seemed to be developing, but he had to work at great speed—greater speed than previously, perhaps, for he daren't use the M-A 19 again and there was nothing else left of much good.

His brain cleared as he once again got interested in his notes. He worked for two hours, making fresh notes, equations, checking his knowledge against the stack of earlier research notes by the wall near his camp-bed.

Dawn was coming as he realised suddenly that he was suffering from thirst. His throat was bone dry, as were his mouth and lips. He got up and his legs felt weak. He staggered, almost knocking over the chair. With a great effort he righted it and, leaning for support on the bed, got himself to the hand-basin. It was filled by a tank near the roof and he had used it sparsely. But this time he didn't care. He stuck his head under the tap and drank the stale water greedily. It did no good. His whole body now seemed cold, his skin tight, his heart thumping heavily against his ribs. His head was aching horribly and his breathing increased.

He went and lay down on the bed, hoping the feeling would leave him.

It got worse. He needed something to cure himself.

What? he asked.

M-A 19, he answered.

NO!

But—Yes, yes, yes. All he needed was a small shot of the drug and he would be all right. He knew it.

And with knowing that, he realised something else.

He was hooked.

The drug was habit-forming.

3

He found the half-full M-A 19 ampoule under the bed where it had rolled. He found the needle on the table where he had left it, buried under his notes. He found a vein in his forearm and shot himself full. There was no thought to Seward's action. There was just the craving and the chance of satisfying that craving.

The M-A 19 began to swim leisurely through his veins, drifting up his spine—

It hit his brain with a powerful explosion.

He was walking through a world of phosphorescent rain, leaping over large purple rocks that welcomed his feet, drew them down towards them. All was agony and startling Now.

No-time, no-space, just the throbbing voice in the air above him. It was talking to him.

DOOM, Seward. DOOM, Seward. DOOM, Seward.

"Seward is doomed!" he laughed. "Seward is betrayed!"

Towers Advance. Towers Recede. Towers Rotate At Normal Speed.

Carnival Aktion. All Carnivals To Explode.

Up into the back-brain, into the mid-brain, on to the fore-brain.

EXPLOSION ALL CENTRES!

He was back in the torture-chamber, though standing up. In the corner near the brazier the grotesque pair were muttering to one another. Mr. Hand darted him an angry glance; his lips drawn over his gums in an expression of outrage.

"Hello, Seward," said the Man Without A Navel behind him. "So you're back."

"Back," said Seward heavily. "What more do you want?"

"Only your All, Seward, old man. I remember a time in Dartford before the war…"

"Which war?"

"Your war, Seward. You were too young to share any other. You don't remember *that* war. You weren't born. Leave it to those who *do*, Seward."

Seward turned. "My war?" He looked with disgust at the Man Without A Navel; at his reptilian blue skin and his warm-cold, dark-light, good-evil eyes. At his small yet well-formed body.

The Man Without A Navel smiled. "*Our* war, then, old man. I won't quibble."

"You made me do it. I think that somehow you made me suggest Experiment Restoration!"

"I said we won't quibble, Seward," said the man in an authoritative tone. Then, more conversationally: "I remember a time in Dartford before the war, when you sat in your armchair—one rather like mine—at your brother-in-law's house. Remember what you said, old man?"

Seward remembered well. "If," he quoted, "if I had a button and could press it and destroy the entire universe and myself with it, I would. For no reason other than boredom."

"Very good, Seward. You have an excellent memory."

"Is that all you're going on? Something I said out of frustration because nobody was recognising my work?" He paused as he realised something else. "You know all about me, don't you?" he said bitterly. There seemed to be nothing he didn't know. On the other hand Seward knew nothing of the man. Nothing of this world. Nothing of where it was in space and time. It was a world of insanity, of bizarre contrasts. "*How* do you know all this?"

"Inside information, Seward, old boy."

"You're mad!"

The Man Without A Navel returned to his earlier topic. "Are you bored now, Seward?"

"Bored? No. Tired, yes."

"Bored, no—tired, yes. Very good, Seward. You got here later than expected. What kept you?" The man laughed.

"I kept me. I held off taking the M-A 19 for as long as I could."

"But you came to us in the end, eh? Good man, Seward."

"You knew the M-A 19 was habit-forming? You knew I'd have to take it, come back here?"

"Naturally."

He said pleadingly: "Let me go, for God's sake! You've made me. Made me..."

"Your dearest wish almost come true, Seward. Isn't that what you wanted? I made you come close to destroying the world? Is that it?"

"So you *did* somehow influence Experiment Restoration!"

"It's possible. But you haven't done very well either way. The world is in shambles. You can't reverse that. Kill it off. Let's start fresh, Seward. Forget your experiments with the tranquilomats and help us."

"No."

The Man Without A Navel shrugged. "We'll see, old boy."

He looked at the mumbling men in the corner. "Morl—Hand—take Professor Seward to his room. I don't want any mistakes this time. I'm going to take him out of your hands. Obviously we need subtler minds put on the problem."

The pair came forward and grabbed Seward. The Man Without A Navel opened the door and they went through it first, forcing Seward ahead of them.

He was too demoralised to resist much, this time. Demoralised by the fact that he was hooked on M-A 19. What did the junkies call it? The Habit. He had The Habit. Demoralised by his inability to understand the whereabouts or nature of the world he was on. Demoralised by the fact that the Man Without A Navel seemed to know everything about his personal life on Earth. Demoralised that he had fallen into the man's trap. Who had developed M-A 19? He couldn't remember. Perhaps the Man Without A Navel had planted it? He supposed it might be possible.

He was pushed along another series of corridors, arrived at another door. The Man Without A Navel came up behind them and unlocked the door.

Seward was shoved into the room. It was narrow and low—coffinlike.

"We'll be sending someone along to see you in a little while, Seward," said the man lightly. The door was slammed.

Seward lay in pitch blackness.

He began to sob.

Later, he heard a noise outside. A stealthy noise of creeping feet. He shuddered. What was the torture going to be this time?

He heard a scraping and a muffled rattle. The door opened.

Against the light from the passage, Seward saw the man clearly. He was a big, fat negro in a grey suit. He wore a flowing, rainbow-coloured tie. He was grinning.

Seward liked the man instinctively. But he no longer trusted his instinct. "What do you want?" he said suspiciously.

The huge negro raised his finger to his lips. "Ssshh," he whispered. "I'm going to try and get you out of here."

"An old Secret Police trick on my world," said Seward. "I'm not falling for that."

"It's no trick, son. Even if it is, what can you lose?"

"Nothing." Seward got up.

The big man put his arm around Seward's shoulders. Seward felt comfortable in the grip, though normally he disliked such gestures.

"Now, son, we go real quietly and we go as fast as we can. Come on."

Softly, the big man began to tiptoe along the corridor. Seward was sure that TV cameras, or whatever they were, were following him, that the Man Without A Navel, the monk, the two torturers, the Laughing Cavalier, were all waiting somewhere to seize him.

But, very quickly, the negro had reached a small wooden door and was drawing a bolt. He patted Seward's shoulder and held the door open for him. "Through you go, son. Make for the red car."

It was morning. In the sky hung a golden sun, twice the size of Earth's. There was a vast expanse of lifeless rock in all directions, broken only by a white road which stretched into the distance. On the road, close to Seward, was parked a car something like a Cadillac. It was fire-red and bore the registration plates YOU 000. Whoever these people were, Seward decided, they were originally from Earth—all except the Man Without A Navel, perhaps. Possibly this was his world and the others had been brought from Earth, like him.

He walked towards the car. The air was cold and fresh. He stood by the convertible and looked back. The negro was running over the rock towards him. He dashed round the car and got into the driver's seat. Seward got in beside him.

The negro started the car, put it into gear and shoved his foot down hard on the accelerator pedal. The car jerked away and had reached top speed in seconds.

At the wheel, the negro relaxed. "Glad that went smoothly. I didn't expect to get away with it so easily, son. You're Seward, aren't you?"

"Yes. You seem to be as well-informed as the others."

"I guess so." The negro took a pack of cigarettes from his shirt pocket. "Smoke?"

"No thanks," said Seward. "That's one habit I don't have."

The negro looked back over his shoulder. The expanse of rock seemed never-ending, though in the distance the fortress was disappearing. He flipped a cigarette out of the pack and put it between his lips. He unclipped the car's lighter and put it to the tip of the cigarette. He inhaled and put the lighter back. The cigarette between his lips, he returned his other hand to the wheel.

He said: "They were going to send the Vampire to you. It's lucky I reached you in time."

"It could be," said Seward. "Who are you? What part do you play in this?"

"Let's just say I'm a friend of yours and an enemy of your enemies. The name's Farlowe."

"Well, I trust you, Farlowe—though God knows why."

Farlowe grinned. "Why not? I don't want your world destroyed any more than you do. It doesn't much matter, I guess, but if there's a chance of restoring it, then you ought to try."

"Then you're from my world originally, is that it?"

"In a manner of speaking, son," said Farlowe.

Very much later, the rock gave way to pleasant, flat countryside with trees, fields and little cottages peaceful under the vast sky. In the distance, Seward saw herds of cattle and sheep, the occasional horse. It reminded him of the countryside of his childhood, all clear and fresh and sharp with the clarity that only a child's eye can bring to a scene before it is obscured and tainted by the impressions of adulthood. Soon the flat country was behind them and they were going through an area of low, green hills, the huge sun flooding the scene with its soft, golden light. There were no clouds in the pale blue sky.

The big car sped smoothly along and Seward, in the comfortable companionship of Farlowe, began to relax a little. He felt almost happy, would have felt happy if it had not been for the nagging knowledge that somehow he had to get back and continue his work. It was not merely a question of restoring sanity to the world, now—he had also to thwart whatever plans were in the mind of the Man Without A Navel.

After a long silence, Seward asked a direct question. "Farlowe, where is this world? What are we doing here?"

Farlowe's answer was vague. He stared ahead at the road. "Don't ask me that, son. I don't rightly know."

"But you live here."

"So do you."

"No—I only come here when—when..."

"When what?"

But Seward couldn't raise the courage to admit about the drug to Farlowe. Instead he said: "Does M-A 19 mean anything to you?"

"Nope."

So Farlowe hadn't come here because of the drug. Seward said: "But you said you were from my world originally."

"Only in a manner of speaking." Farlowe changed gears as the road curved steeply up a hill. It rose gently above the idyllic countryside below.

Seward changed his line of questioning. "Isn't there any sort of organisation here—no government. What's the name of this country?"

Farlowe shrugged. "It's just a place—no government. The people in the fortress run most things. Everybody's scared of them."

"I don't blame them. Who's the Vampire you mentioned?"

"He works for the Man."

"What is he?"

"Why—a vampire, naturally," said Farlowe in surprise.

The sun had started to set and the whole countryside was bathed in red-gold light. The car continued to climb the long hill.

Farlowe said: "I'm taking you to some friends. You ought to be fairly safe there. Then maybe we can work out a way of getting you back."

Seward felt better. At least Farlowe had given him some direct information.

As the car reached the top of the hill and began to descend Seward got a view of an odd and disturbing sight. The sun was like a flat, round, red disc—yet only half of it was above the horizon. *The line of the horizon evenly intersected the sun's disc!* It was some sort of mirage—yet so convincing that Seward looked away, staring instead at the black smoke which he could now see rolling across the valley below. He said nothing to Farlowe.

"How much further?" he asked later as the car came to the bottom of the hill. Black night had come, moonless, and the car's headlights blazed.

"A long way yet, I'm afraid, son," said Farlowe. "You cold?"

"No."

"We'll be hitting a few signs of civilisation soon. You tired?"

"No—why?"

"We could put up at a motel or something. I guess we could eat anyway."

Ahead, Seward saw a few lights. He couldn't make out where they came from. Farlowe began to slow down. "We'll risk it," he said. He pulled in towards the lights and Seward saw that it was a line of fuel pumps. Behind the pumps was a single-storey building, very long and built entirely of timber by the look of it. Farlowe drove in between the pumps and the building. A man in overalls, the top half of his face shadowed by the peak of his cap, came into sight.

Farlowe got out of the car with a signal to Seward to do the same. The negro handed his keys to the attendant. "Fill her full and give her a quick check."

Could this be Earth? Seward wondered. Earth in the future—or possibly an Earth of a different space-time continuum. That was the likeliest explanation for this unlikely world. The contrast between recognisable, everyday things and the grotesqueries of the fortress was strange—yet it could be explained easily if these people had contact with his world. That would explain how they had things like cars and fuel stations and no apparent organisation necessary for producing them. Somehow, perhaps, they just—*stole* them?

He followed Farlowe into the long building. He could see through the wide windows that it was some kind of restaurant. There was a long, clean counter and a few people seated at tables at the far end. All had their backs to him.

He and Farlowe sat down on stools. Close to them was the largest pin-table Seward had ever seen. Its lights were flashing and its balls were clattering, though there was no one operating it. The coloured lights flashed series of numbers at him until his eyes lost focus and he had to turn away.

A woman was standing behind the counter now. Most of her face was covered by a yashmak.

"What do you want to eat, son?" said Farlowe, turning to him.

"Oh, anything."

Farlowe ordered sandwiches and coffee. When the woman had gone to get their order, Seward whispered: "Why's she wearing that thing?"

Farlowe pointed at a sign Seward hadn't noticed before. It read THE HAREM HAVEN. "It's their gimmick," said Farlowe.

Seward looked back at the pin-table. The lights had stopped flashing, the balls had stopped clattering. But above it suddenly appeared a huge pair of disembodied eyes. He gasped.

Distantly, he heard his name being repeated over and over again. "Seward. Seward. Seward. Seward..."

He couldn't tell where the voice was coming from. He glanced up at the ceiling. Not from there. The voice stopped. He looked back at the pin-table. The eyes had vanished. His panic returned. He got off his stool.

"I'll wait for you in the car, Farlowe."

Farlowe looked surprised. "What's the matter, son?"

"Nothing—it's okay—I'll wait in the car."

Farlowe shrugged.

Seward went out into the night. The attendant had gone but the car was waiting for him. He opened the door and climbed in.

What did the eyes mean? Were the people from the fortress following him in some way. Suddenly an explanation for most of the questions bothering him sprang into his mind. Of course—telepathy. They were probably telepaths. That was how they knew so much about him. That could be how they knew of his world and could influence events there—they might never go there in person. This comforted him a little, though he realised that getting out of this situation was going to be even more difficult than he'd thought.

He looked through the windows and saw Farlowe's big body perched on its stool. The other people in the café were still sitting with their backs to him. He realised that there was something familiar about them.

He saw Farlowe get up and walk towards the door. He came out and got into the car, slamming the door after him. He leaned back in his seat and handed Seward a sandwich. "You seem worked up, son," he said. "You'd better eat this."

Seward took the sandwich. He was staring at the backs of the other customers again. He frowned.

Farlowe started the car and they moved towards the road. Then Seward realised who the men reminded him of. He craned his head back in the hope of seeing their faces, but it was too late. They had reminded him of his dead assistants—the men who'd committed suicide.

They roared through dimly seen towns—all towers and angles. There seemed to be nobody about. Dawn came up and they still sped on. Seward realised that Farlowe must have a tremendous vitality, for he didn't seem to tire at all. Also, perhaps, he was motivated by a desire to get as far away from the fortress as possible.

They stopped twice to refuel and Farlowe bought more sandwiches and coffee which they had as they drove.

In the late afternoon Farlowe said: "Almost there."

They passed through a pleasant village. It was somehow alien, although very similar to a small English village. It had an oddly foreign look which was hard to place. Farlowe pulled in at what seemed to be the gates of a large public park. He looked up at the sun. "Just made it," he said. "Wait in the park—someone will come to collect you."

"You're leaving me?"

"Yes. I don't think they know where you are. They'll look but, with luck, they won't look around here. Out you get, son. Into the park."

"Who do I wait for?"

"You'll know her when she comes."

"Her?" He got out and closed the door. He stood on the pavement watching as, with a cheerful wave, Farlowe drove off. He felt a tremendous sense of loss then, as if his only hope had been taken away.

Gloomily, he turned and walked through the park gates.

4

As he walked between low hedges along a gravel path, he realised that this park, like so many things in this world, contrasted with the village it served. It was completely familiar just like a park on his own world.

It was like a grey, hazy winter's afternoon, with the brittle, interwoven skeletons of trees black and sharp against the cold sky. Birds perched on trees and bushes, or flew noisily into the silent air.

Evergreens crowded upon the leaf-strewn grass. Cry of sparrows. Peacocks, necks craned forward, dived towards scattered bread. Silver birch, larch, elm, monkey-puzzle trees, and swaying white ferns, each one like an ostrich feather stuck in the earth. A huge, ancient, nameless trunk from which, at the top, grew an expanse of soft, yellow fungus; the trunk itself looking like a Gothic cliff, full of caves and dark windows. A grey-and-brown pigeon perched motionless on the slender branches of a young birch. Peacock chicks the size of hens pecked with concentration at the grass.

Mellow, nostalgic smell of winter; distant sounds of children playing; lost black dog looking for master; red disc of sun in the cool, darkening sky. The light was sharp and yet soft, peaceful. A path led into the distance towards a flight of wide stone steps, at the top of which was the curving entrance to an arbour, browns, blacks and yellows of sapless branches and fading leaves.

From the arbour a girl appeared and began to descend the steps with quick, graceful movements. She stopped when she reached the path. She looked at him. She had long, blonde hair and wore a white dress with a full skirt. She was about seventeen.

The peace of the park was suddenly interrupted by children rushing from nowhere towards the peacocks, laughing and shouting. Some of the boys saw the tree-trunk and made for it. Others stood looking upwards at the sun as it sank in the cold air. They seemed not to see either Seward or the girl. Seward looked at her. Did he recognise her? It wasn't possible. Yet she, too, gave him a look of recognition, smiled shyly at him and ran towards him. She reached him, stood on tiptoe and gave him a light kiss on the cheek.

"Hello, Lee."

"Hello. Have you come to find me?"

"I've been looking for you a long time."

"Farlowe sent a message ahead?"

She took his hand. "Come on. Where have you been, Lee?"

This was a question he couldn't answer. He let her lead him back up the steps, through the arbour. Between the branches he glanced a garden and a pool. "Come on," she said. "Let's see what's for dinner. Mother's looking forward to meeting you."

He no longer questioned how these strange people all seemed to know his name. It was still possible that all of them were taking part in the conspiracy against him.

At the end of the arbour was a house, several storeys high. It was a pleasant house with a blue-and-white door. She led him up the path and into a hallway. It was shining with dark polished wood and brass plates on the walls. From a room at the end he smelled spicy cooking. She went first and opened the door at the end. "Mother—Lee Seward's here. Can we come in?"

"Of course." The voice was warm, husky, full of humour. They went into the room and Seward saw a woman of about forty, very well preserved, tall, large-boned with a fine-featured face and smiling mouth. Her eyes also smiled. Her sleeves were rolled up and she put the lid back on a pan on the stove.

"How do you do, Professor Seward. Mr. Farlowe's told us about you. You're in trouble, I hear."

"How do you do, Mrs.—"

"Call me Martha. Has Sally introduced herself?"

"No," Sally laughed. "I forgot. I'm Sally, Lee."

Her mother gave a mock frown. "I suppose you've been calling our guest by his first name, as usual. Do you mind, professor?"

"Not at all." He was thinking how attractive they both were, in their different ways. The young, fresh girl and her warm, intelligent mother. He had always enjoyed the company of women, but never so much, he realised, as now. They seemed to complement one another. In their presence he felt safe, at ease. Now he realised why Farlowe had chosen them to hide him. Whatever the facts, he would *feel* safe here.

Martha was saying: "Dinner won't be long."

"It smells good."

"Probably smells better than it tastes," she laughed. "Go into the lounge with Sally. Sally, fix Professor Seward a drink."

"Call me Lee," said Seward, a little uncomfortably. He had never cared much for his first name. He preferred his middle name, William, but not many others did.

"Come on, Lee," she took his hand and led him out of the kitchen. "We'll see what there is." They went into a small, well-lighted lounge. The furniture, like the whole house, had a look that was half-familiar, half-alien—obviously the product of a slightly different race. Perhaps they deliberately imitated Earth culture, without quite succeeding. Sally still gripped his hand. Her hand was warm and her skin smooth. He made to drop it but, involuntarily, squeezed it gently before she took it away to deal with the drink. She gave him another shy smile. He felt that she was as attracted to him as he to her. "What's it going to be?" she asked him.

"Oh, anything," he said, sitting down on a comfortable sofa. She poured him a dry martini and brought it over. Then she sat demurely down beside him and watched him drink it. Her eyes sparkled with a mixture of sauciness and innocence which he found extremely appealing. He looked around the room.

"How did Farlowe get his message to you?" he said.

"He came the other day. Said he was going to try and get into the fortress and help you. Farlowe's always flitting about. I think the people at the fortress have a price on his head or something. It's exciting, isn't it?"

"You can say that again," Seward said feelingly.

"Why are they after you?"

"They want me to help them destroy the world I come from. Do you know anything about it?"

"Earth, isn't it?"

"Yes." Was he going to get some straightforward answers at last?

"I know it's very closely connected with ours and that some of us want to escape from here and go to your world."

"Why?" he asked eagerly.

She shook her head. Her long, fine hair waved with the motion. "I don't really know. Something about their being trapped here—something like that. Farlowe said something about you being a 'key' to their release. They can only do what they want to do with your agreement."

"But I could agree and then break my word!"

"I don't think you could—but honestly, I don't know any more. I've probably got it wrong. Do you like me, Lee?"

He was startled by the directness of her question. "Yes," he said, "very much."

"Farlowe said you would. Good, isn't it?"

"Why—yes. Farlowe knows a lot."

"That's why he works against *them*."

Martha came in. "Almost ready," she smiled. "I think I'll have a quick one before I start serving. How are you feeling, Lee, after your ride?"

"Fine," he said, "fine." He had never been in a position like this one—with two women both of whom were extremely attractive for almost opposite reasons.

"We were discussing why the people at the fortress wanted my help," he said, turning the conversation back the way he felt it ought to go if he was ever going to get off this world and back to his own and his work.

"Farlowe said something about it."

"Yes, Sally told me. Does Farlowe belong to some sort of underground organisation?"

"Underground? Why, yes, in a way he does."

"Aren't they strong enough to fight the Man Without A Navel and his friends?"

"Farlowe says they're strong enough, but divided over what should be done and how."

"I see. That's fairly common amongst such groups, I believe."

"Yes."

"What part do you play?"

"None, really. Farlowe asked me to put you up—that's all." She sipped her drink, her eyes smiling directly into his. He drained his glass.

"Shall we eat?" she said. "Sally, take Lee into the dining room."

The girl got up and, somewhat possessively Seward thought, linked her arm in his. Her young body against his was distracting. He felt a little warm. She took him in. The table was laid for supper. Three chairs and three places. The sun had set and candles burned on the table in brass candelabra. She unlinked her arm and pulled out one of the chairs.

"You sit here, Lee—at the head of the table." She grinned. Then she leaned forward as he sat down. "Hope mummy isn't boring you."

He was surprised. "Why should she?"

Martha came in with three covered dishes on a tray. "This may not have turned out quite right, Lee. Never does when you're trying hard."

"I'm sure it'll be fine," he smiled. The two women sat down one either side of him. Martha served him. It was some sort of goulash with vegetables. He took his napkin and put it on his lap.

As they began to eat, Martha said: "How is it?"

"Fine," he said. It was very good. Apart from the feeling that some kind of rivalry for his attentions existed between mother and daughter the air of normality in the house was comforting. Here, he might be able to do some constructive thinking about his predicament.

When the meal was over, Martha said: "It's time for bed, Sally. Say goodnight to Lee."

She pouted. "Oh, it's not fair."

"Yes it is," she said firmly. "You can see Lee in the morning. He's had a long journey."

"All right." She smiled at Seward. "Sleep well, Lee."

"I think I will," he said.

Martha chuckled after Sally had gone. "Would you like a drink before you go to bed?" She spoke softly.

"Love one," he said.

They went into the other room. He sat down on the sofa as she mixed the drinks. She brought them over and sat down next to him as her daughter had done earlier.

"Tell me everything that's been happening. It sounds so exciting."

He knew at once he could tell her all he wanted to, that she would listen and be sympathetic. "It's terrifying, really," he began, half-apologetically. He began to talk, beginning with what had happened on Earth. She listened.

"I even wondered if this was a dream world—a figment of my imagination," he finished, "but I had to reject that when I went back to my own. I had rope marks on my wrists—my hair was soaking wet. You don't get that in a dream!"

"I hope not," she smiled. "We're different here, Lee, obviously. Our life doesn't have the—the *shape* that yours has. We haven't much direction, no real desires. We just—well—*exist*. It's as if we're waiting for something to happen. As if—" she paused and seemed to be looking down deep into herself. "Put it this way—Farlowe thinks you're the key figure in some development that's happening here. Supposing—supposing we were some kind of—of experiment..."

"Experiment? How do you mean?"

"Well, from what you say, the people at the fortress have an advanced science that we don't know about. Supposing our parents, say, had been kidnapped from your world and—made to think—what's the word—"

"Conditioned?"

"Yes, conditioned to think they were natives of this world. We'd have grown up knowing nothing different. Maybe the Man Without A Navel is a member of an alien race—a scientist of some kind in charge of the experiment."

"But why should they make such a complicated experiment?"

"So they could study us, I suppose."

Seward marvelled at her deductive powers. She had come to a much firmer theory than he had. But then he thought, she might subconsciously *know* the truth. Everyone knew much more than they knew, as it were. For instance, it was pretty certain that the secret of the tranquilomat was locked somewhere down in his unconscious if only he could get at it. Her explanation was logical and worth thinking about.

"You may be right," he said. "If so, it's something to go on. But it doesn't stop my reliance on the drug—or the fact that the Man and his helpers are probably telepathic and are at this moment looking for me."

She nodded. "Could there be an *antidote* for the drug?"

"Unlikely. Drugs like that don't really need antidotes—they're not like poisons. There must be some way of getting at the people in the fortress—some way of putting a stop to their plans. What about an organised revolution? What has Farlowe tried to do?"

"Nothing much. The people aren't easy to organise. We haven't much to do with one another. Farlowe was probably hoping you could help—think of something he hasn't. Maybe one of those machines you mentioned would work against the fortress people?"

"No, I don't think so. Anyway, the hallucinomats are too big to move from one place to another by hand—let alone from one world to another."

"And you haven't been able to build a tranquilomat yet?"

"No—we have a lot of experimental machines lying around at the lab—they're fairly small—but it's a question of modifying them—that's what I'm trying to do at the moment. If I could make one that works it would solve part of my problem—it would save my world and perhaps even save yours, if you *are* in a state of conditioning."

"It sounds reasonable," she dropped her eyes and looked at her drink. She held the glass balanced on her knees which were pressed closely together, nearly touching him. "But," she said, "they're going to catch you sooner or later. They're very powerful. They're sure to catch you. Then they'll make you agree to their idea."

"Why are you so certain?"

"I know them."

He let that go. She said: "Another drink?" and got up.

"Yes please." He got up, too, and extended his glass, then went closer to her. She put bottle and glass on the table and looked into his face. There was compassion, mystery, tenderness in her large, dark eyes. He smelled her perfume, warm, pleasant. He put his arms around her and kissed her. "My room," she said. They went upstairs.

Later that night, feeling strangely revitalised, he left the bed and the sleeping Martha and went and stood beside the window overlooking the silent park. He felt cold and he picked up his shirt and trousers, put them on. He sighed. He felt his mind clear and his body relax. He must work out a way of travelling from this world to his own at will—that might put a stop to the plans of the Man Without A Navel.

He turned guiltily as he heard the door open. Sally was standing there. She wore a long, white, flowing nightdress.

"Lee! I came to tell mummy—what are you doing in here?" Her eyes were horrified, accusing him. Martha sat up suddenly.

"Sally—what's the matter!"

Lee stepped forward. "Listen, Sally. Don't—"

Sally shrugged, but tears had come to her eyes. "I thought you wanted *me*! Now I know—I shouldn't have brought you here. Farlowe said—"

"What did Farlowe say?"

"He said you'd want to marry me!"

"But that's ridiculous. How could he say that? I'm a stranger here. You were to hide me from the fortress people, that's all."

But she had only picked up one word. "Ridiculous. Yes, I suppose it is, when my own mother..."

"Sally—you'd better go to bed. We'll discuss it in the morning," said Martha softly. "What was it you came in about?"

Sally laughed theatrically. "It doesn't matter now." She slammed the door.

Seward looked at Martha. "I'm sorry, Martha."

"It wasn't your fault—or mine. Sally's romantic and young."

"And jealous," Seward sat down on the bed. The feeling of comfort, of companionship, of bringing some order out of chaos—it had all faded. "Look, Martha, I can't stay here."

"You're running away?"

"If you like—but—well—the two of you—I'm in the middle."

"I guessed that. No you'd better stay. We'll work something out."

"Okay." He got up, sighing heavily. "I think I'll go for a walk in the park—it may help me to think. I'd just reached the stage where I was getting somewhere. Thanks for that, anyway, Martha."

She smiled. "Don't worry, Lee. I'll have everything running smoothly again by tomorrow."

He didn't doubt it. She was a remarkable woman.

He put on his socks and shoes, opened the door and went out onto the landing. Moonlight entered through a tall, slender window at the end. He went down the two flights of stairs and out of the front door. He turned into the lane and entered the arbour. In the cool of the night, he once again was able to begin some constructive thinking.

While he was on this world, he would not waste his time, he would keep trying to discover the necessary modifications to make the tranquilomats workable.

He wandered through the arbour, keeping any thoughts of the two women out of his mind. He turned into another section of the arbour he hadn't noticed before. The turnings became numerous but he was scarcely aware of them. It was probably some sort of child's maze.

He paused as he came to a bench. He sat down and folded his arms in front of him, concentrating on his problem.

Much later he heard a sound to his right and looked up.

A man he didn't know was standing there, grinning at him.

Seward noticed at once that the man had overlong canines, that he smelled of damp earth and decay. He wore a black, polo-neck pullover and black, stained trousers. His face was waxen and very pale.

"I've been looking for you for ages, Professor Seward," said the Vampire.

5

Seward got up and faced the horrible creature. The Vampire continued to smile. He didn't move. Seward felt revulsion.

"It's been a long journey," said the Vampire in a sibilant voice like the sound of a frigid wind blowing through dead boughs. "I had intended to visit you at the fortress, but when I got to your room you had left. I was disappointed."

"Doubtless," said Seward. "Well, you've had a wasted journey. I'm not going back there until I'm ready."

"That doesn't interest me."

"What does?" Seward tried to stop himself from trembling.

The Vampire put his hands into his pockets. "Only you."

"Get away from here. You're outnumbered—I have friends." But he knew that his tone was completely unconvincing.

The Vampire hissed his amusement. "They can't do much, Seward."

"What are you—some sort of android made to frighten people?"

"No." The Vampire took a pace forward.

Suddenly he stopped as a voice came faintly from somewhere in the maze.

"Lee! Lee! Where are you?"

It was Sally's voice.

"Stay away, Sally!" Lee called.

"But I was going to warn you. I saw the Vampire from the window. He's somewhere in the park."

"I know. Go home!"

"I'm sorry about the scene, Lee. I wanted to apologise. It was childish."

"It doesn't matter." He looked at the Vampire. He was standing in a relaxed position, hands in pockets, smiling. "Go home, Sally!"

"She won't, you know," whispered the Vampire.

Her voice was closer. "Lee, I must talk to you."

He screamed: "Sally—the Vampire's here. Go home. Warn your mother, not me. Get some help if you can—but go home!"

Now he saw her enter the part of the maze he was in. She gasped as she saw them. He was between her and the Vampire.

"Sally—do what I told you."

But the Vampire's cold eyes widened and he took one hand out of his pocket and crooked a finger. "Come here, Sally."

She began to walk forward.

He turned to the Vampire. "What do you want?"

"Only a little blood—yours, perhaps—or the young lady's."

"Damn you. Get away. Go back, Sally." She didn't seem to hear him.

He daren't touch the cold body, the earth-damp clothes. He stepped directly between the girl and the Vampire.

He felt sick, but he reached out his hands and shoved at the creature's body. Flesh yielded, but bone did not. The Vampire held his ground, smiling, staring beyond Seward at the girl.

Seward shoved again and suddenly the creature's arms clamped around him and the grinning, fanged face darted towards his. The thing's breath disgusted him. He struggled, but could not break the Vampire's grasp.

A cold mouth touched his neck. He yelled and kicked. He felt a tiny pricking against his throat. Sally screamed. He heard her turn and run and felt a fraction of relief.

He punched with both fists as hard as he could into the creature's solar plexus. It worked. The Vampire groaned and let go. Seward was disgusted to see that its fangs dripped with blood.

His blood.

Now rage helped him. He chopped at the Vampire's throat. It gasped, tottered, and fell in a sprawl of loose limbs to the ground.

Panting, Seward kicked it in the head. It didn't move.

He bent down and rolled the Vampire over. As far as he could tell it was dead. He tried to remember what he'd read about legendary vampires. Not much.

Something about a stake through its heart. Well, that was out.

But the thought that struck him most was that he had fought one of the fortress people—and had won. It was possible to beat them!

He walked purposefully through the maze. It wasn't as tortuous as he'd supposed. Soon he emerged at the arbour entrance near the house. He saw Sally and Martha running towards him. Behind them, another figure lumbered. Farlowe. He had got here fast.

"Seward," he shouted. "They said the Vampire had got you!"

"I got him," said Seward as they came up and stopped.

"What?"

"I beat him."

"But—that's impossible."

Seward shrugged. He felt elated. "Evidently, it's possible," he said. "I knocked him out. He seems to be dead—but I suppose you never know with vampires."

Farlowe was astonished. "I believe you," he said, "but it's fantastic. How did you do it?"

"I got frightened and then angry," said Seward simply. "Maybe you've been overawed by these people too long."

"It seems like it," Farlowe admitted. "Let's go and have a look at him. Sally and Martha had better stay behind."

Seward led him back through the maze. The Vampire was still where he'd fallen. Farlowe touched the corpse with his foot.

"That's the Vampire all right." He grinned. "I knew we had a winner in you, son. What are you going to do now?"

"I'm going straight back to the fortress and get this worked out once and for all. Martha gave me an idea yesterday evening and she may well be right. I'm going to try and find out anyway."

"Better not be over-confident, son."

"Better than being over-cautious."

"Maybe," Farlowe agreed doubtfully. "What's this idea Martha gave you?"

"It's really her idea, complete. Let her explain. She's an intelligent woman—and she's bothered to think about this problem from scratch. I'd advise you to do the same."

"I'll hear what it is, first. Let's deal with the Vampire and then get back to the house."

"I'll leave the Vampire to you. I want to use your car."

"Why?"

"To go back to the fortress."

"Don't be a fool. Wait until we've got some help."

"I can't wait that long, Farlowe. I've got other work to do back on my own world."

"Okay," Farlowe shrugged.

Farlowe faded.

The maze began to fade.

Explosions in the brain.

Vertigo.

Sickness.

His head ached and he could not breathe. He yelled, but he had no voice. Multicoloured explosions in front of his eyes. He was whirling round and round, spinning rapidly. Then he felt a new surface dragging at his feet. He closed his eyes and stumbled against something. He fell onto something soft.

It was his camp-bed. He was back in his laboratory.

Seward wasted no time wondering what had happened. He knew more or less. Possibly his encounter with the Vampire had sent him back—the exertion or—of course—the creature had drawn some of his blood. Maybe that was it. He felt the pricking sensation, still. He went to the mirror near the wash-stand. He could just see the little marks in his neck. Further proof that wherever that world was it was as real as the one he was in now.

He went to the table and picked up his notes, then walked into the other room. In one section was a long bench. On it, in various stages of dismantling, were the machines that he had been working on, the tranquilomats that somehow just didn't work. He picked up one of the smallest and checked its batteries, its lenses and its sonic agitator. The idea with this one was to use a combination of light and sound to agitate certain dormant cells in the brain. Long since, psychophysicists had realised that mental abnormality had a chemical as well as a mental cause. Just as a patient with a psychosomatic illness produced all the biological symptoms of whatever disease he thought he had, so did chemistry play a part in brain disorders. Whether the change in the brain cells came first or afterwards they weren't sure. But the fact was that the cells could be agitated and the mind, by a mixture of hypnosis and conditioning, could be made to work normally. But it was a long step from knowing this and being able to use the information in the construction of tranquilomats.

Seward began to work on the machine. He felt he was on the right track, at least.

But how long could he keep going before his need for the drug destroyed his will?

He kept going some five hours before his withdrawal symptoms got the better of him.

He staggered towards one of the drug-drawers and fumbled out an ampoule of M-A 19. He staggered into his bedroom and reached for the needle on the table.

He filled the syringe. He filled his veins. He filled his brain with a series of explosions which blew him clean out of his own world into the other.

Fire flew up his spine. Ignited back-brain, ignited mid-brain, ignited fore-brain. Ignited all centres.

EXPLOSION ALL CENTRES.

This time the transition was brief. He was standing in the part of the maze where he'd been when he'd left. The Vampire's corpse was gone. Farlowe had gone, also. He experienced a feeling of acute frustration that he couldn't continue with his work on KLTM-8—the tranquilomat he'd been modifying when his craving for the M-A 19 took over.

But there was something to do here, too.

He left the maze and walked towards the house. It was dawn and very cold. Farlowe's car was parked there. He noticed the licence number. It seemed different. It now said YOU 009. Maybe he'd mistaken the last digit for a zero last time he'd looked.

The door was ajar. Farlowe and Martha were standing in the hall.

They looked surprised when he walked in.

"I thought the Vampire was peculiar, son," said Farlowe. "But yours was the best vanishing act I've ever seen."

"Martha will explain that, too," Seward said, not looking at her. "Has she told you her theory?"

"Yes, it sounds feasible." He spoke slowly, looking at the floor. He looked up. "We got rid of the Vampire. Burned him up. He burns well."

"That's one out of the way, at least," said Seward. "How many others are there at the fortress?"

Farlowe shook his head. "Not sure. How many did you see?"

"The Man Without A Navel, a character called Brother Sebastian who wears a cowl and probably isn't human either, two pleasant gentlemen called Mr. Morl and Mr. Hand—and a man in fancy dress whose name I don't know."

"There are one or two more," Farlowe said. "But it's not their numbers we've got to worry about—it's their power!"

"I think maybe it's overrated," Seward said.

"You may be right, son."

"I'm going to find out."

"You still want my car?"

"Yes. If you want to follow up behind with whatever help you can gather, do that."

"I will." Farlowe glanced at Martha. "What do you think, Martha?"

"I think he may succeed," she said. "Good luck, Lee." She smiled at him in a way that made him want to stay.

"Right," said Seward. "I'm going. Hope to see you there."

"I may be wrong, Lee," she said warningly. "It was only an idea."

"It's the best one I've heard. Goodbye."

He went out of the house and climbed into the car.

6

The road was white, the sky was blue, the car was red and the countryside was green. Yet there was less clarity about the scenery than Seward remembered. Perhaps it was because he no longer had the relaxing company of Farlowe, because his mind was working furiously and his emotions at full blast.

Whoever had designed the set-up on this world had done it well, but had missed certain details. Seward realised that one of the "alien" aspects of the world was that everything was just a little too new. Even Farlowe's car looked as if it had just been driven off the production line.

By the early afternoon he was beginning to feel tired and some of his original impetus had flagged. He decided to move in to the side of the road and rest for a short time, stretch his legs. He stopped the car and got out.

He walked over to the other side of the road. It was on a hillside and he could look down over a wide, shallow valley. A river gleamed in the distance, there were cottages and livestock in the fields. He couldn't see the horizon. Far away he saw a great bank of reddish-looking clouds that seemed to swirl and seethe like a restless ocean. For all the *signs* of habitation, the countryside had taken on a desolate quality as if it had been abandoned. He could not believe that there were people living in the cottages and tending the livestock. The whole thing looked like the set for a film. Or a play—a complicated play devised by the Man Without A Navel and his friends—a play in which the fate of a world—possibly two worlds—was at stake.

How soon would the play resolve itself? he wondered, as he turned back towards the car.

A woman was standing by the car. She must have come down the hill while he was looking at the valley. She had long, jet-black hair and big, dark eyes. Her skin was tanned dark gold. She had full, extraordinarily sensuous lips. She wore a well-tailored red suit, a black blouse, black shoes and black handbag. She looked rather sheepish. She raised her head to look at him and as she did so a lock of her black hair fell over her eyes. She brushed it back.

"Hello," she said. "Am I lucky!"

"Are you?"

"I hope so. I didn't expect to find a car on the road. You haven't broken down, have you?" She asked this last question anxiously.

"No," he said. "I stopped for a rest. How did you get here?"

She pointed up the hill. "There's a little track up there—a cattle-track, I suppose. My car skidded and went into a tree. It's a wreck."

"I'll have a look at it for you."

She shook her head. "There's no point—it's a write-off. Can you give me a lift?"

"Where are you going?" he said unwillingly.

"Well, it's about sixty miles that way," she pointed in the direction he was going. "A small town."

It wouldn't take long to drive sixty miles on a road as clear as this with no apparent speed-limit. He scratched his head doubtfully. The woman was a diversion he hadn't expected and, in a way, resented. But she was very attractive.

He couldn't refuse her. He hadn't seen any cart-tracks leading off the road. This, as far as he knew, was the only one, but it was possible he hadn't noticed since he didn't know this world. Also, he decided, the woman evidently wasn't involved in the struggle between the fortress people and Farlowe's friends. She was probably just one of the conditioned, living out her life completely unaware of where she was and why. He might be able to get some information out of her.

"Get in," he said.

"Oh, thanks." She got in, seeming rather deliberately to show him a lot of leg. He opened his door and slid under the wheel. She sat uncomfortably close to him. He started the engine and moved the car out onto the road again.

"I'm a stranger here," he began conversationally. "What about you?"

"Not me—I've lived hereabouts all my life. Where do you come from—stranger?"

He smiled. "A long way away."

"Are they all as good-looking as you?" It was trite, but it worked. He felt flattered.

"Not any more," he said. That was true. Maniacs never looked very good. But this wasn't the way he wanted the conversation to go, however nice the direction. He said: "You're not very heavily populated around here. I haven't seen another car, or another person for that matter, since I set off this morning."

"It does get boring," she said. She smiled at him. That and her full body, her musky scent and her closeness, made him breathe more heavily than he would have liked. One thing about this world—the women were considerably less inhibited than on his own. It was a difference in population, perhaps. In an overcrowded world your social behaviour must be more rigid, out of necessity.

He kept his hands firmly on the wheel and his eyes on the road, convinced that if he didn't he'd lose control of himself and the car. The result might be a sort of femme fatality. His attraction towards Sally and Martha had not been wholly sexual. Yet he had never before experienced anything like the purely animal attraction which this woman radiated. Maybe, he decided, she didn't know it. He glanced at her. There again, maybe she did.

It said a lot for the woman if she could take his mind so completely off his various problems.

"My name's Magdalen," she smiled. "A bit of a mouthful. What's yours?"

It was a relief to find someone here who didn't already know his name. He rejected the unliked Lee and said: "Bill—Bill Ward."

"Short and sweet," she said. "Not like mine."

He grunted vaguely, consciously fighting the emotions rising in him. There was a word for them. A simple word—short and sweet—lust. He rather liked it. He'd been somewhat repressed on his home world and had kept a tight censorship on his feelings. Here it was obviously different.

A little later, he gave in. He stopped the car and kissed her. He was surprised at the ease with which he did it. He forgot about the tranquilomats, about the M-A 19, about the fortress. He forgot about everything except her, and that was maybe why he did what he did.

It was as if he was drawn into yet another world—a private world where only he and she had any existence. An enclosed world consisting only of their desire and their need to satisfy it.

Afterwards he felt gloomy, regretful and guilty. He started the car savagely. He knew he shouldn't blame her, but he did. He'd wasted time. Minutes were valuable, even seconds. He'd wasted hours.

Beside him she took a headscarf from her bag and tied it over her hair. "You're in a hurry."

He pressed the accelerator as far down as he could.

"What's the problem?" she shouted as the engine thudded noisily.

"I've wasted too much time already. I'll drop you off wherever it is you want."

"Oh, fine. Just one of those things, eh?"

"I suppose so. It was my fault, I shouldn't have picked you up in the first place."

She laughed. It wasn't a nice laugh. It was a mocking laugh and it seemed to punch him in the stomach.

"Okay," he said, "okay."

He switched on the headlamps as dusk became night. There was no milometer on the dashboard so he didn't know how far they'd travelled, but he was sure it was more than sixty miles.

"Where is this town?" he said.

"Not much further." Her voice softened. "I'm sorry, Lee. But what *is* the matter?"

Something was wrong. He couldn't place it. He put it down to his own anger.

"You may not know it," he said, "but I suspect that nearly all the people living here are being deceived. Do you know the fortress?"

"You mean that big building on the rock wastes?"

"That's it. Well, there's a group of people there who are duping you and the rest in some way. They want to destroy practically the whole of the human race by a particularly nasty method—and they want me to do it for them."

"What's that?"

Briefly, he explained.

Again she laughed. "By the sound of it, you're a fool to fight this Man Without A Navel and his friends. You ought to throw in your lot with them. You could be top man."

"Aren't you angry?" he said in surprise. "Don't you believe me?"

"Certainly. I just don't share your attitude. I don't understand you turning down a chance when it's offered. I'd take it. As I said, you could be top man."

"I've already been top man," he said, "in a manner of speaking. On my own world. I don't want that kind of responsibility. All I want to do is save something from the mess I've made of civilisation."

"You're a fool, Lee."

That was it. She shouldn't have known him as Lee but as Bill, the name he'd introduced himself by. He stopped the car suddenly and looked at her suspiciously. The truth was dawning on him and it made him feel sick at himself that he could have fallen for her trap.

"You're working for him, aren't you? The Man?"

"You seem to be exhibiting all the symptoms of persecution mania, Seward. You need a good psychiatrist." She spoke coolly and reached into her handbag. "I don't feel safe with you."

"It's mutual," he said. "Get out of the car."

"No," she said quietly. "I think we'll go all the way to the fortress together." She put both hands into her bag. They came out with two things. One was a half bottle of brandy.

The other was a gun.

"Evidently my delay tactics weren't effective enough," she mocked. "I thought they might not be, so I brought these. Get out, yourself, Seward."

"You're going to kill me?"

"Maybe."

"But that isn't what the Man wants, is it?"

She shrugged, waving the gun.

Trembling with anger at his own gullibility and impotence, he got out. He couldn't think clearly.

She got out, too, keeping him covered. "You're a clever man, Seward. You've worked out a lot."

"There are others here who know what I know."

"What do they know?"

"They know about the set-up—about the conditioning."

She came round the car towards him, shaking her head. Still keeping him covered, she put the brandy bottle down on the seat.

He went for the gun.

He acted instinctively, in the knowledge that this was his only chance. He heard the gun go off, but he was forcing her wrist back. He slammed it down on the side of the car. She yelled and dropped it. Then he did what he had never thought he could do. He hit her, a short, sharp jab under the chin. She crumpled.

He stood over her, trembling. Then he took her headscarf and tied her limp hands behind her. He dragged her up and dumped her in the back of the car. He leaned down and found the gun. He put it in his pocket.

Then he got into the driving seat, still trembling. He felt something hard under him. It was the brandy bottle. It was what he needed. He unscrewed the cap and took a long drink.

His brain began to explode even as he reached for the ignition.

It seemed to crackle and flare like burning timber. He grabbed the door handle. Maybe if he walked around...

He felt his knees buckle as his feet touched the ground. He strained to keep himself upright. He forced himself to move round the car. When he reached the bonnet, the headlamps blared at him, blinded him.

They began to blink rapidly into his eyes. He tried to raise his hands and cover his eyes. He fell sideways, the light still blinking. He felt nausea sweep up and through him. He saw the car's licence plate in front of him.

YOU 099

YOU 100

YOU 101

He put out a hand to touch the plate. It seemed normal. Yet the digits were clocking up like the numbers on an adding machine.

Again his brain exploded. A slow, leisurely explosion that subsided and brought a delicious feeling of well-being.

Green clouds like boiled jade, scent of chrysanthemums. Swaying lilies. Bright lines of black and white in front of his eyes. He shut them and opened them again. He was looking up at the blind in his bedroom.

As soon as he realised he was back, Seward jumped off the bed and made for the bench where he'd left the half-finished tranquilomat. He remembered something, felt for the gun he'd taken off the girl. It wasn't there.

But he felt the taste of the brandy in his mouth. Maybe it was as simple as that, he thought. Maybe all he needed to get back was alcohol.

There was sure to be some alcohol in the lab. He searched through cupboards and drawers until he found some in a jar. He filled a vial and corked it. He took off his shirt and taped the vial under his armpit—that way he might be able to transport it from his world to the other one.

Then he got down to work.

Lenses were reassembled, checked. New filters went in and old ones came out. He adjusted the resonators and amplifiers. He was recharging the battery which powered the transistorised circuits, when he sensed the mob outside. He left the little machine on the bench and went to the control board. He flicked three switches down and then, on impulse, flicked them off again. He went back to the bench and unplugged the charger. He took the machine to the window. He drew the blind up.

It was a smaller mob than usual. Evidently some of them had learned their lesson and were now avoiding the laboratory.

Far away, behind them, the sun glinted on a calm sea. He opened the window.

There was one good way of testing his tranquilomat. He rested it on the sill and switched it to ATTRACT. That was the first necessary stage, to hold the mob's attention. A faint, pleasant humming began to come from the machine. Seward knew that specially shaped and coloured lenses were whirling at the front. The mob looked up towards it, but only those in the centre of the group were held. The others dived away, hiding their eyes.

Seward felt his body tightening, growing cold. Part of him began to scream for the M-A 19. He clung to the machine's carrying handles. He turned a dial from Zero to 50. There were 100 units marked on the indicator. The machine was now sending at half-strength. Seward consoled himself that if anything went wrong he could not do any more harm to their ruined minds. It wasn't much of a consolation.

He quickly saw that the combined simulated brain-waves, sonic vibrations and light patterns were having some effect on their minds. But what was the effect going to be? They were certainly responding. Their bodies were relaxing, their faces were no longer twisted with insanity. But was the tranquilomat actually doing any constructive good—what it had been designed to do? He upped the output to 75 degrees.

His hand began to tremble. His mouth and throat were tight and dry. He couldn't keep going. He stepped back. His stomach ached. His bones ached. His eyes felt puffy. He began to move towards the machine again. But he couldn't make it. He moved towards the half-full ampoule of M-A 19 on the table. He filled the blunt hypodermic. He found a vein. He was weeping as the explosions hit his brain.

7

This time it was different.

He saw an army of machines advancing towards him. An army of malevolent hallucinomats. He tried to run, but a thousand electrodes were clamped to his body and he could not move. From nowhere, needles entered his veins. Voices shouted SEWARD! SEWARD! SEWARD! The hallucinomats advanced, shrilling, blinking, buzzing—*laughing*. The machines were laughing at him.

SEWARD!

Now he saw Farlowe's car's registration plate.

YOU 110

YOU 111

YOU 119

SEWARD!

YOU!

SEWARD!

His brain was being squeezed. It was contracting, contracting. The voices became distant, the machines began to recede. When they had vanished he saw he was standing in a circular room in the centre of which was a low dais. On the dais was a chair. In the chair was the Man Without A Navel. He smiled at Seward.

"Welcome back, old boy," he said.

Brother Sebastian and the woman, Magdalen, stood close to the dais. Magdalen's smile was cool and merciless, seeming to anticipate some new torture that the Man and Brother Sebastian had devised.

But Seward was jubilant. He was sure his little tranquilomat had got results.

"I think I've done it," he said quietly. "I think I've built a workable tranquilomat—and, in a way, it's thanks to you. I had to speed my work up to beat you—and I did it!"

They seemed unimpressed.

"Congratulations, Seward," smiled the Man Without A Navel. "But this doesn't alter the situation, you know. Just because you *have* an antidote doesn't mean we have to use it."

Seward reached inside his shirt and felt for the vial taped under his arm. It had gone. Some of his confidence went with the discovery.

Magdalen smiled. "It was kind of you to drink the drugged brandy."

He put his hands in his jacket pocket.

The gun was back there. He grinned.

"What's he smiling at?" Magdalen said nervously.

"I don't know. It doesn't matter. Brother Sebastian, I believe you have finished work on your version of Seward's hypnomat?"

"I have," said the sighing, cold voice.

"Let's have it in. It is a pity we didn't have it earlier. It would have saved us time—and Seward all his efforts."

The curtains behind them parted and Mr. Hand, Mr. Morl and the Laughing Cavalier wheeled in a huge, bizarre machine that seemed to have a casing of highly polished gold, silver and platinum. There were two sets of lenses in its domed, headlike top. They looked like eyes staring at Seward.

Was this a conditioning machine like the ones they'd probably used on the human populace? Seward thought it was likely. If they got him with that, he'd be finished. He pulled the gun out of his pocket. He aimed it at the right-hand lens and pulled the trigger.

The gun roared and kicked in his hand, but no bullet left the muzzle. Instead there came a stream of small, brightly coloured globes, something like those used in the attraction device on the tranquilomat. They sped towards the machine, struck it, exploded. The machine buckled and shrilled. It steamed and two discs, like lids, fell across the lenses. The machine rocked backwards and fell over.

The six figures began to converge on him, angrily.

Suddenly, on his left, he saw Farlowe, Martha and Sally step from behind a screen.

"Help me!" he cried to them.

"We can't!" Farlowe yelled. "Use your initiative, son!"

"Initiative?" He looked down at the gun. The figures were coming closer. The Man Without A Navel smiled slowly. Brother Sebastian tittered. Magdalen gave a low, mocking laugh that seemed—strangely—to be a criticism of his sexual prowess. Mr. Morl and Mr. Hand retained their mournful and cheerful expressions respectively. The Laughing Cavalier flung back his head and—laughed. All around them the screens, which had been little more than head-high were lengthening, widening, stretching up and up.

He glanced back. The screens were growing.

He pulled the trigger of the gun. Again it bucked, again it roared—and from the muzzle came a stream of metallic-grey particles which grew into huge flowers. The flowers burst into flame and formed a wall between him and the six.

He peered around him, looking for Farlowe and the others. He couldn't find them. He heard Farlowe's shout: "Good luck, son!" He heard Martha and Sally crying goodbye.

"Don't go!" he yelled.

Then he realised he was alone. And the six were beginning to advance again—malevolent, vengeful.

Around him the screens, covered in weird designs that curled and swirled, ever-changing, were beginning to topple inwards. In a moment he would be crushed.

Again he heard his name being called. SEWARD! SEWARD!

Was it Martha's voice? He thought so.

"I'm coming," he shouted, and pulled the trigger again.

The Man Without A Navel, Magdalen, Brother Sebastian, the Laughing Cavalier, Mr. Hand and Mr. Morl—all screamed in unison and began to back away from him as the gun's muzzle spouted a stream of white fluid which floated into the air.

Still the screens were falling, slowly, slowly.

The white fluid formed a net of millions of delicate strands. It drifted over the heads of the six. It began to descend. They looked up and screamed again.

"Don't, Seward," begged the Man Without A Navel. "Don't, old man—I'll make it worth your while."

Seward watched as the net engulfed them. They struggled and cried and begged.

It did not surprise him much when they began to shrink.

No! *They* weren't shrinking—he was growing. He was growing over the toppling screens. He saw them fold inwards. He looked down and the screens were like cards folding neatly over the six little figures struggling in the white net. Then, as the screens folded down, the figures were no longer in sight. It got lighter. The screens rolled themselves into a ball.

The ball began to take on a new shape.

It changed colour. And then, there it was—a perfectly formed human skull.

Slowly, horrifyingly, the skull began to gather flesh and blood and muscles to itself. The stuff flowed over it. Features began to appear. Soon, in a state of frantic terror, Seward recognised the face.

It was his own.

His own face, its eyes wide, its lips parted. A tired, stunned, horrified face.

He was back in the laboratory. And he was staring into a mirror.

He stumbled away from the mirror. He saw he wasn't holding a gun in his hand but a hypodermic needle. He looked round the room.

The tranquilomat was still on the window-sill. He went to the window. There, quietly talking among the ruins below, was a group of sane men and women. They were still in rags, still gaunt. But they were sane. That was evident. They were saner than they had ever been before.

He called down to them, but they didn't hear him.

Time for that later, he thought. He sat on the bed, feeling dazed and relieved. He dropped the needle to the floor, certain he wouldn't need to use it again.

It was incredible, but he thought he knew where he had been. The final image of his face in the mirror had given him the last clue.

He had been inside his own mind. The M-A 19 was merely an hallucinogenic after all. A powerful one, evidently, if it could give him the illusion of rope marks on his wrists, bites on his neck and the rest.

He had escaped into a dream world.

Then he wondered—but why? What good had it done?

He got up and went towards the mirror again.

Then he heard the voice. Martha's voice.

SEWARD! SEWARD! Seward, listen to me!

No, he thought desperately. No, it can't be starting again. There's no need for it.

He ran into the laboratory, closing the door behind him, locking it. He stood there, trembling, waiting for the withdrawal symptoms. They didn't come.

Instead he saw the walls of the laboratory, the silent computers and meters and dials, begin to blur. A light flashed on above his head. The dead banks of instruments suddenly came alive. He sat down in a big chrome, padded chair which had originally been used for the treating of test-subjects.

His gaze was caught by a whirling stroboscope that had appeared from nowhere. Coloured images began to form in front of his eyes. He struggled to get up but he couldn't.

YOU 121

YOU 122

YOU 123

Then the first letter changed to a V.

VOU 127

SEWARD!

His eyelids fell heavily over his eyes.

"Professor Seward." It was Martha's voice. It spoke to someone else. "We may be lucky, Tom. Turn down the volume."

He opened his eyes.

"Martha."

The woman smiled. She was dressed in a white coat and was leaning over the chair. She looked very tired. "I'm not—Martha—Professor Seward. I'm Doctor Kalin. Remember?"

"Doctor Kalin, of course."

His body felt weaker than it had ever felt before. He leaned back in the big chair and sighed. Now he was remembering.

It had been his decision to make the experiment. It had seemed to be the only way of speeding up work on the development of the tranquilomats. He knew that the secret of a workable machine was imbedded in the deepest level of his unconscious mind. But, however much he tried—hypnosis, symbol-association, word-association—he couldn't get at it.

There was only one way he could think of—a dangerous experiment for him—an experiment which might not work at all. He would be given a deep-conditioning, made to believe that he had brought disaster to the world and must remedy it by devising a tranquilomat. Things were pretty critical in the world outside, but they weren't as bad as they had conditioned him to believe. Work on the tranquilomats *was* falling behind—but there had been no widespread disaster, *yet.* It was bound to come unless they could devise some means of mass-cure for the thousands of neurotics and victims of insanity. An antidote for the results of mass-tension.

So, simply, they conditioned him to think his efforts had destroyed civilisation. He must devise a working tranquilomat. They had turned the problem from an intellectual one into a personal one.

The conditioning had apparently worked.

He looked around the laboratory at his assistants. They were all alive, healthy, a bit tired, a bit strained, but they looked relieved.

"How long have I been under?" he asked.

"About fourteen hours. That's twelve hours since the experiment went wrong."

"Went wrong?"

"Why, yes," said Doctor Kalin in surprise. "Nothing was happening. We tried to bring you round—we tried every darned machine and drug in the place—nothing worked. We expected catatonia. At least we've managed to save you. We'll just have to go on using the ordinary methods of research, I suppose." Her voice was tired, disappointed.

Seward frowned. But he *had* got the results. He knew exactly how to construct a working tranquilomat. He thought back.

"Of course," he said. "I was only conditioned to believe that the world was in ruins and I had done it. There was nothing about—about—the *other* world."

"What other world?" Macpherson, his Chief Assistant asked the question.

Seward told them. He told them about the Man Without A Navel, the fortress, the corridors, the tortures, the landscapes seen from Farlowe's car, the park, the maze, the Vampire, Magdalen... He told them how, in what he now called Condition A, he had believed himself hooked on a drug called M-A 19.

"But we don't have a drug called M-A 19," said Doctor Kalin.

"I know that now. But I didn't know that and it didn't matter. I would have found something to have made the journey into—the other world—a world existing only in my skull. Call it Condition B, if you like—or Condition X, maybe. The unknown. I found a fairly logical means of making myself *believe* I was entering another world. That was M-A 19. By inventing symbolic characters who were trying to stop me, I made myself work harder. Unconsciously I knew that Condition A was going wrong—so I escaped into Condition B in order to put right the damage. By acting out the drama I was able to clear my mind of its confusion. I had, as I suspected, the secret of the tranquilomat somewhere down there all the time. Condition A failed to release that secret—Condition B succeeded. I can build you a workable tranquilomat, don't worry."

"Well," Macpherson grinned. "I've been told to use my imagination in the past—but you *really* used yours!"

"That was the idea, wasn't it? We'd decided it was no good just using drugs to keep us going. We decided to use our drugs and hallucinomats directly, to condition me to believe that what we feared will happen *had* happened."

"I'm glad we didn't manage to bring you back to normality, in that case," Doctor Kalin smiled. "You've had a series of classic—if more complicated than usual—nightmares. The Man Without A Navel, as you call him, and his 'allies' symbolised the elements in you that were holding you back from the truth—diverting you. By 'defeating' the Man, you defeated those elements."

"It was a hell of a way to get results," Seward grinned. "But I got them. It was probably the only way. Now we can produce as many tranquilomats as we need. The problem's over. I've—in all modesty—" he grinned, "saved the world before it needed saving. It's just as well."

"What about your 'helpers,' though," said Doctor Kalin helping him from the chair. He glanced into her intelligent, mature face. He had always liked her.

"Maybe," he smiled, as he walked towards the bench where the experimental tranquilomats were laid out, "maybe there was quite a bit of wish-fulfilment mixed up in it as well."

"It's funny how you didn't realise that it wasn't real, isn't it?" said Macpherson behind him.

"Why is it funny?" He turned to look at Macpherson's long, worn face. "Who knows what's real, Macpherson? This world? That world? Any other world? I don't feel so adamant about this one, do you?"

"Well..." Macpherson said doubtfully. "I mean, you're a trained psychiatrist as well as everything else. You'd think you'd recognise your own symbolic characters?"

"I suppose it's possible." Macpherson had missed his point. "All the same," he added. "I wouldn't mind going back there some day. I'd quite enjoy the exploration. And I liked some of the people. Even though they were probably wish-fulfilment figures. Farlowe—father—it's possible." He glanced up as his eye fell on a meter. It consisted of a series of code-letters and three digits. VOU 128 it said now. There was Farlowe's number-plate. His mind had turned the V into a Y. He'd probably discover plenty of other symbols around, which he'd turned into something else in the other world. He still couldn't think of it as a dream world. It had seemed so real. For him, it was still real.

"What about the woman—Martha?" Doctor Kalin said. "You called *me* Martha as you were waking up."

"We'll let that one go for the time being," he grinned. "Come on, we've still got a lot of work to do."

The Birds of the Moon (1995)

"The Birds of the Moon" is, by a narrow margin, probably my favourite Michael Moorcock story. It was originally commissioned for, submitted to (on time) and apparently accepted by the magazine *New Statesman & Society*.

For some reason, however, it never appeared.

It was to have formed part of a special feature which the magazine had intended to run on the twenty-fifth anniversary of the Glastonbury music festival.

The issue in question was due for publication on 23rd June, 1995, two days after the Summer Solstice which, for a quarter of a century, had loomed large over Glastonbury and its folklore.

Having missed this window, the story was to have awaited publication as the epilogue to *Fabulous Harbours* later in 1995.

So, upon its non-appearance in *New Statesman & Society*, I wasted no time in asking if I could publish the story first in its own one-off edition.

Not long after that—and not *that* long after the event it was written to commemorate—it was finally published by Jayde Design in July 1995.

A Travellers' Tale

For Jon Trux

The established migratory patterns of certain species of birds are now well understood. While some birds fly South in the Winter or North in the Summer, others migrate regularly to the Moon where, at the warm heart of our Satellite, they feed off a rich diet of moon-worms and other grubs. The great under-ground Gardens of the Moon, developed from the natural character of the Asteroid by generations of settlers, are a source of wonder to all travellers privileged to visit them.

James Audubon,
The Birds of the Moon
New Orleans, 1926

I Avoiding Diversions

Tommy Beck pulled the Tranny over to the side of the road and brought it to a careful stop with the engine running. He needed some sleep. Against the grey horizon and the rising sun, a milk float and a breakdown lorry had looked like a police blockade. He folded back his map and checked his route. He needed to start turning west just after Witney, following the invisible lines as best he could, taking the roads they most closely paralleled. He hoped this time he would get where he wanted to go. Every summer for twenty-three years he had retraced their journey back and forth across the country, trying to match exactly the meandering route he and Joany and the kids had taken for Glastonbury and the first festival.

Even his friends weren't too sure of Tommy's sanity. People thought Joany had run off. Someone had even said he'd abused his children.

Tommy knew what had really happened. He ignored the scepticism, the antagonism, the zealots who wanted to use his experience for themselves. He kept his own counsel and his own course.

Since that first Glastonbury Tommy Beck had attempted to reproduce their original route. He spent much of his spare time reading and studying for it. Every year he arrived at Glastonbury Tor and climbed to where caution had betrayed him, where he had seen the air, stinking of roses and vanilla, seal itself over an impossible view, separating him from his wife and children, dooming him to all these years of self-disgust and obsession. He knew what had happened, even if he no longer spoke of it to anyone. He had last seen Joany and the kids standing on that broad band of road, like a wide shaft of moonlight, arcing into the richly coloured darkness of the ether: he had the impression of great caravans of people and animals flowing back and forth, as if every creature that had ever existed was still alive.

Tommy Beck had always been of a practical disposition, valuable to the communes he joined. He smoked a modest amount of dope and did the odd tab of acid only if it was really good. He was widely read and could repair any small engine ever made. His attraction to Glastonbury had been entirely social. He had never been prepared for what had happened twenty-four years ago.

In their old Commer van, full of friends, looking forward to listening to some music and having a good time in the sun, they had left their Notting Dale squat and headed west. It felt wonderful, as if the millennium were just around the corner. If they hadn't quite made it to a universal utopia, at least they seemed to be on the right road. Ultimately they might even stop the Vietnam War and see a world at peace.

Tommy woke up suddenly. A young policeman was banging on his passenger door. Tommy got ready for the familiar ritual.

The copper wasn't about to start anything. "You all right, mate?"

"Yeah," said Tommy. "I got a bit tired driving."

"If you need to kip there's a lay-by about half a mile up the road."

"Gotcher," said Tommy, putting the van into gear. "Thanks, mate."

And he drove to the lay-by, wondering if pulling in at all had been a mistake. They hadn't stopped here the first time they went to Glastonbury.

They hadn't planned on this long a journey.

2 Alternative Routes

He moved through the fair, smiling vaguely, greeting old acquaintances, pausing at stalls to inspect anything which resembled a map. All the regulars knew him. Most welcomed him, but others were impatient with his obsession and dismissed his quietly intense questions. Some were convinced he'd murdered his family. A lot believed privately that Joany had simply got tired of living with a loony.

Tommy kept listening to the music from the stage. He was hoping to hear what he had heard that first time, as they stood on the crest of the Tor, wondering at the sudden silence, the sense of expectation. The music, they thought, had been nothing more than a penny whistle, a Celtic drum and high, melodic voices.

They had begun the climb in darkness, somehow avoiding all barriers, all witnesses, the kids scrambling up ahead while Tommy and Joany followed, hand in hand. They planned to watch the sun rise.

They had half-expected to be stopped. In the silver pre-dawn light they paused on the path to look back. There were camps down there which they didn't recognise. Morning smoke was mingling with the thick mist. Tommy thought he heard horses. Harness.

There was no sign of the festival. They might have been the only human beings in the world. Tommy sniffed at the scented, dew-laden grass and lush foliage, looking up just as the first rays touched the chapel stones. The ruin was in better condition than he expected. He glanced around. The children were just out of sight. He heard Joany call to them, drawing their attention to the view.

The water was everywhere now. A wide, glinting marsh, from which birds rose suddenly, their wings noisy against the warming air. Tommy thought he saw a small boat moving in the reeds. There were what looked like thatched outbuildings raised on platforms above the water. He saw no roads, no real houses. Apart from the hills, nothing was familiar.

"Joany?"

There was a quick, unfamiliar pulse in his head, a chill in his bones.

"Joany?"

"It's amazing, isn't it," she said. "Now I know why they said the view was worth it. Nothing's changed!"

She was excited, thoroughly at ease with what was beginning to alarm Tommy. The mist from the water rose around the base of the Tor like a tide, creating this eery illusion. He remembered coming into Yarmouth years before, when a sea-fog filled the streets, wiping out the new concrete and emphasising the old, red brick, so that the entire town looked as it had at the height of its Edwardian success. It was odd. He couldn't distinguish as much as a power line. Pulling himself together he turned to look up. The kids were staring at the tower and wondering if they were allowed to go in. Joany was just behind them. She turned enquiringly to Tommy.

He spread his hands. He had understood the place to be National Trust which you could only officially visit at certain times. But there were no notices, no signs or warnings, no fences.

Butch was pressing his grubby fists against an oiled oak door whose hinges, of beaten iron, glinted like new. Climbing closer to the tower, Tommy admired the restoration job. He hadn't realised they had done so much. It was very different from the outline you saw below. It seemed much slenderer, and there was an extraordinary glow to the limestone. The oriental origins of the Gothic style were obvious. The doorway was as beautiful as anything Tommy had seen in Granada or Marrakech. The windows' rich stained glass burned with vibrant light.

"Whoever built this place really loved it," said Joany. "I didn't realise it was so recent, did you?"

"I'll have to take a guide book out when we get home," Tommy said. "It's an amazing building." He was tearful with enthusiasm. "Look how that roof curves, the cut of the slate, and the stonework. Imagine the skill of the blokes who made all this!"

"It's like a story." Joany followed the carving around the tower, where it joined the roof. "People on quests and stuff. Some of those King Arthur nuts probably paid for it." She knew a lot more about architecture than he did. "It's no older than the oldest pre-Raphaelite! But it's the work of real artists, you can tell. See, the glass has the same style—and it's in scenes. Joseph of Arimathea, I'd guess. And Sir Percival, or someone like him. And the Grail, of course, it's in all seven of these windows. Some romantic Birmingham ironmaster or Liverpool soap-maker commissioned this. There's a William Morris design like it at the V&A. Blimey! That cross must be pure gold!"

The crimson sun had touched the spire. Tommy guessed there were strips of brass and copper in the roof. It seemed blood streamed down all four quadrants. The cross was unfamiliar, probably Celtic, possibly pagan, hard to see. The sun was above the horizon now, flecking the ruby water with skipping gold and silver. The pole houses were black outlines. Figures moved on the platforms, getting into little boats. A light breeze rippled the water. The whole scene blazed, almost blinding him.

Tommy was still waiting for the mist to clear and reveal the evidence of civilisation when Butch shouted "It opens, Mum!" and slipped inside the unlatched door, Liz at his heels.

Joany dived after them, but the door was hard to push wider and she was still trying to struggle in when Tommy arrived. "Give it a shove, love, I'm stuck."

Tommy found that the door moved easily under his hand. "You must have loosened it up, like a jar top," he said as they entered. "Don't touch anything, you two."

It was a relief not to be looking at that weird landscape.

Tommy was fond of saying that he didn't have a mystical bone in his body. He had never been interested in all that crap about Arthur and Glastonbury and ley-lines. But if that was what inspired the pre-Raphaelites to build this, it must have had something going for it.

As they got used to the jewelled gloom of the chapel, the kids fell silent with delight. Rustling silk banners, embroidered in extraordinary colours, hung from a central brass bracket suspended over a small altar of carved granite worked with silver, gold, iron and copper. The blazing windows, the richest glass Tommy had ever seen, were even more impressive from within, showing what he took to be various aspects of the Grail legend. With their intricate detail and accuracy of observation, the postures of the stylised figures displaying enormous meaning, they were the work of a master artist, with a powerful, indefinable spiritual content Tommy had never noticed in ordinary church art.

In Brookgate, where Tommy came from, near the Old Sweden Street market, most pre-War churches had been bombed and the new ones had never interested him. After his first tab of acid, at fourteen, he'd never needed an old building for a buzz.

Tommy noticed a goblet standing on the altar. By the style of the designs around the rim, it was probably Jewish, though there were also Romano-Celtic motifs, now that he looked, and even Anglo-Saxon, and what might be Sanskrit and Chinese. The whole design was surprisingly coherent. He couldn't believe the Trust allowed something so valuable to be unprotected. The workmanship made it priceless, but the precious metals and gems alone were worth a million in cold cash.

The precision achieved with simple tools always amazed him. "It must be a fake," he said.

"What?" Joany was irritated by his interruption of the silence.

"The cup—the goblet there."

She turned, frowning. "What bloody cup?"

And then Butch had run up to the altar and was reaching for it.

Tommy controlled his impulse to shout. "Better not, Butchy," he said evenly. "It would take a lot of pocket money to repair that!" But Liz, younger and less responsive, was now also grabbing up at the cup.

"What are you talking about?" said Joany. "There's nothing there."

"You're barmy," said Tommy. "It's not exactly an Ovaltine mug. I bet this place is normally locked. We're probably trespassing."

"You're suddenly very respectful of private property." But she was grave. "It is beautiful. It would be horrible if somebody vandalised it."

Tommy crossed to the altar and picked up a protesting Lizzy as she struggled to put her tiny hands on the cup.

"What on Earth's got into you?" said Joany. "Don't spoil it, Tom. We're not doing any harm."

"Maybe it's a fake," said Tommy. "In which case it's still amazing. I'm just worried they'll think we were trying to pinch it."

She snatched Liz from him. "What have you been smoking?"

Liz was quiet. Her eyes over Joan's shoulder were fixed on the goblet. Butch had a similar expression. He was smiling.

Tommy Beck sighed and turned to look up at the windows, the intricate stone, the delicately carved wood worked with precious metals. "If all churches were like this," he said, "you couldn't keep me out of them. We'll have to come back here, Joan."

"As long as you don't start having visions," she said. She shifted Liz onto her other side and took his arm. "Are you really nervous someone'll do us for trespass? It's a church. They're supposed to be open to everybody."

"I don't want to spoil the holiday. We came for the music, remember."

Then Tommy screwed up his face at a sound, like a human voice's highest, loudest vibrato. "Christ! Some sort of alarm system. Come on everyone!" He got to the door and pulled it back. Joany and Liz went first, but Butch was slow. Tommy could hardly see. Security shutters were probably coming down. "Hurry up, lad."

They were outside, with the door slammed behind them, before Tommy realised Butch had pinched the cup.

He tried the latch. He pushed at the heavy oak. It had locked.

"I suppose we might as well just sit here now and wait for the police." Tommy was bitter.

When he looked, he hoped that at least the water would be gone.

The water was still there. Only the village had vanished.

3 Heavy Traffic

Tommy had no problem getting onto the Tor. He knew the whole area intimately, by night, by day, by the seasons. He could tell if a particular stone had been disturbed or a patch of wild-flowers failed to reseed. He was protective of the Tor. The Tor was his way back to Joany and the kids, to that moment when they had heard a soft humming sound, like a bee-swarm, and had gone round to the eastern side of the tower, Butch in the lead with his treasure held to his chest, and had seen the tall figure, thin as a Masai, her brooding eyes on the goblet, smiling at them, beckoning them forward. The humming now sounded human, and there was a pipe again, and a drum. A long way off... This woman was probably with a band...

The tall woman had a slender spear in her hand. She turned the spear and it seemed to expand, grow wider, until it formed a narrow doorway which opened onto teeming colour, swiftly changing shapes, an impression of myriad order, through which wound, like a moonbeam, a great silver road. Far away ahead on the road, tiny figures came and went as casually as if they strolled in Old Sweden Street on a Saturday afternoon. And there were other moonbeams, other roads, winding through that tapestry of restless colour. It was as if, suddenly, he was permitted a glimpse of actuality, a vision of wholeness.

The air reeked of roses and vanilla.

Tommy had felt a painful yearning, as if recollecting a forgotten loss. Even as Butch ran past the woman and through the gateway, brandishing the cup like a passport, Tommy was overcome with euphoria, a feeling of intense optimism as he realised the implications of what he had seen through that opening in the fabric of his own, small sphere of reality.

"No, Liz!" Joany went after the little girl. Now all three were through, staring ahead. The tall woman smiled and beckoned to Tommy. It was as if she could only keep the gate open for a little while.

Tommy looked into the teeming possibilities of suprareality and he suddenly hesitated. "Better not," he had said as the woman stepped through her own gateway, drew the spear back to her body and vanished.

Tommy closed his eyes, as if to dismiss a bad dream. When he opened them the water had gone. The landscape was familiar and modern. Everything was perfectly normal. He was alone.

Tommy's shout of agony had been heard across Glastonbury.

Twenty-four years later, Tommy Beck stood with his back against the cold stones of the ruined chapel and prayed to stare down through the mist and see wide water glinting. Far away, someone was tapping a drum to the thin sound of a penny whistle.

Standing where they had emerged from the door, Tommy began to retrace their steps round to the eastern side, where the sun was crimson against the pale blue horizon, where the woman with the spear had opened a gateway which Tommy had been too slow to enter.

For twenty-three years Tommy Beck had stood here at exactly the same time, trying to reproduce exactly the same movements, in exactly the same conditions which had granted them their original vision of the moonbeam road and then separated them.

"There's only one problem, old dear," said a voice from the other side of the wall. "You haven't got the Grail any more, have you? I've had the devil of a job tracking you down. I thought you lived in Brookgate."

"I haven't lived in Brookgate for nearly thirty years." Tommy controlled his fear. He hated mind-games. This bloke sounded like a weirdo, a sadist, maybe.

"I frequently fall down on the fine tuning." The speaker stepped from around the wall. "Well, you know, it's not exactly time travel we do, but that comes into it. I get confused. I have a message. Are you interested in resuming your relationship with your wife Joan and your kids Benjamin and Elizabeth?"

Tommy could only nod. He realised he had given up hope. This could be some foul practical joke.

The pale-haired messenger was dressed in a '60s-revival long, tight-waisted jacket, flared trousers and a frilly shirt. All the dandified aspects of the period. Tommy hated everything the style stood for.

"You look like an old crack dealer," he said. "I don't do that stuff. I didn't ask for any help in this."

"I was looking for you," declared the dandy, "but I went a bit off my route. I had no intention of getting up your nose. In any way."

"I think you'd better bugger off." Tommy was wild with despair.

"Don't worry about them," said the dandy, looking down at the stilt village. "Their superstitions tend to work in our favour."

From somewhere under his coat, the stranger produced a sword of dark, glowing iron. "Eternity awaits you."

He added: "You'll need the cup. It's in that black plastic bag at your feet. Go on, open it. You'll see it, if I can't. It's in your blood."

As Tommy Beck bent to pick up the Grail, the dandy lifted the heavy sword high above his head.

"Excalibur," he explained.

4 Abandoned Vehicle

The festival had been over a week before the police had time to trace the ownership of the abandoned Transit van.

Eventually a constable turned up in Sporting Club Square, Hammersmith, looking for a Mr. Thomas Beck and was told by Beck's flatmates that Tommy had gone to Glastonbury and had never returned.

They also mentioned Tommy's obsession, which they described as freak-burn, and when the officer passed this on to the sergeant and the sergeant had passed the report back to Somerset, Tommy was assumed to have wandered off with some bunch of like-minded loonies. There was nothing remarkable about his disappearance. He would turn up soon enough. They always did.

~ ~

THERE'S A ROAD between the worlds which shimmers and curves like an erratic moonbeam. It carries a multitude of travellers. Those of us able to walk such roads, and move back and forth at will across the myriad dimensions of existence, call this particular path The Grail. From a distance off, it resembles a mighty cup.

These paths are reproduced over and over again, in millions of scales, each slightly different, yet each a detailed version of the other. They weave the fabric of the multiverse together. They are the means by which human intercourse is achieved and the soul, as well as the species, sustained.

Ordinary people walk these roads. For them Time is not a linear medium and Space has a thousand dimensions. They live to taste the textures and music of the multiverse. They live to explore their experience and to share their wisdom with anyone who desires it. They are entirely purposeful. Their spirits are rich beyond our imagining. They are fully and immortally alive.

Other species also have come to inhabit the roads between the worlds. Many follow migratory paths, making long, difficult journeys between entire universes. Some use the paths only briefly, like the lemmings and the reindeer, or the birds which every year fly between Earth and the Moon. Some, like those who investigate the darkest depths of our struggling world, are always restless, perpetually seeking fresh roads through the myriad scales of space and time.

Such creatures call themselves the Just and they exist to make our noblest dreams come true.

The Cairene Purse (1990)

Moorcock's enduring love for North Africa has never been better nor more poignantly encapsulated than in the longest story in this collection, "The Cairene Purse," which was originally published in 1990, in an anthology, *Zenith 2* (Orbit), edited by David Garnett.

The Cairene Purse

1 Her First Fond Hope of Eden Blighted

On the edge of the Nile's fertile shadow, pyramids merged with the desert and from the air seemed almost two-dimensional in the steady light of late morning. Spreading now beyond the town of Giza, Cairo's forty million people threatened to engulf, with their old automobiles, discarded electronics and every dusty non-degradable of the modern world, the grandiose tombs of their ancestors.

Though Cairo, like Calcutta, was a monument to the enduring survival of our race, I was glad to leave. I had spent only as much time as I needed, seeking information about my archaeologist sister and discovering that everyone in the academic community thought she had returned to England at least a year ago. The noise had begun to seem as tangible as the haze of sand which hung over the crowded motorways, now a mass of moving flesh, of camels, donkeys, horses, mules and humans hauling every variety of vehicle and cargo, with the occasional official electric car or, even rarer, petrol-driven truck.

I suppose it had been a tribute to my imagined status that I had been given a place on a plane, rather than having to take the river or the weekly train to

Aswan. Through the porthole of the little VW8 everything but the Nile and its verdant borders were the colours of sand, each shade and texture of which still held meaning for the nomad Arab, the Bedouin who had conquered the First Kingdom and would conquer several others down the millennia. In the past only the Ptolomies, turning their backs on the Nile and the Sahara, ever truly lost the sources of Egypt's power.

My main reason for accepting the assignment was personal rather than professional. My sister had not written for some months and her letters before that had been disconnected, hinting at some sort of emotional disturbance, perhaps in connection with the dig on which I knew she had been working. An employee of UNEC, I had limited authority in Egypt and did not expect to discover any great mysteries at Lake Nasser, which continued to be the cause of unusual weather. The dam's builders somewhat typically had refused to anticipate this. They had also been warned by our people in the 1950s that the New High Dam would eventually so poison the river with bilharzia that anyone using its water would die. The rain, some of it acid, had had predictable effects, flooding quarries and washing away towns. The local Nubians had long since been evicted from their valleys to make way for the lake. Their new settlements, traditionally built, had not withstood the altered environment, so the government had thrown up concrete shells for them. The road to Aswan from the airport was lined with bleak, half-built structures of rusted metal girders and cinder blocks. Today's Egyptians paid a high price for regulated water.

From the airport my horse-drawn taxi crossed the old English dam with its sluices and gigantic gauges, a Victorian engineer's dream of mechanical efficiency, and began the last lap of the journey into town. Aswan, wretched as much of it is, has a magic few Nile settlements now possess, rising from the East Bank to dominate the coppery blue waters and glinting granite islands of the wide river where white-sailed feluccas cruise gracefully back and forth, ferrying tourists and townspeople between the two sides. The heights, massive grey boulders, are commanded by a beautiful park full of old eucalyptus, poplars and monkey-puzzle trees. Above this, the stately Edwardian glory of Cook's Cataract Hotel is a marvellous example of balconied and shuttered rococo British orientalism at its finest.

The further up-river one goes the poorer Aswan becomes, though even here the clapboard and corrugated iron, the asbestos sheeting and crumbling mud walls are dominated by a splendid hill-top mosque in the grand Turkish style. I had asked to be billeted at a modest hotel in the middle of town, near the Souk. From the outside, the Hotel Osiris, with its pale pink and green pseudo-neon, reminded me of those backstreet Marseilles hotels where once you could take your partner for a few francs an hour. It had the same romantic attraction, the same impossible promises. I found that, once within its tiny fly-thick lobby—actually the communal hallway leading directly to the courtyard—I was as lost to its appeal as any pop to his lid. I had discovered a temporary spiritual home.

The Osiris, though scarcely more than a bed-and-breakfast place by London standards, boasted four or five porters, all of them eager to take my bag to the rooms assigned me by a Hindu lady at the desk. I let one carry my canvas grip up two flights of dirty stairs to a little tiled, run-down apartment looking into the building's central well where two exhausted dogs, still coupled, panted on their sides in the heat. Giving him a five-pound note, I asked my porter on the off-chance if he had heard of an Englishwoman called Noone or Pappenheim living in Aswan. My sister had used the *poste restante* and, when I had last been here, there were few Europeans permanently living in town. He regretted that he could not help. He would ask his brother, who had been in Aswan several months. Evidently, now that I had as it were paid for the information in advance he felt obliged to me. The *bakshish* custom is usually neither one of bribery nor begging in any European sense, but has a fair amount to do with smooth social intercourse. There is always, with legitimate *bakshish*, an exchange. Some measure of mutual respect is also usual. Most Arabs place considerable emphasis on good manners and are not always tolerant of European coarseness.

I had last been in Egypt long before the great economic convulsion following that chain-reaction of destruction or near-exhaustion of so many resources. Then Aswan had been the final port of call for the millions of tourists who cruised the Nile from dawn to dusk, the sound of their dance music, the smell of their barbecues, drifting over fields and mud villages which had remained unchanged for five thousand years.

In the '80s and '90s of the last century Aswan had possessed, among others, a Hilton, a Sheraton, a Ritz-Carlton and a Holiday Inn, but now the luckiest local families had requisitioned the hotels and only the State-owned Cataract remained, a place of pilgrimage for every wealthy enthusiast of 1930s detective stories or autobiographies of the twentieth-century famous. Here, during wartime, secret meetings had been held and mysterious bargains struck between unlikely participants. Today on the water below the terrace some tourists still sailed, the Israelis and the Saudis on their own elegant schoomers, while other boats carried mixtures of Americans, Italians and Germans, French, English, Swedes, Spaniards, Japanese and Hungarians, their women dressed and painted like pagan temptresses of the local soap-operas, displaying their bodies naked on the sundecks of vast slow-moving windliners the size of an earlier era's ocean-going ships, serving to remind every decent Moslem exactly what the road to hell looked like. No eighteenth-century English satirist could have provided a better image.

As an officer of the U.N.'s Conservation and Preservation Department I knew all too well how little of Egypt's monuments were still visible, how few existed in any recognisable state. Human erosion, the dam raising the water-table, the volume of garbage casually dumped in the river, the activities of archaeologists and others, of tourists encouraged in their millions to visit the great sites and bring their hard currency, the two-year Arabian war, all had created a situation where those monuments still existing were banned to everyone but the desperate restorers. Meanwhile replicas had been made by the Disney Corporation and located in distant desert settlements surrounded by vacation towns, artificial trees and vast swimming pools, built by French and German experts and named "Rameses City," "Land of the Gods" or "Tutankhamen World." I was sure that this was why my sister had been secretive about her team's discoveries, why it was important to try to avoid the circumstances which now made Abu Simbel little more than a memory of two great engineering miracles.

When I had washed and changed I left the Osiris and strolled through busy alleys in the direction of the corniche, the restored Victorian riverfront promenade which reminded me more than anywhere of the old ocean boulevard at Yalta. Without her earlier weight of tourists, Aswan had developed a lazy, decayed glamour. The foodstalls, the fake antiquities, the flimsy headdresses and *gelabeas* sold as traditional costume, the souvenir shops and postcard stands, the "cafetrias" offering "Creme Teas" and "Mix Grile," were still patronised by a few plump Poles and tomato-coloured English who had been replaced in the main by smaller numbers of blond East Africans, Swedes and Nigerians affecting the styles and mannerisms of thirty or forty years earlier and drawn here, I had heard, by a Holy Man on the outskirts of Aswan who taught a peculiar mixture of orthodox Sunni Islam and his own brand of mysticism which accepted the creeds of Jews and Christians as well as the existence of other planetary populations, and spoke of a "pure" form of Islam practised in other parts of the galaxy.

Aswan's latter-day hippies, wearing the fashions of my own youthful parents, gave me a queer feeling at first, for although Egypt offers several experiences akin to time travel, these images of recent history, perhaps of a happier period altogether, were somehow more incongruous than a broken-down VW, for instance, being dragged behind a disgusted camel. There was a greater preponderance of charm-sellers and fortune-tellers than I remembered, together with blank-eyed European men and women, some of them with babies or young children, who begged me for drug-money on the street. With the rise of Islamic-Humanism, the so-called Arab Enlightenment, coupled to the increasing power of North Africa and the Middle East in world politics, the drug laws, introduced originally to placate foreign tour operators and their governments, had been relaxed or formally abolished. Aswan, I had heard, was now some kind of Mecca for privileged youngsters and visionary artists, much as Haight-Ashbury or Ladbroke Grove had been in the 1960s. Romanticism of that heady, exaggerated, rather mystical variety was once again loose in the world and the comforts it offered seemed to me almost like devilish temptations. But I was of that puritanical, judgemental generation which had rejected the abstractions of its parents in favour of more realistic, as we saw it, attitudes. A good many of us had virtually rejected the entire Western Enlightenment itself and retreated into a kind of liberal mediaevalism not incompatible with large parts of the Arab world. In my own circles I was considered something of a radical.

I had to admit however that I found these new Aswanians attractive. In many ways I envied them. They had never known a time when Arabia had not been a major power. They came here as equals with everyone and were accepted cheerfully by the Nubians who treated them with the respect due to richer pilgrims and potential converts to the divine revelation of Islam.

Again in common with my generation, I was of a secular disposition and saw only damaging, enslaving darkness in any religion. We had even rejected the received wisdoms of Freud, Jung, Marx and their followers and embraced instead a political creed which had as its basis the eminent likelihood of ecological disaster and the slight possibility of an economic miracle. They called us the Anaemic Generation now; a decade or more that was out of step with the progress of history as it was presently interpreted. It suited me to know that I was an anachronism; it afforded me a special kind of security. Very few people took me seriously.

An Egyptian army officer marched past me as I crossed to the river-side of the corniche to look down at the half-completed stairways, the crumbling, poorly mixed concrete and the piles of rat-infested rubble which the Korean engineers, who had put in the lowest tender for the work, had still neither repaired nor cleared. The officer glanced at me as if he recognised me but then went past, looking, with his neatly trimmed moustache and rigid shoulders, the perfect image of a World War Two English Guards captain. Even his uniform was in the English style. I suppose Romans coming to fifth-century Britain after some lapse of time would have been equally impressed to see a Celt striding through the streets of Londinium, impeccable in a slightly antiquated centurion's kit. The whole casual story of the human race seemed to be represented in the town as I paused to look at the hulks of converted pleasure boats, home to swarms of Nubian families impoverished by the altered climate and the shift of tourism towards the Total Egypt Experience found in the comfort of Fort Sadat and New Memphis. Despite the piles of filthy garbage along the shore, Aswan had acquired the pleasant, nostalgic qualities of unfashionable British resorts like Morecambe or Yarmouth, a local population careless of most strangers save sometimes for the money they brought.

About halfway along the corniche I stopped at a little café and sat down on a cane chair, ordering mint tea from a proprietor whose ancient tarboosh might have escaped from the costume department of a touring production of *Death on the Nile*. He addressed me as *"effendi"* and his chosen brand of English seemed developed from old British war movies. Like me, I thought, he was out of step with the times. When he brought the tea I told him to keep the change from a pound and again on the off-chance asked after my sister. I was surprised by the enthusiasm of his response. He knew the name Pappenheim and was approving when I told him of our relationship. "She is very good," he said. "A tip-top gentlewoman. But now, I think, she is unwell. It is hard to see the justice of it."

Pleased and a little alarmed, I asked if he knew where she lived.

"She lived in *Sharri al Sahahaldeen*, just off the *Sharri al Souk*." He pointed with his thumb back into town. "But that was more than a year ago. Oh, she is very well known here in Aswan. The poor people like her immensely. They call her *Saidneh Duukturah*."

"Doctor?" My sister had only rudimentary medical training. Her doctorate had been in archaeology. "She treats the sick?"

"Well, not so much any more. Now only if the hospitals refuse help. The Bisharim, in particular, love her. You know those nomads. They trust your sister only. But she moved from Sahahaldeen Street after some trouble. I heard she went to the English House over on the West Bank, but I'm not so sure. Perhaps you should ask the Bisharim." He raised his hand in welcome to a small man in a dark blue *gelabea* who walked briskly into the darkness of the shop's interior. "A customer." From his pocket he took a cut-throat razor. "*Naharak sa'id*," he called and, adopting the swagger of the expert barber, waved farewell to me and entered his shop.

"*Fi amani 'llah.*" Picking up my hat I crossed to a rank where the usual two or three ill-used horses stood between the shafts of battered broughams, still the commonest form of taxi in Aswan. I approached the first driver, who stood flicking at flies with his ragged whip while he smoked a cigarette and chatted with his fellows. He wore an American sailor's hat, a faded T-shirt advertising some Russian artpopper, a pair of traditional baggy trousers exposing ulcerated calves and, on his feet, pink and black Roos. From the state of his legs I guess he had retained the habit, against all current warnings, of wading into the Nile to urinate. I asked him to take me first to the dam's administration office where, for courtesy's sake, I presented myself and made an appointment with my old acquaintance Georges Abidos, the Chief Press Officer, who had been called out to the northern end of the lake. His secretary said he was looking forward to seeing me tomorrow and handed me a welcoming note. I then asked the calash-driver if he knew the Bisharim camp on the outskirts of town. I had heard that in recent years the tribe had returned to its traditional sites. He was contemptuous. "Oh, yes, sir. The barbarians are still with us!" I told him I would give him another ten pounds to take me there and return. He made to bargain but then accepted, shrugging and gesturing for me to get in his carriage. I guessed he was maintaining some kind of face for himself. In my travels I had grown used to all kinds of mysterious body-language, frequently far harder to interpret than any spoken tongue.

We trotted back to town and jogged beside a river strewn with old plastic water-bottles, with all the miscellaneous filth from the boats that no legislation appeared able to limit, past flaking quasi-French façades still bearing the crests of Farouk and his ancestors and each now occupied by twenty or thirty families whose washing hung over the elaborate iron balconies and carved stone sphinxes like bunting celebrating some joyous national holiday. We passed convents and churches, mosques and graveyards, shanties, monuments, little clumps of palm-trees sheltering donkeys and boys from a sun which as noon approached grew steadily more intense.

We went by the English holiday villas where hippies nowadays congregated; we passed the burned-out shells of warehouses and storerooms, victims of some forgotten riot, the stained walls sprayed with the emerald-coloured ankh of the Green Jihad, and eventually, turning inland again, reached the old Moslem necropolis, almost a mile long and half a mile across, surrounded by a low, mud wall and filled with every shape and size of stone or sarcophagus. Beyond this, further up the hill, I made out clumps of palms and the dark woollen tents of the Bisharim.

My driver reined in his horse some distance from the camp, beside a gate into the graveyard. "I will wait for you here," he said significantly.

2 Ah, Whence, and Whither Flown Again, Who Knows?

The nomad camp, showing so few outward signs of Western influence, had the kind of self-contained dignity which city Arabs frequently manage to re-create in their homes and yet which is not immediately noticed by those visitors merely disgusted by, for instance, Cairo's squalor.

Sheikh Khamet ben Achmet was the patriarch of this particular clan. They had come in a month ago, he said, from the Sudan, to trade horses and camels. They all knew my sister but she had disappeared. He employed a slow, classical Arabic which was easy for me to understand and in which I could easily respond. "God has perhaps directed thy sister towards another vocation," he suggested gently. "It was only a short time since she would visit us whenever we put down our tents here. She had a particularly efficient cure for infections of the eye, but it was the women who went to her, chiefly." He looked at me with quiet amusement. "The best type of Englishwoman, as we say. Sometimes God sends us his beneficence in strange forms."

"Thou has no knowledge of her present dwelling?" I sipped the coffee a servant brought us. I was glad to be in the cool tent. Outside it was now at least thirty-five degrees. There was little danger of freak rain today.

He looked up at me from his ironic grey eyes. "No," he said. "She always visits us. When we needed her we would send messages to the Copt's house. You know, the carpenter who lives on the street leading from the great mosque to the Souk."

I did not know him, I said.

"He is as gold-haired as thou. They nickname him The German, but I know he is a Copt from Alexandria. I think he is called Iskander. I know that he is easily found."

"Thou knowest my sister was an archaeologist?" I was a little hesitant.

"Indeed, I do! We discussed all manner of ancient things together and she had the courtesy to say that I was at least as informative as the great Egyptian Museum in Cairo!" He was amused by what he perceived as elegant flattery. My sister, if I still knew her, had done no more than to state her direct opinion.

It would have been ill-mannered of me to have left as soon as I had the information I sought, so I spent two further hours answering the Sheikh's questions about current American and European politics. I was not surprised that he was well-informed. I had seen his short-wave radio (doubtless full of *piles noires*) standing on the ivory-inlaid chest on the far side of the tent. I was also unsurprised by his interpretations of what he had learned. They were neither cynical nor unintelligent, but they were characteristic of certain desert Arabs who see everything in terms of power and opportunity and simply cannot grasp the reverence for political institutions we have in the West. For a few minutes I foolishly tried to re-educate him until it became clear I must give offence. Recalling my old rules, I accepted his terms. As a result we parted friends. Any South African apologist for apartheid could not have been more approving of my good manners.

When I got up to leave, the old man took my arm and wished me God's grace and help in finding my sister. "She was associated with Jews." He spoke significantly. "Those who did not like her said that she was a witch. And it is true that two of my women saw her consorting with the spell-seller from the Souk. The one called Lallah Zenobia. The black woman. Thou and I art men of the world and understand that it is superstitious folly. But thou knowest how women are. And they are often," he added in an even lower tone, "susceptible to Yehudim flattery and lies."

It was by no means the first time I had to accept such sentiments from the mouth of one who was otherwise hospitality, tolerance and kindness personified. To persuade a desert Arab that Jews are not in direct and regular touch with Satan and all his minions is still no easier than persuading a Dixie Baptist that the doors of a Catholic Church are not necessarily a direct gateway to hell. One is dealing with powerful survival myths which only direct experience will disprove. In such circumstances I never mention my mother's family. I said I would visit Iskander the Carpenter. At this point a braying, bellowing and snorting chorus grew so loud I could barely hear his elaborate goodbyes. The stock was being beaten back from the water. As I emerged from the tent I saw my driver in the distance. He was sitting on the wall of the cemetery feinting with his whip at the boys and girls who flowed like a tide around him, daring one another to run within his range.

3 Crystal to the Wizard Eye

I had no difficulty in discovering Iskander the Carpenter. He was a slight man wearing a pair of faded denim overalls. Sanding off a barley-sugar chairleg, he sat just inside his workshop, which was open to the street and displayed an entire suite of baroque bedroom and living-room furniture he had almost completed. He chose to speak in French. "It is for a couple getting married this weekend. At least they are spending their money on furniture rather than the wedding itself!" He put down his chairleg and shook my hand. He was fair-skinned and blond, as Sheikh Achmet had said, though I could not have taken him for anything but Egyptian. His features could have come straight from the Egyptian Museum's clay statue displays of ancient tradespeople. He might have been a foreman on a Middle Kingdom site. He turned up a chair which still had to have the upholstery over its horsehair seat, indicated that I should sit and sent his son to get us a couple of bottles of Pyramid beer.

"Of course I know Saidneh Duukturah. She was my friend. That one," he pointed to his disappearing boy, "owes his life to her. He was poisoned. She treated him. He is well. It is true I knew where she lived and would get

not, as I had hoped, from my sister, but a letter welcoming me to Aswan, a short personal note from my friend Georges, a list of appointments with various engineers and officials, some misleading publicity about the dam, consisting mainly of impressive photographs, a variety of press releases stressing the plans for "an even better dam" and so on. I went out again having glanced at them. I was obsessed with all the mysteries with which I had been presented in a single day. How had my sister metamorphosed from a dedicated archaeologist to some kind of local Mother Theresa?

Disturbed by my own speculations I forced myself to think about the next day's work when I would be discussing methods of reducing pollution in all its varieties and rebuilding the dam to allow silt down to the arable areas. The signs of serious "redesertization," as ugly official jargon termed it, were now found everywhere in the Nile valley. In other words, the Aswan Dam was now seriously contributing to ecological damage as well as helping to wipe out our most important links with the remote past. I could not believe how intelligent scientists, who were not those industrial developers motivated only by greed, failed to accept the dreadful psychic damage being done to people whose whole identities were bound up with a particular and very specific landscape. My own identity, for instance, was profoundly linked to a small Oxfordshire village which had remained unchanged for hundreds of years after successfully resisting developers wanting to surround it with high-quality modern properties instead of its existing beeches and oaks.

Few Egyptians were in such comfortable circumstances or could make any choice but the one promising the most immediate benefit, yet they had the same understanding of their tribal homes and what values they represented, and still resisted all attempts to force them to lose their traditional clothes, language and attitudes and make them modern citizens of their semi-democratic society. Unfortunately, this attitude also extended to a dam now much older than many of its staff and never at any time an engineering miracle. UNEC had plans for a replacement. Currently they and the Rajhidi government were arguing over the amounts each would contribute. Happily, that was not my problem.

With a slightly clearer head, I walked to the post office on the corner of Abdel el Taheer Street. Though almost fifty years had passed since the First Revolution, the building still bore the outlines of earlier royal insignia. The elaborate cast-ironwork on doors and windows was of that "Oriental" pattern exported from the foundries of Birmingham to adorn official buildings throughout the Empire east of Gibraltar. Even by the 1970s the stuff was still available from stock, during the brief period after the death of Britain's imperial age and before the birth of that now much-despised and admittedly reckless Thatcher period known ironically as "the Second Empire," the period which had shaped my own expectations of life as well as those of uncounted millions of my fellows, the period in which my uncle had died, a soldier in the Falklands cause.

I entered the main door's cool archway and walked through dusty shafts of light to a tiled counter where I asked to speak to the Post Master. After a moment's wait I was shown into his little gloomy mahogany office, its massive fan constantly stirring piles of documents which moved like a perpetually unsettled flight of doves. A small, handsome Arab entered and closed the door carefully behind him. His neat, Abraham Lincoln beard suggested religious devotion. I told him that my name was Pappenheim and I was expecting mail. I handed him an envelope I had already prepared. On the outside was my name and occupation. Inside was the conventional "purse"—actually another envelope containing a few pounds. I said I would appreciate his personal interest in my mail and hoped he could ensure it was available to me the moment it arrived. Absently, he took the envelope and put it in his trouser pocket. He had brightened at the sound of my name. "Are you related to that woman of virtue whom we know here in Aswan?" He spoke measured, cultured Arabic with the soft accents of Upper Egypt.

"My sister." I was trying to locate her, I said. Perhaps her mail was delivered here?

"It has not been collected, Si Pappenheim, for several months. Yet she has been seen in Aswan recently. There was a small scandal. I understand that El Haj Sheikh Ibrahim Abu Halil intervened. Have you asked him about your sister?"

"Is he the governor?"

He laughed. Clearly the idea of the governor intervening on behalf of an ordinary member of the public amused him. "No. Sheikh Abu Halil is the gentleman so many come to Aswan to see these days. He is the great Sufi now. We are blessed in this. God sends us everything that is good, even the rain. So much more grows and blooms. People journey to us from all over the world. Here, God has chosen to reveal a glimpse of paradise."

I was impressed by his optimism. I told him I would go to see Sheikh Abu Halil as soon as possible. Meanwhile I had an appointment with the police chief. At this his face grew a little uncertain, but his only response was some conventional greeting concerning Allah's good offices.

Police Inspector el-Bayoumi was one of those suave career officers produced by the new academies. His manners were perfect, his hospitality generous and discreet, and when I had replied to his question, telling him where I had been born in England, he confessed affectionate familiarity with another nearby Cotswold village. Together, we deplored the damage tourism had done to the environment and confessed it to be a major problem in both our countries, which depended considerably on the very visitors who contributed to the erosion. He sighed. "I think the human race has rather foolishly cancelled many of its options."

Since he preferred to speak it, I replied in English. "Perhaps our imaginative resources are becoming as scarce as our physical ones?"

"There has been a kind of psychic withering," he agreed. "And its worst symptom, in my view, Mr. Pappenheim, is found in the religious and political fundamentalism to which so many subscribe. As if, by some sort of sympathetic magic, the old, simpler days will return. We live in complicated times with complicated problems. It's a sad fact that they require sophisticated solutions."

I admitted I had been schooled in many of those fundamentalist notions and sometimes found them difficult to resist. We chatted about this for a while. Coffee was brought, together with a selection of delicious *gurrahiya* pastries, whose secret the Egyptians inherited from the Turks, and we talked for another half-hour, during which time we took each other's measure and agreed the world would be a better place if civilised people like ourselves were allowed a greater voice. Whereupon, in that sometimes abrupt change of tone Arabs have, which can mislead Europeans into thinking they have somehow given offence, Inspector el-Bayoumi asked what he could do for me.

"I'm looking for my sister. She's an economic archaeologist who came here two-and-a-half years ago with the Burbank College Project. It was an international team. Only about half were from California and those returned the next year, after the big earthquake. Most of them, of course, had lost relatives. My sister stayed on with the remaining members." I did not mention her talk of a wonderful discovery out in the Western Sahara. Their sonavids had picked up a New Kingdom temple complex almost perfectly preserved but buried some hundred feet under the sand. My sister had been very excited about it. It was at least on a par with the discovery of the Tutankhamen treasures and probably of far greater historical importance. She and the team kept the discovery quiet, of course, especially since so many known monuments had suffered. Naturally, there were some conflicts of interest. There was little she could tell me in a letter and most of that was a bit vague, making reference to personal or childhood incidents whose relevance escaped me. I added delicately, "You know about the discovery, naturally."

He smiled as he shook his handsome head. "No, Mr. Pappenheim, I don't. I think an elaborate dig would not escape my notice." He paused, asking me if he might smoke. I told him I was allergic to cigarette smoke and he put his case away. Regretfully, he said: "I should tell you that your sister is a little disturbed. She was arrested by us about a year ago. There was something we had to follow up. An outbreak of black magic amongst the local people. We don't take such things very seriously until it's possible to detect a cult growing. Then we have to move to break it up as best we can. Such things are not a serious problem in London, but for a policeman in Aswan they are fairly important. We arrested a known witch, a Somali woman they call Madame Zenobia, and with her an Englishwoman, also rumoured to be practising. That was your sister, Mr. Pappenheim. She was deranged and had to be given a sedative. Eventually, we decided against charging her and released her into the custody of Lady Roper."

"The Consul's wife?"

"He's the Honorary Consul here in Aswan now. They have a large house on the West Bank, not far from the Ali Khan's tomb. You can't see it from this side. It is our miracle. Locally, it's called the English House. More recently they've called it the Rose House. You'll find no mysteries there!"

"That's where my sister's staying?"

"No longer. She left Aswan for a while. When she came back she joined the community around Sheikh Abu Halil and I understand her to be living in the old holiday villas on the Edfu road, near the race course. I'll gladly put a man to work on the matter. We tend not to pursue people too much in Aswan. Your sister is a good woman. An honest woman. I hope she has recovered herself."

Thanking him I said I hoped my search would not involve the time of a hardworking police officer. I got up to leave. "And what happened to Madame Zenobia?"

"Oh, the courts were pretty lenient. She got a year, doing quarry work for the Restoration Department in Cairo. She was a fit woman. She'll be even fitter now. Hard labour is a wonderful cure for neurosis! And far more socially useful than concocting love potions or aborting cattle."

He sounded like my old headmaster. As an afterthought, I said, "I gather Sheikh Abu Halil took an interest in my sister's case."

He flashed me a look of intelligent humour. "Yes, he did. He is much respected here. Your sister is a healer. The Sufi is a healer. He sometimes makes an accurate prophecy. He has a following all over the world, I believe."

I appreciated his attempt at a neutral tone, given his evident distaste for matters psychic and mystical. We shared, I think, a similar outlook.

I found myself asking him another question. "What was the evidence against my sister, Inspector?"

He had hoped I would not raise the matter, but was prepared for it. "Well," he began slowly, "for instance, we had a witness who saw her passing a large bag of money to the woman. The assumption was that she was paying for a spell. A powerful one. A love philtre, possibly, but it was also said that she wanted a man dead. He was the only other member of her team who had remained behind. There was some suggestion, Mr. Pappenheim," he paused again, "that he made her pregnant. But this was all the wildest gossip. He did in fact die of a heart attack shortly after the reported incident. Sometimes we must treat such cases as murder. But we only had circumstantial evidence. The man was a drug addict and apparently had tried to force your sister to give him money. There was just a hint of blackmail involved in the case, you see. These are all, of course, the interpretations of a policeman. Maybe the man had been an ex-lover, no more. Maybe she wanted him to love her again?"

"It wasn't Noone, was it?"

"It was not her estranged husband. He is, I believe, still in New Zealand."

"You really think she got tangled up in black magic?"

"When confused, men turn to war and women to magic. She was not, as the Marrakshim say, with the caravan." He was just a little sardonic now. "But she was adamant that she did not wish to go home."

"What did she tell you?"

"She denied employing the witch. She claimed the Somali woman was her only friend. Otherwise she said little. But her manner was all the time distracted, as if she imagined herself to be surrounded by invisible witnesses.

We were not unsympathetic. The psychiatrist from the German hospital came to see her. Your sister is a saintly woman who helped the poor and the sick and asked for no reward. She enriched us. We were trying to help her, you know."

He had lost his insouciance altogether now and spoke with controlled passion. "It could be that your sister had an ordinary breakdown. Too much excitement in her work, too much sun. Caring too much for the hardships of others. She tried to cure the whole town's ills and that task is impossible for any individual. Her burden was too heavy. You could see it written in every line of her face, every movement of her body. We wanted her to recover. Some suspected she was in the witch's power, but in my own view she carried a personal weight of guilt, perhaps. Probably pointlessly, too. You know how women are. They are kinder, more feeling creatures than men."

5 The Seasons of Home—Aye, Now They Are Remembered!

That evening, while there was still light, I took the felucca across the Nile, to the West Bank. The ferryman, clambering down from his high mast where he had been reefing his sail, directed me through the village to a dirt road winding up the hillside a hundred yards or so from the almost austere resting place of the Ali Khan. "You will see it," he assured me. "But get a boy."

There were a couple of dozen children waiting for me on the quay. I selected a bright-looking lad of about ten. He wore a ragged Japanese T-shirt with the inscription I LOVE SEX WAX, a pair of cut-off jeans and Adidas trainers. In spite of the firmness with which I singled him out, we were followed by the rest of the children all the way to the edge of the village. I had a couple of packs of old electronic watches which I distributed, to a pantomime of disappointment from the older children. Watches had ceased to be fashionable currency since I had last been in Aswan. Now, from their requests, I learned it was "real" fountain pens. They showed me a couple of Sheaffers some tourist had already exchanged for their services as guides and companions of the road.

I had no fountain pen for the boy who took me to the top of the hill and pointed down into the little valley where, amongst the sand and the rocks, had been erected a large two-storey house, as solidly Edwardian as any early twentieth-century vicarage. Astonishingly, it was planted with cedars, firs and other hardy trees shading a garden to rival anything I had ever seen in Oxfordshire. There were dozens of varieties of roses, of every possible shade, as well as hollyhocks, snapdragons, foxgloves, marigolds and all the flowers one might find in an English July garden. A peculiar wall about a metre high surrounded the entire mirage and I guessed that it disguised some kind of extraordinarily expensive watering and sheltering apparatus which had allowed the owners to do the impossible and bring a little bit of rural England to Upper Egypt. The grounds covered several acres. I saw some stables, a garage, and a woman on the front lawn. She was seated in a faded deckchair watching a fiche-reader or a video which she rested in her left hand. With her right hand she took a glorious drink from the little table beside her and sipped through the straw. As I drew nearer, my vision was obscured by the trees and the wall, but I guessed she was about sixty-five, dressed in a thoroughly unfashionable Marks and Ashley smock, a man's trilby hat and a pair of rubber-tyre sandals. She looked up as I reached the gate and called "Good afternoon." Happy with cash, my boy departed.

"Lady Roper?"

She had a quick, intelligent, swarthy face, her curls all grey beneath the hat, her long hands expressive even when still. "I'm Diana Roper."

"My name's Paul Pappenheim. I'm Beatrice's brother."

"The engineer!" She was full of welcome. "My goodness, you know, I think Bea could foretell the future. She *said* you'd be turning up here about now."

"I wrote and told her!" I was laughing as the woman unlocked the gate and let me in. "I knew about this job months ago."

"You're here on business."

"I'm going through the rituals of sorting out a better dam and trying to do something about the climatic changes. I got sent because I know a couple of people here—and because I asked to come. But there's little real point to my being here."

"You don't sound very hopeful, Mr. Pappenheim." She led me towards the back of the house, to a white wrought-iron conservatory which was a relatively recent addition to the place and must have been erected by some forgotten imperial dignitary of the last century.

"I'm always hopeful that people will see reason, Lady Roper."

We went into the sweet-smelling anteroom, whose glass had been treated so that it could admit only a certain amount of light, or indeed reflect all the light to perform some needed function elsewhere. Despite its ancient appearance, I guessed the house to be using up-to-date EE technologies and to be completely self-sufficient. "What an extraordinary garden," I said.

"Imported Kent clay." She offered me a white basket chair. "With a fair bit of Kenyan topsoil, I understand. We didn't have it done. We got it all dirt cheap. It takes such a long time to travel anywhere these days, most people don't want the place. It belonged to one of the Fayeds, before they all went off to Malaysia. But have you looked carefully at our roses, Mr. Pappenheim? They have a sad air to them, a sense of someone departed, someone mourned. Each bush was planted for a dead relative, they say." Her voice grew distant. "Of course, the new rain has helped enormously. I've survived because I know the rules. Women frequently find their intuition very useful in times of social unrest. But things are better now, aren't they? We simply refuse to learn. We refuse to learn."

Grinning as if enjoying a game, a Nubian girl of about sixteen brought us a tray of English cakes and a pot of Assam tea. I wondered how I had lost the thread of Lady Roper's conversation.

"We do our best," I said, letting the girl take tongs to an éclair and with a flourish pop it on my plate. "I believe Bea lived here for a while."

"My husband took quite a fancy to her. As did I. She was a sweetie. And so bright. Is that a family trait? Yes, we shared a great deal. It was a luxury for me, you know, to have such company. Not many people have been privileged as she and I were privileged." She nodded with gentle mystery, her eyes in the past. "We were friends of your uncle. That was the funny thing we found out. All at Cambridge together in the late '60s. We thought conservation an important subject *then*. What? Fifty years ago, almost? Such a jolly boy. He joined up for extremely complicated reasons, we felt. Did you know why?"

I had never really wondered. My picture of my mother's brother was of the kind of person who would decide on a military career, but evidently they had not been acquainted with that man at all. Finding this disturbing, I attempted to return to my subject. "I was too young to remember him. My sister was more curious than I. Did she seem neurotic to you, while she was here?"

"On the contrary. She was the sanest of us all! Sound as a bell upstairs, as Bernie always said. Sharp intelligence. But, of course, she had been there, you see. And could confirm everything we had been able to piece together at this end."

"You're referring to the site they discovered?"

"That, of course, was crucial. Especially at the early stages. Yes, the site was extraordinary. We went out to see it with her, Bernie and I. What a mind-blower, Paul! Amazing experience. Even the small portion they had excavated. Four mechanical sifters just sucking the sand gradually away. It would have taken years in the old days. Unfortunately three of the operators left after the earthquake and the sifters were recalled for some crucial rescue work over in Sinai. And then, of course, everything changed."

"I'm not sure I'm…"

"After the ship came and took Bea."

"A ship? On the Nile?"

She frowned at me for a moment and then her tone changed to one of distant friendliness. "You'll probably want a word with Bernie. You'll find him in his playroom. Nadja will take you. And I'm here if you need to know anything."

She glanced away, through the glass walls of the conservatory and was at once lost in melancholy reflection of the roses and their guardian trees.

6 The Smoke Along the Track

A tape of some antique radio programme was playing as I knocked on the oak door and was admitted by a white-haired old man wearing a pair of overalls and a check shirt, with carpet slippers on his feet. His skin had the healthy sheen of a sun-baked reptile and his blue eyes were brilliant with trust. I was shocked enough to remain where I was, even as he beckoned me in. He turned down his stereo, a replica of some even older audio contraption, and stood proudly to display a room full of books and toys. One wall was lined with glass shelves on which miniature armies battled amidst a wealth of tiny trees and buildings. "You don't look much like a potential playmate!" His eyes strayed towards the brilliant jackets of his books.

"And you're not entirely convincing as Mr. Dick, sir." I stood near the books, which were all well-ordered, and admired his illustrated Dickens. The temperature in the room was, I guessed, thoroughly controlled. Should the power fail for just a few hours the desert would fade and modify this room as if it had been a photograph left for an hour in the sun.

My retort seemed to please him. He grinned and came forward. "I'm Bernie Roper. While I have no immediate enemies, I enjoy in this room the bliss of endless childhood. I have my lead soldiers, my bears and rabbits, my model farm, and I read widely. *Treasure Island* is very good, as are the 'William' books, and Edgar Rice Burroughs and, as you say, Charles Dickens, though he's a bit on the scary side sometimes. E. Nesbit and H. G. Wells and Shaw. I enjoy so much. For music I have the very best of *Children's Favourites* from the BBC—a mixture of comic songs, Gilbert and Sullivan, *Puff the Magic Dragon*, *The Laughing Policeman*, popular classics and light opera. Flanders and Swann, Danny Kaye, *Sparky's Magic Piano*, *Peter and the Wolf* and *Song of the South*. Do you know any of those? But I'm a silly chap! You're far too young. They'd even scrapped *Children's Hour* before you were born. Oh, dear. Never to enjoy *Larry the Lamb* or Norman and Henry Bones, the Boy Detectives! Oh!" he exclaimed with a knowing grin. "Calamity!" Then he returned his attention to his toys for a moment. "You think I should carry more responsibility?"

"No." I had always admired him as a diplomat. He deserved the kind of retirement that suited him.

"I feel sorry for the children," he said. "The pleasures of childhood are denied to more and more of them as their numbers increase. Rajhid and Abu Halil are no real solution, are they? We who remember the Revolution had hoped to have turned the desert green by now. I plan to die here, Mr.—?"

"My name's Pappenheim. I'm Bea's brother."

"My boy! Thank goodness I offered an explanation. I'm not nearly as eccentric as I look! 'Because I could not stop for Death, He kindly stopped for me. We shared a carriage, just we two, and Immortality.' Emily Dickinson, I believe. But I could also be misremembering. 'The child is Father to the Man,' you know. And the lost childhood of Judas. Did you read all those poems at school?"

"I was probably too young again," I said. "We didn't do poetry as such."

"I'm so sorry. All computer studies nowadays, I suppose."

"Not all, sir." The old-fashioned courtesy surprised us both. Sir Bernard acted as one cheated and I almost apologised. Yet it was probably the first time I had used the form of address without irony. I had, I realised, wanted to show respect. Sir Bernard had come to the same understanding. "Oh, well. You're a kind boy. But you'll forgive me, I hope, if I return to my preferred world."

"I'm looking for my sister, Sir Bernard. Actually, I'm pretty worried about her."

Without irritation, he sighed. "She was a sweet woman. It was terrible. And nobody believing her."

"Believing what, Sir Bernard?"

"About the spaceship, you know. But that's Di's field, really. Not my area of enthusiasm at all. I like to make time stand still. We each have a different way of dealing with the fact of our own mortality, don't we?" He strolled to one of his displays and picked up a charging 17th Lancer. "Into the Valley of Death rode the six hundred."

"Thank you for seeing me, Sir Bernard."

"Not at all, Paul. She talked about you. I liked her. I think you'll find her either attending Abu Halil's peculiar gymnasium or at the holiday homes. Where those Kenyan girls and boys are now living."

"Thank you. Goodbye, sir."

"Bye, bye!" Humming some stirring air, the former Director General of the United Nations hovered, contented, over his miniature Death-or-Glory Boys.

7 Another Relay in the Chain of Fire

Lady Roper had remained in her conservatory. She rose as I entered. "Was Bernie able to help?"

"I could be narrowing things down." I was anxious to get back to the East Bank before dark. "Thank you for your kindness. I tried to find a phone number for you."

"We're not on the phone, lovie. We don't need one."

"Sir Bernard mentioned a spaceship." I was not looking forward to her reply.

"Oh, dear, yes," she said. "The flying-saucer people. I think one day they will bring us peace, don't you? I mean one way or another. This is better than death for me, at any rate, Paul. But perhaps they have a purpose for us. Perhaps an unpleasant one. I don't think anybody would rule that out. What could we do if that were the case? Introduce a spy? That has not proved a successful strategy. We know that much, sadly. It's as if all that's left of Time is here. A few shreds from a few ages."

Again I was completely nonplussed and said nothing.

"I think you share Sir B's streak of pessimism. Or realism is it?"

"Well, we're rather different, actually…" I began to feel foolish.

"He was happier as Ambassador, you know. Before the U.N. And then we were both content to retire here. We'd always loved it. The Fayeds had us out here lots of times, for those odd parties. We were much younger. You probably think we're both barking mad." When I produced an awkward reply she was sympathetic. "There *is* something happening here. It's a *centre.* You can feel it everywhere. It's an ideal place. Possibly we shall be the ones left to witness the birth of the New Age."

At that moment all I wished to do was save my sister from that atmosphere of half-baked mysticism and desperate faith, to get her back to the relative reality of London and a doctor who would know what was wrong with her and be able to treat it.

"Bea was never happier than when she was in Aswan, you know," said Lady Roper.

"She wrote and told me as much."

"Perhaps she risked a bit more than was wise. We all admire her for it. What I don't understand is why she was so thick with Lallah Zenobia. The woman's psychic, of course, but very unsophisticated."

"You heard about the witness? About the purse?"

"Naturally."

"And you, too, are sure it was a purse?"

"I suppose so. It's Cairo slang, isn't it, for a lot of money? The way the Greeks always say 'seven years' when they mean a long time has passed. Bernie's actually ill, you realise? He's coherent much of the time. A form of P.D., we were told. From the water when we were in Washington. He's determined to make the best of it. He's sweet, isn't he?"

"He's an impressive man. You don't miss England?"

She offered me her hand. "Not a bit. You're always welcome to stay if you are bored over there. Or the carping materialism of the Old Country gets to you. Simplicity's the keynote at the Rose House. Bernie says the British have been sulking for years, like the Lost Boys deprived of their right to go a-hunting and a-pirating at will. I'm afraid, Paul, that we don't think very much of home any more."

8 And All These in Their Helpless Days…

The great Egyptian sun was dropping away to the horizon as, in the company of some forty blue-cowled Islamic schoolgirls and a bird-catcher, I sailed back to the East. Reflected in the Nile the sky was the colour of blood and saffron against every tone of dusty blue; the rocks, houses and palms dark violet silhouettes, sparkling here and there as lamps were lit, signalling the start of Aswan's somewhat orderly nightlife. Near the landing stage I ate some *mulakhiya*, rice and an antique salad at Mahommeds' Cafetria, drank some mint tea and went back to the Osiris, half expecting to find that my sister had left word, but the Hindu woman had no messages and handed me my key with a quick smile of encouragement.

I slept poorly, kept awake by the constant cracking of a chemical "equaliser" in the basement and the creak of the all but useless wind-generator on the roof. It was ironic that Aswan, so close to the source of enormous quantities of electricity, was as cruelly rationed as everyone.

I refused to believe that my sister, who was as sane as I was and twice as intelligent, had become entangled with a black-magic flying-saucer cult. Her only purpose for associating with such people would be curiosity, perhaps in pursuit of some anthropological research connected with her work. I was, however, puzzled by her secrecy. Clearly, she was deliberately hiding her whereabouts. I hoped that, when I returned the next day, I would know where she was.

My meetings were predictably amiable and inconsequential. I had arrived a little late, having failed to anticipate the levels of security at the dam. There were police, militia and security people everywhere, both on the dam itself and in all the offices and operations areas. I had to show my pass to eleven different people. The dam was under increased threat from at least three different organisations, the chief being Green Jihad. Our main meetings were held in a large, glass-walled room overlooking the lake. I was glad to meet so many staff, though we all knew that any decisions about the dam would not be made by us but by whoever triumphed in the Geneva negotiations. It was also good to discover that earlier attitudes towards the dam were changing slightly and new thinking was being done. Breakfasted and lunched, I next found myself guest of honour at a full-scale Egyptian dinner which must have taken everyone's rations for a month, involved several entertainments and lastly a good deal of noisy toasting, in cokes and grape juice, our various unadmired leaders.

At the Hotel Osiris, when I got back that night, there was no note for me so I decided next day to visit the old vacation villas before lunching as arranged at the Cataract with Georges Abidos, who had told me that he was retiring as Public Relations officer for the dam. I had a hunch that my sister was probably living with the neo-hippies. The following morning I ordered a calash to pick me up and sat on the board beside the skinny, cheerful driver as his equally thin horse picked her way slowly through busy Saturday streets until we were on the long, cracked concrete road with the railway yards on one side and the river on the other, flanked by dusty palms, which led past the five-storey Moorish-style vacation complex, a tumble of typical tourist architecture of the kind once found all around the Mediterranean, Adriatic and parts of the Black and Red Seas. The white stucco was patchy and the turquoise trim on window-frames and doors was peeling, but the new inhabitants, who had occupied it when the Swedish owners finally abandoned it, had put their stamp on it. Originally the place had been designed for Club Med, but had never sustained the required turnover, even with its special energy dispensations, and had been sold several times over the past ten years. Now garishly dressed young squatters from the wealthy African countries, from the Australias, North and South America, as well as Europe and the Far East, had covered the old complex with their sometimes impressive murals and decorative graffiti. I read a variety of slogans. LET THE BLOOD CONSUME THE FIRE, said one. THE TYGERS OF THE MIND RULE THE JUNGLE OF THE HEART, said another. I had no relish for such undisciplined nonsense and did not look forward to meeting the occupants of this bizarre New New Age fortress. Psychedelia, even in its historical context, had never attracted me.

As I dismounted from the calash I was greeted by a young woman energetically cleaning the old Club Med brass plate at the gate. She had those startling green eyes in a dark olive skin which one frequently comes across everywhere in Egypt and are commonly believed to be another inheritance from the Pharaonic past. Her reddish hair was braided with multicoloured ribbons and she wore a long green silk smock which complemented her eyes.

"Hi!" Her manner was promiscuously friendly. "I'm Lips. Which is short for Eclipse, to answer your question. Don't get the wrong idea. You're here to find a relative, right?" Her accent was Canadian with a trace of something else, possibly Ukrainian. "What's your name?"

"Paul," I said. "My sister's called Bea. Are the only people who visit you trying to find relatives?"

"I just made an assumption from the way you look. I'm pretty good at sussing people out." Then she made a noise of approving excitement. "Bea Porcupine, is it? She's famous here. She's a healer and an oracle. She's special."

"Could you take me to her apartment?" I did my best not to show impatience with the girl's nonsense.

"Lips" answered me with a baffled smile. "No. I mean, sure I could take you to one of her rooms. But she's not here now."

"Do you know where she went?"

The girl was vaguely apologetic. "Mercury? Wherever the ship goes."

My irritation grew more intense. But I controlled myself. "You've no idea when the ship gets back?"

"Now? Yesterday? There's so much time-bending involved. No. You just have to hope."

I walked past her into the complex.

9 Fast Closing Toward the Undelighted Night...

By the time I had spoken to a dozen or so *enfants des fleurs* I had found myself a guide who introduced himself as Magic Mungo and wore brilliant face-paint beneath his straw hat. He had on an old pair of glitterjeans which whispered and flashed as he walked. His jacket announced in calligraphic Arabic phonetic English: THE NAME IS THE GAME. He was probably no older than thirteen. He asked me what I did and when I told him he said he, too, planned to become an engineer "and bring back the power." This amused me and restored my temper. "And what will you do about the weather?" I asked.

"It's not the weather," he told me, "not Nature—it's the ships. And it's not the dam, or the lake, that's causing the storms and stuff. It's the Reens."

I misheard him. I thought he was blaming the Greens. Then I realised, belatedly, that he was expressing a popular notion amongst the New New

Agers, which by the time I had heard it several times more had actually begun to improve my mood. The Reens, the flying-saucer people, were used by the hippies as an explanation for everything they couldn't understand. In rejecting Science, they had substituted only a banal myth. Essentially, I was being told that the gods had taken my sister. In other words they did not know where she was. At last, after several further short but keen conversations, in various rug-strewn galleries and cushion-heavy chambers smelling strongly of kif, incense and patchouli, I met a somewhat older woman, with grey streaks in her long black hair and a face the colour and texture of well-preserved leather.

"This is Ayesha." Mungo gulped comically. "She-who-must-be-obeyed!" He ran to the woman who smiled a perfectly ordinary smile as she embraced him. "We encourage their imaginations," she said. "They read books here and everything. Are you looking for Bea?"

Warily expecting more Reen talk, I admitted that I was trying to find my sister.

"She went back to Aswan. I think she was at the *medrassah* for a bit—you know, with the Sufi—but after that she returned to town. If she's not there, she's in the desert again. She goes there to meditate, I'm told. If she's not there, she's not anywhere. Around here, I mean."

I was relieved by the straightforward nature of her answer. "I'm greatly obliged. I thought you, too, were going to tell me she was taken into space by aliens!"

Ayesha joined in my amusement. "Oh, no, of course not. That was more than a year ago!"

10 Thoughts of Too Old a Colour Nurse My Brain

I decided to have a note delivered to the Sufi, El Haj Ibrahim Abu Halil, telling him that I planned to visit him next day, then, with a little time to spare before my appointment, I strolled up the corniche, past the boat-ghetto at the upper end, and along the more fashionable stretches where some sporadic attempt was made to give the railings fresh coats of white paint and where a kiosk, closed since my first time here, advertised in bleached Latin type the *Daily Telegraph*, *Le Monde* and the *New York Herald-Tribune*. A few thin strands of white smoke rose from the villages on Elephantine Island; and from *Gazirat-al-Bustan*,

Plantation Island, whose botanical gardens, begun by Lord Kitchener, had long since mutated into marvellously exotic jungle, came the laughter of the children and teenagers who habitually spent their free days there.

Outside the kiosk stood an old man holding a bunch of faded and ragged international newspapers under one arm and *El Misr* under the other. "All today!" he called vigorously in English, much as a London coster shouted "All fresh!" A professional cry rather than any sort of promise. I bought an *El Misr*, only a day old, and glanced at the headlines as I walked up to the park. There seemed nothing unusually alarming in the paper. Even the E.C. rate had not risen in the last month. As I tried to open the sheet a gust came off the river and the yellow-grey paper began to shred in my hands. It was low-density recyke, unbulked by the sophisticated methods of the West. Before I gave up and dumped the crumpled mess into the nearest reclamation bin I had glimpsed references to the UNEC conference in Madagascar and something about examples of mass hysteria in Old Paris and Bombay, where a group called *Reincarnation* was claiming its leader to be a newly born John Lennon. There were now about as many reincarnated Lennons abroad as there had been freshly risen Christs in the early Middle Ages.

I stopped in the park to watch the gardeners carefully tending the unsweet soil of the flower-beds, coaxing marigolds and nasturtiums to bloom at least for a few days in the winter, when the sun would not burn them immediately they emerged. The little municipal café was unchanged since British days and still served only ice creams, tea, coffee or soft-drinks, all of them made with non-rationed ingredients and all equally tasteless. Pigeons wandered hopelessly amongst the débris left by customers, occasionally pecking at a piece of wrapping or a sliver of *Sustenance* left behind by some poor devil who had been unable to force his stomach to accept the high-concentrate nutrients we had developed at UNEC for his benefit.

The Cataract's entrance was between pillars which, once stately, Egyptianate and unquestionably European, were now a little the worse for wear, though the gardens on both sides of the drive were heavy with freshly planted flowers. Bougainvillaeas of every brilliant variety covered walls behind avenues of palms leading to a main building the colour of Nile clay, its shutters and ironwork a dark, dignified green, the kind of colour Thomas Cook himself would have picked to represent the security and solid good service which established him as one of the Empire's noblest champions.

I walked into the great lobby cooled by massive carved mahogany punkahs worked on hidden ropes by screened boys. Egypt had had little trouble implementing many of the U.N.'s mandatory energy-saving regulations. She had either carried on as always or had returned, perhaps even with relief, to the days before electricity and gas had become the necessities rather than the luxuries of life.

I crossed the lobby to the wooden verandah where we were to lunch. Georges Abidos was already at our table by the rail looking directly over the empty swimming pool and, beyond that, to the river itself. He was drinking a cup of Lipton's tea and I remarked on it, pointing to the label on the string dangling from his tiny metal pot. "Indeed!" he said. "At ten pounds the pot why shouldn't the Cataract offer us Lipton's, at least!" He dropped his voice. "Though my guess is the teabag has seen more than one customer through the day's heat. Would you like a cup?"

I refused. He hadn't, I said, exactly sold me on the idea. He laughed. He was a small, attractively ugly Greek from Alexandria. Since the flooding, he had been driven, like so many of his fellow citizens, to seek work inland. At least half the city had not been thought worth saving as the sea-level had steadily risen to cover it.

"Can't you," he asked, "get your American friends to do something about this new embargo? One misses the cigarettes and I could dearly use a new John B." He indicated his stained Planter's straw and then picked it up to show me the label on the mottled sweatband so that I might verify it was a genuine product of the Stetson Hat Co. of New Jersey. "Size seven and a quarter. But don't get anything here. The Cairo fakes are very close. Very good. But they can't fake the finish, you see."

"I'll remember," I promised. I would send him a Stetson next time I was in the U.S.A.

I felt we had actually conducted our main business before we sat down. The rest of the lunch would be a social affair with someone I had known both professionally and as a close personal acquaintance for many years.

As our mixed *hors d'oeuvres* arrived, Georges Abidos looked with a despairing movement of his mouth out towards the river. "Well, Paul, have you solved any of our problems?"

"I doubt it," I said. "That's all going on in Majunga now. I'm wondering if my function isn't as some kind of minor smokescreen."

"I thought you'd volunteered."

"Only when they'd decided that one of us had to come. It was a good chance, I thought, to see how my sister was. I had spare relative allowance and lots of energy and travel owing, so I got her a flight out with me. It took for ever! But I grew rather worried. The last note I had from her was three months ago and very disjointed. It didn't tell me anything. I'd guessed that her husband had turned up. It was something she said. That's about all I know which would frighten her that much. My mistake, it's emerged. Then I wondered if she wasn't pregnant. I couldn't make head nor tail of her letters. They weren't like her at all."

"Women are a trial," said Georges Abidos. "My own sister has divorced, I heard. But then," as if to explain it, "they moved to Kuwait." He turned his eyes back to the river which seemed almost to obsess him. "Look at the Nile. An open sewer running through a desert. What has Egypt done to deserve rescue? She gave the world the ancestors who first offered Nature a serious challenge. Should we be grateful for that? From Lake Nasser to Alexandria the river remains undrinkable and frequently unusable. She once replenished the earth. Now, what with their fertilisers and sprays, she helps poison it." It was as if all the doubts he had kept to himself as a publicity officer were now being allowed to emerge. "I listen to Blue Danube Radio from Vienna. The English station. It's so much more reliable than the World Service. We are still doing less than we could, they say, here in Egypt."

The tables around us had begun to fill with Saudis and wealthy French people in fashionable silk shifts, and the noise level rose so that it was hard for me to hear my acquaintance's soft tones.

We discussed the changing nature of Aswan. He said he would be glad to get back to Cairo where he had a new job with the Antiquities Department raising money for specific restoration or reconstruction projects.

We had met at the re-opening of the Cairo Opera House in 1989, which had featured the Houston Opera Company's *Porgy and Bess*, but had never become more than casual friends, though we shared many musical tastes and he had an extraordinary knowledge of modern fiction in English. His enthusiasm was for the older writers like Gilchrist or DeLillo, who had been amongst my own favourites at college.

We were brought some wonderfully tasty Grönburgers and I remarked that the cuisine had improved since I was last here. "French management," he told me. "They have one of the best teams outside of Paris. They all came from Nice after the troubles. Lucky for us. I might almost be tempted to stay! Oh, no! I could not. Even for that! Nubian music is an abomination!"

I told him about my sister, how I was unable to find her and how I was beginning to fear the worst. "The police suggested she was mad."

Georges was dismissive of this. "A dangerous assumption at any time, Paul, but especially these days. And very difficult for us to define here, in Egypt, just as justice is at once a more brutal and a subtler instrument in our interpretation. We never accepted, thank God, the conventional wisdoms of psychiatry. And madness here, as elsewhere, is defined by the people in power, usually calling themselves the State. Tomorrow those power holders could be overthrown by a fresh dynasty, and what was yesterday simple common sense today becomes irresponsible folly. So I do not like to make hasty judgements or pronounce readily on others' moral or mental conditions—lest, indeed, we inadvertently condemn ourselves." He paused. "They say this was not so under the British, that it was fairer, more predictable. Only real troublemakers and criminals went to jail. Now it isn't as bad as it was when I was a lad. Then anyone was liable to arrest. If it was better under the British, then that is our shame." And he lowered his lips to his wineglass.

We had slipped, almost automatically, into discussing the old, familiar topics. "It's sometimes argued," I said, "that the liberal democracies actually stopped the flow of history. A few hundred years earlier, as feudal states, we would have forcibly Christianised the whole of Islam and changed the entire nature of the planet's power struggle. Indeed, all the more childish struggles might have been well and truly over by now!"

"Or it might have gone the other way," Georges suggested dryly, "if the Moors had reconquered France and Northern Europe. After all, Islam did not bring the world to near-ruin. What has the European way achieved except the threat of death for all?"

I could not accept an argument which had already led to massive conversions to Islam amongst the youth of Europe, America and Democratic Africa, representing a sizeable proportion of the vote. This phenomenon had, admittedly, improved the tenor of world politics, but I still deplored it.

"Oh, you're so thoroughly out of step, my friend." Georges Abidos smiled and patted my arm. "The world's changing!"

"It'll die if we start resorting to mystical Islamic solutions."

"Possibly." He seemed unconcerned. I think he believed us unsaveable.

A little drunk, I let him take me back to the Osiris in a calash. He talked affectionately of our good times, of concerts and plays we had seen in the world's capitals before civilian flight had become so impossibly expensive, of the Gilbert and Sullivan season we had attended in Bangkok, of Wagner in Bayreuth and Britten in Glyndebourne. We hummed a snatch from *Iolanthe* before we parted.

When I got up to my room all the shutters had been drawn back to give the apartment the best of the light. I recognised the subtle perfume even as my sister came out of the bathroom to laugh aloud at my astonishment.

11 Saw Life to Be a Sea Green Dream

Beatrice had cut her auburn hair short and her skin was paler than I remembered. While her blue eyes and red lips remained striking, she had gained an extra beauty. I was overjoyed. This was the opposite of what I had feared to find.

As if she read my mind, she smiled. "Were you expecting the Mad Woman of Aswan?" She wore a light blue cotton skirt and a darker blue shirt.

"You've never looked better." I spoke the honest truth.

She took both my hands in hers and kissed me. "I'm sorry I didn't write. It began to seem such as sham. I couldn't write for a while. I got your letters today, when I went to the post office. What a coincidence, I thought—my first sally into the real world and here comes good old Paul to help me. If anyone understands reality, you do."

I was flattered and grinned in the way I had always responded to her half-mocking praise. "Well, I'm here to take you back to it, if you want to go. I've got a pass for you on the Cairo plane in four days' time, and from there we can go to Geneva or London or anywhere in the Community."

"That's marvellous," she said. She looked about my shabby sitting room with its cracked foam cushions, its stained tiles. "Is this the best you get at your rank?"

"This is the best for any rank, these days. Most of us don't travel at all and certainly not by plane."

"The schoomers are still going out of Alex, are they?"

"Oh, yes. To Genoa, some of them. Who has the time?"

"That's what I'd thought of, for me. But here you are! What a bit of luck!"

I was immensely relieved. "Oh, Bea. I thought you might be dead—you know, or worse."

"I was selfish not to keep you in touch, but for a while, of course, I couldn't. Then I was out there for so long..."

"At your dig, you mean?"

She seemed momentarily surprised, as if she had not expected me to know about the dig. "Yes, where the dig was. That's right. I can't remember what I said in my letters."

"That you'd made a terrific discovery and that I must come out the first chance I got. Well, I did. This really was the first chance. Am I too late? Have they closed down the project completely? Are you out of funds?"

"Yes," she smiled. "You're too late, Paul. I'm awfully sorry. You must think I've brought you on a wild goose chase."

"Nonsense. That wasn't why I really came. Good Lord, Bea, I care a lot for you!" I stopped, a little ashamed. She was probably in a more delicate condition than she permitted me to see. "And, anyway, I had some perks coming. It's lovely here, still, isn't it? If you ignore the rubbish tips. You know, and the sewage. And the Nile!" We laughed together.

"And the rain and the air," she said. "And the sunlight! Oh, Paul! What if this really is the future?"

12 A Man in the Night Flaking Tombstones

She asked if I would like to take a drive with her beside the evening river and I agreed at once. I was her senior by a year but she had always been the leader, the initiator and I admired her as much as ever.

We went up past the ruins of the Best Western and the Ramada Inn, the only casualties of a shelling attack in '02, when the Green Jihad had attempted to hole the dam and six women had died. We stopped near the abandoned museum and bought a drink from the ice-stall. As I turned, looking out at the river, I saw the full moon, huge and orange, in the cloudless night. A few desultory mosquitoes hung around our heads and were easily fanned away as we continued up the corniche, looking out at the lights from the boats, the flares on the far side, the palms waving in the soft breeze from the north.

"I'm quitting my job," she said. "I resigned, in fact, months ago. I had a few things to clear up."

"What will you do? Get something in London?"

"Well, I've my money. That was invested very sensibly by Jack before our problems started. Before we split up. And I can do freelance work." Clearly, she was unwilling to discuss the details. "I could go on living here."

"Do you want to?"

"No," she said. "I hate it now. But is the rest of the world any better, Paul?"

"Oh, life's still a bit easier in England. And Italy's all right. And Scandinavia, of course, but that's closed off, as far as residency's concerned. The population's dropping quite nicely in Western Europe. Not everything's awful. The winters are easier."

She nodded slowly as if she were carefully noting each observation. "Well," she said, "anyway, I don't know about Aswan. I'm not sure there's much point in my leaving Egypt. I have a permanent visa, you know."

"Why stay, Bea?"

"Oh, well," she said. "I suppose it feels like home. How's Daddy? Is everything all right in Marrakech?"

"Couldn't be better, I gather. He's having a wonderful time. You know how happy he always was there. And with the new government! Well, you can imagine."

"And Mother?"

"Still in London. She has a house to herself in West Hampstead. Don't ask me how. She's installed the latest EE generators and energy storers. She's got a TV set, a pet option and a gas licence. You know Mother. She's always had the right contacts. She'll be glad to know you're okay."

"Yes. That's good, too. I've been guilty of some awfully selfish behaviour, haven't I? Well, I'm putting all that behind me and getting on with my life."

"You sound as if you've seen someone. About whatever it was. Have you been ill, Bea?"

"Oh, no. Not really." She turned to reassure me with a quick smile and a hand out to mine, just as always. I nearly sang with relief. "Emotional trouble, you know."

"A boyfriend?"

"Well, yes, I suppose so. Anyway, it's over."

"All the hippies told me you'd been abducted by a flying saucer!"

"Did they?"

I recognised her brave smile. "What's wrong? I hadn't meant to be tactless."

"You weren't. There are so many strange things happening around here. You can't blame people for getting superstitious, can you? After all, we say we've identified the causes, yet can do virtually nothing to find a cure."

"Well, I must admit there's some truth in that. But there are still things we can do."

"Of course there are. I didn't mean to be pessimistic, old Paul." She punched me on the arm and told the driver to let his horse trot for a bit, to get us some air on our faces, since the wind had dropped so suddenly.

She told me she would come to see me at the same time tomorrow and perhaps after that we might go to her new flat. It was only a temporary place while she made up her mind. Why didn't I just go to her there? I said. Because, she said, it was in a maze. You couldn't get a calash through and even the schoolboys would sometimes mislead you by accident. Write it down, I suggested, but she refused with an even broader smile. "You'll see I'm right. I'll take you there tomorrow. There's no mystery. Nothing deliberate."

I went back into the damp, semi-darkness of the Osiris and climbed through black archways to my rooms.

13 You'll Find No Mirrors in that Cold Abode

I had meant to ask Beatrice about her experience with the Somali woman and the police, but her mood had swung so radically I had decided to keep the rest of the conversation as casual as possible. I went to bed at once more hopeful and more baffled than I had been before I left Cairo.

In the morning I took a cab to the religious academy, or *medrassah*, of the famous Sufi, El Haj Sheikh Ibrahim Abu Halil, not because I now needed his help in finding my sister, but because I felt it would have been rude to cancel my visit without explanation. The *medrassah* was out near the old obelisk quarries. Characteristically Moslem, with a tower and a domed mosque, it was reached on foot or by donkey, up a winding, artificial track that had been there for at least two thousand years. I climbed to the top, feeling a little dizzy as I avoided looking directly down into the ancient quarry and saw that the place was built as a series of stone colonnades around a great courtyard with a fountain in it. The fountain, in accordance with the law, was silent.

The place was larger than I had expected and far more casual. People, many obviously drugged, of every age and race sat in groups or strolled around the cloisters. I asked a pale young woman in an Islamic *burqa* where I might find Sheikh Abu Halil. She told me to go to the office and led me as far as a glass door through which I saw an ordinary business layout of pens and paper, mechanical typewriters, acoustic calculators and, impressively, an EMARGY console. I felt as if I were prying. My first job, from which I had resigned, was as an Energy Officer. Essentially the work involved too much peeping-tomism and too little real progress.

A young black man in flared Mouwes and an Afghan jerkin signalled for me to enter. I told him my business and he said, "No problem, man." He asked me to wait in a little room furnished like something still found in any South London dentist's. Even the magazines looked familiar and I did not intend to waste my battery ration plugging in to one. A few minutes later the young man returned and I was escorted through antiseptic corridors to the Sufi's inner sanctum.

I had expected some rather austere sort of Holy Roller's Executive Suite, and was a trifle shocked by the actuality which resembled a scene from *The Arabian Nights.* The Sufi was clearly not celibate, and was an epicurean rather than ascetic. He was also younger than I had expected. I guessed he was no more than forty-five. Dressed in red silks of a dozen shades, with a massive scarlet turban on his head, he lay on cushions smoking from a silver-and-brass hookah while behind him on rich, spangled divans lolled half a dozen young women, all of them veiled, all looking at me with frank, if discreet, interest. I felt as if I should apologise for intruding on someone's private sexual fantasy, but the Sufi grinned, beckoned me in, then fell to laughing aloud as he stared into my face. All this, of course, only increased my discomfort. I could see no reason for his amusement.

"You think this a banal piece of play-acting?" He at once became solicitous. "Pardon me, *Herr Doktor.* I misunderstood your expression for a moment. I thought you were an old friend." Now he was almost grave. "How can I help you?"

"Originally," I said, "I was looking for my sister Beatrice. I believe you know her." Was this my sister's secret? Had she involved herself with a charismatic charlatan to whom even I felt drawn? But the banality of it all! True madness, like true evil, I had been informed once, was always characterised by its banality.

"That's it, of course. Bea Porcupine was the name the young ones used. She is a very good friend of mine. Are you looking for her no longer, Dr. Porcupine?"

I pointed out that Pappenheim was the family name. The hippies had not made an enormously imaginative leap.

"Oh, the children! Don't they love to play? They are blessed. Think how few of us in the world are allowed by God to play."

"Thou art most tolerant indeed, sidhi." I used my best classical Arabic, at which he gave me a look of considerable approval and addressed me in the same way.

"Doth God not teach us to tolerate, but not to imitate, all the ways of mankind? Are we to judge God, my compatriot?" He had done me the honour, in his own eyes, of addressing me as a co-religionist. When he smiled again his expression was one of benign happiness. "Would you care for some coffee?" he asked in educated English. "Some cakes and so on? Yes, of course." And he clapped his hands, whispering instructions to the nearest woman who rose and left. I was so thoroughly discomforted by this outrageously old-fashioned sexism which, whatever their private practices, few sophisticated modern Arabs were willing to admit to, that I remained silent.

"And I trust that you in turn will tolerate my stupid self-indulgence," he said. "It is a whim of mine—and these young women—to lead the life of Haroun-el-Raschid, eh? Or the great chiefs who ruled in the days before the Prophet. We are all nostalgic for that, in Egypt. The past, you know, is our only escape. You don't begrudge it us, do you?"

I shook my head, although by training and temperament I could find no merit in his argument. "These are changing times," I said. "Your past is crumbling away. It's difficult to tell good from evil or right from wrong, let alone shades of intellectual preference."

"But I can tell you really do still think there are mechanical solutions to our ills."

"Don't you, sidhi?"

"I do. I doubt though that they're much like a medical man's."

"I'm an engineer, not a doctor of medicine."

"Pardon me. It's my day for gaffs, eh? But we're all guilty of making the wrong assumptions sometimes. Let us open the shutters and enjoy some fresh air." Another of the women went to fold back the tall wooden blinds and let shafts of sudden sunlight down upon the maroons, burgundies, dark pinks, bottle-greens and royal blues of that luxurious room. The woman sank into the shadows and only Sheikh Abu Halil remained with half his face in light, the other in shade, puffing on his pipe, his silks rippling as he moved a lazy hand. "We are blessed with a marvellous view."

From where we sat it was possible to see the Nile, with its white sails and flanking palms, on the far side of an expanse of glaring granite.

"My sister—" I began.

"A remarkable woman. A saint, without doubt. We have tried to help her, you know."

"I believe you're responsible for getting her out of police custody, sidhi."

"God has chosen her and has blessed her with unusual gifts. Dr. Pappenheim, we are merely God's instruments. She has brought a little relief to the sick, a little consolation to the despairing."

"She's coming home with me. In three days."

"A great loss for Aswan. But perhaps she's more needed out there. Such sadness, you know. Such deep sadness." I was not sure if he described my sister or the whole world. "In Islam, you see," an ironic twitch of the lip, "we share our despair. It is a democracy of misery." And he chuckled. "This is blasphemy I know, in the West. Especially in America."

"Well, in parts of the North maybe." I smiled. My father was from Mississippi and settled first in Morocco, then in England after he came out of the service. He said he missed the old, bitter-sweet character of the U.S. South. The New South, optimistic and, in his view, Yankified, no longer felt like home. He was more in his element in pre-Thatcher Britain. When she, too, began a programme of "Yankification" of her own he retreated into fantasy, leaving my mother and going to live in a working-class street in a run-down north-eastern town where he joined the Communist Party and demonstrated against closures in the mining, fishing and steel industries. My mother hated it when his name appeared in the papers or, worse in her view, when he wrote intemperate letters to the weekly journals or the heavy dailies.

But "Jim Pappenheim" was a contributor to *Marxism Today* and, later, *Red is Green* during his brief flirtation with Trotskyist Conservationism. He gave that up for anarcho-socialism and disappeared completely into the world of the abstract. He now wrote me letters describing the "Moroccan experiment" as the greatest example of genuinely radical politics in action. I had never completely escaped the tyranny of his impossible ideals. This came back to me, there and then, perhaps because in some strange way I found this sufi as charming as I had once found my father. "We say that misery loves company. Is that the same thing?" I felt I was in some kind of awful contest. "Is that why she wanted to stay with you?"

"I knew her slightly before it all changed for her. Afterwards, I knew her better. She seemed very delicate. She came back to Aswan, then went out to the dig a couple more times, then back here. She was possessed of a terrible restlessness she would allow nobody here to address and which she consistently denied. She carried a burden, Dr. Pappenheim." He echoed the words of Inspector el-Bayoumi. "But perhaps we, even we, shall never know what it was."

14 On Every Hand—The Red Collusive Stain

She arrived at the Osiris only a minute or two late. She wore a one-piece work-suit and a kind of bush-hat with a veil. She also carried a briefcase which she displayed in some embarrassment. "Habit, I suppose. I don't need the maps or the notes. I'm taking you into the desert, Paul. Is that okay?"

"We're not going to your place?'

"Not now."

I changed into more suitable clothes and followed her down to the street. She had a calash waiting which carried us to the edge of town, to a camel camp where, much to my dismay, we transferred to grumbling dromedaries. I had not ridden a camel for ten years, but mine proved fairly tractable once we were moving out over the sand.

I had forgotten the peace and the wonderful smell of the desert and it was not long before I had ceased to pay attention to the heat or the motion and had begun to enjoy a mesmeric panorama of dunes and old rock. My sister occasionally used a compass to keep course but sat her high saddle with the confidence of a seasoned drover. We picked up speed until the heat became too intense and we rested under an outcrop of red stone which offered the only shade. It was almost impossible to predict where one would find shade in the desert. A year ago this rock might have been completely invisible beneath the sand; in a few months it might be invisible again.

"The silence is seductive," I said after a while.

My sister smiled. "Well, it whispers to me, these days. But it is wonderful, isn't it? Here you have nothing but yourself, a chance to discover how much of your identity is your own and how much is actually society's. And the ego drifts away. One becomes a virgin beast."

"Indeed!" I found this a little too fanciful for me. "I'm just glad to be away from all that…"

"You're not nervous?"

"Of the desert?"

"Of getting lost. Nothing comes out here, ever, now. Nomads don't pass by and it's been years since a motor vehicle or plane was allowed to waste its E.R. on mere curiosity. If we died, we'd probably never be found."

"This is a bit morbid, isn't it, Bea? It's only a few hours from Aswan, and the camels are healthy."

"Yes." She rose to put our food and water back into their saddlebags, causing a murmuring and an irritable shifting of the camels. We slept for a couple of hours. Bea wanted to be able to travel at night, when we would make better time under the full moon.

The desert at night will usually fill with the noises of the creatures who waken as soon as the sun is down, but the region we next entered seemed as lifeless as the Bical flats, though without their aching mood of desolation. The sand still rose around our camels' feet in silvery gasps and I wrapped myself in the other heavy woollen *gelabea* Beatrice had brought. We slept again, for two or three hours, before continuing on until it was almost dawn and the moon faint and fading in the sky.

"We used to have a gramophone and everything," she said. "We played those French songs mainly. The old ones. And a lot of classic Rai. It was a local collection someone had brought with the machine. You wouldn't believe the mood of camaraderie that was here, Paul. Like Woodstock must have been. We had quite a few young people with us—Egyptian and European mostly—and they all said the same. We felt privileged."

"When did you start treating the sick?" I asked her.

"Treating? Scarcely that! I just helped out with my First Aid kit and whatever I could scrounge from a pharmacy. Most of the problems were easily treated, but not priorities as far as the hospitals are concerned. I did what I could whenever I was in Aswan. But the kits gradually got used and nothing more was sent. After the quake, things began to run down. The Burbank Foundation needed its resources for rebuilding at home."

"But you still do it. Sometimes. You're a legend back there. Ben Achmet told me."

"When I can, I help those nomads cure themselves, that's all. I was coming out here a lot. Then there was some trouble with the police."

"They stopped you? Because of the Somali woman?"

"That didn't stop me." She raised herself in her saddle suddenly. "Look. Can you see the roof there? And the pillars?"

They lay in a shallow valley between two rocky cliffs and they looked in the half-light as if they had been built that very morning. The decorated columns and the massive flat roof were touched a pinkish gold by the rising sun and I could make out hieroglyphics, the blues and ochres of the Egyptian artist. The building, or series of buildings, covered a vast area. "It's a city," I said. I was still disbelieving. "Or a huge temple. My God, Bea! No wonder you were knocked out by this!"

"It's not a city or a temple, in any sense *we* mean." Though she must have seen it a hundred times, she was still admiring of the beautiful stones. "There's nothing like it surviving anywhere else. No record of another. Even this is only briefly mentioned and, as always with Egyptians, dismissively as the work of earlier, less exalted leaders, in this case a monotheistic cult which attempted to set up its own god-king and, in failing, was thoroughly destroyed. Pragmatically, the winners in that contest re-dedicated the place to Sekhmet and then, for whatever reasons—probably economic—abandoned it altogether. There are none of the usual signs of later uses. By the end of Nyusere's reign no more was heard of it at all. Indeed, not much more was heard of Nubia for a long time. This region was never exactly the centre of Egyptian life."

"It was a temple to Ra?"

"Ra, or a sun deity very much like him. The priest here was represented as a servant of the sun. We call the place Onu'us, after him."

"Four thousand years ago? Are you sure this isn't one of those new Dutch repros?" My joke sounded flat, even to me.

"Now you can see why we kept it dark, Paul. It was an observatory, a scientific centre, a laboratory, a library. A sort of university, really. Even the hieroglyphics are different. They tell all kinds of things about the people and the place. And, it had a couple of other functions." Her enthusiasm died and she stopped, dismounting from her camel and shaking sand from her hat. Together we watched the dawn come up over the glittering roof. The pillars, shadowed now, stood only a few feet out of the sand, yet the brilliance of the colour was almost unbelievable. Here was the classic language of the fifth dynasty, spare, accurate, clean. And it was obvious that the whole place had only recently been refilled. Elsewhere churned, powdery earth and overturned rock spoke of vigorous activity by the discovering team; there was also, on the plain which stretched away from the southern ridge, a considerable area of fused sand. But even this was now covered by that desert tide which would soon bury again and preserve this uncanny relic.

"You tried to put the sand back?" I felt stupid and smiled at myself.

"It's all we could think of in the circumstances. Now it's far less visible than it was a month ago."

"You sound very proprietorial." I was amused that the mystery should prove to have so obvious a solution. My sister had simply become absorbed in her work. It was understandable that she should.

"I'm sorry," she said. "I must admit..."

For a moment, lost in the profound beauty of the vision, I did not realise she was crying. Just as I had as a little boy, I moved to comfort her, having no notion at all of the cause of her grief, but assuming, I suppose, that she was mourning the death of an important piece of research, the loss of her colleagues, the sheer disappointment at this unlucky end to a wonderful adventure. It was plain, too, that she was completely exhausted.

She drew towards me, smiling an apology. "I want to tell you everything, Paul. And only you. When I have, that'll be it. I'll never mention it again. I'll get on with some sort of life. I'm sick of myself at the moment."

"Bea. You're very tired. Let's go home to Europe where I can coddle you for a bit."

"Perhaps," she said. She paused as the swiftly risen sun outlined sunken buildings and revealed more of a structure lying just below the surface, some dormant juggernaut.

"It's monstrous," I said. "It's the size of the large complex at Luxor. But this is different. All the curved walls, all the circles. Is that to do with sun worship?"

"Astronomy, anyway. We speculated, of course. When we first mapped it on the sonavids. This is the discovery to launch a thousand theories, most of them crackpot. You have to be careful. But it felt to us to be almost a contrary development to what was happening at roughly the same time around Abu Ghurab, although of course there were sun-cults there, too. But in Lower Egypt the gratification and celebration of the Self had reached terrible proportions. All those grandiose pyramids. This place had a mood to it. The more we sifted it out the more we felt it. Wandering amongst those light columns, those open courtyards, was marvellous. All the turquoises and reds and bright yellows. This had to be the centre of some ancient Enlightenment. Far better preserved than Philae, too. And no graffiti carved anywhere, no Christian or Moslem disfigurement. We all worked like maniacs. Chamber after chamber was opened. Gradually, of course, it dawned on us! You could have filled this place with academic people and it would have been a functioning settlement again, just as it was before some petty Pharaoh or local governor decided to destroy it. We felt we were taking over from them after a gap of millennia. It gave some of us a weird sense of responsibility. We talked about it. They knew so much, Paul."

"And so little," I murmured. "They only had limited information to work with, Bea..."

"Oh, I think we'd be grateful for their knowledge today." Her manner was controlled, as if she desperately tried to remember how she had once talked and behaved. "Anyway, this is where it all happened. We thought at first we had an advantage. Nobody was bothering to come out to what was considered a very minor find and everyone involved was anxious not to let any government start interfering. It was a sort of sacred trust, if you like. We kept clearing. We weren't likely to be found. Unless we used the emergency radio nobody would waste an energy unit on coming out. Oddly, we found no monumental statuary at all, though the engineering was on a scale with anything from the nineteenth dynasty—not quite as sophisticated, maybe, but again far in advance of its own time."

"How long did it take you to uncover it all?"

"We never did. We all swore to reveal nothing until a proper international preservation order could be obtained. This government is as desperate for cruise-schoomer dollars as anyone..."

I found myself interrupting her. "This was all covered by hand, Bea?"

"No, no." Again she was amused. "No, the ship did that, mostly. When it brought me back."

A sudden depression filled me. "You mean a spaceship, do you?"

"Yes," she said. "A lot of people here know about them. And I told Di Roper, as well as some of the kids, and the Sufi. But nobody ever believes us—nobody from the real world, I mean. And that's why I wanted to tell you. You're still a real person, aren't you?"

"Bea—you could let me know everything in London. Once we're back in a more familiar environment. Can't we just enjoy this place for what it is? Enjoy the world for what it is?"

"It's not enjoyable for me, Paul."

I moved away from her. "I don't believe in spaceships."

"You don't believe in much, do you?" Her tone was unusually cool.

I regretted offending her, yet I could not help but respond. "The nuts and bolts of keeping this ramshackle planet running somehow. That's what I believe in, Bea. I'm like that chap in the first version of *The African Queen*, only all he had to worry about was a World War and a little beam-engine. Bea, you were here alone and horribly overtired. Surely…?"

"Let me talk, Paul." There was a note of aching despair in her voice which immediately silenced me and made me lower my head in assent.

We stood there, looking at the sunrise pouring light over that dusty red-and-brown landscape with its drowned architecture, and I listened to her recount the most disturbing and unlikely story I was ever to hear.

The remains of the team had gone into Aswan for various reasons and Bea was left alone with only a young Arab boy for company. Ali worked as a general servant and was as much part of the team as anyone else, with as much enthusiasm. "He, too, understood the reasons for saying little about our work. Phil Springfield had already left to speak to some people in Washington and Professor al-Bayumi, no close relative of the Inspector, was doing what he could in Cairo, though you can imagine the delicacy of his position. Well, one morning, when I was cleaning the dishes and Ali had put a record on the gramophone, this freak storm blew up. It caused a bit of panic, of course, though it was over in a minute or two. And when the sand settled again there was the ship—there, on that bluff. You can see where it came and went."

The spaceship, she said, had been a bit like a flying saucer in that it was circular, with deep sides and glowing horizontal bands at regular intervals. "It was more drum-shaped, though there were discs—I don't know, they weren't metal, but seemed like visible electricity, sort of protruding from it, half on the inside, half on the outside. Much of that moved from a kind of hazy gold into a kind of silver. There were other colours, too. And, I think, sounds. It looked a bit like a kid's tambourine—opaque, sparkling surfaces top and bottom—like the vellum on a drum. And the sides went dark sometimes. Polished oak. The discs, the flange things, went scarlet. They were its main information sensors."

"It was organic?"

"It was a bit. You'd really have to see it for yourself. Anyway, it stood there for a few minutes and then these figures came out. I thought they were test-pilots from that experimental field in Libya and they'd made an emergency landing. I was going to offer them a cup of tea when I realised they weren't human. They had dark bodies that weren't suits exactly but an extra body you wear over your own. Well, you've seen something like it. We all have. It's Akhenoton and Nefertiti. Those strange abdomens and elongated heads, their hermaphroditic quality. They spoke a form of very old-fashioned English. They apologised. They said they had had an instrument malfunction and had not expected to find anyone here. They were prepared to take us with them, if we wished to go. I gathered that these were standard procedures for them. We were both completely captivated by their beauty and the wonder of the event. I don't think Ali hesitated any more than I. I left a note for whoever returned, saying I'd had to leave in a hurry and didn't know when I'd be back. Then we went with them."

"You didn't wonder about their motives?"

"Motives? Yes, Paul, I suppose hallucinations have motives. We weren't the only Earth-people ever to go. Anyway, I never regretted the decision. On the dark side of the moon the main ship was waiting. That's shaped like a gigantic dung-beetle. You'll laugh when I tell you why. I still find it funny. They're furious because their bosses won't pay for less antiquated vessels. Earth's not a very important project. The ship was designed after one of the first organisms they brought back from Earth, to fit in with what they thought was a familiar form. Apparently their own planet has fewer species but many more different sizes of the same creature. They haven't used the main ship to visit Earth since we began to develop sensitive detection equipment. Their time is different, anyway, and they still find our ways of measuring and recording it very hard to understand."

"They took you to their planet?" I wanted her story to be over. I had heard enough to convince me that she was in need of immediate psychiatric help.

"Oh, no. They've never been there. Not the people I know. Others have been back, but we never communicated with them. They have an artificial environment on Mercury." She paused, noticing my distress. "Paul, you know me. I hated that von Däniken stuff. It was patently rubbish. Yet this was, well, horribly like it. Don't think I wasn't seriously considering I might have gone barmy. When people go mad, you know, they get such ordinary delusions. I suppose they reflect our current myths and apocrypha. I felt foolish at first. Then, of course, the reality grew so vivid, so absorbing, I forgot everything. I could not have run away, Paul. I just walked into it all and they let me. I'm not sure why, except they know things—even circumstances, if you follow me—and must have felt it was better to let me. They hadn't wanted to go underwater and they'd returned to an old location in the Sahara. They'd hoped to find some spares, I think. I know it sounds ridiculously prosaic.

"Well, they took us with them to their base. If I try to pronounce their language it somehow sounds so ugly. Yet it's beautiful. I think in their atmosphere it works. I can speak it, Paul. They can speak our languages, too. But there's no need for them. Their home-planet's many light years beyond the Solar System which is actually very different to Earth, except for some colours and smells, of course. Oh, it's so lovely there, at their base. Yet they complain all the time about how primitive it is and long for the comforts of home. You can imagine what it must be like.

"I became friends with a Reen. He was exquisitely beautiful. He wasn't really a he, either, but an androgyne or something similar. There's more than one type of fertilisation, involving several people, but not always. I was completely taken up with him. Maybe he wasn't so lovely to some human eyes, but he was to mine. He was golden-pale and looked rather negroid, I suppose, like one of those beautiful Masai carvings you see in Kenya, and his shape wasn't altogether manlike, either. His abdomen was permanently rounded—most of them are like that, though in the intermediary sex I think there's a special function. My lover was of that sex, yet he found it impossible to make me understand how he was different. Otherwise they have a biology not dissimilar to ours, with similar organs and so on. It was not hard for me to adapt. Their food is delicious, though they moan about that, too. It's sent from home. Where they can grow it properly. And they have extraordinary music. They have recordings of English TV and radio—and other kinds of recordings, too. Earth's an entire department, you see. Paul," she paused as if regretting the return of the memory, "they have recordings of events.

Like battles and ceremonies and architectural stuff. He—my lover—found me an open-air concert at which Mozart was playing. It was too much for me. An archaeologist, and I hadn't the nerve to look at the past as it actually was. I might have got round to it. I meant to. I'd planned to force myself, you know, when I settled down there."

"Bea, don't you know how misanthropic and nuts that sounds?"

"They haven't been 'helping' us or anything like that. It's an observation team. We're not the only planet they're keeping an eye on. They're academics and scientists like us." She seemed to be making an effort to convince me and to repeat the litany of her own faith, whatever it was that she believed kept her sane. Yet the creatures she described, I was still convinced, were merely the inventions of an overtaxed, isolated mind. Perhaps she had been trapped somewhere underground?

"I could have worked there, you see. But I broke the rules."

"You tried to escape?" Reluctantly I humoured her.

"Oh, no!" Her mind had turned backward again and I realised then that it was not any far-off interstellar world but her own planet that had taken her reason. I was suddenly full of sorrow.

"A flying saucer, Bea!" I hoped that my incredulity would bring her back to normality. She had been so ordinary, so matter-of-fact, when we had first met.

"Not really," she said. "The hippies call them Reens. They don't know very much about them, but they've made a cult of the whole thing. They've changed it. Fictionalised it. I can see why that would disturb you. They've turned it into a story for their own purposes. And Sheikh Abu Halil's done the same, really. We've had arguments. I can't stand the exploitation, Paul."

"That's in the nature of a myth." I spoke gently, feeling foolish and puny as I stood looking down on that marvellous construction. I wanted to leave, to return to Aswan, to get us back to Cairo and from there to the relative sanity of rural Oxfordshire, to the village where we had lived with our aunt during our happiest years.

She nodded her head. "That's why I stopped saying anything.

"You can't imagine how hurt I was at first, how urgent it seemed to talk about it. I still thought I was only being taught a lesson and they'd return for me. It must be how Eve felt when she realised God wasn't joking." She smiled bitterly at her own naïveté, her eyes full of old pain. "I was there for a long time, I thought, though when I got back it had only been a month or two and it emerged that nobody had ever returned here from Aswan. There had been that Green Jihad trouble and everyone was suddenly packed off back to Cairo and from there, after a while, to their respective homes. People assumed the same had happened to me. If only it had! But really Paul I wouldn't change it."

I shook my head. "I think you were born in the wrong age, Bea. You should have been a priestess of Amon, maybe. Blessed by the gods."

"We asked them in to breakfast, Ali and me." Shading her eyes against the sun, she raised her arm to point. "Over there. We had a big tent we were using for everything while the others were away. Our visitors didn't think much of our C-Ral and offered us some of their own rations which were far tastier. It was just a scout, that ship. I met my lover later. He had a wonderful sense of irony. As he should, after a thousand years on the same shift."

I could bear no more of this familiar modern apocrypha. "Bea. Don't you think you just imagined it? After nobody returned, weren't you anxious? Weren't you disturbed?"

"They weren't away long enough. I didn't know they weren't coming back, Paul. I fell in love. That wasn't imagination. Gradually, we found ourselves unable to resist the mutual attraction. I suppose I regret that." She offered me a sidelong glance I might have thought cunning in someone else. "I don't blame you for not believing it. How can I prove I'm sane? Or that I was sane then?"

I was anxious to assure her of my continuing sympathy. "You're not a liar, Bea. You never were."

"But you think I'm crazy." All at once her voice became more urgent. "You know how terribly dull madness can be. How conventional most delusions are. You never think you could go mad like that. Then maybe it happens. The flying saucers come down and take you off to Venus, or paradise, or wherever, where war and disease and atmospheric disintegration are long forgotten. You fall in love with a Venusian. Sexual intercourse is forbidden. You break the law. You're cast out of paradise. You can't have a more familiar myth than that, can you, Paul?" Her tone was disturbing. I made a movement with my hand, perhaps to silence her.

"I loved him," she said. "And then I watched the future wither and fade before my eyes. I would have paid any price, done anything, to get back."

That afternoon, as we returned to Aswan, I was full of desperate, bewildered concern for a sister I knew to be in immediate need of professional help. "We'll sort all this out," I reassured her, "maybe when we get to Geneva. We'll see Frank."

"I'm sorry, Paul." She spoke calmly. "I'm not going back with you. I realised it earlier, when we were out at the site. I'll stay in Aswan, after all."

I resisted the urge to turn away from her, and for a while I could not speak.

15 Whereat Serene and Undevoured He Lay...

The flight was leaving in two days and there would be no other ticket for her. After she went off, filthy and withered from the heat, I rather selfishly used my whole outstanding water allowance and bathed for several hours as I tried to separate the truth from the fantasy. I thought how ripe the world was for Bea's revelation, how dangerous it might be. I was glad she planned to tell no one else, but would she keep to that decision? My impulse was to leave, to flee from the whole mess before Bea started telling me how she had become involved in black magic. I felt deeply sorry for her and I felt angry with her for not being the strong leader I had looked up to all my life. I knew it was my duty to get her back to Europe for expert attention.

"I'm not interested in proving what's true or false, Paul," she had said after agreeing to meet me at the Osiris next morning. "I just want you to *know*. Do you understand?"

Anxious not to upset her further, I had said that I did.

That same evening I went to find Inspector el-Bayoumi in his office. He put out his cigarette as I came in, shook hands and, his manner both affable and relaxed, offered me a comfortable leather chair. "You've found your sister, Mr. Pappenheim. That's excellent news."

I handed him a "purse" I had brought and told him, in the convoluted manner such occasions demand, that my sister was refusing to leave, that I had a ticket for her on a flight and that it was unlikely I would have a chance to return to Aswan in the near future. If he could find some reason to hold her and put her on the plane, I would be grateful.

With a sigh of regret—at my folly, perhaps—he handed back the envelope. "I couldn't do it, Mr. Pappenheim, without risking the peace of Aswan, which I have kept pretty successfully for some years. We have a lot of trouble with Green Jihad, you know. I am very short-staffed as a result. You must convince her, my dear sir, or you must leave her here. I assure you, she is much loved and respected. She is a woman of considerable substance and will make her own decisions. I promise, however, to keep you informed."

"By the mail packet? I thought you wanted me to get her out of here!"

"I had hoped you might *persuade* her, Mr. Pappenheim."

I apologised for my rudeness. "I appreciate your concern, Inspector." I put the money back in my pocket and went out to the corniche, catching the first felucca across to the West Bank where this time I paid off my guides before I reached the English House.

The roses were still blooming around the great brick manor and Lady Roper was cutting some of them, laying them carefully in her bucket. "Really, Paul, I don't think you must worry, especially if she doesn't want to talk about her experiences. *We* all know she's telling the truth. Why don't you have a man-to-man with Bernie? There he is, in the kitchen."

Through the window, Sir Bernard waved with his cocoa cup before making a hasty and rather obvious retreat.

16 Your Funeral Bores Them with Its Brilliant Doom

Awaking at dawn the next morning I found it impossible to return to sleep. I got up and tried to make some notes but writing down what my sister had told me somehow made it even more difficult to understand. I gave up. Putting on a cotton *gelabea* and some slippers I went down to the almost empty street and walked to the nearest corner café where I ordered tea and a couple of rolls. All the other little round tables were occupied and from the interior came the sound of a scratched Oum Kal Thoum record. The woman's angelic voice, singing the praises of God and the joys of love, reminded me of my schooldays in Fèz, when I had lived with my father during his brief entrepreneurial period, before he had returned to England to become a Communist. Then Oum Kal Thoum had been almost a goddess in Egypt. Now she was as popular again, like so many of the old performers who had left a legacy of 78 rpms which could be played on spring-loaded gramophones or the new clockworks which could also play a delicate LP but which few Egyptians could afford. Most of the records were re-pressed from ancient masters purchased from Athenian studios which, fifty years earlier, had mysteriously manufactured most Arabic recordings. The quality of her voice came through the surface noise as purely as it had once sounded through fractured stereos or on crude pirate tapes in the days of licence and waste. "Inte el Hob," wistful, celebratory, thoughtful, reminded me of the little crooked streets of Fèz, the stink of the dyers and tanners, the extraordinary vividness of the colours, the pungent mint bales, the old men who loved to stand and declaim on the matters of the day with anyone who would listen, the smell of fresh saffron, of lavender carried on the backs of donkeys driven by little boys crying "*balek*!" and insulting, in the vocabulary of a professional soldier, anyone who refused to move aside for them. Life had been sweet then, with unlimited television and cheap air-travel, with any food you could afford and any drink freely available for a few dirhams, and every pleasure in the reach of the common person. The years of Easy, the years of Power, the paradise from which our lazy greed and hungry egos banished us to eternal punishment, to the limbo of the Age of Penury, for which we have only ourselves to blame! But Fèz was good, then, in those good, old days.

A little more at peace with myself, I walked down to the river while the muezzin called the morning prayer and I might have been back in the Ottoman Empire, leading the simple, steady life of a small land-owner or a civil servant in the family of the Bey. The débris of the river, the ultimate irony of the Nile filling with all the bottles which had held the water needed because we had polluted the Nile, drew my attention. It was as if the water industry had hit upon a perfect means of charging people whatever they wanted for a drink of *eau naturelle*, while at the same time guaranteeing that the Nile could never again be a source of free water. All this further reinforced my assertion that we were not in the Golden Age those New New Aquarians so longed to re-create. We were in a present which had turned our planet into a single, squalid slum, where nothing beautiful could exist for long, unless in isolation, like Lady Roper's rose garden. We could not bring back the Golden Age. Indeed we were now paying the price of having enjoyed one.

I turned away from the river and went back to the café to find Sheikh Abu Halil sitting in the chair I had recently occupied. "What a coincidence, Dr. Pappenheim. How are you? How is your wonderful sister?" He spoke educated English.

I suspected for a moment that he knew more than he allowed but then I checked myself. My anxiety was turning into paranoia. This was no way to help my sister.

"I was killing time," he said, "before coming to see you. I didn't want to interrupt your beauty sleep or perhaps even your breakfast, but I guessed aright.

You have the habits of Islam." He was flattering me and this in itself was a display of friendship or, at least, affection.

"I've been looking at the rubbish in the river." I shook his hand and sat down in the remaining chair. "There aren't enough police to do anything about it, I suppose."

"Always a matter of economics." He was dressed very differently today in a conservative light-and-dark blue *gelabea*, like an Alexandrian businessman. On his head he wore a discreet, matching cap. "You take your sister back today, I understand, Dr. Pappenheim."

"If she'll come."

"She doesn't want to go?" The Sufi's eyelid twitched almost raffishly, suggesting to me that he had been awake most of the night. Had he spent that time with Bea?

"She's not sure now," I said. "She hates flying."

"Oh, yes. Flying is a very difficult and unpleasant thing. I myself hate it and would not do it if I could."

I felt he understood far more than that and I was in some way relieved. "You couldn't persuade her of the wisdom of coming with me, I suppose, sidhi?"

"I have already told her what I think, Paul. I think she should go with you. She is unhappy here. Her burden is too much. But she would not and will not listen to me. I had hoped to congratulate you and wish you God Speed."

"You're very kind." I now believed him sincere.

"I love her, Paul." He gave a great sigh and turned to look up at the sky. "She's an angel! I think so. She will come to no harm from us."

"Well—" I was once again at a loss. "I love her too, sidhi. But does she want our love? I wonder."

"You are wiser than I thought, Paul. Just so. Just so." He ordered coffee and sweetac for us both. "She knows only the habit of giving. She has never learned to receive. Not here, anyway. Especially from you."

"She was always my best friend." I said. "A mother sometimes. An alter-ego. I want to get her to safety, Sheikh Abu Halil."

"Safety?" At this he seemed sceptical. "It would be good for her to know the normality of family life. She has a husband."

"He's in New Zealand. They split up. He hated what he called her 'charity work.'"

"If he was unsympathetic to her calling, that must be inevitable."

"You really think she has a vocation?" The coffee came and the oversweetened breakfast cakes which he ate with considerable relish. "We don't allow these at home. All those chemicals!" There was an element of self-mockery in his manner now that he was away from his *medrassah*. "Yes. We think she has been called. We have many here who believe that of themselves, but most are self-deluding. Aswan is becoming a little over-stocked with mystics and wonder-workers. Eventually, I suppose, the fashion will change, as it did in Nepal, San Francisco or Essaouira. Your sister, however, is special to us. She is so sad, these days, doctor. There is a chance she might find happiness in London. She is spending too long in the desert."

"Isn't that one of the habitual dangers of the professional mystic?" I asked him.

He responded with quiet good humour. "Perhaps of the more old-fashioned type, like me. Did she ever tell you what she passed to Lallah Zenobia that night?"

"You mean the cause of her arrest? Wasn't it money? A purse. The police thought it was."

"But if so, Paul, what was she buying?"

"Peace of mind, perhaps," I said. I asked him if he really believed in people from space, and he said that he did, for he believed that God had created and populated the whole universe as He saw fit.

"By the way," he said, "are you walking up towards the Cataract? There was some kind of riot near there an hour or so ago. The police were involved and some of the youngsters from the holiday villas. Just a peaceful demonstration, I'm sure. That would be nothing to do with your sister?"

I shook my head.

"You'll go back to England, will you, Dr. Pappenheim?"

"Eventually," I told him. "The way I feel at the moment I might retire. I want to write a novel."

"Oh, your father was a vicar, then?"

I was thoroughly puzzled by this remark. Again he began to laugh. "I do apologise. I've always been struck by the curious fact that so much enduring English literature has sprung, as it were, from the loins of the minor clergy. I wish you luck, Dr. Pappenheim, in whatever you choose to do. And I hope your sister decides to go with you tomorrow." He kissed me three times on my face. "You both need to discover your own peace. *Sabah el Kher.*"

"Allah yisabbe'h Kum bil-Kher."

The holy man waved a dignified hand as he strolled down towards the corniche to find a calash.

By now the muezzin was calling the mid-morning prayer. I had been away from my hotel longer than planned. I went back through the crowds to the green-and-white entrance of the Osiris and climbed slowly to my room. It was not in my nature to force my sister to leave and I felt considerably ashamed of my attempt to persuade Inspector el-Bayoumi to extradite her. I could only pray that, in the course of the night, she had come to her senses. My impulse was to seek her out but I still did not know her address.

I spent the rest of the morning packing and making official notes until, at noon, she came through the archway, wearing a blue cotton dress and matching shawl. I hoped this was a sign she was preparing for the flight back to civilisation. "You haven't eaten, have you?" she said.

She had booked a table on the Mut, a floating restaurant moored just below the Cataract. We boarded a thing resembling an Ottoman pleasure barge, all dark green trellises, scarlet fretwork and brass ornament, while inside it was more luxurious than the Sufi's "harem." "It's hardly used, of course, these days," Bea said. "Not enough rich people wintering in Aswan any more. But the atmosphere's nice still. You don't mind? It's not against your puritan nature, is it?"

"Only a little." I was disturbed by her apparent normality. We might never have ridden into the desert together, never have talked about aliens and spaceships and Ancient Egyptian universities. I wondered, now, if she were not seriously schizophrenic.

"You do seem troubled, though." She was interrupted by a large man in a dark yellow *gelabea* smelling wildly of garlic who embraced her with affectionate delight. "Beatrice! My Beatrice!" We were introduced. Mustafa shook hands with me as he led us ecstatically to a huge, low table looking over the Nile, where the feluccas and great sailing barges full of holidaymakers came close enough to touch. We sat on massive brocaded foam cushions.

I could not overcome my depression. I was faced with a problem beyond my scope. "You've decided to stay, I take it?"

The major-domo returned with two large glasses of Campari Soda. "Compliments of the house." It was an extraordinary piece of generosity. We saluted him with our glasses, then toasted each other.

"Yes." She drew her hair over her collar and looked towards the water. "For a while, anyway. I won't get into any more trouble, Paul, I promise. And I'm not the suicide type. That I'm absolutely sure about."

"Good." I would have someone come out to her as soon as possible, a psychiatrist contact in MEDAC who could provide a professional opinion. "You'll tell me your address?"

"I'm moving. Tomorrow. I'll stay with the Ropers if they'll have me. Any mail care of them will be forwarded. I'm not being deliberately mysterious, dear, I promise. I'm going to write. And meanwhile, I've decided to tell you the whole of it. I want you to remember it, perhaps put it into some kind of shape that I can't. It's important to me that it's recorded. Do you promise?"

I could only promise that I would make all the notes possible.

"Well, there's actually not much else."

I was relieved to know I would not for long have to suffer those miserably banal inventions.

"I fell in love, you see."

"Yes, you told me. With a spaceman."

"We knew it was absolutely forbidden to make love. But we couldn't help ourselves. I mean, with all his self-discipline he was as attracted to me as I was to him. It was important, Paul."

I did my best to give her my full attention while she repeated much of what she had already told me in the desert. There was a kind of biblical rhythm to her voice. "So they threw me out. I never saw my lover again. I never saw his home again. They brought me back and left me where they had found me. Our tents were gone and everything was obviously abandoned. They let their engines blow more sand over the site. Well, I got to Aswan eventually. I found water and food and it wasn't too hard. I'm not sure why I came here. I didn't know then that I was pregnant. I don't think I knew you could get pregnant. There isn't a large literature on sexual congress with semi-males of the alien persuasion. You'd probably find him bizarre, but for me it was like making love to an angel. All the time. It was virtually our whole existence. Oh, Paul!" She pulled at her collar. She smoothed the table-cloth between her knife and fork. "Well, he was wonderful and he thought I was wonderful. Maybe that's *why* they forbid it. The way they'd forbid a powerful habit-forming stimulant. Do you know I just this second thought of that?"

"That's why you were returned here?" I was still having difficulty following her narrative.

"Didn't I say? Yes. Well, I went to stay with the Ropers for a bit, then I stayed in the commune and then the *medrassah*, but I kept going out to the site. I was hoping they'd relent, you see. I'd have done almost anything to get taken back, Paul."

"To escape from here, you mean?"

"To be with him. That's all. I was—I am—so lonely. Nobody could describe the void."

I was silent, suddenly aware of her terrible vulnerability, still convinced she had been the victim of some terrible deception.

"You're wondering about the child," she said. She put her hand on mine where I fingered the salt. "He was born too early. He lived for eight days. I had him at Lallah Zenobia's. You see, I couldn't tell what he would look like. She was better prepared, I thought. She even blessed him when he was born so that his soul might go to heaven. He was tiny and frail and beautiful. His father's colouring and eyes. My face, I think, mostly. He would have been a *wunderkind*, I shouldn't be surprised. Paul..." Her voice became a whisper. "It was like giving birth to the Messiah."

With great ceremony, our meal arrived. It was a traditional Egyptian *meze* and it was more and better food than either of us had seen in years. Yet we hardly ate.

"I took him back to the site." She looked out across the water again. "I'd got everything ready. I had some hope his father would come to see him. Nobody came. Perhaps it needed that third sex to give him the strength? I waited, but there was not, as the kids say, a Reen to be seen." This attempt at humour was hideous. I took firm hold of her hands. The tears in her eyes were barely restrained.

"He died." She released her hands and looked for something in her bag. I thought for a frightening moment she was going to produce a photograph. "Eight days. He couldn't seem to get enough nourishment from what I was feeding him. He needed that—whatever it was he should have had." She took a piece of linen from her bag and wiped her hands and neck. "You're thinking I should have taken him to the hospital. But this is Egypt, Paul, where people are still arrested for witchcraft and here was clear evidence of my having had congress with an *ifrit*. Who would believe my story? I was aware of what I was doing. I'd never expected the baby to live or, when he did live, to look the way he did. The torso was sort of pear-shaped and there were several embryonic limbs. He was astonishingly lovely. I think he belonged to his father's world. I wish they had come for him. It wasn't fair that he should die."

I turned my attention to the passing boats and controlled my own urge to weep. I was hoping she would stop, for she was, by continuing, hurting herself. But, obsessively, she went on. "Yes, Paul. I could have gone to Europe as soon as I knew I was pregnant and I would have done if I'd had a hint of what was coming, but my instincts told me he would not live or, if he did live, it would be because his father returned for him. I don't think that was self-deception. Anyway, when he was dead I wasn't sure what to do. I hadn't made any plans. Lallah Zenobia was wonderful to me. She said she would dispose of the body properly and with respect. I couldn't bear to have some future archaeologist digging him up. You know, I've always hated that. Especially with children. So I went to her lean-to in Shantytown. I had him wrapped in a shawl—Mother's lovely old Persian shawl—and inside a beautiful inlaid box. I put the box in a leather bag and took it to her."

"That was the Cairene Purse? Or did you give her money, too?"

"Money had nothing to do with it. Do the police still think I was paying her? I offered Zenobia money but she refused. 'Just pray for us all,' was what she said. I've been doing it every night since. The Lord's prayer for everyone. It's the only prayer I know. I learned it at one of my schools."

"Zenobia went to prison. Didn't you try to tell them she was helping you?"

"There was no point in mentioning the baby, Paul. That would have constituted another crime, I'm sure. She was as good as her word. He was never found. She made him safe somewhere. A little funeral boat on the river late at night, away from all the witnesses, maybe. And they would have found him if she had been deceiving me, Paul. She got him home somehow."

Dumb with sadness, I could only reach out and stroke her arms and hands, reach for her unhappy face.

We ate so as not to offend our host, but without appetite. Above the river the sun was at its zenith and Aswan experienced the familiar, unrelenting light of an African afternoon.

She looked out at the river with its day's flow of débris, the plastic jars, the used sanitary towels, the paper and filth left behind by tourists and residents alike.

With a deep, uneven sigh, she shook her head, folded her arms under her breasts and leaned back in the engulfing foam.

All the *fhouls* and the marinated salads, the *ruqaq* and the meats lay cold before us as, from his shadows, the proprietor observed us with discreet concern.

There came a cry from outside. A boy perched high on the single mast of his boat, his white *gelabea* tangling with his sail so that he seemed all of a piece with the vessel, waved to friends on the shore and pointed into the sky. One of our last herons circled overhead for a moment and then flew steadily south, into what had been the Sudan.

My sister's slender body was moved for a moment by some small, profound anguish.

"He could not have lived here."

Chapter Quotes: 1 Hood; 2 Khayyám FitzGerald; 3 AE; 4 Dylan Thomas; 5 Wheldrake; 6 Yokum; 7 Aeschylus MacNeice; 8 Vachel Lindsay; 9 F. Thompson; 10 Peake; 11 Treece; 12 Duffy; 13 Nye; 14 C. D. Lewis; 15 E. St. V. Millay; 16 Nye.

A Slow Saturday Night at the Surrealist Sporting Club (2001)

"A Slow Saturday Night..." is the second of two homages Moorcock has written to Maurice Richardson's famous creation, Engelbrecht the surrealist boxer, immortalised in Richardson's 1950 book (and its recent reprint), *The Exploits of Engelbrecht*.

The story was originally published in 2001, in an anthology, *Redshift* (Roc), edited by Al Sarrantonio.

A Slow Saturday Night at the Surrealist Sporting Club*

Being a Further Account of Engelbrecht the Boxing Dwarf and His Fellow Members

After Maurice Richardson

I happened to be sitting in the snug of the Strangers' Bar at the Surrealist Sporting Club on a rainy Saturday night, enjoying a well mixed Existential Fizz (2 pts Vortex Water to 1 pt Sweet Gin) and desperate to meet a diverting visitor, when Death slipped unostentatiously into the big chair opposite, warming his bones at the fire and remarking on the unseasonable weather. There was sure to be a lot of flu about. It made you hate to get the tube but the buses were worse and had I seen what cabs were charging, these days? He began to drone on as usual about the ozone layer and the melting pole, how we were poisoning ourselves on G.M. foods and feeding cows to cows and getting all that pollution and cigarette smoke in our lungs and those other gloomy topics he seems to relish, which I suppose makes you appreciate it when he puts you out of your misery.

I had to choose between nodding off or changing the subject. The evening being what it was, I made the effort and changed the subject. Or at least, had a stab at it.

"So what's new?" It was feeble, I admit. But, as it happened, it stopped him in mid-moan.

"Thanks for reminding me," he said, and glanced at one of his many watches. "God's dropping in—oh, in about twelve minutes, twenty-five seconds. He doesn't have a lot of time, but if you've any questions to ask him, I suggest you canvass the other members present and think up some good ones in a hurry. And he's not very fond of jokers, if you know what I mean. So stick to substantial questions or he won't be pleased."

"I thought he usually sent a seraphim ahead for this sort of visit?" I queried mildly. "Are you all having to double up or something? Is it overpopulation?" I didn't like this drift, either. It suggested a finite universe, for a start.

Our Ever-Present Friend rose smoothly. He looked around the room with a distressed sigh, as if suspecting the whole structure to be infected with dry rot and carpenter ants. He couldn't as much as produce a grim brotherly smile for the deathwatch beetle which had come out especially to greet him. "Well, once more into the breach. Have you noticed what it's like out there? Worst on record, they say. Mind you, they don't remember the megalithic. Those were the days, eh? See you later."

"Be sure of it." I knew a moment of existential angst.

Sensitively, Death hesitated, seemed about to apologise, then thought better of it. He shrugged. "See you in a minute," he said. "I've got to look out for God in the foyer and sign him in. You know." He had the air of one who had given up worrying about minor embarrassments and was sticking to the protocol, come hell or high water. He was certainly more laconic than he had been. I wondered if the extra work, and doubling as a seraphim, had changed his character.

With Death gone, the Strangers' was warming up rapidly again and I enjoyed a quiet moment with my fizz before rising to amble through the usual warped and shrieking corridors to the Members' Bar, which appeared empty.

"Are you thinking of dinner?" Lizard Bayliss, looking like an undisinfected dishrag, strolled over from where he had been hanging up his obnoxious cape. Never far behind, out of the W.C., bustled Engelbrecht the Dwarf Clock Boxer, who had gone ten rounds with the Greenwich Atom before that over-refined chronometer went down to an iffy punch in the eleventh. His great, mad eyes flashed from under a simian hedge of eyebrow. As usual he wore a three-piece suit a size too small for him, in the belief it made him seem taller. He was effing and blinding about some imagined insult offered by the taxi-driver who had brought them back from the not altogether successful Endangered Sea Monsters angling contest in which, I was to learn later, Engelbrecht had caught his hook in a tangle of timeweed and wound up dragging down the *Titanic*, which explained that mystery. Mind you, he still had to come clean about the R101. There was some feeling in the club concerning the airship, since he'd clearly taken bets against himself. Challenged, he'd muttered some conventional nonsense about the Maelstrom and the Inner World, but we'd heard that one too often to be convinced. He also resented our recent rule limiting all aerial angling to firedrakes and larger species of pterodactyls.

Lizard Bayliss had oddly coloured bags under his eyes, giving an even more downcast appearance to his normally dissolute features. He was a little drained from dragging the Dwarf in by his collar. It appeared that, seeing the big rods, the driver had asked Bayliss if that was his bait on the seat beside him. The irony was, of course, that the Dwarf had been known to use himself as bait more than once and there was still some argument over interpretation of the rules in that area, too. The Dwarf had taken the cabby's remark to be specific not because of his diminutive stockiness, but because of his sensitivity over the rules issue. He stood to lose a few months, even years, if they reversed the result.

He was still spitting on about "nit-picking fascist anoraks with severe anal-retention problems" when I raised my glass and yelled: "If you've an important question for God, you'd better work out how to phrase it. He's due in any second now. And he's only got a few minutes. At the Strangers' Bar. We could invite him in here, but that would involve a lot of time-consuming ritual and so forth. Any objection to meeting him back there?"

The Dwarf wasn't sure he had anything to say that wouldn't get taken the wrong way. Then, noticing how low the fire was, opined that the Strangers' was bound to offer better hospitality. "I can face my maker any time," he pointed out, "but I'd rather do it with a substantial drink in my hand and a good blaze warming my bum." He seemed unusually oblivious to any symbolism, given that the air was writhing with it. I think the *Titanic* was still on his mind. He was trying to work out how to get his hook back.

By the time we had collected up Oneway Ballard and Taffy Sinclair from the dining room and returned to the Strangers', God had already arrived. Any plans the Dwarf had instantly went out of the window, because God was standing with his back to the fire, blocking everyone's heat. With a word to Taffy not to overtax the Lord of Creation, Death hurried off on some urgent business and disappeared back through the swing doors.

"I am thy One True God," said Jehovah, making the glasses and bottles rattle. He cleared his throat and dropped his tone to what must for him have been a whisper. But it was unnatural, almost false, like a TV presenter trying to express concern while keeping full attention on the autoprompt. Still, there was something totally convincing about God as a presence. You knew you were in his aura and you knew you had Grace, even if you weren't too impressed by his stereotypical form. God added: "I am Jehovah, the Almighty. Ask of me what ye will."

Lizard knew sudden inspiration. "Do you plan to send Jesus back to Earth and have you any thoughts about the 2:30 at Aintree tomorrow?"

"He is back," said God, "and I wouldn't touch those races, these days. Believe me, they're all bent, one way or another. If you like the horses, do the National... Take a chance. Have a gamble. It's anybody's race, the National."

"But being omniscient," said Lizard slowly, "wouldn't you know the outcome anyway?"

"If I stuck by all the rules of omniscience it wouldn't exactly be sporting, would it?" God was staring over at the bar, checking out the Corona-Coronas and the melting marine chronometer above them.

"You don't think it's hard on the horses?" asked Jillian Burnes, the transsexual novelist, who could be relied upon for a touch of compassion. Being almost seven feet tall in her spike heels, she was also useful for getting books down from the higher shelves and sorting out those bottles at the top of the bar which looked so temptingly dangerous.

"Bugger the horses," said God, "it's the race that counts. And anyway, the horses love it. They love it."

I was a little puzzled. "I thought we had to ask only substantial questions?"

"That's right?" God drew his mighty brows together in enquiry.

I fell into an untypical silence. I was experiencing a mild revelation concerning the head of the Church of England and her own favourite pasatiempi, but it seemed inappropriate to run with it at that moment.

"What I'd like to know is," said Engelbrecht, cutting suddenly to the chase, "who gets into heaven and why?"

There was a bit of a pause in the air, as if everyone felt perhaps he'd pushed the boat out a little too far, but God was nodding. "Fair question," he said. "Well, it's cats, then dogs, but there's quite a few human beings, really. But mostly it's pets."

Lizard Bayliss had begun to grin. It wasn't a pretty sight with all those teeth which he swore weren't filed. "You mean you like animals better than people? Is that what you're saying, Lord?"

"I wouldn't generalise." God lifted his robe a little to let the fire get at his legs. "It's mostly cats. Some dogs. Then a few people. All a matter of proportion, of course. I mean, it's millions at least, probably billions, because I'd forgotten about the rats and mice."

"You like those, too?"

"No. Can't stand their hairless tails. Sorry, but it's just me. They can, I understand, be affectionate little creatures. No, they're for the cats. Cats are perfectly adapted for hanging out in heaven. But they still need a bit of a hunt occasionally. They get bored. Well, you know cats. You can't change their nature."

"I thought you could," said Oneway Ballard, limping up to the bar and ringing the bell. He was staying the night because someone had put a Denver Boot on his Granada and he'd torn the wheel off, trying to reverse out of it. He was in poor spirits because he and the car had been due to be married at St. James's, Spanish Place, next morning and there was no way he was going to get the wheel back on and the car spruced up in time for the ceremony. He'd already called the vicar. Igor was on tonight and had trouble responding. We watched him struggle to get his hump under the low doorway. "Coming, Master," he said. It was too much like *Young Frankenstein* to be very amusing.

"*I* can change nature, yes," God continued. "I said *you* couldn't. Am I right?"

"Always," said Oneway, turning to order a couple of pints of Ackroyd's. He wasn't exactly looking on fate with any favour at that moment. "But if you can..."

"There are a lot of things I could do," God pointed out. "You might have noticed. I could stop babies dying and famines and earthquakes. But I don't, do I?"

"Well, we wouldn't know about the ones you'd stopped," Engelbrecht pointed out, a bit donnishly for him. "So when the heavens open on the day of resurrection, it really will rain cats and dogs. And who else? Jews?"

"Some Jews, yes." In another being, God's attitude might have seemed defensive. "But listen, I want to get off the race issue. I don't judge people on their race, colour or creed. I never have. Wealth," he added a little sententiously, "has no colour. If I've said who I favour and some purse-mouthed prophet decides to put his name in instead of the bloke I chose, then so it goes. It's free will in a free market. And you can't accuse me of not supporting the free market. Economic liberalism combined with conservative bigotry is the finest weapon I ever gave the chosen people. One thing you can't accuse me of being and that's a control freak."

"See," said Lizard, then blushed. "Sorry, God. But you just said it yourself—chosen people."

"Those are the people I choose," said God with a tinge of impatience. "Yes."

"So—the Jews."

"No. The moneylenders are mostly wasps. The usurers. Oil people. Big players in Threadneedle Street and Wall Street. Or, at least, a good many of them. Very few Jews, as it happens. And most of them, in heaven, are from show business. Look around you and tell me who are the chosen ones. It's simple. They're the people in the limousines with great sex lives and private jets. Not cats, of course, who don't like travel. Otherwise, the chosen are very popular with the public or aggressively wealthy, the ones who have helped themselves. And those who help themselves God helps."

"You're a Yank!" Engelbrecht was struck by a revelation. "There are rules in this club about Yanks."

"Because Americans happen to have a handle on the realities doesn't mean I'm American." God was a little offended. Then he softened. "It's probably an easy mistake to make. I mean, strictly speaking, I'm prehistoric. But, yes, America has come up trumps where religious worship is concerned. No old-fashioned iconography cluttering up their vision. There's scarcely a church in the nation which isn't a sort of glorified business seminar nowadays. God will help you, but you have to prove you're serious about wanting help. He'll at least match everything you make, but you have to make a little for yourself first, to show you can. It's all there. Getting people out of the welfare trap."

"Aren't they all a bit narrow-minded?" asked Taffy Sinclair, the metatemporal pathologist, who had so successfully dissected the Hess quins. "They are where I come from, I know." His stern good looks demanded our attention. "Baptists!" He took a long introspective pull of his shant. The massive dome of his forehead glared in the firelight.

God was unmoved by Sinclair's point. "Those Baptists are absolute wizards. They're spot on about me. And all good Old Testament boys. They use the Son of God as a source of authority, not as an example. The economic liberalism they vote for destroys everything of value worth conserving! It drives them nuts, but it makes them more dysfunctional and therefore more aggressive and therefore richer. Deeply unhappy, they turn increasingly to the source of their misery for a comfort that never comes. Compassionate consumption? None of your peace and love religions down there. Scientology has nothing on that little lot. Amateur, that Hubbard. But a bloody good one." He chuckled affectionately. "I look with special favour on the Southern Baptist Convention. So there does happen to be a preponderance of Americans in paradise, as it happens. But ironically no Scientologists. Hubbard's as fond of cats as I am, but he won't have Scientologists. I'll admit, too, that not all the chosen are entirely happy with the situation, because of being pretty thoroughly outnumbered, just by the Oriental shorthairs. And they do like to be in control. And many of them are bigots, so they're forever whining about the others being favoured over them.

"Of course, once they get to heaven, I'm in control. It takes a bit of adjustment for some of them. Some of them, in fact, opt for hell, preferring to rule there than serve in heaven, as it were. Milton was on the money, really, if a bit melodramatic and fanciful. Not so much a war in heaven as a renegotiated contract. A pending paradise."

"I thought you sent Jesus down as the Prince of Peace," said Lizard a little dimly. The black bombers were wearing off and he was beginning to feel the effects of the past few hours.

"Well, in those days," said God, "I have to admit, I had a different agenda. Looking back, of course, it was a bit unrealistic. It could never have worked. But I wouldn't take no for an answer, and you know the rest. New Testament and so on? Even then Paul kept trying to talk to me, and I wouldn't listen. Another temporary fix-up as it turned out. He was right. I admitted it. The problem is not in the creating of mankind, say, but in getting the self-reproducing software right. Do that and you have a human race with real potential. But that's always been the hurdle, hasn't it? Now lust and greed are all very well, but they do tend to involve a lot of messy side-effects. And, of course, I tried to modify those with my ten commandments. Everyone was very excited about them at the time. A bit of fine tuning I should have tried earlier. But we all know where that led. It's a ramshackle world at best, I have to admit. The least I can do is shore a few things up. I tried some other belief systems. All ended the same way. So the alternative was to bless the world with sudden rationality. Yet once you give people a chance to think about it, they stop reproducing altogether. Lust is a totally inefficient engine for running a reproductive programme. It means you have to override the rational processes so that they switch off at certain times. And we all know where that leads. So, all in all, while the fiercest get to the top, the top isn't worth getting to and if it wasn't for the cats I'd wind the whole miserable failure up. In fact I was going to until Jesus talked me into offering cloning as an alternative. I'd already sent them H. G. Wells and the Universal Declaration of Human Rights, the United Nations and all the rest of it. I'm too soft, I know, but Jesus was always my favourite, and he's never short of a reason for giving you all another chance. So every time I start to wipe you out, along he comes with that bloody charm of his and he twists me round his little finger. Well, you know the rest. One World War interrupted. Started again. Stopped again. Couple more genocides. Try again. No good. So far, as you've probably noticed, you haven't exactly taken the best options offered. Even Jesus is running out of excuses for you. So I'm giving it a few years and then, no matter what, I'm sending a giant comet. Or I might send a giant cat. It'll be a giant something anyway. And it'll be over within an instant. Nothing cruel. No chance to change my mind."

Death was hovering about in the shadows, glancing meaningfully at his watches.

"That's it, then, is it?" Jillian Burnes seemed a bit crestfallen. "You've come to warn us that the world has every chance of ending. And you offer us no chance to repent, to change, to make our peace?" She tightened her lips. God could tell how she felt.

"I didn't offer," God reminded her. "Somebody asked. Look, I am not the Prince of Lies. I am the Lord of Truth. Not a very successful God of Love, though I must say I tried. More a God of, well, profit, I suppose. I mean everyone complains that these great religious books written in my name are incoherent, so they blame the writers. Never occurs to them that I might not be entirely coherent myself. On account of being—well, the supreme being. If I am existence, parts of existence are incoherent. Or, at least, apparently incoherent..." He realised he'd lost us.

"So there's no chance for redemption?" said Engelbrecht looking about him. "For, say, the bohemian sporting fancy?"

"I didn't say that. Who knows what I'll feel like next week? But I'll always get on famously with cats. Can't resist the little beggars. There are some humans who are absolutely satisfied with the status quo in heaven. But all cats get a kick out of the whole thing. The humans, on the quiet, are often only there to look after the cats."

"And the rest?"

"I don't follow you," said God. "Well, of course, being omniscient, I could follow you. What I should have said was 'I'm not following you.'"

"The rest of the people. What happens to them. The discards. The souls who don't make it through the pearly gates, as it were?" Engelbrecht seemed to be showing unusual concern for others.

"Recycled," said God. "You know—thrown back in the pot—what do the Celts call it?—the Mother Sea? After all, they're indistinguishable in life, especially the politicians. They probably hardly notice the change."

"Is that the only people who get to stay?" asked the Dwarf. "Rich people?"

"Oh, no," said God. "Though the others do tend to be funny. Wits and comics mostly. I love Benny Hill, don't you? He's often seated on my right side, you might say. You need a lot of cheering up in my job."

Jillian Burnes was becoming sympathetic. She loved to mother power. "I always thought you were a matron. I felt ashamed of you. It's such a relief to find out you're male." There was a sort of honeyed criticism in her voice, an almost flirtatious quality.

"Not strictly speaking male," said God, "being divine, sublime and, ha, ha, all things, including woman, the eternal mime."

"Well, you sound very masculine," she said. "White and privileged."

"Absolutely!" God reassured her. "I approve of your method. That's exactly who I am and that's who I like to spend my time with, if I have to spend it with human beings at all."

Engelbrecht had bared his teeth. He was a terrier. "So can I get in, is what I suppose I'm asking?"

"Of course you can."

"Though I'm not Jewish."

"You don't have to be Jewish. I can't stress this too often. Think about it. I haven't actually favoured the main mass of Jews lately, have I? I mean, take the twentieth century alone. I'm not talking about dress codes and tribal loyalties."

God spread his legs a little wider and hefted his gown to let the glow get to his divine buttocks. If we had not known it to be a noise from the fire, we might have thought he farted softly. He sighed. "When I first got into this calling there were all kinds of other deities about, many of them far superior to me in almost every way. More attractive. More eloquent. More easy-going. Elegant powers of creativity. Even the Celts and the Norse gods had a bit of style. But I had ambition. Bit by bit I took over the trade until, bingo, one day there was only me. I am, after all, the living symbol of corporate aggression, tolerating no competition and favouring only my own family and its clients. What do you want me to do? Identify with some bloody oik of an East Timorese who can hardly tell the difference between himself and a tree? Sierra Leone? Listen, you get yourselves into these messes, you get yourselves out."

"Well it's a good world for overpaid CEOs…" mused Lizard.

"In this world and the next," confirmed God. "And it's a good world for overpaid comedians, too, for that matter."

"So Ben Elton and Woody Allen…"

God raised an omnipotent hand. "I said comedians."

"Um." Engelbrecht was having difficulties phrasing something. "Um…" He was aware of Death hovering around and ticking like a showcase full of Timexes. "What about it?"

"What?"

"You know," murmured Engelbrecht, deeply embarrassed by now, "the meaning of existence? The point."

"Point?" God frowned. "I don't follow."

"Well you've issued a few predictions in your time…"

Death was clearing his throat. "Just to remind you about that policy subcommittee," he murmured. "I think we told them half-eight."

God seemed mystified for a moment. Then he began to straighten up. "Oh, yes. Important committee. Might be some good news for you. Hush, hush. Can't say any more."

Lizard was now almost falling over himself to get his questions in. "Did you have anything to do with global warming?"

Death uttered a cold sigh. He almost put the fire out. We all glared at him, but he was unrepentant. God remained tolerant of a question he might have heard a thousand times at least. He spread his hands. "Look. I plant a planet with sustainable wealth, ok? Nobody tells you to breed like rabbits and gobble it all up at once."

"Well, actually, you did encourage us to breed like rabbits," Jillian Burnes murmured reasonably.

"Fair enough," said God. "I have to agree corporate expansion depends on a perpetually growing population. We found that out. Demographics are the friend of business, right?"

"Well, up to a point, I should have thought," said Lizard, aware that God had already as good as told him a line had been drawn under the whole project. "I mean it's a finite planet and we're getting close to exhausting it."

"That's right." God glanced at the soft Dalí watches over the bar, then darted an enquiry at Death. "So?"

"So how can we stop the world from ending?" asked Engelbrecht.

"Well," said God, genuinely embarrassed, "you can't."

"Can't? The end of the world is inevitable?"

"I thought I'd answered that one already. In fact, it's getting closer all the time." He began to move towards the cloakroom. God, I understood, couldn't lie. Which didn't mean he always liked telling the truth. And he knew anything he added would probably sound patronising or unnecessarily accusatory. Then the taxi had turned up, and Death was bustling God off into it.

And that was that. As we gathered round the fire, Lizard Bayliss said he thought it was a rum do altogether and God must be pretty desperate to seek out company like ours, especially on a wet Saturday night. What did everyone else make of it?

We decided that nobody present was really qualified to judge, so we'd wait until Monday, when Monsignor Cornelius returned from Las Vegas. The famous Cowboy Jesuit had an unmatched grasp of contemporary doctrine.

But this wasn't good enough for Engelbrecht, who seemed to have taken against our visitor in a big way.

"I could sort this out," he insisted. If God had a timepiece of any weight he'd like to back, Engelbrecht would cheerfully show it the gloves.

That, admitted Jillian Burnes with new admiration, was the true existential hero, forever battling against fate, and forever doomed to lose. Engelbrecht, scenting an opportunity he hadn't previously even considered, became almost egregious, slicking back his hair and offering the great novelist an engaging leer.

When the two had gone off, back to Jillian's Tufnell Hill eyrie, Lizard Bayliss offered to buy the drinks, adding that it had been a bloody awful Friday and Saturday so far, and he hoped Sunday cheered up because if it didn't the whole weekend would have been a rotten write-off.

I'm pleased to say it was Taffy Sinclair who proposed we all go down to the Woods of Westermaine for some goblin shooting, so we rang up Count Dracula to tell him we were coming over to *Dunsuckin*, then all jumped onto our large black Fly and headed for fresher fields, agreeing that it had been one of the most depressing Saturdays any of us had enjoyed in centuries and the sooner it was behind us, the better.

With respectful acknowledgements to Maurice Richardson and The Exploits of Engelbrecht, *published by Savoy Books, Manchester, U.K., and Port Sabatini, Texas.*

AFTERWORD

THE JOKE GOES a little like this: "Michael Moorcock has written for so long in so many different genres that there's something for every reader to hate." If you're an iconic post-WWII literary figure whose résumé includes everything from creating a mythic heroic fantasy anti-hero to editing *New Worlds*, the magazine that gave voice to the New Wave and the careers of writers like J. G. Ballard and M. John Harrison, then it's very much true, simply because few readers can keep up with the protean *reach* of this giant.

How, then, to edit a "best" of Moorcock's short fiction? How to even create a short list? Luckily, our task was simplified by the brilliant work of John Davey, who had already compiled a 250,000-word manuscript and who deserves the bulk of the praise for its success.

From that manuscript, with Davey's notes on individual stories in mind, the final volume of approximately 150,000 words took shape. Even so, several admittedly invasive decisions had to be made in compiling the final contents. We decided to leave Elric largely to the excellent new series of reprints from Del Rey, opting to begin this volume with a later Elric story. We also decided that Jerry Cornelius—a Moorcock character who has come to serve as a kind of running commentary on the state of the world—could only be excerpted in a way that would seem incomplete, and thus we left that fine fellow largely to his own devices (for now).

Which brings us to a very important point: *This writer, without the aid of those two robust companions, would* still *have had an amazing career.* That career, in the short form, breaks down roughly into stories that fall under the rubric of fantasy/SF and, using a hated term, the literary mainstream. There is some overlap, for those who grade on taxonomy. For example, Moorcock's "World War Three" stories appear to partake of a variety of influences in style and execution—part of what makes them still seem contemporary. It is this overlap, along with the guiding intelligence and wit of the author, that provides coherence to this collection.

We are sure that many of these choices will be hotly debated, and we welcome that debate. Let anyone who dares stand in our shoes for a month or two, looking out over the depth and breadth of Moorcock's oeuvre. From that perspective, we think any reasonable person will agree on how devilishly hard it is to say *this* and *not this, that* but *not that.*

Ultimately, our rôle in editing this collection is a personal thank you to a man and a writer we love deeply: Michael Moorcock, whose genius is only matched by his generosity. We believe both of those qualities exist, in quantity, in this book.

ANN & JEFF VANDERMEER

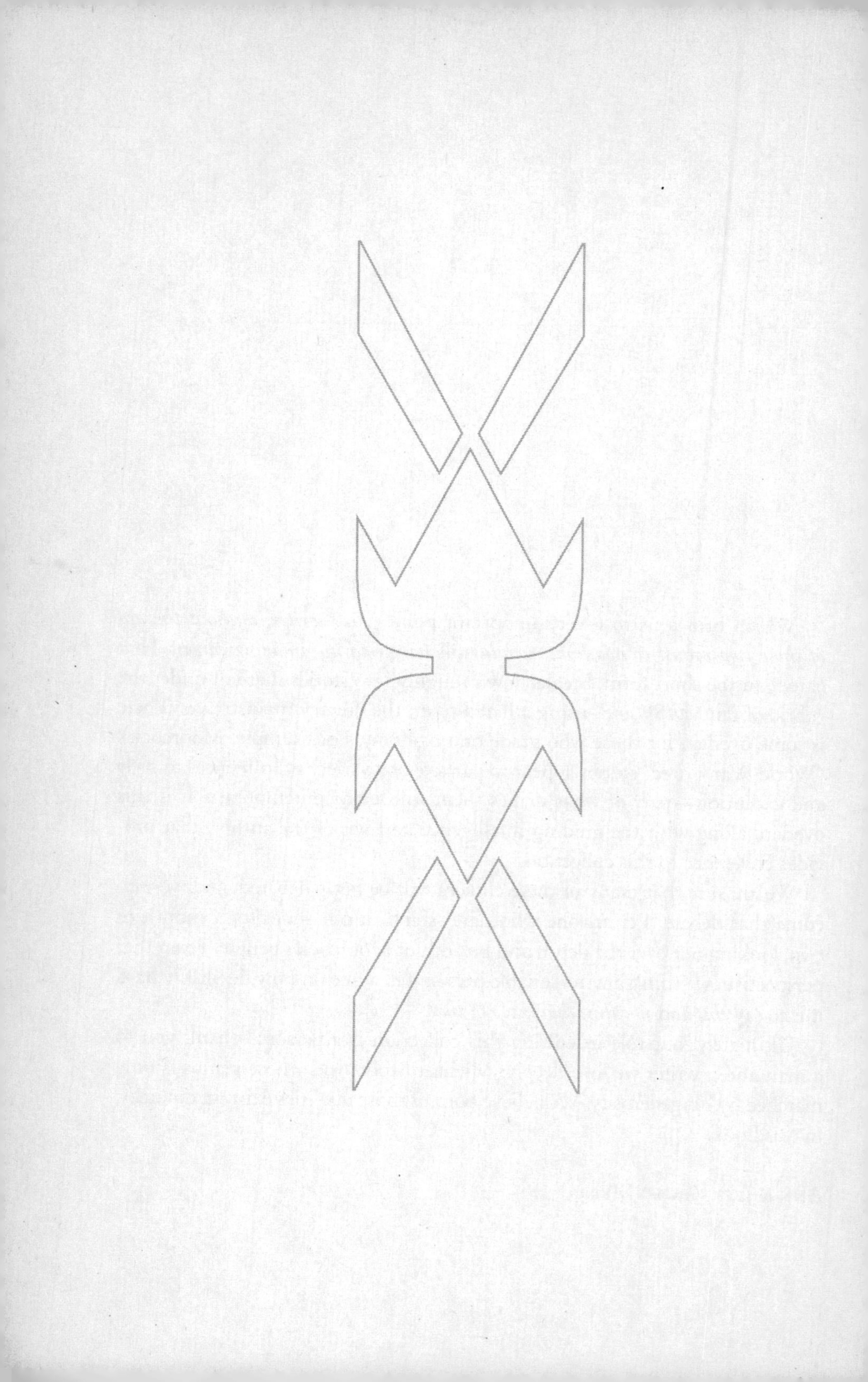